PENGUIN BOOKS

Stones of Fire

Born in Washington DC, C. M. Palov graduated from George Mason University with a degree in art history. The author's résumé includes working as a museum guide, teaching English in Seoul, Korea and managing a bookshop. Twin interests in art and arcana inspired the author to write esoteric thrillers. C. M. Palov currently lives in West Virginia.

Stones of Fire

C. M. PALOV

PENGUIN BOOKS

PENGUIN BOOKS

First published 2009

1

Copyright © C. M. Palov, 2009

The moral right of the author has been asserted

Typeset by Rowland Phototypesetting Ltd, Bury St Edmunds, Suffolk
Printed in England by Clays Ltd, St Ives plc

ISBN: 978-0-141-04123-0

www.greenpenguin.co.uk

Mixed Sources
Product group from well-managed
forests and other controlled sources
www.fsc.org Cert no. SA-COC-1592
© 1996 Forest Stewardship Council

Penguin Books is committed to a sustainable future
for our business, our readers and our planet.
The book in your hands is made from paper
certified by the Forest Stewardship Council.

To Ria Palov for keeping the faith.
And Steve Kasdin for taking a chance.

I

.

His movements slow and deliberate, the curator ran his fingertips over the small bronze coffer, lightly grazing the incised Hebrew letters. A lover's caress.

Holding his breath, he opened the box.

'*Claves regni caelorum,*' he whispered, entranced by the relic nestled within the box. Like Eve gazing upon the forbidden fruit, he stared at the twelve polished gemstones anchored in an ancient gold setting.

The keys to the kingdom of heaven.

Dr Jonathan Padgham, chief curator at the Hopkins Museum of Near Eastern Art, reached into the coffer, carefully removing what had once been a gem-encrusted breastplate. *Once.* Long ago. More than three thousand years ago by his reckoning.

Although bits and pieces of the gold scapular still precariously clung to the setting, the relic was scarcely recognizable as a breastplate, the chains that originally secured the gem-studded shield to the wearer's body having long since vanished. Only the stones, set in four rows of three, gave any indication as to the relic's original rectangular shape, the breastplate measuring some five inches by four.

'That's some real bling-bling, huh?'

Annoyed by the disruption, Padgham glanced at the curly-haired woman engaged in placing a camera on a tripod. Not for the first time, he wondered what possessed her to pair black leather motorcycle boots with a long tartan skirt.

A cheeky grin on her face, Edie Miller stepped over to his desk, bending her head to peer at the relic. Since immigrating to 'the land of the free' he'd come to realize that American females were far more brazen than their English cousins. Ignoring her, Padgham arranged the breastplate upon a square piece of black velvet, readying it to be photographed.

'Wow. There's a diamond, an amethyst, and a sapphire.' As she spoke, the Miller woman pointed to each stone she named. Padgham was tempted to snatch her hand, afraid she might actually touch the precious relic. A freelance photographer hired by the Hopkins to digitally archive the collection, she was not trained to handle rare artefacts.

'And there's an emerald! Which, by the by, happens to be my birthstone,' she continued. 'What do you think that is, about five carats?'

'I have no idea,' he said dismissively, gemology not his strong suit. Hers either, he suspected.

'How old do you think it is?'

Barely glancing at the plaid-garbed magpie, he again replied, 'I have no idea.'

'I'm guessing *really* old.'

To be certain, the age of the breastplate was

punctuated by a very large question mark. So, too, its provenance. Although he had an inkling.

Again, Padgham ran the tip of a manicured finger over the engraved symbols that adorned the bronze coffer in which the breastplate had been housed. He only recognized one word – יהוה – the Hebrew Tetragrammaton. The unspeakable four-letter name of God. It had been placed on the coffer as a talisman to ward off the curious, the covetous, the greedy who gobbled up ancient relics like sugar-coated sweeties.

How in God's name did an ancient Hebrew relic end up in Iraq?

Although the museum director Eliot Hopkins had been very hush-hush, he had let slip that the relic originated in Iraq. Padgham had been entrusted by the old man with the initial evaluation of the be-jewelled breastplate. He'd also been cautioned to keep mum. Padgham was no fool. Far from it. He knew the relic had been bought on the black market.

Risky business, the purchase of stolen relics. In recent years a curator at the renowned Getty had been brought to trial by Italian prosecutors for having knowingly purchased pinched artefacts. The black-market antiquities trade was a billion-dollar business, particularly with the unabated pilfering of Iraqi relics, Babylonian art popping up all over the place these days. Many in the museum world turned a blind eye, jaded enough to believe that they were preserving, not stealing, ancient culture. Padgham concurred. After all, had it not been for European art thieves, the world would have been deprived of such treasures as the Rosetta Stone and the Elgin Marbles.

'There's too much backlight falling on it. Do you mind if I adjust the window shades?'

Padgham drew his gaze away from the relic. 'Hmm? No, no, of course not. This is your arena, as it were.' He pasted a smile on his face, needing the woman's cooperation. He'd been ordered not to show the relic to anyone on the museum staff. It was the reason he was conducting his preliminary evaluation on a Monday – the museum closed to the public, no staff on the premises. Of course, the photographer didn't count, the woman a freelance contractor who didn't know a breastplate from a bas-relief. *Who would she tell?* As far as he knew, aside from the two guards in the museum lobby, they were the only two bodies present.

A flash of light momentarily illuminated the dimmed office.

'Looks good,' the photographer remarked, reviewing the image on the camera display. She deftly pushed several buttons on the camera. 'I'll just snap a back-up copy.' No sooner did a second flash go off than she gestured to the bronze coffer. 'Do you want a shot of the metal box as well?'

'Is Queen Anne dead?' Then, catching himself, he added in a more congenial tone, 'If you would be so kind.'

Padgham stood aside as the photographer re-positioned the tripod. Contemplating the beautiful relic, he worriedly bit his lower lip. As curator of Babylonian antiquities, he'd been given custody of the breastplate because it had been found in the deserts of Iraq. The museum director assumed he'd be able to put flesh to bone, to discover the four Ws of provenance – who, where, when and why. To Padgham's consternation, those answers eluded him. The breastplate was most definitely of Hebrew derivation and his knowledge of the ancient Israelites was sketchy at best. Thus, the reason for the digital photograph.

As fate would have it, an old Oxford chum, Cædmon Aisquith, was currently in Washington on a publicity junket for his newly released book *Isis Revealed*, one of those faux histories that purported to expose the arcane secrets of the long-buried past. Never one to gawk at the proverbial gift horse, upon reading the newspaper review Padgham immediately rang up Aisquith's publishers, got the number of his hotel, and called him. Last he'd heard, old Aisquith had inherited some money, absconded to Paris and opened an antiquarian bookshop on the Left Bank. Drinking Beaujolais and banging French tarts, the man should have his head examined. Although they hadn't set eyes on one another in nearly twenty years, Aisquith had agreed to meet him later that evening for drinks. Hoping to pique his interest – and in the process glean some kernel of information about the mysterious Hebrew relic – he intended to email Aisquith the digital photographs. A true Renaissance man with an encyclopedic knowledge of ancient history, Cædmon Aisquith would hopefully be able to shed some much-needed light. As with the freelance photographer, Padgham did not deem the secrecy stipulated by the museum director applicable to his Oxford chum.

'All finished,' the photographer announced. Popping open the digital camera, she removed a tiny rectangle of plastic and handed it to him.

He stared at the minuscule object. 'And what am I supposed to do with *this*? I asked you to take a photograph.'

'And I did just that. There's your photograph. On the memory card.' She stuffed the camera into her pocket, her outlandish garb topped by a khaki-coloured waistcoat.

Cheeky cow, Padgham thought. Although only forty-two years of age, he often felt as though the modern world and all its technical sleights of hand were passing him by at a dizzying speed.

As she dismantled the tripod, Padgham repeated his question. 'What am I supposed to do with this?'

'You're supposed to download it on your computer. Once you do that, you can print it, email it, doctor it up, whatever.'

There being no staff available to assist him, Padgham was forced to grovel. 'I would be most appreciative if –'

Just as he hoped, she snatched the memory card

out of his hand. Bending at the waist, she inserted it into the computer tower under his desk.

Biting back a pleased smile, he pointed to a note-pad inscribed with the museum logo. 'I would like to send the photographs, via email, to that address.'

'Yes, sire. I live to serve.'

Padgham turned a deaf ear on her disgruntled mumblings. 'You're most kind, Miss Miller.'

'You say that only because you don't know me.' She seated herself at his carved mahogany desk. 'All right, let me get this straight. You want me to send the pics to one C.Aisquith at lycos.com?' When he nodded, she said, 'Probably best if we send the photos as JPEGs.'

'Yes, well, I'll leave it up to you.'

She quickly and deftly tapped away on the key-board. Then, getting up from his executive-style chair, she said, 'Okay, I want you to pull up your email account.'

'I would be only too happy to oblige.' Padgham seated himself at the desk. 'What the bloody hell!'

'What's wrong?'

'Are you blind, woman? The screen has gone blank.' He pointed an accusing finger at the monitor.

'Calm down. No need to have a conniption. It's probably just a loose cable.'

'Hmm . . .' He peered under the desk then glanced at his Gieves and Hawkes hand-tailored trousers. The problem had but one solution. 'Since you so easily diagnosed the problem, would you be a dear and . . . ?'

'You do know that this is *not* in my job description,' Edie Miller griped as she scrambled to her knees. There being no room to pull the computer tower forward, she was forced to wedge herself under the desk in order to check the cables. Padgham glanced at the Waterford dish on the nearby console, thinking he might offer her a cellophane-wrapped sweet. Recompense for a job well done.

As the woman under the desk silently went about her business, Padgham picked up the ancient breastplate, returning it to the incised bronze coffer.

'Ah, let there be light,' he murmured a moment later, pleased that a spark of life now emanated from his computer, the monitor flickering the familiar Dell logo. Out of the corner of his eyes Padgham saw a third person enter the office. Surprised to see a man attired in grey overalls, a black balaclava pulled over his head, he imperiously demanded, 'Who the devil are you?'

The man made no reply. Instead, he raised a gun and pointed it at Padgham's head, his finger poised on the trigger.

Death almost instantaneous, Padgham experienced a sharp, piercing pain in his right eye socket. Then, like the flickering lights on his computer monitor, he saw an explosion of colour before the world around him turned a deep, impenetrable shade of black.

2

'Who the devil are you?'

Pop.

Crash!

Thud.

Those sounds registered on Edie Miller's brain in such quick succession, it wasn't until she saw Dr Padgham's lifeless body sprawled on the Persian carpet three feet from her huddled position under the desk that she realized what had happened.

She stifled a shriek of terror. Like a freight train that had jumped the tracks, her heart slammed against her chest. In a state of shock, her brain sent a series of urgent messages. *Don't move. Don't speak. Don't twitch so much as a finger.*

Terrified, Edie heeded the commands.

And then her fear turned to joy.

Several seconds had passed since Dr Padgham hit the floor and she was still alive. *It was her lucky day.* The killer didn't know she was crouched in the knee well under the desk. Covered on three sides by antique mahogany, she was hidden from view. In order to see her, the killer would have to bend down and peer under the desk.

From her vantage point, Edie saw a pair of

grey-clad legs come into view. At the end of those legs was a pair of tan military-style boots. Next to those legs hung a large masculine hand wrapped around a pistol that had a silencer attached to it. As though she were looking through the lens of a camera, she focused on that ham-fisted hand, noticing the hairy knuckles and the unusual silver ring made up of interconnected crosses. The notion that she and the killer might actually pray to the same God caused her to bite down on her lip *hard*, a hysterical burst of laughter threatening to escape.

And that's when the killer did the completely unexpected.

Stepping over Dr Padgham's body, he set the gun on top of the desk and began clicking away on the computer keyboard. A few seconds later, Edie heard him softly swear under his breath as he yanked open a drawer.

He was looking for something.

Edie barely had time to wrap her mind around that thought when the killer reached under the desk and removed the digital memory card from the computer.

She held her breath, praying to God, Jesus, anyone who would listen, that the killer didn't see her. It stood to reason that you couldn't plead with a man who sneaked up on his victims and killed in unpitying silence.

Only able to see the killer from the waist down, she watched as he unclipped a mobile phone from his belt. Then she listened and was able to hear seven digital beeps. A local phone number. He was calling someone in the Washington DC metropolitan area.

'Let me speak to the colonel.' Several moments passed in silence before he again spoke. 'Sir, I've got the breastplate. I've also got a problem.'

The breastplate, she belatedly realized. *Dr Padgham had been killed because of the jewelled breastplate.*

'I'm not sure, but I think the little English homo sent digital photos of the relic to someone outside the museum. I found a tripod on the desk, a memory card with photos of the breastplate and an email address.' Edie heard a sheet of paper being ripped from a pad. 'C.Aisquith at lycos.com.' A short pause. The killer carefully spelled out the email address. Another pause ensued. 'No. I couldn't find the camera ... Yes, sir, I took care of the guards ... Don't worry, sir, I'll cover my tracks.'

Edie heard another beep, the call disconnected. She then heard the metallic *whhsh* of a zipper. The killer was putting the bronze box with the breastplate inside some sort of carrying case.

And then he was gone, exiting the office as unobtrusively as he had entered.

Edie slowly counted to twenty before she crawled out from under the desk. Forced to straddle Dr Padgham's corpse, she took one look at his bloody, mutilated eye socket ... and promptly threw up. All over the Persian carpet. Not that it mattered – the carpet was already stained with blood and brain matter.

Still on all fours, she wiped her mouth on her sweater sleeve. She had never liked Jonathan Padgham. But someone else had liked him even less. Enough to kill him in cold blood. *Correction.* Warm blood. Warm, wet, coppery-smelling blood.

Lurching to her feet, Edie picked up the telephone. *Nothing but dead air.* The killer had disabled the phone line. With a sinking heart she remembered that her BlackBerry was still plugged into the battery charger on her kitchen counter. So much for calling the cops to come to the rescue. Since the killer had 'taken care' of the two guards downstairs, Edie knew she was on her own.

Her goal being to get out of the museum as quickly as possible, she left the office and headed for the main corridor. The Hopkins Museum was housed in a four-storey nineteenth-century Beaux Art mansion located in the heart of the Dupont Circle area, a vibrant commercial and residential district. Once out of the museum, help was only a shout away.

Coming to a halt at the end of the hall that led to the main corridor, Edie tentatively peered around the corner.

'Oh God.'

Stunned to see the killer, Edie caught herself in mid-gasp. A behemoth of a man in grey overalls with a black ski mask pulled over his head, he was standing in front of the wall monitor and security keypad next to the door leading out of the administration area. In order to gain access to this area, each and every employee, regardless of rank, had to key a personal ID number into the security system, the procedure repeated when one left. The code activated the lock on the intimidating steel door. The computer system enabled museum security to monitor all employees' whereabouts.

It occurred to Edie that in order to enter the office suite, the murderer must have had a valid security code. *How did he get a hold of a code?*

At the moment that didn't matter. All that mattered was that she was stuck on the fourth floor with a murderer. To get to the lift or stairs, she had to pass through the steel door. Meaning she'd have to wait him out. Once he left the premises, she could escape the building.

Wondering what the killer was doing, Edie watched his super-sized hand move across the keypad with surprising dexterity. She knew from experience that it took no more than two seconds to key in a five-digit code and unlock the door, but by her reckoning the killer had been standing in front of the monitor and keypad a good thirty seconds.

So just leave already.

'Fucking shit!' she heard the killer mutter as he removed a notepad and pencil from his breast pocket.

As she watched him scribble something onto the notepad, Edie went slack-jawed. Although the monitor was too far away to be sure, she suspected the killer had accessed the computer security log. If true, that meant 'E. Miller' had just popped up on the monitor. Beside her name would be the exact date – 12/1/08 – and time – 13:38:01 – that she had entered the fourth floor. Even more damning, there would be no date or time indicated in the 'Depart' column.

Edie had watched enough crime dramas on TV to know she'd been made.

She had to find a hiding place. *Now*. This very instant.

Terrified the Neanderthal in the grey overalls would somehow home in on her, Edie slowly eased away from the corner. She then ran down the hall grateful for the hideous maroon carpet that muffled her footfalls, past the office with the sprawled corpse on the floor.

Turning right, she headed down another hall, this one dead-ending at a storeroom. Lined with shelving units stacked with boxes, it would make an excellent hiding place.

Or would have made an excellent hiding place had it been open.

She stared at the locked door.

Now what?

If she could get downstairs to the exhibition galleries, she could yank an artefact off the wall, instantly triggering the museum alarm system. The DC police would arrive within minutes, maybe even seconds if there happened to be a squad car in the area. But to do that, she'd have to first sneak past Dr Padgham's killer.

Too faint of heart to give this idea further consideration, Edie spun on her booted heel. As she did, she caught sight of a bright red sign with bold white lettering.

The fire escape.

Hope renewed at seeing the word EXIT, Edie rushed down the hall. When she reached the door, she grabbed the bar handle and pushed, bracing herself for what she assumed would be a very loud alarm.

3

'I think Isis is like the total embodiment of the wise woman. That's why my magic circle practises a devotional ritual to invoke the power of Isis at each full moon.'

Cædmon Aisquith glanced at the pierced and tattooed speaker, who clutched an autographed copy of *Isis Revealed* to her breast.

'Do you by any chance mention the rites of Isis in your book?'

About to answer with a terse negative, Cædmon caught himself. His American readers tended to fall into two categories: the erudite and the asinine. Not that it mattered, as he'd been ordered by his publicist – who looked on with the stern demeanour of an English headmistress – to treat all questions, no matter how inane or idiotic, with due consideration. Particularly if the questioner had already purchased a copy of his book.

Cædmon schooled his features into an attentive expression. 'Er, no. I am afraid there are no magical rituals detailed in the text. However, you are quite correct in that Isis, like her Greek counterpart Sophia, represents wisdom in all its myriad forms.'

Apple polished, Cædmon thanked the young

woman for her interest in ancient mysteries and cordially took his leave of her. A private man, he was uncomfortable in the role of public author, finding the meet-and-greet segment of book signings a tiresome exercise in the art of chinwagging, an art he'd never quite mastered.

His belly aching from the cheap champagne and his facial muscles aching from the fool's grin he'd been forced to wear since entering the bookshop, he was actually relieved when his mobile began to softly vibrate, the incoming call a perfect excuse to turn his back on the nattering group crowded into the diminutive confines of Dupont Books. To lessen his publicist's displeasure, he made a big to-do of raising his mobile to his left ear, silently signaling that he needed to take the call. This being the last leg of a twelve-city tour, they'd had their fill of one another, Cædmon anxious to return to the quiet monotony of pen and ink.

'Yes, hello,' he said, always feeling like a bit of an ass speaking into, essentially, thin air.

'Cædmon Aisquith?'

Politely correcting the man's butchered pronunciation of his name, he said, 'Who's calling, please?'

The question met with a long silence followed by a *click*, the call abruptly disconnected.

'Bloody hell,' Cædmon muttered, yanking the mobile from his ear. The hairs on the back of his neck suddenly bristled. He didn't give out his number. Hit with the unnerving sensation that he was being watched by someone who had no interest in discussing ancient lore or swilling free bubbly, he turned on his heel. Slowly. Calmly. A man with nothing to fear.

Only he knew such posturing was an outright lie.

Using the training ingrained from the eleven years he'd spent indentured in Her Majesty's Security Service, he casually glanced about the bookshop, searching for the face that did not belong in the crowd, the telltale flush, the quick, breakaway glance of the guilty. No suspect characters prowling about, he next glanced out the plate-glass windows that opened onto Connecticut Avenue, the city pavement teeming with holiday shoppers.

Nothing appearing out of the ordinary, he quietly released a pent-up breath.

All quiet on the western front.

Like most men with a price on his head, he didn't know how it would end, if the day just lived would be his last. All he knew was that when the thugs of the Real Irish Republican Army did finally catch up with him, they would see to it that he died a barbaric death indeed. An eye for an eye and all that.

Five years ago he had avenged the death of his lover by tracking down an RIRA chieftain and killing the bastard in the streets of Belfast. Such deeds did not go unpunished. Forced to go to ground, he'd spent the last several years living in Paris. A stranger in a strange land. Although he'd spent the time wisely, writing his first book, a treatise on the esoteric traditions of the ancient world. Lulled into a sense of security, he'd decided against using a pseudonym, thinking he'd fallen off the RIRA radar screen.

Only now did it dawn on him that that bit of arrogance might cost him dearly.

Ah, the folly of a first-born son still trying to impress the long-dead father.

He rechecked the digital readout on his mobile. BLOCKED CALL was prominently displayed.

'Why am I not surprised?' he murmured. Again he scanned the bookshop, certain he was being stalked.

His gaze fell on a volume of Byron propped on a nearby book shelf.

'For the Angel of Death spread his wings on the blast . . .'

As the long-forgotten line popped into his head, he bit back a caustic laugh, knowing he'd been that same dark angel. Once. A long time ago.

Still holding the mobile in his hand, he strolled over to his publicist. 'My hotel just rang me,' he blithely lied, falling back on lessons learned at MI5. 'A bit of bother with the bill. Something about my credit card being refused.' He pointedly glanced around the bookshop, the shelves littered with abandoned champagne flutes. 'Seeing as how the festivities are winding down, you won't mind if I dash off and take care of it?'

His publicist, a touchy woman with the ironic surname of Huffman, stared at him from behind the frames of her ruby-red spectacles. 'Do you need me to call the front desk for you?'

'No problem,' he replied with a shake of the head. 'I'm a big boy. Although perhaps I should fortify myself before battling the dragon.' He picked up a full champagne flute from a nearby tray, ignoring the fact that it had long since gone flat. 'Cheers.'

Taking his leave of her, the flute still clutched in his right hand, he headed to the back of the bookshop, veering down a hall marked EMPLOYEES ONLY. Blatantly ignoring the admonition, he continued until he came to a room stacked with cardboard boxes, the sole inhabitant a lank-haired young man unpacking a crate with the desultory air of an underpaid cog who didn't much care if or when the wheel turned.

Cædmon nodded, acting as though he had every right to be there. 'The exit, if you please.'

The young man jerked his head at the door opposite.

On the other side of the service exit, Cædmon found himself standing on a cigarette-strewn pavement behind the bookshop, the concrete walls covered in ribald graffiti.

No sooner did the exit door close behind him than he smashed his champagne flute against the wall.

Weapon in hand, he waited.

Come out, come out, wherever you are, he silently taunted, readying himself to do combat with his unseen nemesis.

A full minute passed in tense silence.

Realizing he'd given in to his fears, he derisively snorted.

'The ghost of Irishmen past,' he murmured, tossing the jagged-edged flute to the pavement.

The moment of lunacy having passed, he flipped up the collar of his jacket, warding off the cold. He recalled seeing a coffee shop several blocks away. In dire need of caffeine, he headed in that direction.

Although he knew he was being paranoid, Cædmon couldn't shake off the unnerving feeling that an Irish militant who refused to accept the peace had tracked him to the far side of the Atlantic. Where he intended to settle a very old, yet still outstanding score.

Who else would have called him on his mobile? As if to say, we can see you, but you can't see us.

4

To Edie's surprise, no fire alarm sounded. There was only the reverberating *clunk* of the bar handle as she swung open the fire door.

The killer had disabled the alarm system.

Hit by a blast of cold wintry air, she found herself over the precipice between the open door and an external fire escape that zigzagged down the rear of the museum. Completely enclosed in black chain link, the escape was designed so that only those inside the museum had access to it, keeping vagrants and thieves at bay.

No time to worry that it was lightly snowing, that she had no coat or that she was afraid of heights, Edie stepped across the threshold into the caged stairwell, the fire door swinging shut behind her. She kept her gaze on the alley below, knowing that if she looked anywhere else but down, she'd get dizzy, maybe even faint. Like that time she watched the Fourth of July fireworks from a friend's rooftop patio.

A white-knuckled grip on the railing, she made her descent. The sound of her boots hitting the metal steps echoed in the alley below. At the bottom she opened the cage door, emerging into the alleyway. As with the emergency exit above, the door automatically closed and locked behind her.

Hurriedly she glanced around, disoriented, uncertain in which direction to go. Like a weird nether world, the alley was filled with bins, skips, SUV-sized air conditioning condensers and parked vans. Against an adjacent building there was a tall pile of discarded office furniture, the offices recently remodelled, the old stuff still waiting to be taken away. Given it was December, every window that looked onto the alley was closed. And since no one wanted a bird's eye view of big blue rubbish bins, the blinds were all pulled shut.

From above her, Edie heard a door suddenly swing open.

The killer had found the fire escape.

Not wasting a second, she ducked behind a condenser, praying she hadn't been spotted. If she hurried, she could escape the alley before he reached the bottom. But she couldn't exit the alley without moving into the killer's line of sight. That left only one option – she had to hide.

Keeping to the shadows, she dashed some fifteen feet to the heap of jumbled chairs, their wooden arms and legs jutting into the air at odd angles. Like so many broken bones. As far as hiding places went, it was pretty pathetic. The pile wouldn't stop a bullet. Or prevent a big, meaty fist from grabbing her. But it was the best that she could do at short notice.

Espying a small opening at the bottom of the pile,

she got down on her hands and knees and crawled into the hole. It was no more than twenty inches in height and she had to navigate with care. One wrong move and the heap of furniture could well tumble to the ground. With her underneath. Unable to crawl any farther into the pile, she came to a halt. Tucking her legs beneath her body, she made herself as small as possible. Invisible would have been better. Better because she knew with a sickening sense of certainty that the man on the fire escape wouldn't hesitate to kill her.

Hearing the rattle of a metal door, she peered through the jumble of furniture, watching as the killer exited the fire escape. He had removed his ski mask. Edie could see that he sported a military-style buzz cut. His face mottled with what looked like rage, he seemed on the verge of a steroid-induced rampage.

In hunting mode, the killer swivelled his head from side to side, scanning the alley. Edie saw a large bulge at the back of his waist. *The gun that had killed Dr Padgham.* Methodically, the man's gaze moved from target to target: blue bins, green condenser, white van. And then his gaze zeroed in on the furniture pile.

These might very well be the last few moments before my death.

Edie envisioned her bleeding body sprawled beneath a pile of discarded chairs. No doubt that's who would find her, the orange-suited guys from the sanitation department.

Holding her breath, Edie slowly counted backwards from ten.

Ten, nine, eight, seven —

The killer's gaze suddenly swung to the other side of the alley, where a group of recycling bins overflowed with cans.

She'd gone undetected.

Surprisingly light-footed for such a large man, the killer walked all the way down the alley towards 21st Street before turning round and heading back to the fire escape. As he did, a police cruiser pulled into the alley from the opposite direction. Relieved beyond words, Edie released a pent-up breath. Opening the door to the fire escape had obviously triggered a silent alarm. The DC police had arrived to investigate.

For some strange reason the killer didn't seem the least bit perturbed by the sudden appearance of the cop car, actually raising his hand to flag down the cruiser. *Why would he do that?* she wondered. *Might as well announce that he set off the alarm.*

A few seconds later she had her answer. A uniformed police officer got out of the cruiser and approached the killer, who removed a bag from his shoulder and handed it to the cop.

The breastplate.

The cop was in on it.

The cavalry had come to kill her.

'Looks like the op is a go,' Edie overheard the cop say as he took custody of the stolen relic. 'We fly to London at nineteen hundred hours.'

The killer shook his head. 'We've got loose ends. Someone else was in the museum besides Padgham and the two guards. The little shit escaped down the fire escape.'

A resounding bang ensued as the cop slammed his fist down on the bonnet of the police cruiser. 'Shit! We're fucked! The English fag was supposed to have been the only staff person in the building.'

'It gets even worse,' the killer said. Reaching into his breast pocket he removed the same notepad that Edie had seen earlier. 'Padgham may have emailed photos of the breastplate. I notified the tac team at Rosemont. They're hunting down the person at the other end of Padgham's email.'

Watching the exchange, Edie took slow, deep breaths, willing her cramped legs to stop quivering, her body protesting the straitjacket confinement.

'This was supposed to have been a simple snatch and go,' the cop muttered.

'And sometimes a mission gets bogged down in the mire. What we need to do is find this fucker – what's his name – E. Miller and get things tidied up.'

Thank you, God. A small break. They thought she was a man. They would be looking for a man, not a woman. They also didn't know that Padgham never sent the email. But that wasn't her problem. Her problem was getting free and clear of the alley.

'So far, there's been no calls made to 911.'

'When Miller does call, I want to know ASAP.'

'Don't worry. I'm on it,' the cop said before getting into his cruiser.

The knot in Edie's stomach tightened painfully. If she contacted the police, the killer would know where to find her. And since one of the killer's cohorts – maybe more – wore a police uniform, she'd have no way of distinguishing the good guys from the bad.

More scared than ever, Edie watched as the cruiser drove away. The exchange ended, the killer walked over to the service entrance of the museum and punched in a code, the locked door buzzing open. *Like he owned the place.* Padgham's killer went back inside the museum.

Edie hurriedly backed out of her hidey-hole. Standing upright, she took a big gulp of air. The alley reeked of urine and rotting garbage, the stench so strong her eyes welled with tears.

Hearing a loud mechanical rattle, she spun on her heel.

Across the alleyway a garage door slowly opened. She could exit the alley without having to go past the museum. No sooner did a black BMW emerge from the underground garage than Edie broke into a run towards the door. Or at least tried to. Hobbling on her cramped leg muscles, she lurched forward. The driver turned his head and glanced at her – a wild-haired terrified woman with an ungraceful gait – then just as quickly glanced away.

'Obviously one of the apathetic multitudes,' Edie

mumbled under her breath as she dodged into the garage.

Seeing a lift, she headed towards it. Not until she was safe inside the elevator, the doors closing with a melodic chime, did she permit herself a sigh of relief. Although in actuality it was more like a sag of relief, her body going into an old-lady slump, her legs barely able to support her weight.

A few seconds later the elevator doors opened onto what looked like an upmarket apartment building lobby. Straight ahead a pair of plate-glass doors beckoned. Overcome with a sudden burst of giddiness, she limped towards the beautiful doors with their big beautiful brass handles. Yanking the door on the right side wide open, Edie barely restrained herself from hugging a postman in the vestibule, who was busy inserting letters into rows of identical-looking mailboxes. Instead, she smiled at him. A big, toothy, glad-to-be-alive smile.

Just then a cab pulled up to the kerb in front of the apartment building.

Free at last. Thank God Almighty, free at last.

5

Like a man who'd just been baptized in the cool waters of the Jordan, retired Marine Corps Colonel Stanford J. MacFarlane stared at the jewel-encrusted breastplate.

The Stones of Fire.

Arguably one of the most sacred of all biblical relics, third only to the Ark of the Covenant and the Holy Grail.

'Mine eyes have seen the glory of the coming of the Lord.'

Stan MacFarlane knew from his Bible studies that the twelve inlaid stones had originally been entrusted to Lucifer when he was still God's favourite. After the expulsion from heaven, the stones were retrieved by God and later given to Moses, who created the breastplate according to God's specific instruction. Worn only by the high priest of the Jews, the breastplate came to be known as the Stones of Fire. Hidden within the sacred confines of the Jerusalem Temple, the breastplate was plundered by the Babylonians when Nebuchadnezzar's army sacked the holy city in the sixth century BC. For the next twenty-six centuries the holy relic had remained hidden in the deserts of Babylon in what is now Iraq. More than one treasure hunter lost his head attempting to find the breast-plate, learning, too late, that the caliphs, sultans and dictators who ruled Mesopotamia did not take kindly to foreign trespassers.

All that changed when the American army marched into Baghdad.

Knowing he would need an expert, Stan hired an Iraqi archaeologist more interested in making a buck than safeguarding his country's national treasures. Before the conquest the archaeologist had been in charge of a site where a cache of ancient Hebrew objects had been uncovered. Stan was certain those were some of the holy relics stolen from the Temple and that more digging would unearth the Stones of Fire. But he wasn't the only man searching for the breastplate. Eliot Hopkins, director of the Hopkins Museum of Near Eastern Art, beat him to the prize. Not about to let the relic elude him a second time, Stan sent his most trusted aide to retrieve the breast-plate.

Except his trusted aide had made a very careless mistake.

'"And the serpent cast out of his mouth water as a flood after the woman that he might cause her to be carried away of the flood,"' he hissed to the man who stood at attention in front of him. His temper rising, he stared down his red-faced subordinate. 'So tell me, Gunny, how did this Miller woman get away from you? Do you think she hitched a ride on Satan's dinghy?'

The penitent, former Gunnery Sergeant Boyd Braxton, shook his head. 'I told you, sir. I don't know what happened. I didn't even know that she was a woman until I found her purse in the museum.'

'The weaker sex, yet still she eluded you.' MacFarlane stepped towards the gunnery sergeant, jabbing him in the chest with his finger. 'Boy, you're not going soft on me, are you? I hate to think that you've been pussy-whipped.'

'No, sir. You don't need to worry about that, sir.'

'You make certain of it, Gunny. Each and every day, you make certain.'

His subordinate properly chastened, Stan Mac-Farlane stepped back, such discipline necessary to keep order in the ranks. A lesson he had learned during his thirty-one years in the Corps.

A full colonel when he left the service, he'd still be in uniform had his career not been abruptly derailed two years ago by the Pentagon watchdog group FREEDOM NOW!, a godless cabal made up of left-wing lawyers and activists. They targeted him soon after he was promoted to the intelligence office of the undersecretary of defense. Hypocrites, one and all, they claimed their purpose was to protect religious freedom in the US military. Because of his strict adherence to the word of God, FREEDOM NOW! had branded him a religious fanatic bent on converting the whole of the US military to the evangelical faith.

Well, guess what, you godless hippie freaks? It was already happening.

When FREEDOM NOW! caught wind of the weekly prayer meeting he held in the Pentagon's executive dining room, they wasted no time blowing the whistle, somehow getting their lily-white hands on a photo of him standing in a prayer circle with other uniformed officers. The photo made the front page of the *Washington Post*. In the accompanying article several junior officers claimed they'd been personally harassed by him, told they would eternally burn in hell if they didn't attend the prayer meetings.

Left-wing pundits, Washington politicos and military-bashers unwilling to let the story drop had had a field day. Soon after, he'd been relieved of his command.

God, however, worked in mysterious ways.

No sooner did the furore die down than Stan founded Rosemont Security Consultants. In recent years private contractors had become the mercenary might behind the US military, tens of thousands of private fighters hired in Iraq alone. With his top-level Pentagon contacts, he was soon making money hand over balled fist. Made up entirely of former special ops soldiers, Rosemont was twenty thousand strong. As leader of this well-armed flock, Stan made certain there wasn't a pluralist or atheist or agnostic among them. Holy warriors, each and every one.

'Sir, what do you want me to do about the woman?'

MacFarlane glanced at his subordinate, the former gunnery sergeant a member of his handpicked Praetorian Guard. His eyes and ears in the nation's capital, this elite team were embedded in law enforcement agencies all over the city. Contemplating how best to clean up the mess, he opened the satchel that had been retrieved from the museum and removed a leather wallet. For several seconds he stared at the driver's licence photo of a thirty-seven-year-old curly-haired woman.

'You heard Gunny ... What shall we do with you, Eloise Darlene Miller?' he contemplatively murmured.

A quick background check had uncovered the fact that the Miller woman had been arrested in 1991 for protesting against the First Gulf War. In Stan's book that made her a Chardonnay-sipping left-wing tree hugger. Like the bastards who had derailed his military career.

Nothing like a 'terrible swift sword' to keep an unruly woman in her place.

'Any word on the whereabouts of –' Stan glanced at the name scrawled on a sheet of paper '– Cædmon Aisquith?' A similar background check had turned up a noticeable dearth of information, prompting Stan to order his intelligence team to dig deeper.

'Aisquith managed to slip out of the bookstore undetected. We're keeping a close watch on his hotel, but he's yet to show up,' the sergeant informed him.

'Hmm.' Stan MacFarlane contemplatively rolled

the silver ring that he wore on his right hand, the intertwined crosses worn smooth over the years. 'This man Aisquith is another loose end we can't afford to let dangle.'

'I hear ya, Colonel.'

'Then hear this.' Stanford MacFarlane looked his subordinate straight in the eye so there would be no misunderstanding. 'You will search. You will find. And you will destroy.'

The order clearly to his liking, the gunnery sergeant smiled. 'By day's end, sir.'

6

Feeling like she'd gone fifteen rounds with the heavyweight champ, Edie Miller dragged herself out of the cab. From her skirt pocket she removed a crumpled ten-dollar bill. She handed it to the driver. If the dark-skinned man with the turban thought it odd that she'd made him pull into the alley behind her terraced house rather than dropping her at the front, he gave no indication.

Relieved to be back on familiar terrain, Edie raised a weary hand, letting the cabbie know that no change was necessary. Small recompense for whisking her to safety, the driver of the plum-coloured cab a godsend. Her Mini Cooper, her purse and her keys had all been left behind at the museum. But she'd got out with her life and the digital camera she'd stuffed in her waistcoat pocket right before Jonathan Padgham had been killed. And that's all that mattered.

What a nightmare, she thought, still in a daze. *What a surreal, unbelievable nightmare.* The cops were actually in on the murder. Moreover she had no idea how many other people were involved in the theft of the breast-plate. All she knew was that they had no inhibitions about resorting to murder to achieve their objective.

And right now their objective was to 'get things tidied up'.

Shuddering, she bent down and lifted a long-dead chrysanthemum out of a terracotta pot. Holding it by the stem, she shook a key out of the clump of brown compost. With a quick backward glance, she scurried up the patio steps. Unlocking the back door, she stepped inside her kitchen.

Spirulina. Barley grass. Pysllium husks. She glanced at the worktop and the neatly lined-up containers of vile-tasting health concoctions that were supposed to ensure a long life and laughed aloud. A waste of time if the grim reaper, dressed in grey overalls, came a-calling. Although all she wanted to do was stuff her face with Häagen-Dazs ice cream, she couldn't afford the time. She had to quickly gather her things and get out. Before they found her. Before they did to her what they had done to Jonathan Padgham.

Edie snatched a canvas shopping bag from a peg on the back of the kitchen door. Bag in hand, she opened the freezer and removed a box of spinach. Not bothering to open the box, she tossed it into the bag. Having learned at a tender age the importance of having a ready supply of cash on hand, she always kept five thousand dollars hidden in the freezer. Money stowed, she grabbed a vintage motorcycle jacket from the next peg. Pulling off her bloodstained khaki fisherman's waistcoat, she stuffed it into the bag. Hurriedly she donned the jacket.

Next she strode down the hall into the small home

office at the front of the house. Yanking open a filing cabinet, she thumbed through the dog-eared folders until she found the one marked 'Personal Documents'. Inside was her passport, her birth certificate, the deeds to the house, the results of her last cervical smear and an official copy of her college transcripts. She unceremoniously dumped the contents of the file into the canvas bag.

About to head upstairs to get her toiletries, Edie stopped at a sound outside. Peering through the window, she saw a dark blue Ford saloon pull up in front of the house. Behind the wheel was the buzz-cut killer. At his side, the bent cop.

Quickly she ducked away from the window.

The killer must have found her satchel.

Knowing she only had a few seconds to escape through the back door, Edie closed the filing cabinet. She slung the canvas bag over her shoulder and retreated to the kitchen, where she grabbed her BlackBerry out of its charger. She then snatched a set of keys out of a brightly coloured ceramic fruit bowl, souvenir of a fun-filled vacation in Morocco.

Keys in hand, she let herself out the back door, taking a second to lock the dead bolt. She didn't want anyone to know she'd been home. She then tiptoed down the circular staircase that led to the alley below. She paused a moment, listening. She heard Spanish music emanating from the apartment building opposite. But no voices from her house. *So far, so good.*

Not knowing how long her luck would last, Edie squeezed past her neighbour's parked Jeep Wrangler and hurried up the adjoining set of stairs to his house. Garrett was in Chicago on business. He was frequently in Chicago on business. And when he was, she watered his plants and fed his cat. Good friends, they each kept a set of keys to the other's house.

Grateful for the well-oiled lock, she opened the back door and rushed inside, ignoring the huge marmalade cat asleep on the kitchen counter. She then ran down the hall to the living room, taking up a position at the sash window that overlooked the street.

Standing in the crease of a full-length velvet curtain, she pulled back the purple fabric a scant half-inch, giving herself a sliver of a peephole.

The two men were already out of the Ford, the cop halfway to her front porch.

Edie held her breath as he banged on the door.

'Open up! DC police!'

When he got no response, he banged again.

Then he did exactly what Edie expected him to do – he unlocked her front door using the keys the killer had undoubtedly found in her satchel at the museum.

Since the two residences shared a common wall, Edie could hear the soft reverberations as the cop charged up her wooden staircase. That was followed by the slamming of several doors. Then he stomped back down the stairs. She wasn't sure, but she thought she heard the back door open. All the while, the killer stood sentry beside the Ford.

A few moments later the cop emerged from the house.

'She hasn't been here,' he announced to his partner, who joined him on the porch. Standing side by side, Edie could see that the two men were near equal in height, giants both of them.

'You certain?'

The cop nodded. 'Nothing's been touched in the bathroom. I can't imagine a chick hitting the road without her electric razor and make-up bag.'

'Fuck! Where the hell is she?'

'Dunno. According to the background search, she has no living relatives and there doesn't appear to be a significant other in the picture.'

Edie tightened her hold on the curtain, disbelieving what she'd just heard. They'd done a background check on her. They knew all about her. Her friends. Her family. Or lack thereof. Everything. They held all the cards and she ... she was about to pee her pants.

Even if she hid in Garrett's house – and the thought was awfully tempting – she figured that sooner or later they'd come banging on the front door. Not having a key, they'd probably kick it in when no one answered.

'Where the fuck is she?' the killer again snarled.

'Don't worry. We'll find her. Without a wallet she's not going to get very far.'

'Don't be so sure. She got out of the museum, didn't she?'

Smirking, the cop said, 'Hey, don't pin that on me. As I recall, that happened on your watch, not mine.'

The killer countered with a glare. Of the two, he was definitely the more frightening. 'You've got the first watch. I want to know the second the bitch shows up,' he growled before stomping down the steps. The cop, relegated to guard duty, stayed behind on the porch.

Moments later, seeing a plume of white smoke rise from the Ford's exhaust, Edie let go of the curtain.

Time suddenly a precious commodity, she rushed into the kitchen, threw open a cabinet door and grabbed a roasting pan off the shelf. Filling it with dried cat food, she placed it on the floor. She then got a large mixing bowl from the same cabinet, filled it with tap water and placed it beside the food. She figured it would do until Garrett returned at the weekend.

As she locked the back door behind her, she prayed that Garrett had filled up his Jeep before leaving for Chicago. Along with the keys to his house, she had the keys to his wheels. And those wheels were her ticket out of town.

Unlocking the driver's door of the black Wrangler, she slid behind the steering column. As she did so, she slung her bag onto the passenger seat. Seeing the big wet spot on the bag from the melting spinach, she was hit with an onslaught of memories. Of leaving in the middle of the night to escape the land-lord. The bill collector. The abusive boyfriend. The junkie in need of a fix. On any given day, those had been the bit players in her mother's poorly acted psychodrama. Like she had just been dunked in a cold tank of water, the memories crashed in on her. Thirty years had come and gone and she was still that scared little girl huddled in the back seat of her mother's old Buick Le Sabre.

Her hands violently shaking, Edie stared at the steering wheel. She tried to put the key in the ignition, but couldn't, the metal repeatedly sliding off the steering column. She hadn't known how to deal with the fear then. She couldn't deal with it now.

Breathe, Edie, breathe. In and out. Long, slow, deep breaths. It won't conquer the fear, but it will mask it. Just enough so you can put the key in the ignition and start the car.

A lost soul, she obeyed the voice in her head. Breathing deeply, she told herself that she could do this. She could escape the bastards. She'd escaped four different juvenile centres in the span of two years. This was no different.

By the fourth exhalation, she was able to start the Jeep.

She glanced at the fuel gauge.

Thank you, Garrett. I owe you big time.

Driving to the end of the alley, she turned left. Not too fast. Not so slow. She didn't want anyone to later recall having seen the Jeep. As light snow began to dot the windscreen, she reached over and turned on the wipers, still taking deep measured breaths.

At the corner of 18th and Columbia she braked, the light turning red. As though she were an escaped felon, Edie nervously glanced from side to side. On the street corner nearest the Jeep a group of Latino men was huddled in front of a cheque cashing joint. On the opposite corner the owner of the quaint Salvadorian café La Flora was busy opening the shutters on the plate-glass windows that fronted the street. Edie was a frequent patron, having stopped in just that morning for a quick breakfast of *frijoles* and eggs.

Catching her eye, Eduardo raised his hand in greeting.

Edie reluctantly returned the wave, hoping, *praying*, that if the police canvassed the neighbourhood, they steered clear of La Flora.

Taking a small measure of comfort in the fact that there wasn't a dark blue Ford in sight, she put the Jeep into first gear and continued down 18th Street. Reaching over, she retrieved her BlackBerry from the bag. She needed to contact C.Aisquith. His or her life was in grave danger. She didn't know if he/she was a local. Didn't know anything about him/her. She only knew the mystery person's email address. She hoped C.Aisquith was at a computer. And that said computer was in the near vicinity. Otherwise, what she was about to do would be a colossal waste of time. Something that at the moment she didn't have a particularly big supply of.

Like most city dwellers forced to use their vehicle as an office on wheels, Edie was able to drive, text and chew gum all at the same time. Her arms draped over the steering wheel, she quickly moved her thumbs over the keypad.

Finished with the email, she hit 'Send'.

'He'll think I'm a crazy woman,' she muttered, knowing that if the shoe were on the other foot, if she was on the receiving end of that hastily composed message, that's exactly what she would think.

She glanced in the rear-view mirror, her line of sight blocked by an orange and white U-Haul-It van on her tail.

Startled by its shrill ringtone, she glanced at the BlackBerry in her lap, hesitating, the words BLOCKED CALL sending an ominous chill down her spine. Shaking off what she hoped would prove an unfounded fear, she reached for her wireless headset.

'H-hello.'

'Ms Miller, so glad to have reached you,' a masculine voice purred in her ear.

Edie didn't recognize the silky-smooth southern accent.

'Who is this?'

'I mean you no harm, Ms Miller. I'm merely someone who's very interested in your safety and well-being.'

Edie yanked the headset away from her ear.

Oh God.

They had found her.

7

Cædmon Aisquith opened the door to Starbucks, assailed by the inviting aroma of fresh-ground coffee and cinnamon scones.

The comforts of a civilized life.

Such scents made one forget, at least temporarily, that one inhabited a most uncivilized world. A world where brutal acts of violence took place with chilling regularity.

When he reached the head of the queue, Cædmon ordered a hazelnut coffee, wondering who the devil had thought it a clever idea to call the small size a Grande. It made him think of an insecure bloke describing the length of his appendage.

Cup in hand, he glanced about the interior jam-packed with small bistro tables, each customer an island unto him- or herself. Espying a favourable-looking islet he strode in that direction, seating himself next to the window, his own porthole onto the world. His position would enable him to simultaneously keep an eye on the pedestrian traffic outside the window while monitoring each and every customer who entered the shop. Although he tried to shake off his earlier unease, he was still troubled by the anonymous phone call he had received at the bookshop.

Knowing the Irish to be a persistent bunch, he removed his mobile and placed it in clear view on the tabletop. If they made contact again, he would be ready for them.

Christ! To think he was still fighting the old battles after so many years.

The rules of polite behaviour not so rigidly adhered to in the Americas, he dunked his scone into his coffee. Purposefully nonchalant, he took a bite. Then, acting like a man totally absorbed in scone and coffee, he surreptitiously glanced out the window. From his vantage point, he had a view clear across all four lanes of Connecticut Avenue to the Church of Scientology nestled in the trees beyond. Idly, he wondered how long Tom Cruise's marriage to Katie –

'Bloody hell,' he muttered, catching himself pondering the inane.

Although pondering the inane was better by far than pondering old memories.

The memory in question had been named Juliana Howe. A reporter for the BBC, Jules had been a media darling, having acquired a well-earned reputation for edgy reporting.

As fate would have it, their relationship began as a routine undercover operation. When MI5 caught wind of the fact that Juliana Howe was in contact with a North African terrorist cell, they sent him in to assess the situation and uncover her source. Playing the absent-minded but sincere Charing Cross book dealer, Cædmon worked the case for six months. Like a pastry chef applying layers of icing to a wedding cake, he slowly gained Juliana's confidence over drinks at the Fox and Hounds, dinner dates at Le Caprice and evenings spent at Covent Garden. Thus the legend of Peter Willoughby-Jones was born, Cædmon becoming the man that an MI5 background check had indicated would most appeal to the gently bred and well-educated Juliana Howe.

He also became the intelligence officer who committed the unpardonable and tragic sin of falling in love with his target. Tragic because the object of his affection would always know him as Peter Willoughby-Jones. Because of the nature of her work, the background investigators at Thames House deemed Juliana Howe a high-level security risk. Meaning he could never reveal to her his true identity.

After the North African cell had been put under lock and key, Cædmon continued his relationship with Juliana, unable to give her up. He assured his superiors that there was still more intelligence to be gleaned, that being in daily contact with an investigative reporter at the BBC would pay dividends. When the Real Irish Republican Army detonated a bomb in front of the BBC, his section chief suddenly agreed. But the bloody bastards in the RIRA weren't content to stop there. Bent on terrorizing London, they detonated several more bombs that summer, including another at the BBC.

This bomb took from him the woman he loved above all others. And because a man who has lost his heart becomes a heartless bastard, Cædmon took it upon himself to right that horrible wrong. After he hunted down Timothy O'Halloran, the RIRA leader responsible for the bombing campaign, he spent weeks in a pickled state, like an inebriate in a Hogarth engraving. The pain unbearable, he discovered that killing O'Halloran had not exorcised the demons of that fateful explosion. It had merely satisfied his need for revenge. But revenge did not bring solace. Nor redemption. It only taught him that he had the capacity to kill.

Not an easy revelation for any man.

When he finally came to his sober senses, he discovered that MI5 does not abandon its own, no matter the transgression. But it does punish them. Demoted to maintaining a safe house in Paris, it was five years before he was discharged from the service. Finally, a free man.

Cædmon glanced at the mobile on the table, re-collecting the earlier call. Maybe he'd been too quick to cut the old ties.

'Rather late, old boy, for that,' he muttered, garnering a pointed glance from a horse-faced woman at the next table. He smiled apologetically. 'Don't mind me. I tend to ramble on when lost in thought.'

'Glad to hear I'm not the only one who talks to

themselves.' She met his gaze and held it. An overture.

'Yes, quite.' His mobile softly chimed, notifying him of an incoming email. Relieved to have a graceful exit, he picked up the device. 'I apologize, but I must attend to business.'

'Oh, sure.' Blushing all the way to her widow's peak, his neighbour took a sudden interest in adjusting the plastic lid on her coffee cup.

Cædmon accessed his email file. Staring at the log, he drummed his fingers on the tabletop, having no recollection of giving his email address to anyone named Edie Miller. Although that didn't mean his publicist hadn't given it to someone at a book signing. Assuming that to be the case, he opened the email rather than delete it outright.

His eyes narrowed, the missive not what he expected.

From:	Edie Miller
To:	c. aisquith@lycos.com
Date:	12/01/06 2:16:31
Subject:	DANGER!!

urgent i meet w u @ NGA cascade cafe TODAY will wait until closing your life in danger ☥ mine 2

ps im not crazy

edie103@earthlink.net

'Indeed,' he murmured, reading the postscript.

8

Edie Miller replaced the wireless headset in her ear.

She wasn't going to run. She wasn't going to hide. She was going to play dumb.

'My safety and well-being? Um, gee, I have no idea what your t-talking about. I'm doing just fine.' Her voice noticeably warbled, bravado slow in coming.

'Come now, Ms Miller. Let's not play games with one another,' the caller replied, seeing right through her. 'We both know that you were at the Hopkins Muscum earlier today.'

Her hands began to shake, the Jeep straying out of its lane. A UPS truck to the left of her laid on the horn causing Edie to swerve back. Hitting the turn signal, she navigated the Jeep into the inner lane of Dupont Circle.

Back-burner. That's where you need to put the fear.

'Of course I was at the museum,' she replied, the best lies those fashioned from the truth. 'I'm at the museum every Monday. It's the only day of the week that I can take photos of the collection. But you already know that.' She dramatically sighed, hoping she sounded like a whipped and defeated cog. 'Linda in payroll has been threatening for weeks to tell on me for not clocking out when I leave the museum. I know. I know. Really bad habit. Guess you guys in audit finally caught up to me, huh?'

'Is it also your habit to exit the museum via the fire escape?'

'Oh, gosh ... *bus-ted*.' She nervously laughed, the lies fast mounting. 'All these smoke-free buildings make it hard for us addicts to get our nicotine fix.'

'And what of your satchel? You left it on your desk. Is that also another of your bad habits?'

Edie braked to avoid a ridiculously long stretch Hummer. 'Yeah, well, what can I say? Absent-minded is my middle name.'

'According to your driver's licence, your middle name is Darlene. Lovely picture, I might add. But then I've always had a weakness for curly-haired maidens.'

Edie racked her brain for a response, fast running out of lies.

Determined not to end up like Jonathan Padgham, she injected a big dose of fake incredulity into her voice. '*You* have my wallet? Thank God. I was wondering who – You will be a dear and return it, won't you? It'd be such a pain to have to cancel all my cards.'

'No need to worry. I've already taken the liberty of cancelling your credit cards. I've also cleaned out your chequing and savings accounts. My, my, what a thrifty little miser you are. You've hoarded away nearly thirty thousand dollars.'

They cleaned out my accounts. How in God's name did

they get the security codes to – The bent cop. He would have access to God knows what records. Her mobile number. Her social security number. Every Big Brother computerized database under the sun.

'I'd be happy to give you a reward for returning my wallet,' she said, scrambling for a foothold, a limb, a root, *anything* she could hold on to. 'I'd also appreciate if you didn't let payroll know that I left a couple of hours early. I had a killer headache and –'

'Thou shall not lie!' the caller barked into her ear. A half-second later, as though he had reined in his runaway temper, he calmly said, 'Entertaining though they are, I'm beginning to grow weary of your lies, Ms Miller.'

'Lies? What lies?' When that met with silence, she said, 'Look, you've got me confused with another woman in the line-up.' When the silence lengthened, she said, 'That was a joke.' *As in people with something to hide are not capable of cracking a joke.*

'A mailman in the apartment building behind the museum, believing he was performing his civic duty, identified you from your DC driver's licence photo. You see? We know everything about you, Ms Miller. We also know that you were at the museum, on the fourth floor, when Dr Padgham met his unfortunate end.'

Unfortunate end? Was this guy for real? Jonathan Padgham's brains were blown clear out of his head. Talk about wiping the toilet bowl clean.

'Who are you?'

'Who I am is unimportant.' Then, the caller's voice dropping a scary octave, 'Perhaps at this juncture I should mention that you can run but you cannot hide.'

Edie looked in the rear-view mirror.

SUVs. Cars, taxis and delivery trucks of every stripe.

But no dark blue Ford.

And no DC police cruisers.

She decided to call his bluff.

'Word of warning, fella. When trying to threaten a woman, clichés usually don't inspire a whole lot of fear. As for threats, here's one right back at you ... Call me again and I will not *hesitate* to go to the FBI. Normally, I'd call the cops, but I figure I wouldn't get out of the precinct alive. I can just hear the news broadcast now. "Edie Miller, victim of an unfortunate accident, slipped on a recently mopped floor at DC police headquarters, cracking her skull." What do you think? Does that sound about right?'

'I'm certain that the FBI is much too busy tracking jihadist terror cells to take your call let alone give you the time of day.'

'Ah, but like you said, I'm the sole surviving witness to a brutal execution. One that involves a well-organized art ring,' she added, laying all her cards on the table. 'I think the suits at the FBI will be only too happy to spare me a few minutes of their time.'

'How do you know we haven't infiltrated the FBI?'

She didn't. And the cocky bastard knew it.

'What do you want from me?'

'Merely to talk. To clarify the situation so as to alleviate your unwarranted fears. I have very deep pockets, Ms Miller, and would be only too happy to triple the balance in your two bank accounts.'

Yeah, right. Something told her she'd never see a dime.

Accelerating, she jerked the Jeep over one lane. Then another, exiting the traffic circle at Mass Avenue.

'You want to talk? Fine. Here's the only thing I have to say to you –' She dragged out the silence for several seconds then screeched, 'Go to hell!"

Pulling the wireless headset out of her ear, she flung it in the direction of her bag.

Shaking – not like one leaf, but like a whole pile of wind-whipped leaves – she kept her eyes glued to the road, the familiar equestrian monuments passing in a blur as she drove around Scott Circle and under Thomas Circle. She then turned right at 11th, drove a few blocks and made a left turn onto Pennsylvania. In the distance loomed the US Capitol.

The snow started to fall more heavily. Driving on autopilot, she turned up the heater.

At 4th Street, she turned right, the East Building of the National Gallery of Art on her left, the West Building on her right. Not bothering to signal, she made a sharp right into the circular drive next to the museum, pulling the Jeep into the first available parking spot she could find, right behind a snow-covered Lexus. It was a prime parking spot, mere steps from the West Building entrance. It also required a NGA parking sticker.

'So, sue me,' she muttered. It was snowing and she didn't have time to find a legal parking space, the Mall crowded despite the foul weather.

Yanking the keys out of the ignition, she tossed them into her bag and got out of the Jeep. The National Gallery of Art was the most public place she could think of to hide. One of the largest marble buildings in the world, it exuded a sense of strength and security. And there were guards everywhere. Tons of them. As she rushed towards the oversized entry doors, she tried not to think of the two dead guards back at the Hopkins.

Opening a door, she glanced at her watch: 2:30. The museum would be open for another two and a half hours. Enough time to figure out her next move. Hopefully, C.Aisquith had received her email and was on his or her way to the museum.

At the front desk, Edie opened her bag for inspection, the guard giving the contents only a cursory glance. If he noticed the box of spinach, he gave no indication. Edie slung the bag back on her shoulder, unimpressed with the museum's post-9/11 security measures.

Well acquainted with the layout – she had spent many hours perusing the museum's collection since first moving to DC nearly twenty years ago – Edie took the escalator down one floor to the underground concourse that connected the two wings. Passing the Henry Moore sculpture at the base of the escalator, she headed into the gift shop. The muffled hubbub was non-stop. People chatting. People talking on mobiles. People waxing poetic about the beautiful boxed Christmas cards. The mingling of all those voices was a comforting sound, reassuring Edie that she was finally safe.

Reaching the Cascade Café, she stood next to the gushing waterfall that gave the café its name. Enclosed behind a giant screen of glass, pumped water continuously flowed over a wall of corrugated granite. One storey below ground, the protective glass wall was the only source of natural light in the concourse. Edie was able to see the wintry grey sky above.

For the next fifteen minutes, she carefully scrutinized each and every museum patron who entered the concourse. Teens garbed in Gap. Ladies who lunch garbed in Gucci. Museum staff garbed in drab grey. And then she saw him, a tall red-headed man, fortyish, who had about him a discernible air of self-assurance. From the cut of his clothes – expensive navy-blue wool jacket, cream-coloured cable-knit sweater, black leather shoes paired with blue denim jeans – she pegged him for a European.

The red-headed man came to a stop in the middle of the crowded concourse. Turning his head, he glanced at her, held her gaze, then looked away.

Edie purposefully strode towards him. Having spent a summer selling timeshares in Florida, she wasn't afraid of approaching strangers.

The red-headed man's gaze swerved back in her direction, a questioning look on his face.

'C.Aisquith at lycos.com?'

He nodded, blue eyes narrowing. 'And you must be Edie103 at earthlink.com. I would normally say "Pleased to make your acquaintance" but given the dire content of your electronic missive that may be a bit premature.'

Like Jonathan Padgham, he had a cultured English accent.

'I'm curious. How did you recognize me? There must be a hundred people milling about.'

'Lucky guess,' she replied, shrugging. 'That and the fact that you have the same British I'm-so-superior air about you that Dr Padgham had.'

One side of the man's mouth twitched up. 'Had? I can't imagine old Padge has changed all that much.'

Edie swallowed, the moment of truth having arrived much too abruptly.

'I said "had" for a reason. He's dead. Jonathan Padgham was killed a little over an hour ago. And just my luck, I'm the only witness to the murder.'

9

'. . . and if they find us, we're both going to wish we'd had the foresight to pre-purchase a headstone and burial plot.'

For several moments Cædmon Aisquith stared at the paranoid, Pre-Raphaelite beauty standing before him. Like a mad maestro, she used her hands to punctuate the nonsensical words issuing from her chapped lips.

'Why contact me? Why not go to the authorities?' He spoke calmly, not wanting to tip the scales from mad to stark raving mad.

'Because the authorities were in on the kill, that's why. And they mistakenly believe that Dr Padgham sent you an email right before he died,' she answered, clearly unable to speak in coherent sentences. 'That's why they want to kill you. And trust me, killing you would be child's play for these guys. Like the grim reaper pulling that battery bunny right out of a top hat.'

'Mmmm.' He wondered if she had taken some sort of hallucinatory drug.

'Is that all you have to say?'

'I could say that you have a penchant for mixed metaphors.'

'Look, I'm dead serious. Emphasis on *dead* just in case you're too dense to get the message. You still don't believe me? Fine. I've got the proof right here.'

'Indeed.'

She began to rummage through the bag hanging off her leather-clad shoulder. Peering inside, Cædmon caught sight of what looked like a Manila file folder and a box of frozen vegetables.

It was plain as a pikestaff: the woman was absolutely bonkers.

A determined look on her face, she removed a khaki-coloured waistcoat from the bag. Clutching it in her hand, she brandished the garment in front of his face. 'I was wearing this when Dr Padgham was murdered. Then I had to crawl over his body . . .' Her chest visibly heaved. 'That's his blood smeared on the front.'

'May I?' Cædmon touched the bloodstain, surprised to discover that it was damp.

Were it not for the still-tacky bloodstain and the faint smell of vomit, he would have dismissed the woman outright. Instead, he removed his mobile phone from his breast pocket.

'What are you doing?' Edie Miller frantically grabbed him by the arm, preventing him from raising the mobile to his ear. 'If you call the police, we're as good as dead.'

'If you would be so kind as to unhand me, I'm going to ring Padgham.' *And hopefully get to the bottom of this lunacy.*

'Be my guest,' she muttered, releasing her grip.

Having earlier programmed Padge's mobile number into his phone, he quickly made the call. He let it ring five times, disconnecting when an automated message began to play.

'It appears that the old boy has turned off his mobile.'

'Wrong!' Edie Miller screeched at him, earning several sideways glances from passers-by. 'The old boy is lying under his desk in a pool of his own blood.'

Worried she might continue to attract unwanted attention, he motioned to the nearby tables. 'I'm willing to hear you out provided you keep calm. Understood?'

She nodded, actually managing to look contrite.

'Very well then. Do be seated while I get us some coffee. Unless, of course, you prefer tea.'

'No. Coffee is fine.' She glanced at the nearby Espresso Bar. 'A cappuccino would be better.'

'Duly noted. I won't be a moment.'

Aisquith watched her as, like an obedient child, she shuffled over to a small table adjacent to the Espresso Bar. Seating herself, she removed her bag from her shoulder and clutched it to her breast. While the mass of dark brown corkscrew curls was her crowning glory, it was the deep-set brown eyes that drew and held his attention. Accentuated by straight brows, the combination gave her a sombre air wholly at odds with her forceful personality. And wholly at odds with her eccentric attire – a black leather motor-cycle jacket, clunky black boots and a long purple and red tartan skirt.

'God help me for coming to a crazed damsel's rescue,' he muttered under his breath.

The order placed for a cappuccino and a hazelnut coffee, he paid the cashier. Collecting the coffees, he grabbed sugar packets, dairy creamers, plastic stirrers and paper napkins, stuffing them into his jacket pocket. A few seconds later, a coffee cup clutched in each hand, he made his way to the table.

'Not knowing how you take your coffee, I rather overdid it.' He plonked everything onto the middle of the round table.

His noticeably subdued companion reached for two sugar packets. 'I always sweeten the deal with a couple of sugars,' she remarked, snapping the packets to and fro as she spoke. Ripping them open she poured the contents into her cup. 'You know, it's just occurred to me that I don't even know your first name.'

'Cædmon,' he replied, watching her brow wrinkle when she heard the Old English moniker, the un-usual name his father's way of making a man of him, forcing him to face up to the bullies at a tender age.

'I thought the English were all tea drinkers.'

'Rumour has it I'm something of an iconoclast.' Opening a creamer, he poured a dollop into his cup. That done, he began the inquisition. 'How is it that you came to witness this *supposed* murder?'

'You're a hard sell, aren't you? Although I suppose if the boot were on the other foot, I would be as well. To answer your question, I'm a freelance photographer at the Hopkins Museum. That's how I came to witness the murder.' About to raise the cup to her lips, she suddenly lowered it to the table. 'Before I tell you what happened, I need to know in what capacity you knew Dr Padgham,' she abruptly demanded, her lack of subtlety disarming.

'We played cricket together at Oxford. As so often happens with youthful friendships, we eventually lost touch with one another. When Padge learned that I was in Washington on the last leg of a book tour, he rang me up. Suggested we meet for drinks. Talk over old times, that sort of thing. Satisfied?' When she nodded, he said, 'It's now your turn, Miss Miller.'

'A month ago I was hired by Eliot Hopkins to photograph and digitally archive the entire museum collection. I work on Mondays because that's when the museum is closed to the public.'

'Enabling you to take your photographs unimpeded,' he intuited.

'Exactly. But today was unusual.'

'How so?'

'Dr Padgham was in his office. He's *never* in the office on Mondays.'

'Was there anyone else in the museum?'

'As usual, there were two guards downstairs in the main lobby.' She shot him a penetrating glance from deep-set brown eyes. 'You're following all this, right?'

'Yes, yes,' he assured her. 'Please continue.'

'Around one thirty, Dr Padgham called and asked if I would come upstairs to the administration offices.'

'Why did he do that?'

'He wanted me to take some photographs for him. I got the idea that he was working on some kind of special project. That's why he was in the office on his day off. Obedient minion that I am, I went up to the fourth floor and took the pics. I was about to leave his office when a cable came loose on his computer. Dr Padgham conned me into climbing under the desk to fix the connection.'

Cædmon nodded. 'Now *that* sounds like the Padge I know and love.'

'You *knew* and *loved*. I told you he's –'

'I know. No need to labour the point.'

'No need to be so crabby,' she countered, proving she was no shrinking violet. 'Anyway, I was still under the desk when a man walked into Dr Padgham's office and shot him in the head point blank.' As she spoke, her hands began to tremble. She wrapped both of them round her cup. 'He was killed instantly. The killer had no idea that I was under the desk ... that I witnessed the whole thing.'

Cædmon stared at the curly-haired beauty sitting across from him, resisting the urge to pull her to him, to calm the fearful quiver that had travelled from her hands to her entire upper body.

'How did you get away?'

'I climbed down the fire escape. I was hiding in the alley when I saw the killer approach a DC cop. And *this* is where the story takes a turn for the worse.' She looked him in the eye, her gaze disturbingly direct. 'The killer and the cop were in cahoots.'

'Did they see you in the alley?'

'No. But it didn't much matter because the killer had already accessed the museum security logs. That's how they found out I was in the building at the time of the murder. That's why they're looking for me.'

'Would you be able to identify the man?'

'Murderer,' she corrected. 'For starters he had a military-style buzz cut. And he was big. Really, *really* big. Steroid big,' she added, using her hands to indicate height and width. If her gestures were to be believed, the killer had an improbable shoulder span of some four and a half feet. 'That's all I can remember.'

'I see.'

'Wait!' she exclaimed, cappuccino spilling over the brim of her cup as she excitedly jogged the table. 'He wore an unusual silver ring on his right hand.' She hunted around in her bag and pulled out a creased sheet of paper. 'Do you have a pen?'

He wordlessly reached into his breast pocket. Taking his pen, she drew an intricate pattern. Tilting her head to one side, she reviewed her handiwork before sliding the sheet of paper in his direction.

'Sorry, I'm a photographer not an artist.'

Cædmon examined the drawing, instantly recognizing the pattern.

'How interesting ... it's a Jerusalem cross. Also known as the crusader's cross. The four tau crosses represent the Old Testament. That's these T shapes.' He pointed to the arms of the larger cross at the centre. 'And the four smaller Greek crosses are the New Testament. You're certain this is the symbol that was on the, er, killer's ring?'

She nodded. 'Is that significant?'

'It was to the medieval knights who conquered the Holy Land,' he informed her, well acquainted with the topic having developed an interest in the Knights Templar when he was at Oxford. An obsessive interest, as it turned out, one that ultimately cost him his academic career. 'In the twelfth century this particular cross served as the coat of arms for the short-lived kingdom of Jerusalem. Although the European knights ...' He self-consciously cleared his throat. 'I apologize. I'm rambling. Do you recall anything else?'

Edie Miller sucked her lower lip between her teeth, enabling him to see that she had slightly crooked front teeth. And plump beautiful lips.

64

'No, sorry. But you do believe me, don't you? About Dr Padgham being murdered?'

He shook his head, uncertain what to make of her fantastical tale. 'Why in God's name would this masked man kill Jonathan Padgham? Padge was as harmless as the proverbial fly. Annoying, at times, I admit, but utterly harmless.'

She stared at him long and hard. As though he'd just asked a fool's question.

'He was killed on account of the relic.'

'Relic? This is the first that you've made mention of a relic.'

A confused look crept into her eyes. A second later, shaking her head, she said, 'Oh God, I'm sorry. So much has happened. I'm getting everything mixed up. Like my brain is starting to short-circuit.'

Again, he was tempted to pull her into his arms. While her travails may be imaginary, her panic seemed real enough.

'Drink some more coffee.'

She gulped down the last of her cappuccino. Seeing a faint brown smear on her upper lip, he un-thinkingly picked up a paper napkin and wiped the smudge clean. Then, guiltily aware of the trespass, he crumbled the napkin into a ball, tossing it onto the table.

'Dr Padgham was in the process of sending you a digital photo of the relic when he was killed. When the killer left he took the relic.'

'A digital photo? Why would he have done that?'

Opening her bag, she removed a camera. 'He didn't say. As a backup, I saved a photograph on the camera's internal memory. Here.' She shoved the camera at him. 'That's the relic.'

Holding the camera within a few inches of his face, Cædmon examined the digital image as through a glass darkly. His breath caught in his throat, her outlandish story suddenly making perfect sense.

'Bloody hell . . . I don't believe it. I absolutely don't believe it,' he whispered, unable to draw his gaze from the photo.

'I take it from your stupefied expression that the relic is valuable enough to steal.'

'Most assuredly.'

'And how about killing? Is it valuable enough for someone to kill for it?'

He lowered the camera, keenly aware that Edie Miller was in very grave danger.

'Oh, I think a great many people would kill to obtain the fabled Stones of Fire.'

10

'There will be in these last days many deceivers and false prophets and many who will follow them: For many deceivers are entered into the world.'

With reverential care Boyd Braxton closed the book and replaced it in the glove compartment. The Warrior's Bible, leather bound and gilt-embossed with the Rosemont Security Consultants emblem, had been personally given to him by Colonel Stanford MacFarlane. And though Boyd was in a tearing hurry, the colonel always said that it was important to give the Almighty his due.

Reaching under the Bible, Boyd removed an official police permit and placed it on the dash of the Ford. The permit gave him the right to park anywhere in the city. It didn't matter that he wasn't on the force. He looked like a cop. And he drove a cop car. No one would think twice.

Parked directly in front of him, covered in a light layer of newly fallen snow, was a black Jeep Wrangler. Just as he had figured, no sooner had he left her pad than the bitch had crept out of her hidey-hole.

'Stupid cunt,' he muttered, getting out of the Ford. Walking over to the Jeep, he crouched down and slapped a magnetic tracking device on its metal underbelly. He could now monitor the vehicle's every move on his mobile.

'You, bitch, damned near cost me my job,' he muttered as he walked towards the museum.

And being Colonel Stan MacFarlane's right-hand man at Rosemont Security Consultants was a job he took real seriously. Just like he'd taken his stint in the US Marine Corps real seriously. He still wore his hair high and tight, having served fifteen years in the Green Machine. Now he served Stan MacFarlane. If it hadn't been for the colonel, he'd be eating institutional slop and lifting weights alongside the brothers in the state penitentiary. No chance of parole.

Juries don't look kindly upon gunnery sergeants who murder their wife and child.

A lot like that dark day four years ago, he'd fucked up royally today at the Hopkins Museum.

But soon he'd make it right, proving to the colonel that he was still a hard charger. That he was still worthy of his trust. That he was still a holy warrior.

Swinging open the glass door that fronted the 4th Street Entrance, Boyd entered the National Gallery of Art.

Beautiful. Not a metal detector in sight. The Ka-Bar knife and Heckler & Koch Mark 23 pistol would pass undetected.

Like he was on official business, he strode over to the desk. Security didn't amount to much more than a cloth-covered table manned by a pair of renta-cops. Opening the flap of his leather coat, he revealed a very official-looking police badge.

'Is there a problem, Detective Wilson?' the grey-haired guard enquired, straightening his shoulders as he spoke.

'I'm looking for someone. Have you seen this woman?' Boyd held up a photograph of one Eloise Darlene Miller.

The guard reached for the pair of reading glasses hanging from his neck. After several seconds of careful scrutiny, he said, 'Yeah, not too long ago, as a matter of fact. If I'm not mistaken, she headed down to the concourse.'

Never having been inside the National Gallery of Art before, Boyd glanced around the cavernous marble-walled lobby. 'Where's the concourse?'

'At the bottom of the escalator,' the guard said, pointing to the other side of the hall. 'You want me to alert the museum security team?'

'No need. She's not dangerous,' he assured the guard. 'We just need to ask her a few questions.' Returning the photo to his coat pocket, Boyd headed towards the escalator.

At the bottom of the escalator, he took note of the white sculpture, unimpressed.

'If that's art, I'm Pablo Pick-my-ass Picasso,' he muttered, the sculpture looking a lot like the molar he once knocked out of a drunken swabbie's head. For years he'd kept that tooth as a good luck charm, that being his first bar fight of any real note.

Entering a dimly lit gift shop, Boyd saw that the place was overrun with people pushing wheelchairs, people dragging toddlers, people yakking on mobiles. Everywhere he looked there were people meandering about like so many lost sheep. *Perfect.* No one would later be able to recall who did what when, large crowds being the best camouflage a hunter could have.

As he passed a display of cards showing a Nativity scene, he made a mental note that this might be a classy place to do his Christmas shopping. Not that these godless people would even know the meaning of Christmas. Or any other event described in the Bible. Nowadays people put a 'popular' spin on the Word of God, forgetting that biblical text was not subject to New Age feel-good interpretations.

Only a deluded fool would paraphrase the Word of God.

The colonel had taught him that. The colonel had taught him a lot of things since that day four years ago when he had ordered him to get down on his knees before the Almighty. Never having prayed before, Boyd had been wary, but once he got over the initial embarrassment, he discovered it was an easy thing | to beg God's forgiveness. And just like that, in one life-altering moment, he was forgiven all his sins, past and present. The bars, the brothels, the brawls, all forgiven. So, too, the murder of wife and child.

Although it was a daily struggle, he tried mightily to be a perfect holy warrior. He didn't drink. Didn't smoke. Kept his body a temple unto the Lord. He wished that he didn't cuss, but having entered the Corps at the age of seventeen that was proving a hard habit to break.

Always room for improvement, he thought as he left the gift shop and entered the Cascade Café.

Coming to a standstill, he eye-fucked the place.

She was here, somewhere in the crowd. Her fear would make her stand out, having an energy all its own. Its own stink, as it were. Like a bullseye, her fear would lead him to her.

But first he had to cover his ass.

Catching sight of a tall, big-gutted cleaner lack-adaisically pushing a yellow bucket on wheels, Boyd knew he'd found his man. For ten years his father had pushed a similar bucket. Which is why Boyd knew that maintenance workers of every stripe were invisible to the rest of the world. Most people didn't favour them with a polite 'Hello' let alone a sideways glance. Pleased that the op was going so smoothly, he followed the cleaner through a door marked CUSTODIAL STAFF.

In fact he was thinking about his daddy – a mean, drunken bastard till the day he died – when he knocked out the unsuspecting cleaner with one well-aimed punch. Not believing in chance occurrences, Boyd recognized the fortuitous appearance of the cleaner for what it was – a gift from God.

'Since its creation some thirty-five hundred years ago, the Stones of Fire has cost the lives of countless individuals.'

'Including Jonathan Padgham,' Edie pointedly remarked.

'Sadly, I am inclined to agree with you.'

'Well, it's about time. Most people, if you tell them that their life is in danger, are willing to give you the benefit of the doubt.'

His red brows drew together. 'And why is *my* life in danger? I understand why this masked killer would be searching for you since you did, after all, witness Padge's murder. But I have no involvement whatsoever in this nefarious plot.'

'Think again, C.Aisquith at lycos.com. The killer mistakenly believes that Dr Padgham emailed you photos of the relic.' Edie jutted her chin at the camera still clutched in his hand.

Cædmon studied the camera for several seconds, a thoughtful look on his face. 'That can only mean one thing. The thieves don't want anyone to know of the relic's existence. Since the discovery of the Stones of Fire would have made international headlines and set biblical scholars a-twitter, we must assume that the relic came to be at the Hopkins museum via the back door.' Wearing a pensive expression, he slowly shook his head. '"The perfect treasure of his eyesight lost".'

'Are you saying what I think you're saying – that the relic was smuggled out of its country of origin and sold on the black market?' When he nodded, Edie said, 'Well, that would explain why the breastplate isn't listed in the museum's permanent collection. Since I'm archiving the collection, I have the master list of every ancient whatnot owned by the Hopkins. The breastplate was most definitely *not* on the list. Why is it called the Stones of Fire?' she abruptly asked, beginning to suspect that he knew more than he'd so far let on.

Cædmon Aisquith removed his gaze from the digital photo. 'The name was first coined by the Old Testament prophet Ezra. Actually, the relic has been known by quite a few names. The ancient Hebrews called it the Urim and Thummim. There are also several biblical references to the Breastplate of Judgement or the Jewels of Gold.'

'The Stones of Fire. The Urim and Thummim. These names tell me nothing. I feel like the elevator doors just opened on the ground floor of the Tower of Babel.'

'Perhaps I should retrace my steps.' Cædmon pushed his empty coffee cup to the side and positioned the camera in the middle of the table, enabling her to clearly see the photo of the jewel-studded gold breastplate. 'Bearing in mind that everything I am about to say is mere speculation, I believe that this relic,' he pointed to the image on the camera, 'or *askema* as it is known in Hebrew, may have been the actual breastplate worn by the Levite high priest when he performed the sacred temple rituals. What makes the breastplate utterly priceless is the fact that it was created by Moses himself as directed by God. So while not his actual handiwork, the breastplate is nevertheless the design of God.'

Edie, who had been silent up until this point, stubbornly shook her head. 'But I saw it with my own eyes. It was just ... just an old breastplate. You don't really believe that *that* was designed by God?' She tapped the camera display.

'Who am I to dispute the Old Testament prophets? The Bible is inundated with naysayers struck down by the wrath of God.' This droll remark left Edie in some doubt as to what Cædmon Aisquith actually believed.

'Since all that remains of the original breastplate are twelve stones and few bits and pieces of gold, how can you be so sure it's the real deal?'

'The relic would be easy enough to authenticate given the detailed description in the Book of Exodus. Conceived as a square, it originally comprised laced pieces of gold linen inlaid with twelve stones set in four rows of three.' Grabbing the same sheet of paper she'd earlier used to draw the Jerusalem cross, Cædmon sketched out a design. 'Based on the account in Exodus, I believe the breastplate would have looked something like this.' He turned the sketch in her direction.

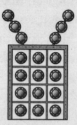

'As you can see, my artistic gifts are rudimentary at best. Be that as it may, each of the twelve gemstones possessed a divine power. In the first row there was a sardius, a topaz and a carbuncle ...' As he spoke, Cædmon carefully wrote the name of each gemstone. 'In the second row an emerald, sapphire and diamond; in the third a ligure, an agate and an amethyst; and finally, in the fourth row, beryl, onyx and jasper. Rather gemmy, don't you think?' He smiled slightly, making Edie realize that he was a handsome man. She didn't usually go for redheads but there was something uniquely appealing about the man sitting across from her. And of course the accent didn't hurt.

She glanced back and forth between the digital photo and penned sketch, suddenly able to see how beautiful the relic must have been aeons ago. 'Is there any significance to the fact there are twelve stones?'

'It's highly significant,' Cædmon replied. 'The number twelve symbolizes the completion of the sacred cycle. In the Torah, the first five books of the Old Testament, it's written that the twelve stones represented the twelve tribes of Israel. Just as each tribe had a unique function, the Levites being of the priestly caste, for instance, so too each of the twelve stones symbolized a hidden truth or virtue.'

'Since emeralds are my birthstone, I know that they symbolize immortality.'

'Rather ironic, what with the relic mysteriously appearing after so many centuries of being hidden away, supposedly lost forever.' The awestruck expression that Edie had seen when Cædmon first looked at the photo returned. 'If the relic can be authenticated, it would be a truly astounding discovery, the Stones of Fire having disappeared from the pages of the Bible several thousand years ago.'

She sat silent. Somewhere in the café Chinese food was being served. Edie could smell stir-fried vegetables and soy sauce. She swallowed a queasy lump in her throat.

'According to biblical scholars, the breastplate disappeared during the Babylonian — Are you all right?'

'No, I feel —' About to tell a lie, she instead said, 'I'm scared, hungry and exhausted. Take your pick.'

'Would you like something to eat?' He gestured to the pastries and desserts on the Espresso Bar.

'I'll pass on the desserts. But if you wouldn't mind getting me another cappuccino . . .'

'I'd be only too happy.'

Excusing himself, Cædmon got up from the table, Edie following him with her gaze. Although he spoke with a proper English accent and possessed a proper English name, albeit an antiquated one, Cædmon Aisquith's red hair, blue eyes and height screamed a Scot in the woodpile. A really smart Scot, the man standing at the Espresso Bar a one-man brains trust. That intelligence was admittedly a turn-on, the mind being the sexiest organ a man could possess. Had she and the strangely named Brit met under different circumstances, she could easily envision herself asking him out on a dinner date.

When Cædmon returned, setting a steaming cup of cappuccino in front of her, Edie smiled her thanks.

'Tell me, when you gazed upon the Stones of Fire, did you notice anything extraordinary, strange or even mystical?'

She gave the question a moment's consideration. 'No. Should I have noticed something out of the ordinary?'

'Difficult to say. Some biblical scholars believe that, once garbed with the breastplate, the high priest could foresee the future, as though the hand of God momentarily pulled back the curtain of time.'

'So the breastplate was used as some sort of divination tool?'

'Only secondarily. The primary function was that of a conduit between the high priest and God.' Cædmon paused a moment, letting the factoid sink in. Or maybe he was considering how much more he should divulge. Decision evidently reached, he continued: 'Specifically, the high priest used the breastplate to control and harness the divine fire contained within the Ark.'

About to take a sip of her cappuccino, Edie lowered her cup to the table.

'The Ark? As in the Ark of the Covenant?'

'None other.'

'" ... blessed be God Most High, who has delivered your enemies into your hand!" Praise be, praise be,' Boyd Braxton whispered as he finished reciting his favourite Bible passage. Buttoning up the cleaner's dark blue shirt, he unzipped the cheap polyester trousers and tucked in the shirt-tails. Then, not willing to mess with his juju, he cupped his balls. 'You're the man, BB. You are the man.'

He'd been out of boot camp only a few weeks when his mess buddies had taken to calling him BB. As in Big Bang. As in the fact that he could outdrink, outfight, outfuck any man in the unit. The fighting part landed him in the brig more times than he could recall, Boyd damned with his father's murderous temper. The colonel said his temper was a cross he had to bear. Like Jesus lugging a hundred and ten pounds of lumber all the way to Calvary. It was a daily struggle. Sometimes he took the day. Sometimes the day took him.

A quick glance at the name badge sewn onto the front of the matching blue jacket indicated that the black man sprawled at his feet was named Walter Jefferson. Blood seeped from his head and dribbled

79

from his snot box, the cleaner having broken his nose when he hit the deck.

'Sorry 'bout that,' Boyd snickered, figuring it'd be a couple of hours before the man came to. Since the colonel had been adamant that everything be by numbers, he'd taken the extra precaution of stuffing a dirty rag into the man's mouth. Then, trussing him up like a big turkey, he'd secured his hands and feet with a belt. He'd fucked up at the Hopkins Museum, but this time there would be no more dumb-ass mistakes.

Boyd popped the mag on his pistol. Fifteen rounds. He only needed one to kill the Miller broad, but it was always a good idea to have extra ammo. Just in case. His movements quick and steady, he screwed a silencer onto the end of the barrel. He shoved the Mark 23 into the small of his back, the jacket hiding the telltale bulge. He jammed a leather scabbard next to the pistol, the Ka-Bar knife his backup weapon of choice. A Ka-Bar could slice and dice a man in less time that it took to say 'Howdy do.' Or a woman, Boyd having killed more than one bitch in his time.

Suited up, he grabbed the mop handle and steered the yellow bucket towards the closed door of the cleaners' storeroom. Grey water sloshed over the sides and Boyd slowed his pace. Opening the door, he rolled the mop and bucket across the threshold. Then, covering his tracks, he reached for the keys dangling from his belt. It took a few tries, but he found the right one, locking Walter Jefferson safely inside. That done, he hid his own clothes, rolled into a ball inside his leather jacket, under a nearby bench. Approaching the crowded concourse, he surveyed the jabbering hordes of tourists. Again he thought they'd make good cover, his plan to kill the Miller bitch, chuck the untraceable gun into the bucket of water and get his hairy ass out of the building before anyone realized what was happening.

Pushing his bucket, Boyd could see that no one paid him any attention. Like he'd figured, he was just a big blue ghost.

Perfect. He loved it when everything came together.

'Cause, God help him, he knew what it was like when the fucking floor gave way. When you were sinking in shit without a buoy in sight. That's how it was back in '04 when he returned from his first deployment in Iraq.

Fallujah. What a fucking shit hole.

Every night he woke up in a cold sweat. One night he actually pissed the bed. If his wife Tammy so much as brushed her bare leg against his, he'd sit bolt upright in the bed, reaching for his M16. Except he didn't have his rifle. Didn't even have a damned sidearm, Tammy refusing to let him bring a loaded anything into the house on account of Baby Ashley. Six months old, Baby Ashley cried all night long. Just like those fucking raghead babies in Fallujah. One night he couldn't take it any longer, Ashley bawling for a milk titty. *Couldn't the brat just shut the fuck up?!*

With each ear-piercing scream, the pounding inside his skull got louder. And louder still.

And then everything went eerily quiet, Ashley's screams muffled with a pillow.

Just like that baby in Fallujah.

That's about the time his wife ran into the room, jumped on his back and actually sank her teeth into the side of his neck, the bitch going for his jugular. He'd had no choice but to fling the rabid cunt off his back. She hit her head on a nearby rocking chair, the blow pretty much killing her on the spot. Not knowing what to do, he telephoned Colonel MacFarlane. Like he was his own flesh and blood, the colonel took care of everything, giving him an airtight alibi, making it look like a robbery gone bad. The local police bought the story. Even the dickheads at the *Daily News* bought it, the local paper speculating that it was one of a series of local robberies committed by strung-out junkies looking to make some quick cash: TRAGEDY BEFALLS WAR HERO.

The colonel said the same thing. Except he went one step further. He said God understood what it was like to be a warrior, to come home from a hard-fought battle only to have to fend off the evil. Colonel Stan MacFarlane was a great and good man, and Boyd owed him. Big time. Not just for saving his ass, but for showing him the Way. For leading him into God's fold. And when the little dick bastards at the Pentagon drummed that great and good man out of the Corps, Boyd went with him.

Pushing his yellow bucket, Boyd scanned the crowd, his nose twitching at the faint smell of stir-fried Chink food.

The Miller bitch is here. Somewhere in the crowd.

Soon enough he'd find her. And when he did, it'd be like shooting ragheads in a rain barrel.

'... the story of the Ark of the Covenant is an operatic drama played out on the stage of the biblical Holy Land,' Cædmon continued in answer to Edie Miller's question.

'Operatic? Don't you think you're laying it on a bit thick?'

'Not in the least. As you undoubtedly know, the Ark of the Covenant, or *aron habrit* in Hebrew, was an ornate chest roughly four feet long, two and a half feet wide, and two and half feet high –' as he spoke Cædmon spanned his hands first in one direction, then another, approximating the proportions in mid-air '– inlaid with hammered gold. But what you may not know is that the Ark of the Covenant was constructed *exactly* like an Egyptian bark.'

'Like the gold boxes I saw last year at the King Tut exhibit, right?'

'Right down to the gold rim on the lid and the winged figures which adorned the top cover. Furthermore, the Egyptian bark and the Ark of the Covenant both had the same purpose: that being to contain their respective deities.'

Her brow furrowed. 'But I thought the Ark of the Covenant was a container for the Ten Commandments. Are you saying that the Ark of the Covenant was some kind of magical God-in-the-box, like in that movie *Raiders of the Lost Ark*?'

Cædmon chuckled, amused by the question. 'Just as the sacred Egyptian bark contained the might and majesty of Aten, so the Ark of the Covenant contained the power and glory of Yahweh. And, once contained, the only way to control all that cosmic power was for the high priest to shield himself with the Stones of Fire.'

Raising her steaming cup to her lips, his companion took several moments to digest what he'd just said. As she did, Cædmon surveyed the throng. Nothing appeared out of the ordinary, his eyes taking in a man pushing a wheelchair-bound octogenarian, a cleaner pushing a yellow bucket and a harried mother pushing a pram. Briefly he noticed two youths, one fuchsia-haired, the other tiger-striped, locked in a passionate embrace in front of the massive glass wall that fronted the waterfall.

'Okay, we know what happened to the breastplate: it was confiscated by Nebuchadnezzar, hidden in Babylon and recently rediscovered and smuggled out of Iraq,' Edie said, drawing his attention back to the matter in hand. 'But what happened to the Ark of the Covenant?'

Ah, a woman after my own heart.

'At some point after the construction of Solomon's famous temple, the Ark of the Covenant disappears from the pages of the Bible. Whether captured, destroyed or hidden, its current where-abouts are unknown.'

She folded her arms across her chest. 'Yeah, well, I seem to recall you saying the same thing about the Stones of Fire, but the breastplate managed to mysteriously turn up. And because of it, you and I are now in serious danger.'

Out of the corner of his eye, Cædmon noticed that the cleaner pushing the yellow bucket had suddenly turned in their direction.

Odd that the man was wearing military-style boots.

The man was also a muscular behemoth. *'He was big. Really, really big. Steroid big.'*

Recalling Edie's earlier description of Padgham's killer, Cædmon felt a prickling sensation on the back of his neck.

'I am beginning to concur with your assessment,' he murmured, his eyes still trained on the giant. The man removed his right hand from the mop handle and reached behind his back.

In that instant Cædmon saw the flash of a silver ring.

In the next instant he caught the dark flash of . . .

He squinted, the object coming into focus.

Bloody hell! The man had a gun!

14

There being no time to think, Cædmon shoved the table aside and hurled himself at Edie Miller, flinging both of them to the floor in one strong-armed motion.

The bullet struck the upturned table and ricocheted off the stone top. Female companion in tow, Cædmon scooted behind a nearby column. The second bullet struck a metal planter – *ping!* – less than a metre from their huddled position.

A woman in the crowd frantically screamed.

A man gruffly shouted, 'He's got a gun!'

Yet another yelled, 'It's a fucking terrorist!'

Several other people joined the cacophony of fear.

Not waiting for the third bullet, Cædmon went on the offensive. Stretching out his right arm, he grabbed a trolley stacked with dirty crockery parked beside the column. With a mighty heave, he propelled the cart forward. Plates crashed to the floor. A smashing diversion.

Catching sight of the motion, the gunman spun on his heel, reflexively firing a third round. The bullet hit the sheet of glass that contained the cascading fountain, the glass shattering on impact. Water gushed into the concourse.

The chaos increased, people running pell-mell in every direction.

Armour-piercing bullets, Cædmon thought, horrified. *That would have been safety glass. The man was using bloody armour-piecing bullets.*

Edie, flattened beneath the weight of his body, shrieked in his ear. Raising his head, Cædmon scanned the panic-stricken crowd, searching for the armed behemoth.

The gunman was nowhere in sight. All that remained was the yellow bucket, a wooden mop handle protruding from its murky depths. He'd fled the scene. Or he'd moved to a different firing position. Either way, they had mere seconds to escape the concourse.

He pushed himself to his knees, yanking Edie off the floor as he did so.

'What's happening?' she asked in a strangled voice.

'Padgham's murderer has just paid his respects.'

'Oh, God! We're not going to get out of here alive!'

Suddenly realizing he might soon have a hysterical woman on his hands, Cædmon roughly grabbed her by the shoulders. 'We *will* escape. But only if you remain calm and do *exactly* as I say. Understood?' When he received no answer, he shook her. Hard. 'Understood?'

She nodded. Satisfied with the mute reply – her input unnecessary and unwanted – he surveyed the damage. The crowd, some running, many crouched on the concourse floor, had become a shouting, screaming mass of collective hysteria. A Bosch painting come to life.

Cædmon directed his gaze first one way then the other, determining how best to navigate through the mêlée. To the right was a tunnel-like hall. To the left was the gift shop. With its dim recessed lighting and numerous display counters, the gift shop offered the best cover. Grabbing Edie by the hand, he ran in that direction.

'Where are we going?' she demanded, huffing as she kept pace with him.

He sidestepped a museum employee, the man actually attempting to direct the frenzied horde, much like a traffic cop directing cars after a pile-up.

'We're going as far from the maddening crowd as possible,' he informed her, having to shout to be heard over the din. Espying a black trench coat draped over a counter, the owner having abandoned it in the rush to escape, he grabbed it as they ran past. He then dodged behind an oversized column. Out of sight, he came to a halt.

'Quickly! Put this on!' Unceremoniously, he shoved the coat at his companion's chest.

'Why would I want to –'

'Your outfit is preposterous. As such, it makes an easy target.'

Removing her bag from her shoulder, Edie shoved her arms into the trench coat. 'With your red hair, you kind of stick out yourself.'

'Point taken.' As he spoke, Cædmon plucked a

beanie from the head of a bespectacled Asian teen-ager as he shot past, the youth too terrified to do anything other than keep on running. Having lived through several RIRA terrorist attacks on London, Cædmon knew that chaos had a way of making even the most truculent uncharacteristically pliant. He shoved the green hat with its gold-lettered PATRIOTS logo onto his head. Then he reached over and yanked the two sides of the much-too-big trench coat across Edie's waist, hurriedly tying the belt around her waist.

Camouflaged, he led them through the gift store in a zigzag pattern, that being the most difficult for the human eye to follow. Hand in hand they darted from sales counter to column to yet another sales counter. A few seconds later they emerged into a well-lit antechamber that housed a Henry Moore sculpture. Quickly, Cædmon assessed their three choices: escalator, lift or staircase.

'Always execute the least likely manoeuvre, that being the only way to escape a determined enemy.'

His MI5 instructors' lesson well-learned, Cædmon grabbed Edie by the shoulder, spinning her towards the stairs.

'But it's quicker to take the escalator.'

'Quicker, perhaps, but far more dangerous.'

Side by side, they ascended the steps, the stair-case deserted, unlike the crowded escalator on the opposite side of the antechamber, people packed onto it like frantic sheep.

At the top of the stairs they found themselves in a

large vestibule, two matched bronze pumas standing sentry. On the far side of the vestibule the lift
opened, half a dozen owl-faced visitors spilling out.
A few feet away, he sighted the public conveniences,
the WCs marked with male and female symbols. Just
beyond the pumas was the 4th Street lobby, the area
a veritable mob scene, frantic museum goers running
to and fro, harried guards attempting to corral them
through the exit.

Like doomed fish in a glass bowl.

Easy pickings for a hungry cat.

The situation evaluated, Cædmon grabbed Edie by
the hand and dragged her towards the WCs. Shoving
his shoulder against the swinging door, he pulled his
companion into the ladies' loo.

'What are you doing?' she screeched, the sound
echoing off the stark white tiles.

'Saving your life, I dare say.'

'But you're a man! You're not allowed in here!'

Ignoring her, he scanned the facilities.

Six stalls. Five sinks. No occupants.

He pushed open one of the middle stall doors.

'Did you hear me, Cædmon? I said that you're not
allowed –'

'Do calm down, will you?' He shoved her inside
the stall, following her. 'And while you're at it, lower
your voice. Getting into a dither will only make
things worse than they already are.'

An adamant look on her face, she continued to
protest, 'But this is the ladies' room.'

'Precisely why I chose it over the little boys' loo. It's only a guess, but I seriously doubt our testosterone-driven assailant will think to look for us in here, the word "ladies" acting as a natural deterrent. For the moment at least, we're safe.'

'Not to mention cramped like peas in a porcelain pod,' she muttered, awkwardly twisting her upper body as she straddled the toilet, the stall barely wide enough to accommodate one person, let alone two.

Stall door locked, Cædmon removed a visitors' guide from his coat pocket, having picked up the map when he arrived at the museum.

'Now what?'

'Now, we work out how best to outwit our nemesis.' Unfolding the map, he held it in front of his chest. Edie, forced to stand on tiptoe, peered over his shoulder. 'According to the map, there are five possible exits from the museum.'

'The nearest is no more than fifty feet away. That one we just passed.' Reaching over his shoulder, she jabbed her index finger at the nearby exit. 'Right there. The 4th Street exit. My Jeep is parked outside the door. We can be out of here in seconds. As in "Gentlemen, start your engines."'

Cædmon rejected her suggestion with a brusque shake of his head. 'I have reason to suspect you were followed to the museum. Which means the 4th Street exit will undoubtedly be manned by either the gunman or an accomplice. Our point of egress should be the most distant exit from our current position.'

She grabbed him by the upper arm, awkwardly turning him towards her. 'Are you crazy? You're talking about the 7th Street exit!' she hissed in a highly agitated whisper. 'That's all the way on the other side of the National Gallery of Art. It's three city blocks from where we're at right now. If you think that's a good plan, you're totally insane!'

'Ah, I see my reputation precedes me.'

His mind made up, he refolded the map, replacing it in his breast pocket. Not bothering to ask permission, he searched the pockets of Edie's pilfered trench coat. Discovering a black canvas rain hat, he handed it to her.

'Here, put this on.'

'Uh uh.' She shook her head, brown curls buoyantly bouncing about her shoulders. 'You might not care if you get a case of head lice, but I –'

'Put it on,' he ordered, thinking her adamance, yet again, misplaced. 'Head lice can be cured with a bit of medicated shampoo. Resurrection is trickier to manage. As I speak, the gunman is searching the museum for two targets: a red-headed chap and a curly-haired maiden. Trust me. We have danger in spades.'

'Not to mention hearts, clubs and diamonds,' she muttered, stuffing her curls into the canvas hat.

'Much better,' he said, nodding his approval. 'Come. We've tarried long enough.' He unlocked the stall and swung it open.

Edie stared at him, her obstinacy now replaced with a look of fearful dread.

'Do you think we've got a chance of getting out of here alive?' she whispered.

Rather than make an empty promise he might not be able to keep, he said, 'We shall find out soon enough.'

15

A fiddle fuck.

That's what he had on his hands, a goddamned fiddle fuck.

Uncertain how things had turned so bad so quick, Boyd Braxton shoved his arms into his black turtle-neck sweater, the unconscious Walter Jefferson still sprawled on the floor of the storeroom. Having retrieved his bundle of clothing from where he'd stowed it, Boyd had returned to the store, needing to reconnoitre. In a big-ass hurry, he yanked his black trousers over the top of the blue pair he already wore. He didn't give a rat's ass how he looked. He just needed to *not* look like a cleaner. Too many people had seen a cleaner firing into the crowd. No way in hell would he be able to get out of the museum decked out like some numb-nuts service worker.

He shoved the Ka-Bar and Mark 23 into his waistband. Next he checked his mobile, which was programmed with a preset number to immediately warn him if Edie Miller's Jeep was moved.

He heaved a sigh of relief; the Jeep was still parked out the front.

The bitch was in the museum. He could make this right. Wherever the bitch went, he would follow.

Yanking open the door of the store, he stepped across the threshold, the museum concourse directly across from his present position.

Quickly he scanned the area. *Blown-out glass. A couple of overturned tables. Some broken plates.* People frantically sloshed through the water from the shattered fountain. A sobbing woman in a tight-fitting suit, hobbled by a pair of stilettos heels, limped past, Boyd nearly gagging in her wake, the broad doused in more perfume than a Bangkok whore.

He heard the blare of at least half a dozen police sirens. Any second the place would be swarming with cops.

No sense looking for the Miller bitch here; he already knew she'd fled the concourse, having earlier caught sight of her and that red-headed bastard heading towards the gift shop.

Just who the fuck was he, anyway?

Obviously, the guy was a player. He had to be. Nobody had reflexes *that* quick unless they'd been trained. Maybe the bastard worked for a law enforcement agency. Whoever he worked for, it meant trouble.

Boyd strode over to where the Miller woman had been sitting, snatching a sheet of paper off the floor.

'Shit!'

On the sodden paper were two sketches, one a drawing of the relic he'd earlier stolen from the Hopkins, the other the Jerusalem cross that he and

96

every other man at Rosemont Security Consultants wore on their right ring finger.

As he continued to stare at the piece of paper, he caught sight of a Muslim couple, the wife's head wrapped in a hijab, propelling a pushchair, the kid bawling its head off. The couple stopped a few feet away from where he stood. The woman peered into the pushchair, the kid bawling even louder.

The bawling baby in the back room was gonna give away their position. There was a sniper in the building across the street and dozens of raghead fuckers prowling the streets of Fallujah in Toyota pickups. If the brat didn't stop bawling, he and his men were gonna end up hanging from a street light with no head and no balls. Burnt toast.

Boyd strode into the back bedroom. 'Hey, Fatima, shut the fucking brat the hell up!' he hissed.

Wrapped in a big black chador, she stared at him. Like he was a freakin' Martian or something.

'Well, fuck that shit!' He was sick and tired of getting his ass shot at for these ungrateful, godless people.

Lunging forward, he slashed the black-swathed woman's throat. Then he grabbed a pillow off the bed and shoved it over the bawling brat's face.

The piece of paper in Boyd's hand began to shake, his head suddenly exploding in a corolla of pain.

Babies crying. Women crying. Everybody and their fucking Uncle Tom crying. Christ, you'd think he'd killed somebody. Like this was a goddamned war zone or something. *This* was nothing. A minor public disturbance. A cleaner gone nuts. Except this time around nobody got killed.

And that was the problem. Somebody was supposed to have ended up dead.

'Kill 'em. Kill 'em all. God will know his own.' Isn't that what the colonel always said?

Still staring at the Muslim couple and their screaming baby, Boyd reached behind his back, his hand curling around the gun grip. Slowly he slid the Mark 23 from his waistband. *Papa, Mama and Baby Bear.* One, two, three.

No sooner did he pull the gun free than his mobile vibrated against his breastbone.

Boyd shoved his piece back into his waistband. Turning his back on the couple and their screaming brat, he reached for his phone. The digital display read 'RSC'. Rosemont Security Consultants.

'Fuck.'

It was the colonel calling for a status report.

Feeling like Joe Shit the Ragman, he pressed 'Answer'. Since the colonel hated what he referred to as circumlocution – what Boyd and everybody else with a 12th-grade education called beating around the bush – he didn't bother with the pleasantries. Instead, he simply said, 'We've got a problem, sir. The target escaped. The place has turned into a three-ring circus, and the cops have just arrived.'

The statrep met with a moment's silence, Boyd bracing himself for a world-class ass-chewing.

'Is the Miller woman still on the premises?' the

colonel asked, his calm tone of voice taking Boyd by surprise. Usually this kind of fuck-up would meet with wrath second only to God Almighty's.

'I believe so, sir. Her Jeep is still parked out front. I found a sheet of paper with two drawings – one of the relic, the other a Jerusalem cross. And one other thing, sir . . .' He hesitated, knowing the colonel would break his balls but good. 'She's hooked up with somebody. A tall guy with red hair. I'm not altogether certain, but he may be a player. What do you want me to do, sir?'

Another silence ensued, then in the background Boyd heard the muffled sounds of several voices. The colonel had put him on the speakerphone. Then he heard what sounded like a file folder being opened.

'Gunnery Sergeant?'

'Yes, sir.'

'Stand by for further instruction.'

16

Colonel Stanford MacFarlane took a moment to review the dossier just handed to him. Turning his back on his chief of staff, he discreetly removed his reading glasses from his breast pocket. He despised weakness of any sort, particularly in himself. Though physically fit, there were days when he felt each and every one of his fifty-three years.

Adjusting the reading glasses on his nose, he glanced at the file. With his contacts inside the intelligence office of the undersecretary of defense, he'd managed to obtain a full dossier on one Cædmon St John Aisquith.

He examined the photo attached to the upper right-hand corner with a paper clip. *Red hair. Blue eyes. Fair complexion.* He next glanced at the physical particulars. *6'3" 190 lbs.* It stood to reason that Aisquith was the 'tall guy with red hair' with the Miller woman at the National Gallery of Art.

Next, he skimmed the personal background material. *DOB 2/2/67. Eton. Queen's College, Oxford. Masters in medieval studies. Recruited MI5 – 1995. Formal resignation – 2006.*

MacFarlane's shoulders sagged ever so slightly as though weighed down with a heavy load.

Why now, God? Why this with the prize so close at hand?

Still clutching the file folder, MacFarlane walked over to the sliding glass door behind his desk and pulled it open, stepping onto the balcony. Gentle snow fell upon the midday traffic that ebbed and flowed ten storeys below on Virginia Avenue, the busy thoroughfare made heavenly with the covering of pristine white flakes. To his left he could see the majestic grey spires of the National Cathedral high above the city; to his right the majestic white spire of the Washington Monument.

God first. Country second.

Words to live by.

A credo to die for.

Again, he glanced at the file folder. MI5 was Britain's security service. *Regnum Defende.* Defenders of the Realm.

How had the Miller woman made the acquaintance of a former British intelligence officer?

The dead curator had been a Brit. Perhaps he arranged the meeting.

But why? And how was it that Aisquith and this woman knew about the Stones of Fire and the Jerusalem cross?

MacFarlane didn't like having more questions than answers.

With Armageddon near at hand, why would God —

It's a trial, he suddenly realized, the weight lifting from his shoulders. *A trial to prove your worthiness to the Almighty. To prove that you can be trusted with God's great*

plan. Shadrach. Meshach. Abed'nego. Like those holy men of
old, you too are being tested by God.

MacFarlane glanced at the beautiful grey spires in the distance, offering up a quick prayer of heart-felt thanks, grateful for the opportunity to prove his worth unto the Lord. Closing the file folder, he stepped back into his office and walked over to the telephone console.

'You listen up, Gunny,' he said without preamble. 'I'm sending in a five-man team, one man to be posted at each museum exit. ETA two minutes. You stay with the Jeep. Edged weapons only. I want Miller and Aisquith in zippered bags before the new hour strikes. You hear me, boy?'

'Yes, sir,' Boyd Braxton replied. 'But what if . . .' MacFarlane could hear the confidence leach from the other man's voice. 'What if the two of 'em manage to slip past us?'

Although gung-ho and loyal to a fault, the former gunnery sergeant lacked decision-making skills. Such men made good followers and even better fodder, but were poor leaders.

'To ensure they don't escape, I want you to rig the Miller woman's vehicle.'

'I hear ya, sir!' Braxton exclaimed, his confidence clearly regained.

'Keep me posted.'

17

Edie and Cædmon emerged from the ladies' room. As they did so, an alarm blared overhead, the teeth-jangling sound accompanied by a continuously repeated prerecorded message. Surreally calm, the disembodied voice stated the obvious: 'The museum alarm has been activated. Immediately make your way to the nearest exit lobby. Thank you.'

'You heard the man. He said "the *nearest* exit lobby". That would be the one right over there.' Nudging her companion in the ribs, Edie pointed to the 4th Street lobby on the other side of the vestibule, the hall still jam-packed with people clamouring and jostling as they headed towards the oversized glass doors.

Intractable, Cædmon simply said, 'I think not.' Grabbing her by the upper arm, he pulled her towards the staircase on the right.

'What are you doing?'

'We're going to take the stairs to the upper level of the museum.'

Jerking her arm free, Edie stared at him.

The main floor of the museum? Was he nuts? They'd have to navigate their way through umpteen art galleries and a couple of sculpture halls.

She shook her head, vetoing the idea. 'It'll be faster if we stay on the lower level of the museum. The main floor will be a mob scene.'

'Yes, I assume that it will. However, a mob scene will serve us well if the beast should again rear his ugly head.'

Refusing to budge, Edie folded her arms over her chest. 'How many times have you visited the National Gallery of Art?'

'This is my maiden voyage.' Again, Cædmon took her by the arm, his grip this time noticeably more firm. 'While you are no doubt well acquainted with the museum floor plan, you are also suffering from delayed shock. Not the best frame of mind for making a decision.'

'Look, I might be losing it, but I still have a mind of my own.'

Ignoring her last remark, Cædmon pulled her towards the staircase. As they ascended, Edie twice stumbled on the steps and he had to catch hold of her.

At the top of the steps she turned to him. 'Now what?'

Rather than answer, Cædmon strode towards an abandoned wheelchair, PROPERTY OF THE NGA stamped across the brown leather back support. Her eyes narrowed as he took hold of it by the handles and wheeled it towards her.

'Bum in the chair,' he brusquely ordered.

She baulked. 'Two fumbles does not an invalid make.'

'The gunman will be searching for a female so high.' Holding out his hand, Cædmon raised it parallel to the top of her head. 'The gunman will not be looking for a wheelchair-bound woman.'

'How do I know that —'

'Seat yourself! Before I put a boot up your Khyber!'

Edie did as ordered, it belatedly dawning on her that she was doing a first-rate job of antagonizing the man who had earlier saved her from a gunman's bullet. At great risk to his own life.

Craning her head to peer at him, she said, 'Look, I'm sorry for being a bitch. I'm just really, really scared.' And unaccustomed to relying on anyone other than herself. Particularly for her safety and well-being. Over the years too many people had let her down.

'You have every right to be frightened,' Cædmon replied, once more the courteous Brit. Releasing the brake, he shoved the wheelchair forward.

Edie removed the bag from her shoulder and clutched it to her chest. Inside its canvas depths was everything she would need to escape this madness.

As Cædmon navigated his way through the crowd, she realized that the wheelchair was an inspired idea, the hordes parting before them like the Red Sea parting before the Israelites. She'd been leery of

Cædmon's plan to take the long route through the museum. Maybe his route, like the wheelchair, would prove a good call after all.

Within seconds they had passed the American paintings gallery, George Bellows' famous pair of boxers eclipsed in a darkly hued blur. A few seconds after that they entered the East Court Garden, the humid air in the cavernous space cloying; even more cloying, the winged cupids astride a giant scallop shell in the dead centre of the courtyard, water merrily tinkling over their chubby feet. Cædmon veered to the right, bypassing the fountain. As he wheeled the chair around the columned perimeter, Edie caught sight of a homeless man sound asleep in a wrought-iron chair, oblivious to the alarm and automated message blaring on the PA system. Exiting the court-yard garden, Cædmon increased his speed as they traversed the long, barrel-vaulted sculpture hall. On either side of her, Edie saw familiar flashes of colour in the adjoining galleries – Toulouse-Lautrec, Renoir – the history of nineteenth-century French art reduced to blips.

Straight ahead of them, like mighty old trees in a virgin forest, loomed the huge black marble columns of the main rotunda.

'We can exit at the rotunda,' she said, turning in her seat to look at him, clasping her hands together in a beseeching gesture.

Her proposal met with a *whirr*, the wheelchair advancing full speed ahead.

It's like entering one of Dante's lower circles, Edie thought, a few seconds later, as they entered the domed rotunda. Everywhere she looked swarms of people were haphazardly congregating in undulating lines that meandered in the direction of the main entrance. In front of the exit doors uniformed guards were patting down each and every visitor before permitting them to leave the premises. Edie assumed they were searching for the gunman.

'It would appear that all roads lead to Rome,' Cædmon remarked as he steered the wheelchair on.

Like the courtyard garden, the rotunda was jungle humid on account of all the potted plants. Afraid Padgham's killer might be lurking, Edie tucked her chin into her chest, making herself as small as possible.

No sooner did they clear the rotunda than Cædmon started running.

Bronze sculptures. Flemish still lifes. Della Robbias.

Famous works of art passed at such a dizzying speed, Edie feared she would lose the contents of her stomach.

'Slow down, will ya? You're giving me a bad case of motion sickness.'

If Cædmon heard her, he gave no indication, the man fast proving himself a well-spoken hard ass.

Having crossed three quarters of the museum in less than two minutes, Cædmon wheeled her into the West Garden Court, a mirror image of the open space at the opposite end of the museum. Swerving sharply to the left, he somehow managed to maintain control as the chair took the turn on one wheel. A few seconds later Edie could see the marble wall that marked the end of the main hall.

'Quick! Put on the brakes!' she screeched, a full-length statue of St John of the Cross looming directly in front of her. She grabbed the padded arms and held on tight as Cædmon brought the wheelchair to an abrupt halt mere inches from the stern-faced saint.

'Bloody hell.' He turned his head from side to side. 'There's supposed to be a lift at the end of ... Ah, yes, there she be, starboard bow.' Cædmon rolled the wheelchair to the elevator, which was tucked away to the right of them.

Edie reached out and pushed the button, the metal doors instantly sliding open. No room to turn the wheelchair around, she sat facing the back wall of the elevator. Within moments, they'd be free of the museum, the 7th Street exit located on the lower level.

Readying herself for the last cavalry charge, she opened her bag. She rummaged through it, her hand finding the now soft-sided box of melted spinach.

'What are you doing?'

Edie spared Cædmon a quick glance. 'I'm searching for the car keys.'

'Driving your vehicle would not be a good idea.'

Placing her arm over the back of the chair, she twisted her upper body so she could look him in the

108

eye. 'You're kidding, right? The Jeep is our only means of escape.'

'How do you think the gunman found you? I'll bet it was no guess.'

'Maybe it was an *educated* guess. And let us not forget about the old lucky guess,' she retorted, then, realizing how childish she sounded, 'Okay, he followed me here. But I can promise you that he won't be following us when we leave. I know this town like the back of my hand. Trust me, Cædmon. I can get us out of here.'

She watched as he mulled over her proposal. He was tempted, she could see it in his eyes.

'There's a back service alley one block away at Federal Triangle. If we're being followed, it's the perfect place to lose a tail.'

The elevator door opened with a melodic *ping*. Cædmon backed the wheelchair out and turned it towards the 7th Street lobby, the scene almost identical to what they had witnessed in the rotunda.

Seeing all the hustle and bustle, the mass confusion, the absolute chaos that reigned within the marble-walled space, Edie breathed a sigh of relief.

The end was in sight.

18

Holding a museum map in front of him, Boyd Braxton rechecked the exits.

He had Sanchez on the Mall exit, Harliss at Constitution, Napier across the street at the East Wing, Agee manning the 4th Street exit and Riggins posted at the 7th Street exit. Experienced war fighters one and all, each was equipped with a Ka-Bar and two ID photos, one of a curly-haired bitch and the other of a tall red-headed bastard. *And the best part?* To a man, they were decked out in DC police uniforms. Given that the National Gallery of Art was swarming with every badge the city could rustle up, no one would give them a second glance.

The op in play, Boyd secured a communication device to his right ear enabling him to speak to all five of his men. 'You've got your orders. Take out both targets. Edged weapons only. We want this to go down swift, silent and deadly.'

'Copy that, Boss Man,' Riggins replied, speaking for the group. An expert at close-quarters fighting, Riggins knew how to wield a knife with lethal proficiency. Better yet, he *enjoyed* wielding a blade, close combat appealing to a particular kind of warrior. That being the kind of warrior who liked to look his victim in the eye when he went in for the kill.

'Okay, boys and girls. Let's go have some fun,' Boyd said, grinning, confident that this time there would be no more fuck-ups. 'And don't forget, we go with God.'

'Amen, brother.' This from Sanchez, a former army ranger and Afghan veteran well experienced in slaying the godless.

As he headed towards the 4th Street exit, Boyd glanced at the ring he wore on his right hand, the cluster of silver crosses a constant reminder that he and his men were soldiers in God's army. Holy warriors not unlike the crusaders of old. The colonel often spoke of the men who a thousand years ago had gone forth to conquer the Holy Land: Hugues of Payen. Godfroi of Bouillon. Yves of Faillon. Boyd felt a kindred link to those knights of old who had fought with a sword in one hand and a Bible in the other. The sword he had great experience with, having spent fifteen years in the Corps. The Bible was something new to him, his old man not holding the good book in very high regard. In fact, Joe Don Braxton hadn't held much of anything except a bottle of Old Crow. And he'd held that damned near every night. Rumour had it there was a half-drunk fifth of bourbon clutched between Joe Don's thighs the night he drove his Dodge pickup into a stand of poplar trees.

Approaching the museum lobby, Boyd jutted his chin at the Rosemont man standing sentry near the cloakroom – Agee, a good man to have in a tight fix. The silent greeting was returned with an innocuous nod.

Not about to stand in line, Boyd slid his hand into his coat pocket and removed a leather wallet. Flipping it open, he thrust the DC police badge at the same guard he had flashed when he entered the museum.

'Detective Wilson,' the guard said by way of greeting. 'Hell of a mess we've got on our hands, huh?'

'Just another day in sin city. Anyone get a look at the bastard who fired the shots?'

'As a matter of fact, one of the museum patrons was able to video some of it on his cell phone.'

Hearing that, Boyd froze.

Within hours his face would be plastered all over YouTube and the major news outlets.

'Glad to hear it,' he replied, his facial muscles taut with a fake smile. 'Keep up the good work –' he glanced at the man's name badge '– Officer Milligan.' He had no idea if security guards were addressed as 'Officer', and at the moment he didn't much care. The fake grin replaced with a grimace, he headed for the doors, shoving aside a couple of jabbering tourists.

Once outside, he came to a standstill, his booted feet planted on the cobbled stone driveway that fronted the entrance. Ignoring the two-way human traffic – badges heading into the museum, tourists heading out – he raised his head to the grey sky above. And prayed.

Dear Lord, help me make this right.

Boyd didn't want to let down the colonel. He owed everything he had to Colonel Stan MacFarlane. Sometimes, when his mind wandered, he liked to imagine that the colonel was the father he never had but always wanted. Stern but fair. Righteous. A man who'd never hit you unless he had just cause.

Like a soothing balm, the gently falling snow cooled his brow, big fluffy flakes sticking to his eyelashes, his lips, the tip of his nose. It put him in mind of the first time he'd ever seen snow fall from the sky. It was during a tour of duty in Japan. A backwater kid from Pascagoula, Mississippi, he'd only seen winter snow on celluloid. He well remembered standing there, a bad-ass two-hundred-and-thirty-pound marine, sorely tempted to lie down, flap his arms and legs like an epileptic and make an angel in the snow. Come to think of it, it'd been snowing the day he made his first kill. A Jap with an attitude had accused him of stiffing on the sake bill and had followed him into the alley, attacking him from behind while he took a piss. He killed the slant-eyed shitbird with a backward jab of the elbow, ramming his nose all the way into his skull. A ruby-red blood-stain on virgin white snow. It had been a beautiful sight. Like a silk-clad whore spreading her legs for a game of peek-a-boo.

Reinvigorated, the blood pumping through his veins fast and furious, Boyd straightened his shoulders as he strode past the black Wrangler. The colonel said that God was a fine one for testing the faithful. Maybe that's what all this fiddle fucking was about – he was being tested.

If that was the case, bring it on!

He was up to the challenge.

Opening the boot of the Ford, he removed a drawstring pouch. Inside the bag were two mobiles, coiled wire, duct tape and a small block of C4 plastic explosive. Everything he needed to make things right.

19

Glancing through the plate-glass doors of the 7th Street exit, Edie imagined the headline story on local TV news: GUNMAN GOES BERSERK INSIDE NATIONAL GALLERY OF ART. Channel 9 and Channel 4 news vans had just pulled up outside the museum, technicians hurriedly unloading equipment. As she continued to observe the action outside, it appeared a great many people were unloading equipment from the back of official-looking vehicles: paramedics with stretchers, firemen hefting axes and water hoses, DC police stacking orange traffic cones. The museum had become a scene of industrious purpose – visitors exiting through one door, emergency services entering through another.

Still in the wheelchair, she sat quietly as Cædmon rolled her over to a large Chinese vase set in a niche.

'Time for Milady to exit her carriage.'

Edie hurriedly extricated herself from the wheelchair, her legs so wobbly she unthinkingly grabbed the Qing Dynasty vase to keep from collapsing.

Cædmon wrapped an arm around her shoulders, gently removing her hand from the priceless *objet d'art*. 'Steady as she goes,' he whispered in her ear. 'Deep breaths will slow your heart rate. At least it always works for me.'

She nodded her thanks, surprised by the admission. Although she barely knew him, Cædmon Aisquith seemed to have been born with the proverbial stiff upper lip. No deep breaths required.

'Given the obviously well-planned attack, we must assume that there are more people involved and that our adversaries will attempt to track our movements via electronic transactions.' Removing his wallet from a trouser pocket, Cædmon peered into the worn brown leather. 'I'm afraid that my assets are somewhat paltry. Seventy-five dollars and three hundred euros. How much do you have?' he bluntly enquired.

The question caught Edie off guard. Her eyes narrowing suspiciously, she said, 'I have five thousand dollars. What's it to you?'

'I say! You must have cleaned out your bank account.'

'In a manner of speaking,' she mumbled, unwilling to elaborate.

'Very well then. I suggest we assume aliases, Mr and Mrs Smythe-Jones or some such, and check into a hotel.'

'The two of us? In a hotel?' Edie had given no thought as to what would happen once they left the museum; if anything, she'd assumed they'd go their separate ways. She'd only come to the National

Gallery of Art to warn him of the danger, not to hook up with him.

Although I suppose there might be some truth in the old adage about safety in numbers.

'Yes, a hotel,' Cædmon reiterated. 'I don't know about you, but I'm in dire need of a soft bed and a stiff drink.'

'Bed and booze. Okay, I'm in.'

Cædmon motioned to the throng exiting the museum. 'Shall we join the multitude?'

As they approached the line of people being searched, Edie surveyed the crowd of visitors, most of whom were excitedly chatting about what they'd seen, what they knew or what they'd heard.

She nudged Cædmon in the arm. 'Did you hear what that man just –' She stopped suddenly, catching sight of a familiar face out of the corner of her eye.

The bent cop in the alley behind the Hopkins Museum.

'To your left! It's the killer's cop buddy!' she hissed out of the corner of her mouth.

Without so much as turning his head, Cædmon swivelled his gaze to the left. 'The bloke with sandy blond hair?' When she nodded, he said, 'Did he catch sight of you at the Hopkins?'

'No. But they have my driver's licence photo. They know what I look like.'

'Right.'

An absent-minded look on his face, Cædmon patted his breast pocket, giving every appearance of being a man searching for a pen or his reading glasses. It took a moment for Edie to realize that he was very carefully casing the joint, his eyes moving from left to right and back again.

'In a few seconds there's going to be a frightful stampede towards the door,' he said in a low voice, taking her firmly by the upper arm as he spoke. 'Be ready to run for your life.'

Edie nodded, knowing he spoke literally, not figuratively.

'Good God!' Cædmon suddenly boomed in a loud, forceful voice. 'There's the gunman! That man standing by the elevator doors!'

At Cædmon's commanding voice – which sounded an awful lot like a Shakespearean actor bellowing about kingdoms and horses – every head in the lobby abruptly turned.

A second of shocked silence ensued, then the façade of order gave way. Those visitors closest to the doors rushed them. The four museum guards and every policeman in sight charged in the opposite direction towards the elevators.

That being their cue, Edie and Cædmon ran for the doors, elbowing their way to the head of the pack.

Several seconds later, they burst free of the building.

'Hurry!' Cædmon ordered, taking her by the hand as he descended the portico steps that fronted the museum. 'I suspect we fooled everyone save the man searching for us. What's that across the street?' He pointed beyond the traffic jam of news vans and patrol cars to a grove of leafless trees on the other side of 7th Street.

'That's the outdoor Sculpture Garden.'

'And in this direction?' He pointed towards Constitution Avenue.

'Federal Triangle.'

'Am I correct in thinking there's a tube station nearby?'

'There's a subway station a couple of blocks away. On the other side of the Archives.'

'Right.' Still holding her by the hand, Cædmon scurried past a line of cops attempting to hold back onlookers with a flimsy strand of yellow crime scene tape.

'In case you've forgotten, my Jeep is parked –'

'Not now!'

Knowing their priority was to escape the sandy-haired cop she'd seen in the lobby, Edie held her tongue. They could thrash out the specifics of the escape plan once they were free and clear of the museum.

Breaking into a run, they crossed 7th Street, Cædmon leading the way to the Sculpture Garden. Through the sparse foliage Edie spotted a steel form on the right and a bronze shape on the left. Ahead of them was an outdoor skating rink, a trio of skaters gracefully gliding across the smooth ice, apparently ignorant of the pandemonium on the other side of the street.

Still leading the way, Cædmon went to the right of the rink, turned right yet again then made a sharp left. For a man unfamiliar with the city, he was doing an excellent job of manoeuvring them through the garden. It wasn't until they emerged onto Constitution Avenue, some two blocks from the 7th Street museum exit, that Cædmon slowed his pace.

Her lungs burning with the frigid December air, Edie came to a grinding halt, unable to catch her breath. When Cædmon put a steadying hand on her shoulder, she instinctively hurled herself at his chest.

'That c-cop would have killed ... If you hadn't ... We would be ...' She burrowed her head into his shoulder, fear causing her thoughts to collide incoherently together.

Cædmon wrapped his arms around her. 'Ssshh. It's all right. We're out of danger,' he murmured, his breath warm against her cheek.

It took a good half-minute before her breathing returned to something approximating normal. Embarrassed that she'd thrown herself at him, Edie pulled free from Cædmon's embrace.

'Better?' he enquired solicitously. Other than the fact that his eyes had turned an iridescent shade of cobalt blue, he showed no outward sign of exertion.

Doing a good imitation of a bobble-head doll, she nodded warily. Warily because she could hear the blare of sirens in the near distance. A police net was being thrown around the National Gallery of Art. If the net was extended, they might yet be ensnared.

She glanced at her watch. Unbelievably, no more than fifteen minutes had passed since the three shots had been fired in the museum concourse. It seemed both longer and shorter, as though time had sped up and slowed down all at once.

'I don't know about you, but I feel like I just got sucked into a killer cyclone, houses, cows and farm fences spinning all around me.'

'I feel much the same.' One side of his mouth twitched up. 'Certainly, this was not how I imagined spending my afternoon.'

'I hear you.' Still embarrassed by her show of weakness, she wiped several wet flakes from her eyelashes. The snow had slowed to a desultory smatter, wispy flakes blowing on a cold westerly wind.

From where they stood, diagonally opposite the National Archives, they had an excellent view in either direction along Constitution Avenue. Spread along the famous thoroughfare were familiar citadels of sanity – hot dog vendors, souvenir stands, T-shirt kiosks – tiny punctuation marks haphazardly placed between the ponderous block-like buildings.

Deciding to take charge, Edie turned to the right, intending to backtrack to her parked vehicle. She'd taken no more than a step when Cædmon grabbed her by the elbow.

'Where do you think you're going?'

'We discussed this already. I'm going to the Jeep. Are you in or are you out?'

'While there are advantages to having a vehicle at

our disposal, there are also certain disadvantages that must be considered.'

Desperate to get back to the Jeep, that being the quickest means of escaping the madness, she straightened her shoulders. No easy feat given that she was bundled in a leather jacket and an oversized trench coat. 'On the count of three: paper-rock-scissors.'

His copper-coloured brows drew together in the middle. 'I beg your pardon?'

'You heard me. Since there's just the two of us, we can't put it to a vote. So instead we'll use paper-rock-scissors to decide. You guys do that in England, don't you?'

'I am familiar with the hand game. In fact, it was invented in the mid-eighteenth century by the Comte de Rochambeau as a means to settle —'

Edie held up a hand, stopping him in mid-flow.

'More information than I need to know.' Tired of being the follower rather than the leader, she met his gaze head on. 'On three.'

In unison, they each moved a balled right fist through the air.

20

A cold wet rain fell upon the heath.

A line straight out of a Victorian novel, Cædmon thought moodily as he pulled back the hotel curtain. Except it wasn't a heath; it was an asphalt car park bounded by eight-foot-high brick walls and a twelve-storey office building directly opposite.

'My, my, what style,' he muttered, releasing the rubber-backed curtain and stepping away from the window. Since paper had beaten rock, they'd left Washington via the subway, checking into a Holiday Inn across the river in Arlington, Virginia. That was two hours ago, and he was still trying to muddle his way through the chain of events that had landed him in this monochromatic hotel room with its uninspiring view.

He glanced at Edie Miller, coiled in a ball on one of the double beds, her mouth slack, her eyes unfocused. His gaze lingered a few impolite moments, Cædmon thinking she looked like a dahlia curled in the frost.

In dire need of refreshment, he strolled over to the counter, the room equipped with a coffee pot, microwave oven and a diminutive refrigerator. He uncapped a bottle of Tanqueray purchased at the shop down the street.

'What are you doing?' A drowsy expression on her face, Edie lifted her head from the pillow.

'I thought I'd make myself a G and T.'

The dahlia instantly revived. 'Make mine a double.'

He obliged and, tumbler in hand, walked over to the bed. As though mocking their dismal plight, the ice cubes merrily clinked against the sides of the glass. 'Sorry, but we're out of lemons,' he said, handing her the half-full tumbler.

Swinging her bare feet over the side of the bed, Edie levered herself into a seated position, the tumbler clasped between her hands. 'AWOL lemons are the least of our worries.'

'Indeed.'

Safe for the moment, Cædmon suspected that they were being hunted by very determined adversaries. And while their adversaries had possession of the prize, the Stones of Fire having been stolen from the Hopkins Museum, they also seemed very keen to erase all traces of the theft.

But why?

The question had been plaguing him for the last two hours. Neither he nor Edie Miller could guess the identity of Jonathan Padgham's killer. Nor did they know the current location of the breastplate.

So why launch a bloodthirsty manhunt?

The manhunt implied that their foe did not want it made public that after several thousand years, the fabled Stones of Fire had been rediscovered. So, their foe had an ulterior purpose for stealing the breast-plate, one that had nothing to do with plunder and profit.

Lost in thought, he belatedly realized he'd depleted his glass.

Careful, old boy. You've already slain that dragon.

Needing to pace himself, Cædmon set his tumbler on the dresser. Drink was a tempting mistress that beckoned when one least expected it.

Bare feet still dangling over the side of the bed, Edie looked at him, her expression forthrightly quizzical. At a loss for words, he returned the stare, enjoying the sight of the long brown curls framing her face and shoulders in a riotous halo. Admiring a woman's attributes was one of those simple pleasures that made a man momentarily forget stress and strife. Like hat pegs, her nipples were visibly prominent through the thin fabric of her silk pullover, Edie having removed her bulky jumper.

'Is something the matter?'

Caught with his hand in the biscuit tin, Cædmon quickly glanced at the television on the other side of the room. His cheeks warm with colour, he picked up his depleted G&T and made a big to-do of swirling the ice cubes in the bottom of the glass.

A sudden knock at the door broke the moment.

'You don't think . . . ?'

'No, I do not,' he replied, striding towards the locked door. A quick glance through the peephole confirmed what he already knew – the porter had arrived. A fortuitous interruption, the room awash with sexual tension.

What did you expect, checking into a hotel room with a lovely American woman?

Unlocking the door, he greeted the porter with a courteous nod, the young man handing him a paper bag emblazoned with the Holiday Inn logo. Before taking custody of the bag, Cædmon reached into his trouser pocket and removed several crumpled notes. The exchange made, he closed and locked the door.

Awkwardly smiling, still conscious of the tension, he hefted the white bag in the air. 'I come bearing gifts, compliments of the establishment.'

Edie patted the mattress. 'Sit yourself here and let's see what's in the gift sack.'

Uncertain what to make of the invitation, he obediently complied. He knew that in the aftermath of bum-clenching terror each person acted differently. Some turned to alcohol, some turned to drugs, and a good many turned to sex. Cædmon preferred the first, had never been interested in the second and wasn't altogether certain how he felt about the latter. While he found Edie Miller attractive, he in no way wanted to take advantage of the situation.

He dumped the contents of the bag onto the bed. 'One tube of toothpaste, two toothbrushes, hand lotion, shaving cream, razor and, alas, only one comb. I'm afraid we'll have to share.'

'I'm kinda getting used to sharing.'

Cædmon assumed the offhand remark had to do with the fact that the room had been paid for with a soggy hundred-dollar bill from her 'spinach fund'. Concerned that electronic transactions would be traced, he had imposed a moratorium on all credit cards. Certain his room at the Churchill would also be monitored, he phoned the hotel and asked them to gather his belongings and put them in storage until such time as he could collect them. He'd also rung up his publicist, informing her that he was catching a late flight back to Paris. If asked, she would lead inquisitors astray.

'Would you mind ... ?' Edie waggled her glass back and forth, indicating she needed a refill.

'Not in the least.' Getting up from the bed, Cædmon walked over to the makeshift bar on the other side of the room. Along the way he collected his own glass.

The silence unnerving, he busied himself with mixing the drinks. Concerned he might cross an invisible line and equally worried his companion might be receptive, he went easy on the gin. His fount of small talk dry, he wordlessly handed Edie a replenished glass.

'Cheers,' he said, clinking his tumbler to hers.

'Actually, more like tears, don't you think?' Her demeanour glum, Edie listlessly raised the tumbler to her lips.

'Myself, I prefer taking the glass-half-full approach.'

'Don't you care that your friend was murdered?'

'Of course I care,' he retorted, not wanting to have this conversation with a woman he barely knew. 'However, experience has taught me that pain only worsens if one wallows in it.'

'Is that what I'm doing, wallowing?'

'No, you are not wallowing. Wallowing is when one forgoes the tonic water.' As well he knew. Hoping to lighten the mood, he said, 'His nickname for me was Mercuriophilus Anglicus.'

'I assume you're referring to Dr Padgham.'

'Padge could never recall anyone's forename.'

'Probably because he was too caught up in his own self-importance.' No sooner did the words escape her lips than Edie slapped a hand over her mouth. 'God, that was horrible! I'm sorry.' Then, laughing, 'Did I mention that I'm a mean drunk? So, what does Mercurio blabediblop mean?'

'It means the English mercury lover.'

Still smiling, she lifted a brow. 'Sounds kinky. Do I really want to know the story behind it?'

Enjoying the silly game, he feigned indignation. 'I can assure you that the story is not nearly as racy as you presume. It so happens that alchemical mercury suffuses all creation. In ancient times it was thought to be the secret essence of the *all* in all things.'

She drew a long face. 'Oh, puh-*lease*. There must be a class you guys take at Oxford where they teach you how to pontificate to us little people.'

'Are you always so frank?'

'Not always.' Her brown eyes twinkled mischievously. 'I do have to sleep.'

Cædmon threw back his head and laughed, her humour growing on him.

'You know, it's crazy,' Edie said, suddenly serious. 'All of this murder and mayhem happening because of an old breastplate.'

He walked over to the striped wingback chair on the far side of the bed and sat down. 'The Stones of Fire are much more than "an old breastplate".'

'You said something about the breastplate being designed by God and manufactured by Moses.'

'So claim a good many biblical scholars.'

'Come on. You don't really think that the breastplate was divinely inspired?'

'Actually, I think the breastplate has a far more –' he paused, not wanting to offend her possible religious beliefs '– *complex* pedigree than that contained within the pages of the Old Testament.'

'What exactly do you mean by "complex"?' Drawing her legs onto the bed, she curled them beneath her bum. 'I thought it was pretty straightforward: Moses would don the breastplate in order to control the . . . how did you phrase it? The "cosmic power" contained within the Ark of the Covenant.'

'Which begs the question, where did Moses learn such a feat? I have long suspected that Moses was not only an Egyptian, but a trained magician at the pharaoh's court.'

'Moses, the guy who led the Jews out of bondage

and commanded the ragtag Hebrew tribes as they wandered the wilderness for forty years, *that* Moses was an Egyptian magician?'

He nodded.

'You know what I think, Mr Cædmon Aisquith? I think you've had *way* too much gin. For starters, the Egyptians were a bunch of pagans. They had – what – like a couple hundred gods.'

'Not nearly as many as all that,' he quietly corrected, well aware that the theory he was about to propose would scandalize many a churchgoer. 'Would it surprise you to learn that the ancient Egyptians were the first people to practise monotheism? Known as Atenism, for several decades it was the state religion, the pharaoh Akhenaton officially declaring that Aten was the only god in the heavens.' Leaning forward, he propped his forearms on his thighs, the point he was about to make key to his argument. 'Aten was not the supreme god; Aten was the *only* god. Furthermore, I believe that Moses, or Tuthmos as he was known at the Egyptian court, was not only an avid follower of Atenism, but he also fused his beliefs into those of the fledgling Hebrew faith.'

Edie stared at him, saucer-eyed. 'What are you saying – that Yahweh and the Egyptian god Aten were one and the same?'

Unwilling to penetrate the murky depths, Cædmon purposefully equivocated. 'I am merely saying that there are areas of overlap between the two religions.'

'Such as . . . ?'

'Such as the Ten Commandments, which are suspiciously similar to the behavioural mandates set out in the Egyptian Book of the Dead, a work that predates the biblical Exodus. And let us not forget circumcision, an unusual practice to say the least. Did you know that circumcision was a ritual procedure amongst the Egyptian royal family and their courtiers? Other similarities include the stricture against graven images, a hereditary priesthood, the sacrifice of animals and the use of a golden ark to contain the might and majesty of what can only be called a very jealous god.' His case made, Cædmon folded his arms across his chest. 'Would you not agree that such similarities give one pause?'

'Yeah, well . . . Right now I need to pause and catch my breath because I'm still grappling with Moses being an Egyptian magician.' Edie took a noisy slurp of her G and T, loudly chomping on an ice cube. 'I'm sorry, Cædmon, but I'm having a hard time accepting that Judaism descended from some long-lost Egyptian religion.'

'I'm not speaking of Judaism as it is practised today, that being a religion primarily created in the sixth century BC during the Babylonian Captivity. I'm speaking of the Hebrew religion as it was practised from the time of the Exodus up until the Babylonian Captivity, a span of roughly seven hundred years.'

'So, which came first, the worship of Aten or the worship of Yahweh?'

'Ah, the chicken-and-egg conundrum. In the same way that Roman religious practices influenced early Christianity, I believe that the enslaved Jews in Egypt influenced, and perhaps even inspired, the worship of Aten. The Old Testament makes mention of Moses having been instructed in "all the wisdom of the Egyptians".'

'What exactly does that mean, "all the wisdom of the Egyptians"?'

The question immense in its scope, Cædmon considered his reply. 'The prescribed Egyptian education included the study of crystals and metals, necromancy and the art of divination, knowledge that Moses put to good use when creating the fabled Stones of Fire.'

'But I saw the breastplate with my own eyes. It was just –' she shrugged '– twelve jewels and some bits of old gold.'

'Yes, but it's those very jewels that give the Stones of Fire its immense power.'

'Okay, I'll nibble. What's so special about those twelve jewels?'

'Allow me to preface my answer by saying that gemstones are not the inert, inanimate objects that most people assume them to be. Indeed, gemstones, as well as crystals, are energy conduits. In Asian cultures such energy is known as chi.'

'I have a girlfriend who's into crystals. She swears that if you hold a crystal long enough in your hand you'll feel a vibratory pulse. Personally, I consider that awfully New Agey.'

'Not if you consider the fact that crystals are used to boost radio waves in a process known as piezo-electricity. In a similar process, the ancients used gemstones and crystals to both generate and enhance energy. A high priest steeped in the mysteries of ancient Egypt, Moses used his vast knowledge of gems and crystals when creating the Stones of Fire. I would even go so far as to say that the breastplate is nothing less than a form of ancient technology, each stone specifically selected for its unique vibratory properties.'

Edie snorted. 'You're kidding, right? I'd hardly call an old breastplate a technological wonder.'

'Ah, but that's exactly what the breastplate was, and perhaps still is. Because SONY isn't stamped on it, that doesn't make it any less sophisticated than the mobile phone in my breast pocket,' he countered, patting said pocket. 'The Stones of Fire, even by twenty-first-century standards, is state-of-the-art.'

She mulled that over for a paltry half-second before uttering a non-committal 'Huh.'

Reaching across to the cabinet that separated the two double beds, Edie grabbed a pink and white bag of Oreo cookies. Using both hands, she ripped it open, slid free a tray of factory-packed, chemical-laced brown biscuits and offered him one.

'No, thank you,' he politely demurred

Her lips curled in a come-hither smile. 'Ah, come on, Cædmon. Try it, you'll like it.'

Realizing how easily Adam had been swayed, he took a creme-filled biscuit.

'Quite tasty,' he remarked a few seconds later.

With a twist of her wrists, Edie unscrewed the two halves of her biscuit. To his lurid fascination, she proceeded to lap at the white creme with her tongue. 'OK, let's suppose for argument's sake that Moses was a member of the Egyptian priesthood. Why would he lead a bunch of Hebrew slaves out of Egypt?'

'Your question presumes that the Jews, and only the Jews, left Egypt.'

'Well, who else would have gone with them?'

'All those in grave danger of losing their lives.' He let that sink in a moment before saying, 'Specifically, the entire court of Akhenaton.'

She lowered her cookie. 'Come again?'

'What you must understand is that when the pharaoh Akhenaton imposed a monotheistic faith upon the inhabitants of Egypt, it was nothing short of a religious revolution. Not unlike the furore that ensued when Martin Luther put nail to paper. Suddenly, overnight, the pantheon of familiar gods and goddesses – Isis, Set, Osiris – was null and void.'

'I'm guessing that what some considered a new religion, others considered out 'n' out heresy,' Edie correctly surmised.

'Indeed. When Akhenaton died, the practitioners of the old religion swooped down upon the royal court. And with a vengeance, I might add. Virtually all traces of Akhenaton and Aten were wiped from the annals of Egyptian history.'

'What happened to those Egyptians who still believed in Aten?'

'They fled Egypt in the dead of night. A vast migration of slaves and nobility.'

'Well, that would explain the passage in the Book of Exodus where the Hebrew slaves supposedly took "jewels of silver and jewels of gold" with them when they fled Egypt. I mean how the heck did a bunch of slaves get that kind of treasure?'

He nodded, surprised that she was so well-versed in scripture. 'In truth, it was not the Hebrew slaves who possessed such wealth, but rather the Egyptian nobility who accompanied them on their flight.'

'Moses leading the way to the land of Canaan.'

'So I believe.'

'While it makes for the greatest story never told, I still need more proof before I chuck away years of Sunday-school indoctrination.' She glanced at the electric alarm clock on the cabinet. 'Time for the six o'clock newscast,' she announced, lunging off the bed.

Aiming the remote at the TV, she hit the 'Power' button. A suited woman sporting a blond bob appeared on the screen.

'In a scene reminiscent of the pandemonium that struck Washington in the wake of 9/11, museum goers at the National Gallery of Art came under terrorist fire earlier today, a gunman shooting into the underground concourse area.'

As the talking head read her script, a grainy video of the 'pandemonium' appeared on the screen, the footage clearly shot by an amateur hand. And a shaking hand at that, there being a decidedly frenetic quality to the images. To Cædmon's relief, neither he nor Edie was visible in the video.

Slack-jawed, Edie turned to him. 'They've got it all wrong. It wasn't a terrorist attack.' Reaching for the remote, she quickly changed channels.

'The shooting spree in the museum's concourse was part of a well-coordinated terrorist attack, a car bomb detonating yards away from the 4th Street entrance. No fatal casualties were reported, although several emergency workers suffered severe burns.'

'Oh God,' she murmured as she watched the accompanying video of the smouldering blast site. Then, her eyes filling with tears, she turned to him. 'That's the Jeep. The same Jeep I wanted us to –'

'Don't say it,' he roughly ordered, equally shocked

by the charred wreckage on the screen. 'By a for-tuitous stroke of luck, we escape the demon.'

'That's crap, and you know it! They're not going to stop until they find us.' She shoved a balled fist into her mouth, her eyes glued to the television screen.

In silence, they watched the remainder of the news, Edie muting the volume when the sports came on.

'Don't you think it's odd there was no mention of Padgham's murder? There are three dead bodies at the Hopkins Museum, yet there's no mention of it on the nightly news.'

'I presume the bodies haven't been discovered.'

She shook her head. 'On Mondays the cleaning crew arrives at four o'clock. Why didn't they –' She gasped. 'Oh God! Maybe they killed the cleaning crew.' Spinning on her heel, she made a grab for the telephone. 'I'm going to make an anonymous call to the DC police and inform them that Dr Padgham and the two security guards were –'

Cædmon yanked the phone out of her hand.

'What are you doing?'

'In this day and age, it's impossible to be truly anonymous,' he matter-of-factly informed her. 'We already know that the local police force has been infiltrated. If you contact the authorities, you may inadvertently lead our adversaries –'

'Right to us.' Grim-faced, Edie sank to the bed.

'I have a far better suggestion.'

137

'Unless it involves a magic wand, I don't know how you're going to make things better.'

Knowing its source, he ignored the sarcasm. 'I propose we do a bit of cyber-sleuthing. High time we met the enemy.' He removed his jacket from the back of the wingback chair.

'But we don't have a computer.'

'True, but the bloke downstairs at the front desk seemed amiable enough.'

2 2

'Boy, you don't know your dick from a stick!' Stanford MacFarlane railed at his subordinate.

Just like Custis. Had he lived, his son Custis would be twenty-eight years old this month. But Custis was dead, the weak-kneed snot having –

MacFarlane shoved the thought to the back of his mind.

The framed photographs had been removed, the name Custis Lee MacFarlane stricken from the family Bible. No sense regurgitating the past. It was over and done with. Mortal man could affect nothing save the here and now. And then only if it was God's wish that he should do so.

'What was running through your gourd, Gunny, detonating that wad of C4 without the Miller woman being in the vehicle? This operation was supposed to have been swift and silent, not a blind-man's game of grab-ass.'

'Sir, the explosives were rigged to go off when the engine was started. I had no way of knowing the C4 would detonate when the tow truck hooked the –'

'Well, you should have known! And how is it that Aisquith and Miller eluded six – count 'em – six men trained in urban warfare.'

'I don't know how they got the slip on us, sir.'

MacFarlane was sorely tempted to ram his knee into his subordinate's crotch. Penance for his sins. Instead, he strode over to his desk. A hardback book, *Isis Revealed*, lay in plain sight on top of his in tray. He grabbed the book, waving it in front of the gunny's face.

'Are you saying that the man who wrote this pack of lies outsmarted six of Rosemont's finest?' He'd earlier had one of his assistants purchase the book, a hunter needing to know the nature of the beast before he laid his traps.

'He's good, sir. That's all I know. Riggins is fairly certain they slipped through the 7th Street exit.'

MacFarlane wasn't fooled by the Brit's bravado. No doubt, Aisquith and the Miller woman were holed up somewhere, trying to figure out their next move. They were afraid, uncertain who they could trust. He had carefully cultivated that mistrust when he had spoken to the woman. The mess at the Hopkins Museum had been swept clean and the fiasco at the National Gallery of Art attributed to a rogue terrorist. But all that could change if Ms Miller gave a statement to the police.

He dismissively tossed the book aside, his gaze momentarily landing on the jacket photograph of a red-haired man in a tweed sports jacket. *There is a special place in hell for men who blaspheme the teachings of the one true God.* Soon enough, the ex-intelligence operative turned faux historian would know the meaning of terror, Aisquith playing with a fire that could not be extinguished.

As the silent seconds ticked past, Boyd Braxton wordlessly stared at him, a 'Help me, I'm drowning' look on his broad face. It put the colonel in mind of the night that the gunny murdered his wife and child. A mistake committed in a moment of unchecked rage, MacFarlane had used the calamitous event to bring the sobbing, baby-faced gunnery sergeant to God. He'd done good work that night, having made a promise not to turn his back on the man who now stood before him.

Ass-chewing administered, Stanford MacFarlane pointed to the parquet floor. 'On your knees, boy. It's time you begged the Almighty's forgiveness.'

A look of relief on his face, Braxton obediently dropped to his knees, his head bowed in prayer. Glancing down, MacFarlane could see the criss-crossed scars that marred his subordinate's skull. Souvenirs of a sinner's life, the scars were undoubtedly the result of a broken beer bottle making contact with Braxton's head.

Stepping back, giving the other man the space he needed to make his peace with God, MacFarlane walked over to a box on the other side of the room, the Stones of Fire packed and ready for transport. Acquiring the breastplate had been the preliminary to a much larger operation. A means to an end. The end being the cleansing of all perversion, all licentiousness.

Like ancient Egypt, America was headed down the path of destruction, the world no different now than it had been in the days of the pharaoh. Plague upon plague had been visited upon the godless pagans, none immune save the God-fearing Moses and his Hebrews. So, too, this epoch would see God's might as never before, his terrible swift sword striking down the false prophets, the feel-good TV shrinks, the prosperity gurus. Those who do not heed the warnings of the Old Testament prophets would discover first hand how God judged sin.

With so little time left, America must have a revival of repentance, the nation having strayed from the tenets of God's word as transcribed by the prophets. A course correction was needed. Holy warriors were needed.

MacFarlane walked over to the framed map that hung behind his desk. Starting at Washington DC, he cast his gaze due east. To Jerusalem.

'O holy city of Zion, God's glittering jewel,' he murmured, 'God said the Temple shall be rebuilt . . . and so it shall.' Rejuvenated, he turned away from the map. 'Rise to your feet, boy, and start acting like the man of God that you are.'

As Braxton shoved himself upright, a disembodied voice came over the telephone intercom. 'They just brought Eliot Hopkins into the waiting room, sir.'

Pleased, MacFarlane turned to his subordinate.

'Show the muscum director into the office. And make sure you give him a hearty Rosemont welcome.'

23

'How is it you know so much about Moses and his Egyptian roots?' Edie enquired as she and Cædmon waited for the computer to boot up.

The hotel night porter, a good-natured student at the nearby George Mason School of Law, had given them access to a computer in the back office. More a storage alcove, the room was stacked with plastic bins and boxes. Sitting side by side at the computer, Cædmon in the lone swivel chair, Edie perched on a bin, they were there to cyber-sleuth. Although what Cædmon thought he'd find was a mystery to her.

'For a brief time I dabbled in Egyptology while an undergraduate at Oxford,' Cædmon said in response to her question. 'That was before I became thoroughly infatuated with the Knights Templar and jumped ship, as you Yanks say.'

'The Knights Templar? Yeah, I can see that.' Volunteering a personal titbit of her own, she said, 'I've got a masters degree in women's studies.'

Grinning, Cædmon winked at her. 'Nearly as obscure a course of study as medieval history. And taking digital photographs at the Hopkins Museum?'

'A girl's got to make a living somehow.'

Enjoying the flirtatious banter, she wondered if anything would come of it. Because of the near-miss at the National Gallery, they'd decided against separate rooms. *Would he make a move once the bed covers were turned down?* Imagining what that might be like, she stared at his hands, admiring the raised pattern of veins. She'd seen those hands before. In Florence on Michelangelo's *David.*

Admittedly intrigued by the brainy, street-smart man with masculine hands, she decided to prise the lid a bit higher. 'Earlier today you said something about being on a book tour.'

'I recently wrote a book about the Egyptian mystery cults. Which permits me to put the word "author" on my curriculum vitae.'

'That would make you – what – a historian?'

Cædmon keyed in the log-on code given to them by the porter. 'Actually, I prefer to think of myself as a rehistorian.'

'Last time I looked, that particular word hadn't made it to the pages of *Webster.*'

'Nor the *Oxford English Dictionary.* But seeing as there's no word to accurately describe what I do, I was forced to improvise.'

'And just how does a rehistorian differ from your standard garden-variety historian?'

'A historian gathers, examines and interprets the material evidence that remains from the near and distant past,' Cædmon replied as he brought up the Google home page. 'In contrast, a rehistorian reveals that which has remained hidden from view; scholarship and speculation going hand in hand.'

She smiled. 'Well, you did lay claim to being an iconoclast.'

'So, I did. But enough about me.' Leaning forward, he grabbed a pad of Holiday Inn notepaper lying on the desk. He then removed a fountain pen from his breast pocket. 'I want you to tell me every pertinent detail you can recall from your earlier ordeal.'

'You mean at the Hopkins Museum?' When he nodded, she propped her chin on her balled fist. 'Well, I already told you about the ring with the Jerusalem cross. But what I didn't tell you is that right after he murdered Dr Padgham, the killer called someone on his cell phone. I counted seven digital beeps, so it had to be a local call.'

Cædmon scribbled 'DC phone call' on the pad.

'And I remember that the killer said something about going to "London at nineteen hundred hours".' Edie bracketed the last five words with air quotation marks. 'Or maybe the cop mentioned London. I'm not sure. Sorry. I don't remember. No! Wait!' Excited, Edie slapped her palm on the desk. 'The killer mentioned a place called Rosemont.'

'Let me make certain that I have this correct: DC phone call, London nineteen hundred hours and Rosemont.' When she nodded, he ripped the sheet of paper from the pad.

'Now what?' Edie dragged the green bin closer to the desk so she could see the computer monitor.

'Now, we delve into the abyss.'

Edie nudged him in the arm with her elbow. 'Thanks for that bit of heightened drama. Like I wasn't scared enough already.'

Cædmon glanced first at his arm, then at her face. For several seconds they wordlessly stared at one another. Two strangers drawn together by a trio of seemingly unconnected clues.

As she continued to gaze into Cædmon's blue eyes, Edie detected a fire. A passion. But for what, she had no idea. History. Religion. The 'occult sciences'. Hard to tell.

The first to break eye contact, Cædmon typed 'Rosemont+DC' into the search field. 'Since the London reference is too vague, we'll start with this.'

'You know, I remember the good ol' days when everyone used to have what was quaintly referred to as a private life.'

'Yes, little did Orwell imagine that Big Brother would come in the guise of a desktop computer.'

'Looks like we've got a hit,' she exclaimed a half-second later, pointing to the computer screen. 'It's a Wikipedia entry for Rosemont Security Consultants.' Quickly, she scanned the brief description. She turned to Cædmon. 'Some sort of security firm headquartered in Washington.'

Cædmon clicked on the link. To her dismay, only one scant paragraph appeared. Cædmon hit 'Print', the HP printer whirring to life.

Edie read the particulars aloud. '"Founded in 2005

by former US Marine Corps Colonel Stanford MacFarlane, Rosemont is one of several security consulting firms created in the wake of the Afghan and Iraq conflicts. Specializing in security consulting, stability operations and tactical support, Rosemont has security contracts in twenty-two nations world-wide."' As the information began to sink in, Edie's shoulders slumped. 'A security consulting firm ... That's a polite way of saying Rosemont specializes in mercenaries.'

'So it would seem.' Cædmon typed a new entry into the search field. 'Damn. Rosemont Security Consultants doesn't have a website. Although I shouldn't be surprised, given such companies prefer to operate out of the public eye.'

'You know what this means, don't you? It means we're not dealing with one or two armed bad men. We're dealing with an entire army of –'

'We don't know that,' Cædmon interjected, still the voice of reason. 'Padgham's killer may simply be in the employ of Rosemont Security Consultants. The firm may have nothing to do with Padgham's murder or the theft of the Stones of Fire.'

Suddenly recalling something she'd failed to mention, Edie threw her right arm into the air, waving it to catch the teacher's attention. 'One last premature leap, okay? I remember that the killer asked to speak to "the colonel".' She snatched the printed sheet out of Cædmon's hands. Turning it towards him, she underlined the first sentence of the Wikipedia entry with her index finger. 'It says here that the man who founded Rosemont Security Consultants is an ex-marine colonel by the name of Stanford MacFarlane. Do you think there's a link? That this might be who the killer called on his cell phone?'

'Possibly,' Cædmon replied, obviously not one to leap without looking. He quickly typed 'Stanford+ MacFarlane' into the search engine. A dozen entries popped up, most of them dated 2005.

'That one,' Edie said. 'The *Washington Post* article dated March 20th.'

Cædmon clicked on the entry.

In silence, they both stared at the photograph that accompanied the front-page story, of a group of military officers, some in dress uniform, some in combat fatigues, linked arm in arm, their heads reverentially bowed.

Edie read the headline aloud. 'PENTAGON TOP AIDE CONDUCTS WEEKLY PRAYER CIRCLE. And according to the photo tagline, that guy in the middle with the thinning grey buzz cut is Colonel Stanford MacFarlane. I think you better –'

'Righto,' Cædmon said, hitting 'Print'.

As the page printed, they silently read the article. Edie's gaze zeroed in on the last paragraph: 'Found guilty of violating military regulations regarding religious expression, Colonel MacFarlane was officially relieved of his duties as intelligence advisor to the undersecretary of defense. In a news conference held late yesterday, Colonel MacFarlane announced that he intended to operate a private security firm specializing in defense contracts while continuing his ongoing work in the religious organization Warriors of God.'

'MacFarlane may have fallen from grace, but it appears he landed a very lucrative career in security contracts.' She derisively snorted, the story a common one in DC. 'Talk about a golden parachute. Last I heard, there's tens of thousands of these armed paramilitary types running around Iraq, most of them ex-special forces.'

'Even more worrying, Colonel MacFarlane probably maintains his high-level contacts within the Pentagon. The man did, after all, work for the undersecretary of defense.'

'I have no idea who's on his Christmas list. All I know is that MacFarlane has at least one inside man working for the DC police. If we go to the authorities, MacFarlane will find us.' Edie stared despondently at the newspaper article. 'Religious fanatics ... not good. Try searching for these Warriors of God, will ya?' She tapped her index finger against the computer screen.

A few seconds later, Cædmon found MacFarlane's website, the domain address none other than www.warriorsofgod.com.

'Did God not make Jonathan Padgham as he made you and me?' Cædmon softly whispered.

'Do you think that's the reason why they killed Dr Padgham, because he was gay?'

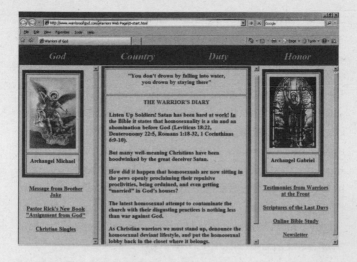

A sad look in his eyes, Cædmon slowly shook his head. 'No, I don't think that was the reason they killed Padge. Although in another place, and at another time, that may have been sufficient reason to take his life. But it wasn't the reason today.'

Edie took several deep breaths, opened her mouth to speak, then found she had nothing to say. The day's events had unravelled in such a helter-skelter fashion, she didn't know if she'd ever be able to untangle the skeins.

'While some might dismiss that –' she jutted her chin at the computer screen '– as your run-of-the-mill hate chatter, it scares the bejesus out of me.'

The hate-filled diatribe bringing to mind her own religious upbringing, Edie turned away from the computer. Her grandfather had been a hard-core evangelical Christian, fervently believing that the Bible was the literal transcription of God's word. And, like the prophets of the Old Testament, Pops had been a rigid taskmaster, daily force-feeding his family an ultra-conservative diet of hellfire and eternal damnation. Finally unable to bear it any longer, her mother had left home at sixteen. Later, Edie had gone to live with her grandparents. She lasted a bit longer, escaping on her eighteenth birthday via a full scholarship to George Washington University. The day she boarded the northbound Greyhound bus was the last day she ever spoke to her maternal grandfather, Conway Miller.

For the first couple of months she'd made half-hearted attempts to keep in touch with her Gran, but when the letters were returned unopened, she got the message. She'd not only left the family, she'd left the flock. She had officially been branded a non-person. It was another fifteen years before she set foot inside a church. The congregation at St Matilda's was an eclectic mix of female priests, gay deacons and multiracial couples. People of all stripes and colours, joined together in mutual joy. A blessed gathering. Edie didn't know if it was a form of rebellion against the religion of her youth, but she loved attending Sunday service at St Mattie's. No doubt, Pops weekly spun in his grave.

'It would appear that Stanford MacFarlane is the big fish in a very murky pond,' Cædmon said, drawing Edie's attention back to the computer screen. 'In my experience, men consumed by hatred who cloak themselves in religion are the most dangerous men on earth.'

'Just read the newspapers. Religious fanaticism is a global phenomenon.'

'Which begs the question, why has a group of fanatical Christians stolen one of the most sacred of all religious relics?'

Edie shrugged. 'I have no idea.'

'Nor I. Although I am keen to uncover the answer.'

24

Outside the hotel room window the day had dawned damp and cold, no glimmer of sunshine to cast even a suggestion of hope. Through the leafless trees Edie stared at the snaking procession of headlights, the early-morning motorists lost in an enviable world of undone Christmas shopping, overdue bills and holiday office parties.

She sighed, her breath condensing into a cloudy smudge as it struck the glass of the window.

'All is not lost,' Cædmon said from behind her, his voice taking her by surprise.

Edie turned to face him, unaware that her glum mood had been so obvious. 'Then why am I having so much trouble finding an answer that makes any sense? I don't know about you, but I tossed and turned all night trying to figure out why an ex-marine colonel who now owns and operates a mercenary-contracting firm would have had Dr Padgham murdered?' She held up her hand, forestalling an objection. 'I know, the Stones of Fire . . . But did they have to go and –'

Hearing a thud, Edie rushed over and unlocked the door to their hotel room, snatching the just-delivered complimentary copy of the *Washington Post* off the mat. Door closed and relocked, she quickly flipped through the newspaper, ignoring the front-page story on the terrorist attack at the National Gallery of Art. Instead, she searched for a headline, a photo, a story tucked away in the 'Metro' section, anything about a triple homicide at the Hopkins Museum.

'There's nothing in the paper. How can that be? Surely by now someone has found Dr Padgham and the two dead guards.' She tossed the newspaper onto her unmade bed.

'It's still less than twenty-four hours since the murders were committed,' Cædmon calmly reminded her. He had just showered and shaved, which ex-plained why he was half-dressed, his red hair matted to his skull. Attired as he was in a white vest, Edie could see that he had broad shoulders and a lean, rangy build.

'Yeah, but the night shift should have found the bodies. The guards are supposed to make the rounds of the museum every thirty minutes. And I know for a fact that Linda Alvarez in payroll arrives at the museum at seven o'clock sharp. She has to walk right past Dr Padgham's office to get to –' Edie stopped, hit with a sudden thought. 'Once they access the computer logs at the museum, the police will know that I was at the museum when Dr Padgham was murdered. Which makes me a fugitive.'

One side of Cædmon's mouth twitched. 'Hardly a fugitive.'

'Well, okay, a person of interest. Isn't that what they call them on cop shows?' She peered at her reflection in the wall mirror. Feeling the sting of tears, she turned her back on Cædmon, worried the dam might burst.

Since yesterday afternoon she'd been fighting the onslaught, and truth be told she was tired. Tired of being strong. She just wanted to curl up in her bed, pull the pile of stiff covers over her head and cry her eyes out. But she couldn't. She barely knew Cædmon Aisquith, and if she scared him off, she'd be left to fend for herself. Like she'd had to do so many times before. When she was a kid, her mother used to ignore her for days on end.

'I'm sorry for getting all emotional on you. I just –' She sank her teeth into her lower lip, struggling to hold back the tears.

As she stood there, her back still turned to him, she heard Cædmon pad over to where she stood. Then she felt a warm hand on her shoulder.

'There's no need to be ashamed of your emotions.'

'Easy for you to say; you're a red-headed pillar of strength.'

'Not true.' Gently he turned her round, pulling her into his arms. Since he stood somewhere in the neighbourhood of six foot three, her head fitted perfectly into his freckled shoulder.

Edie closed her eyes, drinking in his warmth, his solidity. It felt so good to be held in his arms. Good in a way that made her think of the sleepless night just passed. *How many times were you tempted to climb out of bed and get into his?* Too many to count.

Worried she might give in to her urges, sex the best balm of them all, she extricated herself from his arms.

'I need to call the Hopkins and find out what the heck is going on,' she said, striding over to the desk wedged between the TV and the dresser.

'Given we're very much in the dark, I think that's a wise idea. Although make no mention of what you saw yesterday at the museum.'

Nodding, Edie dialled the main number for the museum. When prompted by the automated system, she keyed in the four-digit extension for the payroll department. Hearing a perky voice answer 'Linda Alvarez. How may I help you?' Edie motioned Cædmon to silence.

'Hey Linda, it's Edie Miller. I'm sorry for pestering you so early in the morning, but I really screwed up my timecard yesterday . . . Oh . . . Really? Huh.'

Edie placed her palm over the handset, whispering, 'According to Linda, I never clocked in yesterday. But I know for a fact that I did.'

She removed her hand from the phone. 'Silly me, huh? You'd think after all these weeks I'd be able to get it right. I, um, was in and out so quick that I guess I forgot to –'

Cædmon mouthed, 'Ask for Padgham.'

'Is Dr Padgham in his office by any chance? He asked me to take some photos for a special project and I was just ... Oh, gosh, that's terrible. Well, um, since he's not at the museum, would you be a dear and walk down the hall to his office for me? I spilled a cup of coffee all over his Persian carpet and I just wanted to make sure the cleaning crew took care of – Yeah, he is a bit of a priss, isn't he? Thanks, Linda.'

Again, Edie placed her palm over the handset. 'You're not going to believe this. She claims that Dr Padgham's longtime partner was killed yesterday in a hit-and-run accident and that Dr Padgham flew to London to take care of the burial arrangements.'

Cædmon's blue eyes narrowed. 'They're trying to make it appear that Padge is still among the living. My, my, what a tangled web we weave.'

She again motioned him to silence. 'That's great. Well, I, um, gotta run. Thanks a million, Linda. I'll catch you later.'

Edie hung up the phone, stunned.

'What did she say about the blood-stained carpet?' Cædmon prompted.

'To Linda Alvarez's eagle eye, there's no stain on Dr Padgham's carpet. No bloodied bits of brain matter. No noxious pile of vomit. Nothing but a beautifully vacuumed Persian rug.' Edie pulled out the chair in front of the desk and plopped into it. She glanced at Cædmon's reflection in the wall mirror. 'It's a cover-up. A huge wipe-the-slate-clean cover-up.'

'Since the last thing that the thieves want is for the police to become involved, they'll undoubtedly invent something to kill off Padge in London. No one on this side of the Atlantic would question Padgham's suicide, say, grief-stricken at his partner's death.'

'I think they killed Dr Padgham's partner.'

'More than likely they did,' Cædmon replied, his crisp accent noticeably subdued.

'How in God's name did Rosemont pull off such a well-organized cover-up?'

Cædmon seated himself on the edge of her bed. 'With inside help, I dare say. Who captains the ship?'

'At the Hopkins? That would be the museum director, Eliot Hopkins.'

'Call him. Ask for a meeting for later this morning.'

Edie cast him a long, considering glance. 'Tell me why exactly I want to set up a meeting with the museum director?'

'In the hope that Mr Hopkins will spill some gilded beans.'

'What do I tell him? I can't think of a single reason why Eliot Hopkins would agree to meet with us, let alone give us the straight scoop.'

'Try coming at the problem from a different angle. Why would the venerable Mr Hopkins agree to participate in the theft of a relic he already owned?'

'That's easy. Insurance fraud. He intends to collect on the policy.'

'But I suspect that the Stones of Fire was purchased on the black market.'

'Meaning the relic wasn't insured.' Edie said, beating him to the punch.

'Ergo, Eliot Hopkins had nothing to do with Padge's murder. But I believe he had something to do with the subsequent cover-up.'

'But why cover up the murder? It doesn't make any sense.'

Still sitting on the edge of her bed, Cædmon crossed one jeans-clad leg over the other. 'What would happen if the authorities discovered that the director of the Hopkins Museum had knowingly purchased a stolen relic smuggled out of its country of origin?'

'In addition to a hefty fine, Eliot Hopkins might be sentenced to prison.'

'And in the process, his reputation and good name would be ripped to shreds. All of which makes Eliot Hopkins a very weak link.'

'And you want to find out who's yanking his chain,' Edie said, the reason for the proposed rendezvous suddenly making sense. 'I'm guessing it's the guys at Rosemont. Probably what's his name? Colonel MacFarlane. Who else could it be?'

Rather than answer, Cædmon stretched out along the length of the bed, reaching for a tourist map on top of the bedside cabinet, part of the welcome-to-your-room pack. Unfolding the map, he spread it on his lap. 'The National Zoo, the National Cathedral or the Lincoln Memorial. Which of these are you most familiar with?'

'The zoo,' she answered, wondering where he was headed. 'It's only a few blocks from my house. When the weather is nice, I like to power-walk it.'

Cædmon refolded the map. 'Then the National Zoo it is. Tell Mr Hopkins to be there at ten a.m. Sharp. Do be sure to add that. When talking to thieves and murderers, it's always best to speak with authority, that being the only way to deal with a playground bully.'

'That or kick him in the nuts,' Edie muttered as she reached for the phone.

25

Eliot Hopkins slowly hung up the telephone.

Just as the monsters at Rosemont Security Consultants had predicted, Edie Miller had initiated contact.

The first piece of a very complicated puzzle had fallen into place.

He sighed, a long drawn-out breath that was equal parts regret and pain. Regret because he was fond of the quirky and offbeat Miss Miller. Pain on account of the cracked rib he nursed, courtesy of a muscled behemoth with a misplaced sense of civility, the fiend having grinned and said 'Howdy do' after administering the unexpected blow. The men of Rosemont wanted his cooperation. And they'd gone about gaining it in a most primitive fashion.

Why negotiate when one can use fists and threats to achieve the same end?

Glancing at the imposing John Singer Sargent portrait that hung above the mantel, Eliot thought he caught the hint of a smirk on his great-grandfather's stern visage, the coal magnate having put down more than one strike with clubs and bullets.

Unlike Andrew Carnegie, who had suffered with a guilty conscious, Albert Horatio Hopkins had never lost a single night's sleep worrying about the plight of the men who earned him his immense fortune. A true vandal, Albert Hopkins had raped the West Virginia mountains for their minerals and stripped his employees of their dignity.

Long live King Coal.

While he was the great-grandson of Albert Hopkins, he was also, and more importantly to his mind, the grandson of Oliver Hopkins. In his day and age, that being the feel-good, anything-goes frenzy before the Great Depression, Ollie Hopkins had had a well-deserved reputation as a ne'er-do-well. Turning his back on the family business, he instead supped with African chieftains, rode wild horses with Mongolian warriors and explored the licentious world of the harem with Arab potentates.

Along the way, he had spent a king's ransom searching for the relics of the Exodus.

As a young boy, Eliot would sit for hours at his grandfather's knee, enthralled by his exciting tales, which rivalled any adventure book. His particular favourite had been the time that his grandfather, disguised as a Turk, had tunnelled into the bowels of the Temple Mount, only to be discovered by Sheik Khalil, the hereditary guardian of the Dome of the Rock. Chased through the streets of Jerusalem by an angry mob, his grandfather made his getaway in a motor yacht hijacked from the port of Jaffa.

Considered a wastrel by his father, Oliver was eventually disinherited. Penniless when he died, he had left his favourite grandson the fruits of all his labours – an immense collection of artefacts and relics mined over the course of some fifty years. The collection became the cornerstone of the Hopkins Museum of Near Eastern Art, the museum founded in homage to the man who had given Eliot the only familial affection he ever knew.

His grandfather had also bequeathed to him a magnificent obsession – the Stones of Fire.

It had taken decades of dangled carrots and very large bribes, but he had finally found it.

Only to lose it in the blink of a jaded eye.

Had he been a religious man, he might have thought it God's punishment for daring the unthinkable. Certainly, he'd been a fool to entrust Jonathan Padgham with the holy relic. But the man had been an expert on Near East antiquities and Eliot needed to verify that what he'd found in the sands of Iraq was in fact the fabled Stones of Fire. Blinded by his obsession, he had never considered that there might be others even more intent on finding the treasures of the Bible. Men unfettered by the rule of law.

Wearily, Eliot rose to his feet. There being no time to ponder the ethics of the situation, he walked over to a panelled door on the far side of the rosewood-lined library. Pressing a hidden latch, the door swung open. He turned on the light, the small room windowless. In turn, he surveyed each glass case, his collection of antique weaponry a private passion. Out of respect for his thirteen-year-old daughter Olivia, who had an unnatural fear of guns, he kept his collection out of sight.

Pausing in front of a velvet-lined case, he briefly considered the Colt revolver once owned by gunslinger Buffalo Bill, but in the end settled on a World War II-era Walther PPK. The handgun of choice for the German SS.

Over the years, he'd dealt with greedy dealers, ruthless brokers and pompous curators. Last night was the first time he'd come face to face with religious zealots, the interaction shocking. One could not reason with such men for they served but one master.

One could only acquiesce.

26

'Do you think we're being followed?' Edie asked, glancing into the wing mirror of a parked car.

Cædmon waited until the crossing light at Connecticut Avenue turned yellow. Then, taking her by the elbow, he hustled her across the street towards the main entrance to the National Zoo on the opposite side of the intersection. A few seconds later they passed the two bronze lions that stood guard at the gated entrance.

'If we are being followed, our pursuers have successfully faded into the proverbial woodwork.'

Edie shivered, the previous day's snow having turned into a chill-laden drizzle. She moved closer to Cædmon, the two of them huddled beneath a black umbrella they'd purchased en route. Passing the Visitor Center, she peered at the grounds reflected in the bank of glass doors. No surprise that the zoo was eerily deserted, animal-watching not a big draw in December. But then, they weren't there to see the sights; they were there to meet the man who had illegally purchased the Stones of Fire, setting into motion yesterday's brutal train of events.

'Does your family live in the area?' Cædmon enquired casually. Throughout their subway ride from Arlington, he'd maintained a steady stream of pleasant chit-chat. On to his tricks, Edie assumed the light conversation was more for her benefit than his; Cædmon's way of alleviating her all-too-obvious anxiety. Little did he know that personal questions elicited a similar response.

'My mother and father were both killed in a boating accident off the coast of Florida,' she answered, the lie well honed from twenty-five years of sharpening. Approaching the Small Mammal House, she gestured to the walkway on the right, the zoo grounds a maze of pathways that wound through what was surprisingly hilly terrain. 'It was Labor Day weekend and a drunk in a speedboat rammed right into them. I was only eleven years old when it happened.'

Usually she embroidered the tale, going into great detail as to how the non-existent boater only had to spend two years in prison. But today, for some inexplicable reason, she felt guilty about the fabrication. Although why she should feel any guilt was a mystery. Shame, yes. Guilt, no. After all it wasn't her fault that her father was listed on her birth certificate as 'Unknown' or that her mother had been a junkie, never able to lose her taste for smack. When her mother fatally OD'd, Edie had been forced to spend two and a half years in the Florida foster care system, until a kind-hearted social worker had taken an interest in her case, going the extra two miles to track down her maternal grandparents in Cheraw, South Carolina. Edie never spoke of the thirty nightmarish months spent on the foster care merry-go-round. Not to anyone. There were some things a person couldn't, or shouldn't, share with another human being.

Seeing a vaporous cloud approach, Cædmon waited until a red-faced man decked out in winter Lycra jogged past. A few moments later, he solicitously took her by the elbow, steering her clear of an icy patch. 'Who took care of you?'

'Oh, I, um, went to live with my grandparents in South Carolina. Pops and Gran were great. Really, really great,' she said with a big fake smile. Uncomfortable with the lie, she feigned a sudden interest in the leafless shrubs planted along a low retaining wall. Winter had its claws dug deep, the nearby trees and plantings covered in a crystal shroud. Most of the animals had gone to ground. As they passed the tamarin cage, there wasn't a primate in sight.

'South Carolina ... How interesting. One would think you'd have a more pronounced accent. And you've been in Washington for how long?'

Wishing he'd cease and desist, she said, 'It's coming up on the twenty-year mark. What anniversary is that? Crystal? I'm not sure.'

'I believe that would be china,' he replied, watching her out of the corner of his eye.

Edie cleared her throat, wondering if she'd laid it on too thick about Pops and Gran. As happened with all new acquaintances, she feared that he was on to her.

Hearing a branch snap, Cædmon momentarily paused, the silence filled with several unidentified screeches. Evidently satisfied that the noises were not man made, he said, 'I'm curious. Why did you choose a degree in women's studies?'

'Why do you want to know? You're not a closet chauvinist, are you?'

'Not in the least.'

Satisfied with his reply, Edie shrugged. 'Since someone else was footing the bill for my education, I studied what interested me. At the time I was interested in the role of women in American society.' What she didn't tell him was that she had wanted to find out why women made the choices they did. 'I had an internship at a non-profit organization, but because of budget constraints it didn't pan into a paying gig. Luckily, I found a job at a downtown photo shop.' At the time she hadn't known squat about photography, having charmed her way into the job. But she learned quickly, enamoured with the way that photography could be used to manipulate the real world, to erase the ugliness.

'And how long have you been working as a photographer?'

'Gees, what are you, a Spanish Inquisitor?' Edie retorted, determined to end the personal interrogation. 'You know, I usually love the zoo, but today it's got creepy written all over it.'

Cædmon slowed his step as they wound their way through what looked to be an impenetrable chasm, huge buff-coloured boulders, a full storey in height, lining the pathway. She wondered if the man at her side was thinking what she was thinking – that this would be an excellent place for a gunman to hide.

A few moments later they emerged from the stone-lined path and approached the caged hillside set aside for the Mexican wolves, that being the designated meeting place with Eliot Hopkins. To the right of the enclosure a lone man bundled in an overcoat sat on a bench, a cup of Starbucks coffee clutched in his gloved hand.

'There he is,' Edie said in hushed whisper, fearful her voice might carry. 'I don't know about you, but I fully intend to give the SOB a grilling.'

Cædmon's head jerked in her direction.

'What? Why are you looking at me like that? It's called good cop/bad cop.'

Grabbing her by the upper arm, Cædmon drew her to his side. 'Now is not the time for us to be out of step with one another,' he hissed in her ear. 'We merely want to tickle the man.'

'Yeah, before we move in for the kill.'

27

'Figuratively speaking,' Edie amended.

'I most certainly hope so.' Concerned his companion may have watched too many police dramas on TV, Cædmon tightened his grip on her arm. Like a harried parent with an unruly child.

Surreptitiously, he glanced around. Rock-strewn, treed and hilly, the surrounding terrain could easily conceal a hunter on the prowl. Attired in her red and purple plaid skirt, Edie made an easy target. While warning bells were not yet clanging, they did tinkle, the place having about it a sinister air.

As they approached the bareheaded man seated on the bench, Cædmon closed the black brolly he'd been holding aloft, the wintry rain having dwindled to a faint drizzle. He hooked the curved handle over his bent arm.

'A most interesting place to meet, betwixt and between these two beautiful creatures of prey,' Eliot Hopkins remarked, slowly rising to his feet. He gestured first to a lone wolf warily prowling the fenced hillside beside them. Then he pointed a gloved hand to the bald eagle perched on the opposite hillock. 'Did you know that the eagle has been a symbol of war since Babylonian times?'

With his thatch of wavy white hair, patrician features and ruddy red cheeks, Cædmon thought Eliot Hopkins a grandfatherly-looking man. Dressed in English tweed, he could have passed for a country squire, a harmless dolt who, if prompted, could natter for hours on end about shifting weather patterns and the breeding of Leicester Longwool sheep.

'How about canning the bullshit,' Edie retorted, ignoring Cædmon's admonition. 'Because of you, and your boundless greed, Jonathan Padgham is dead! And don't give me any bunk about him going to London to take care of funeral arrangements. I know what happened yesterday at the museum.'

'Jonathan's death is most unfortunate and, I am sad to say, entirely my fault,' the museum director readily confessed, a morose look in his rheumy grey eyes. 'I had no idea that Jonathan was in danger. Although once the deed was done, I had no choice but to assist in the cover-up.'

'I'm curious to know how you became involved with such a bloodthirsty gang,' Cædmon remarked. 'You don't strike me as moving in the same circles.'

Smiling ever so slightly, Hopkins nodded. 'Shortly after I acquired the Stones of Fire I was approached by a private consortium interested in buying the breastplate at an exorbitant price. When I refused to sell the relic, the consortium resorted to blackmail, demanding that I relinquish custody of the breastplate or they would alert the IARC.'

'Who or what is the IARC?' Edie asked.

'That would be the Illicit Antiquities Research Center. They monitor the international trade in stolen or secretly excavated antiquities.'

'And that would have created quite the public scandal,' she correctly deduced. 'So, why didn't you give the consortium the Stones of Fire? Why take the risk of being exposed?'

'I called their bluff, knowing full well that if the IARC became involved, the consortium would lose all chance of getting their hands on my precious relic. A tragic miscalculation as it turned out.'

'Proving that one cannot trump the devil,' Cædmon muttered, infuriated that this deadly game had cost his old friend his life.

'I can assure you that if I had known several weeks ago what I know now, I would have –'

'Oh, puh-*lease*!' Edie interjected. 'You sound like someone running for public office.' She folded her arms over her chest, a stern headmistress in black leather. 'I just don't get it. Why would this so-called consortium resort to cold-blooded murder to get the Stones of Fire? It's just a bit of gold with twelve gemstones.'

A drawn-out pause ensued, the museum director evidently debating whether or not to answer. 'In and of itself, you're probably correct,' he finally replied. 'But when used in concert with another holy relic, the Stones of Fire becomes a conduit to God. Thus making it a prerequisite for the larger prize.'

. . . another holy relic . . . a prerequisite for the larger prize.

173

Cædmon's mouth slackened, the realization hitting him like a bunch of fives to the belly.

'I don't believe it ... They're actually going after the Ark.'

'The Ark?' Edie's gaze ricocheted between him and Eliot Hopkins. 'As in the Ark of the Covenant?'

'None other,' Hopkins confirmed.

Still in a state of shock, Cædmon pressed harder. 'How do you know that the consortium is searching for the Ark?'

'I know because I was searching for it. Two days before the theft at the museum, my Georgetown home was burglarized. Imagine my surprise when the only thing stolen was my research notes. For some thirty years I've hunted down clues, sent excavation teams into remote areas of the Middle East, continuing the work my grandfather began but could not finish.'

'Good God! Do you mean to say that you're Oliver Hopkins' grandson?' Considered by scholars to be daft as a brush, during the early part of the twentieth century Oliver Hopkins had spent a fortune searching for the Ark of the Covenant. To no avail, the wealthy adventurer barely escaping the Holy Land with his head intact.

'I came considerably closer to finding that elusive jewel in the biblical crown than my grandfather did. And in so doing, I knew that if I was to avoid the curse of Bethshemesh, I had to first find the Stones of Fire.'

Edie snickered derisively. 'The curse of Bethshemesh? Who are you, a character in an Indiana Jones movie?'

'Hardly,' Cædmon replied, the conversation about to darken several shades. 'The punishment for accidentally touching the Ark of the Covenant is a very painful death, Yahweh having a beastly temper. That said, in the Book of Samuel the cautionary tale of the city of Bethshemesh is recounted, Yahweh indiscriminately slaughtering fifty thousand of the residents as punishment for the handful of men who, overtaken with curiosity, had dared to peer inside the Ark.'

'Jesus,' she softly swore. 'God did that?'

'Elsewhere the Bible speaks of the Ark levelling whole mountains, parting rivers, annihilating enemy armies and destroying fortified cities. Those who doubted the Ark's power often found themselves covered in cancerous tumours or painful burns,' he informed her, knowing that most people preferred their God sanitized, the ugliness of the Old Testament swept under a heavenly carpet.

'It sounds more like a weapon than a religious artefact.'

'The Ark of the Covenant was, to use modern parlance, a weapon of mass destruction, enabling the ragtag Israelites to conquer the Holy Land. Shielded with the Stones of Fire, the high priest could channel and control all of that explosive energy.'

'Thus making the Stones of Fire a "prerequisite" to finding the Ark of the Covenant.'

Having stood silent, Eliot Hopkins rejoined the conversation. 'Now you see why I'm convinced that my mysterious consortium is intent on hunting bigger game? Think of the power contained within that precious gold chest. The Ark radiated divine power and might. And if one had a mind to communicate with the celestial spheres, the Ark could summon forth angels and even manifest the Almighty himself.'

The enraptured expression on Eliot Hopkins' visage belonged to that of a man obsessed. Cædmon knew the look well, having once been an obsessed man himself, his fascination with the Knights Templar having bordered on the fanatical – the reason, long years ago, he was expelled from Oxford.

'A lot of people would say that the supposed power of the Ark was nothing but a fanciful myth used to entertain Hebrews gathered around the evening campfire,' Edie argued.

'And there are those who claim that God is dead. I, however, am not one of them.'

'So, what happened to the Ark? Was it stolen? Was it lost? Was it destroyed?' his companion asked in rapid-fire succession.

Eliot Hopkins lifted his wool-clad shoulders in an eloquent shrug. 'The pages of the Old Testament don't give so much as a hint. We know only that Moses constructed the Ark in the fifteenth century BC; five centuries later King Solomon built a lavish temple to house the Ark; and sometime prior to the construction of the Second Temple in 516 BC the Ark vanished, seemingly into the dust of history.'

'Surely there's a theory or two to explain its disappearance,' Edie persisted.

'Most biblical historians concur that there are five probable scenarios to explain the Ark's disappearance,' Cædmon replied, beating the older man to the starting gate. 'The first of these concerns Menelik, King Solomon's son with the Queen of Sheba. Those who adhere to this theory have postulated that Menelik stole the Ark from the Temple around 950 BC and took it to Ethiopia, where it resides to this day.'

'Let's not forget the theory put forth in *Raiders of the Lost Ark*,' Edie said, smirking. 'You know, that the Ark is in Egypt.'

'A valid theory, as it turns out, the adherents of which believe that a few years after Solomon's death the Ark was stolen in a raid by the Pharaoh Shishak and taken to his newly constructed capital of Tanis. Then there are the three remaining theories – which involve the Ark being plundered by the Babylonians, the Greeks or the Romans; take your pick.'

'And I did, painstakingly considering each of those theories in turn,' Eliot Hopkins informed them. 'As you may or may not know, there are nearly two hundred references to the Ark contained within the pages of the Old Testament. Most of those references concern the period between the Exodus from Egypt and the construction of the Temple. This led me to surmise that the Ark of the Covenant disappeared shortly after Solomon constructed his fabulous building.'

Proving herself a sure-footed student, Edie said, 'Then the Ark was either stolen by Menelik or Shishak.'

'I know for a fact that the Ark does not reside in Ethiopia,' the older man quietly asserted.

Hearing that, Cædmon deduced that Eliot Hopkins had very deep pockets, the political situation in Ethiopia dicey to say the least. Obtaining permission to mount a thorough search would have been expensive.

'So, that means Shishak stole the Ark, and it's buried in the pharaoh's tomb.'

'Not necessarily,' the older man said in reply to Edie's deduction. 'Some years back, during a trip I made to the Middle East, a group of Bedouin traders told me the most fascinating tale of an English crusader who, en route between Palestine and Egypt, discovered a gold chest buried in the Plain of Esdraelon amidst the ruins of what had once been an Egyptian temple.'

'I've heard this story,' Cædmon murmured, knocked sideways by memories of his Oxford days.

'Careful, Mr Aisquith. In this game a little knowledge can be a dangerous thing.' Eliot Hopkins smiled, a kindly man offering a sage word of advice. 'If you are familiar with the tale, then you undoubtedly have guessed at the final resting place of the Ark of the Covenant.'

Refusing to take the bait, Cædmon went on the offensive. 'Why are you being so forthcoming with us? For years you've gone to great lengths to keep your pursuit of the Ark a secret.'

Grimacing, the museum director slid his gloved hand inside his overcoat. 'Because it is inconsequential whether you know or don't know.'

'And why is that?'

Eliot Hopkins removed his hand from his coat, a Walther PPK clenched in his fist. 'Because I have been ordered to kill you.'

28

With only a wolf and an eagle to bear witness to their deaths, Cædmon affected a calm he didn't feel. 'I say. That's not very friendly of you.'

'You're a fool to think you can get away with murdering us,' Edie hissed, adopting an entirely different approach.

One side of Eliot Hopkins' mouth lifted in a rueful half-smile. 'Killing you and your charming companion will be the least of my crimes.'

'You're actually going to kill us in cold blood all because of some religious artefact? Gold stuff! That's all it is.'

'None of the artefacts mentioned in the Bible can compare with the Ark of the Covenant,' Hopkins whispered, the gun unsteady in his gloved hand. 'The Ark contains the majesty and glory of Yahweh. It alone could inspire or destroy a nation.'

'Or an innocent couple,' Cædmon murmured, the Ark about to consume its next two victims.

Raising the gun a few inches higher, Hopkins pointed it at Edie's chest. 'I do hope you will forgive me, but if I don't comply with their orders, they'll kill my daughter.'

'"They" being your mysterious consortium, aka the Warriors of God,' said Edie.

Behind her brave facade, Cædmon saw the tremble in Edie's shoulder. Although tempted to put a comforting arm around her shoulders, he refrained. Instead he said, 'I can see to it that no harm comes to your daughter.'

'Olivia presently attends boarding school in Switzerland.' As he spoke, tears welled in Eliot Hopkins' eyes. 'My hands are tied. I have only one child. She alone is my hope for the future. My legacy.'

'I can contact Interpol,' Cædmon pressed, that being the only gambit he could think of. 'Within the half-hour your daughter could be in protective custody.'

'Entrust my daughter to strangers more than three thousand miles away?' The museum director wearily shook his head. 'You ask the impossible.'

Refusing to give up, Cædmon pressed a bit harder. 'Yesterday afternoon, in your museum, Jonathan Padgham was senselessly slain. Let us stop this madness before anyone else is killed.'

'I can't stop the madness,' the older man croaked, barely audible. 'I am truly sorry. I have no choice but to —'

A lion roared in the distance, a deep-throated bawl that rumbled through the leafless trees and echoed off the ice-laden boulders. The stentorian bellow momentarily distracted the elderly angel of death, Eliot Hopkins nervously glancing about.

Divine intervention or serendipity, Cædmon had no way of knowing. He only knew it was the moment to act. Before the window slammed shut.

Carpe diem, he silently invoked, his thighs, buttocks and biceps all tightening as he yanked the closed umbrella from where it hung on his forearm and hurled it like a spear. That done, he shoved Edie out of the line of fire behind a massive concrete rubbish receptacle and watched as the umbrella hit its mark, the stainless-steel tip hitting Eliot Hopkins square in the chest.

Knocked off balance, Hopkins dropped the pistol. The handgun fell to the ground, skittering along the icy surface.

About to retrieve the gun, Cædmon froze as a bullet whizzed past his ear, slamming into Eliot Hopkins' heart, killing him on impact.

There was a sniper on the hillside!

It had been a set-up. None of them was to have left the zoo alive.

Knowing that in combat he who hesitates is lost, Cædmon dived behind the rubbish receptacle, pushing against Edie's quivering backside.

'I'm beginning to think that "land of the free" means free to shoot and kill,' he muttered into her ear.

'He's on the hill above the bald eagle, isn't he?'

Cædmon nodded, assuming the man was a professional assassin. If they showed themselves, he would snap off two kill shots. Men trained to kill at a distance did so without remorse or regret, the action no different than breathing.

Edie peered at him from over her shoulder, a stricken expression on her face. 'Please tell me you've got a plan.'

'I haven't,' he replied truthfully. *Although I had better come up with something bloody quick.* Briefly he considered trying to retrieve Hopkins' pistol. Just as quickly he rejected the idea, certain he'd take a bullet to the head for his troubles.

'May I take a peek inside your bag?' he asked, tugging on the large canvas sack she had clutched to her body.

Edie wordlessly complied, opening it for his inspection. There being no time for niceties, he rifled through the bag's contents. He pulled out her khaki-coloured waistcoat.

'Perfect.' Reaching beside him, he grabbed a fistful of snow.

'What are you doing?'

'Weighing it so I can chuck it in the air. If we're lucky, the sniper will see the sudden motion, take aim and fire. The ruse won't gain us more than a few seconds, but that's all we'll need to get our arses behind those rocks.' With a lift of the chin, he indicated a jumble of boulders some twenty yards from their current position.

If she had misgivings, and no doubt she did, she kept them to herself.

Hoping the venture didn't prove a deadly mistake, Cædmon quickly tied the ends of the waistcoat into a knot, securing the ball of snow. Silently mouthing, 'On three,' he counted to two before throwing the waistcoat through the air. A perfectly bowled cricket delivery.

There being no time to observe the arc and descent of the makeshift decoy, Cædmon snatched Edie by the hand. Bending at the waist, making himself as small a target as possible, he charged towards the clustered rocks. Behind him, he heard a bullet *ping!* off the metal handrail that fronted the Mexican wolf enclosure.

The ruse had worked.

With Edie in tow, he dodged behind a waist-high boulder. Crouching, they pressed themselves against the stone. Quickly, he glanced from side to side. In the hilly terrain above the bald eagles he thought he detected a figure in a black anorak. A deadly predator on the prowl.

'It would be suicide for us to retrace our steps to the main entrance,' he said in a hushed tone, fearful that if they didn't find another means of escape they would meet the same fate as the museum director.

Edie lifted her head a scant few inches, enabling her to glance about furtively. Grimacing, she wiped the base of her palm across the trickle of blood that oozed from a scrape on her upper cheek. With the same hand she gestured uphill.

'If we can get to the Think Tank at the top of the hill, there's a path leading down to Rock Creek. This time of year, the creek should be low enough for us to cross on foot.'

'And the advantage of this escape route?'

'It's the quickest way out of here.' Again she wiped at the scrape on her upper cheek. A blooded huntswoman.

He took a moment to consider the merits of her plan. Although the uphill route would put more strain on lung and leg, the path was hedged with clustered bunches of reedy bamboo, which would provide excellent cover. If they moved quickly and carefully, they could remain hidden from sight. Assuming the sniper had no friends with him.

Cædmon deferred to her plan with a quick nod.

Once again snatching her by the hand, he led the way, running towards the uphill fork in the path. He considered it a good sign that he heard no whizzing bullets. However, the screeching bald eagle did not bode well, signalling that the sniper was in pursuit.

Midway up the hill, Edie started to lag, her ex-halations loud and uneven. There being no time to rally the troops, he yanked her after him. Letting go of her hand, he slung his left arm around her shoulder, pulling her to his side, forcing her to keep pace with him.

'You can catch your breath once we're clear.'

Propelled no doubt by a burst of fearful adrena-line, Edie managed to pick up speed.

A few seconds later the path levelled out.

'The Think Tank is that stone building straight ahead of us,' Edie gasped, pointing to a quaint structure straight out of a Thomas Hardy novel.

Pulling her behind a drystone wall that oozed icicles, he surveyed the area. Dismayed, he could see that they'd have to navigate a long stretch of open path – no trees, rocks or bamboo to obscure their movements.

'There's thirty yards of open terrain between here and the Think Tank. Will you be able to sprint that far?'

She nodded. Then, sinking her fingers into his forearm, she whispered, 'Cædmon, I'm afraid. Really, really afraid.'

'No disgrace in that. I'm feeling a bit unmanned myself.'

Her brown eyes opened wide. 'You're kidding right? You're like one of those guys in the Light Brigade.'

'Yes, well, we know what happened to them, don't we?'

'No, what happened?'

'Nearly half of them perished in the charge.' Not giving her time to contemplate the significance of that bit of British history, he snatched hold of her hand and set off at a run. His gait the longer, she had to move her legs twice as fast to keep up. A lone zookeeper, attired in wellies and a pair of brown overalls, overtook them in a covered golf cart, several

186

buckets of animal feed lashed into the cargo space with bungee cords.

'I'm halfway tempted to hitch a ride,' Edie muttered, puffing heavily as she spoke. Barely able to raise her arm, she pointed to a grotto-like area. 'There's the path – on the other side of the building.'

'Right.' He veered in the direction indicated, 'the path' being a set of boarded steps that snaked down the side of a very steep hillside. At the bottom of the wooden steps Cædmon could see a deserted car park.

'Rock Creek is on the other side of the parking lot,' Edie informed him between two noisy gasps. 'Once we cross the creek, we should be able to hike our way up to Beach Drive, where we can hopefully hail a cab.'

Cædmon directed his gaze beyond the car park. Through a dense grove of leafless trees, he could see a creek winding through tumbled rock. And he could hear a busy motorway on the far side of the ravine, cars moving along at a fast clip. Somehow he had his doubts about hailing a cab.

Keeping his reservations to himself, he led the way down the wooden steps. They made good time, the steps laid in a pattern that allowed for an easy descent of the steep hill. As they neared the bottom, Edie muttered an apology, her heavy-heeled boots repeatedly making rhythmic *thumps* on the weathered wood.

'It might help if you –' He stopped in mid-suggestion, suddenly picking up the vibration of an unseen footfall.

He peered over his shoulder, catching a flash of motion at the top of the steps. His visibility impaired by the thick shrubs and trees on either side of the steps, he had no way of knowing if the third party was a zookeeper, a bystander or a cold-blooded killer.

'We have company,' he whispered in Edie's ear, motioning her to silence.

Frantically, she glanced behind her. He wasn't certain, but he thought she mouthed, 'Oh God.'

A few seconds later, reaching the bottom of the steps, they arrived at a paved road. They crossed it. On the left was the deserted car park, on the right an abandoned greenhouse, sheets of torn plastic eerily waving in the breeze. In front lay a wild hinterland that hadn't seen scythe nor blade in many a year.

'This way,' Edie hissed, lifting her skirt to knee height as she plunged into the wilderness.

Cædmon fell into step, reaching over her head to brush aside hanging limbs and foliage. While the brambles and briars caught on hands, face and clothing, the growth provided excellent cover. Cædmon was still unsure who had followed them down the steps, the intruder having yet to reveal himself.

Reaching the creek bank, they came to an abrupt halt.

'Bloody hell,' he muttered, surprised to see that the creek was far more than the trickle of water he'd imagined. A calf-high torrent of water raged past, creating frothy whitecaps as it hit ice-covered rocks.

'If we attempt to ford this so-called creek, we'll break our –'

Just then, a tree limb plunged into the water, severed from its parent by a high-velocity bullet.

As though pushed by the hand of God, the two of them barrelled into the frigid creek, lingering concerns about the wisdom of braving the treacherous waters shoved aside.

Within seconds Edie had lost her footing, her arms windmilling in the air as she attempted to regain her balance. Cædmon grabbed hold of her tartan skirt, preventing her from pitching forward. Yanking her upright, he released the fistful of fabric only to shove his hand into her waistband, that being the most expedient way to keep her from falling over into what was fast becoming numbingly cold water. Thus linked, they sloshed across the aptly named Rock Creek.

'Oh God!' Edie shrieked as a nearby rock shattered from the impact of another bullet, splashing them both in the face.

Retreat not an option, they emerged from the creek, skirt and jeans saturated with cold water. Their goal being the nearby motorway, they clawed their way up the embankment. After one tumble and an ungainly scramble to keep from sliding back into the creek, they reached the top. In front of them was a four-lane highway, cars whizzing by at forty miles per hour.

'There's a cab!' Edie exclaimed, pointing to a

bright yellow vehicle in the distance. 'Wave your arms so the cabbie can see us.'

Several feet from where they stood, a bullet embedded itself in the asphalt.

Galvanized into action, Edie ran along the hard shoulder, her arms wildly swinging to and fro. Almost instantly, car horns began to blare, one motorist rudely gesturing as he drove past. Cædmon had no choice but to give chase. Drenched to the knees, twigs and debris clinging to their garments, they looked like a pair of escaped asylum inmates.

In a reckless show of heroics, Edie stepped into the roadway, frantically hailing the fast-approaching cab.

The driver swerved into a skid, barely managing to brake his vehicle to a screeching halt several feet from where she stood.

Rushing over, she yanked open the back door.

Like a jack-in-the-box, a wide-eyed passenger popped his immaculately groomed head through the opening. With an upraised arm, he prevented her from getting into the vehicle.

'In case you didn't notice, this cab is already taken.'

Undeterred, Edie shoved her hand into her bag. A second later, she slapped a hundred-dollar bill into the passenger's hand. 'Now shut up and move over!'

The man obediently slid to the far side of the seat.

29

'Drop us off at the next corner,' Edie ordered the cab driver, handing him a ten. Having yet to utter a single word, the cabbie stopped in front of McPherson Square, a city park overrun with homeless men huddled around metal subway grates, their worldly possessions bundled in plastic shopping bags. Still pissed off she'd had to pay a hundred-dollar bribe to the obviously affluent consultant-type, who had got out at a K Street lobbying firm, she grudgingly waved to the driver to keep the change.

No sooner had Cædmon slammed the cab door shut than she turned to him. Confused, angered and more than anything else terrified, she said, 'I can't believe they actually killed Eliot Hopkins.'

'Like you, I didn't foresee today's turn of events.' Sliding an arm around her shoulders, he led her to one of the benches that ringed the park. Although they were both soaked to the knee, no one in the park took any notice of their bedraggled state, more than a few of the bench-warmers in far worse straits. It was no accident that she had picked McPherson Square, the downtown park an excellent place to fade into the city landscape.

'Just as they manipulated yesterday's murder scene

at the Hopkins Museum, no doubt Colonel MacFarlane had planned a similar device for today's bloodshed.'

Edie derisively snorted. 'I can see the headlines now – LOVE TRIANGLE TURNS DEADLY.'

'Or some such tripe.' Cædmon's red brows drew together. 'I think we're both in need of a fortifying cup of hot coffee,' he said, gesturing to a branch of the ubiquitous Starbucks on the nearby street corner.

'Do you mind if I sit here and wait for you? To be honest, I don't know if I'm capable of putting one waterlogged foot in front of the other.'

Cædmon surveyed the park. Not only were there homeless men on nearly every bench, there were homeless men bundled in sleeping bags, the only thing protecting them from the cold, pieces of corrugated cardboard.

'Go on. I'll be perfectly safe. They might look dangerous, but these guys are perfectly harmless,' she assured him.

'Ironic to see so many men living rough while others live in the lap of luxury.' He glanced at the nearby Hilton Hotel.

'Yeah, well, unless we can figure out a safe place to lie low, you and I may be reduced to the same plight come nightfall.'

'A topic we'll discuss when I return.'

Edie nodded, inclined to leave the decision-making to Cædmon. Without his quick thinking, she'd be lying in a puddle of her own blood, the second member of the imaginary love triangle. Whether she liked to admit it or not – and she didn't – she needed his protection.

With a backward wave of the hand, Cædmon departed on his coffee run.

'Don't forget the biscotti,' she yelled at his backside, the shout earning another wave.

Her legs about to give way, Edie sat down on the bench. Within moments it began to hail, pellets of crystallized ice assaulting her person, hitting her on the cheeks, nose and forehead. She hunched forward, tucking her chin into her chest. She listened to the uneven tattoo of ice striking the wood planks of the weathered bench. With nowhere to run, and fast running out of places to hide, she felt imprisoned in a winter canvas of grey, taupe and white. *How appropriate*, she dejectedly thought, her body starting to go into deep freeze, her limbs becoming immobile, her thoughts reduced to a sluggish meander.

Suddenly seeing red instead of winter neutrals, she shoved her hand into her bag, retrieving her BlackBerry. Hopefully, she had enough juice to make a local phone call.

She dialled 411.

The days of speaking to a real person a thing of the past, she slowly said, 'Rosemont Security Consultants,' when prompted by the automated operator. A few seconds later the same computerized voice recited a seven-digit phone number. Edie hit '1', requesting to be connected.

The call was answered on the first ring.

'Rosemont Security Consultants.'

Momentarily taken aback that the office receptionist was a man not a woman, 'I want to speak to Stanford MacFarlane,' she brusquely demanded, hoping the lackey on the other end picked up on her don't-mess-with-me attitude.

He didn't.

'I'm sorry, but the colonel is unavailable to take any calls at this time. If you would like to leave a –'

'Tell him that Edie Miller is on the line. Trust me. He'll take the call.'

The receptionist put her on hold, Edie treated to the annoying strains of elevator music.

Midway into Sinatra's 'My Way', the line re-engaged.

'Ah, Miss Miller. What an unexpected surprise.'

Edie shivered, Stanford MacFarlane eerily cordial.

'I trust that you're feeling –'

'Can the bullshit, MacFarlane. How do you think I feel after watching one of your goons gun down a scared old man?'

'None too well, I suspect. You do know that you're proving a most elusive target.' Edie wasn't certain, but she thought she detected a note of grudging respect in his voice.

Disgusted by the thought that she and Cædmon had become some kind of perverted pastime, she said, 'I know what you're up to, you sick bastard!

Eliot Hopkins told us all about your plan to find the Ark of the —'

From out of nowhere, an unseen hand yanked the BlackBerry away from her ear. Craning her neck, Edie was surprised to find Cædmon standing behind the park bench. In his right hand he held her BlackBerry, in his left, an egg-carton carrier of coffee. Without a word, Cædmon unceremoniously shoved the mobile into his jacket pocket. Then, acting as though nothing was even remotely wrong, he handed her a cup of coffee.

'If I recall correctly, you take two sugars.'

Edie's shock turned to outrage.

'Do you know why the British have never rebelled against the monarchy? Because you're afraid to take action! You're afraid to say, "I'm mad as hell and I'm not going to take it any longer!"'

'Unlike you, I believe that restraint is the better part of valour.'

'Oh, stuff an argyle sock in it, will ya? I'm beginning to think you love the sound of your own voice.'

Cædmon straightened his shoulders, drawing himself to his full imposing height of six foot three. 'Because of your impetuousness, we have lost our only advantage. Not only did you divulge the fact that we know their identities, but you foolishly disclosed the information given to us by the now deceased Mr Hopkins.'

'Look, I don't know about you, but I'm sick and tired of being hunted down like a defenceless animal.

And while you might not give a rat's patootie, I want to know why Colonel MacFarlane ordered Eliot Hopkins to kill us.'

'The answer to that is patently obvious. MacFarlane intended to create yet another subterfuge that would disguise his intentions.' As he spoke, Cædmon sat down beside her. 'The first part of the plan was to have Hopkins kill us. At which point, I suspect, the unwitting museum director would have been forced to put the gun to his own head and pull the trigger.'

Raising a hand to her head, Edie rubbed her temples, grateful she still had a temple to rub.

'This is insane. All of it. Eliot Hopkins pulled a gun on us. And when he didn't shoot us straightaway, they killed him. That makes two men killed before my very eyes in as many days. And they would have killed us if we hadn't slogged across that creek.' Raising her arms, she gestured to the park. 'So, now what? I ask because this doesn't seem like much of a plan.'

'I agree that we need to take a more proactive approach.'

'Proactive? As in going on the offensive?'

'If you like.'

A noticeable pause ensued, Cædmon refusing to elaborate.

'Just how are we going to pull that off?' Edie prodded.

'We know that Colonel MacFarlane is going after

the Ark of the Covenant. And, assuming that Eliot Hopkins spoke the truth, I know where MacFarlane and his gang of cut-throats will be searching.'

Again, Cædmon failed to elaborate, forcing Edie to push him a bit harder. 'So where are they going to put shovel to dirt?'

One side of Cædmon's mouth lifted in a bemused half-smile.

'Of all places, England.'

30

'We're talking about a big island. Where exactly in England might the Ark of the Covenant be hidden?'

'The "where exactly" is a bit thorny,' Cædmon replied in response to Edie's question. 'If you recall, Eliot Hopkins spoke of an English crusader who supposedly discovered a gold chest on the Plain of Esdraelon. He was referring to one Galen of Godmersham, a younger son who, like so many younger sons, went to the Holy Land to seek the fortune denied him by the circumstance of his birth.'

'And did he find his fortune?'

'Indeed, he did, returning to England in 1286 an extremely wealthy man. For centuries whispers and rumours rattled about, some claiming that Galen had uncovered the Spear of Longinus, others claiming he had found Veronica's Veil.' Leaning close enough to brush shoulders, he said in a lowered tone, 'And then there are those who believe that not only did Galen of Godmersham discover the Ark of the Covenant, but that he transported the Ark to his home in Kent, whereupon he promptly buried the holy relic. Admittedly, there's scant evidence for the theory, although that hasn't stopped a legion of treasure hunters from pockmarking the environs of Godmersham.'

'Come on, Cædmon. Even you have to admit the idea of some English knight just happening upon the Ark of the Covenant is hard to swallow.'

'With your own eyes, you saw the sacred Stones of Fire. If the breastplate exists, why not the Ark?'

'Maybe I don't want the Ark to exist,' she answered with her trademark candour. 'If what you say is even partially true, the implications are immense. History-altering, in fact.'

'Do you think that hasn't crossed my mind?'

'Has this thought crossed your mind? Right now, you've got nothing more solid than a rumour about some old knight. Lesson of the day? One crazy rumour does not a fact make.'

'It's thin, I admit, but many an extraordinary discovery has been made by men labelled hare-brained. Most thought Schliemann mad when he went searching for Troy with only a battered copy of Homer as his guide.'

Edie snickered, her breath condensing in the chill air. 'Yeah, well, you know what they say about mad dogs and Englishmen.'

'In defence of my countrymen, I should point out that Heinrich Schliemann was German,' Cædmon retorted, the argument having degenerated into petty tit-for-tat. 'Since the Bible makes no mention of the Ark being destroyed, we must assume that it still exists. While biblical scholars have long denied the rumours regarding Galen of Godmersham, there is a scholar at Oxford, a man by the name of Sir Kenneth

Campbell-Brown, who has devoted his life to studying the thirteenth-century English crusaders. If there is any credence to the notion of an English knight discovering a gold chest on the Plain of Esdraelon, Sir Kenneth would certainly know of it. And given all that has transpired in the last twenty-four hours, we must accept Eliot Hopkins' premise as a viable possibility.'

Folding her arms over her chest, Edie stubbornly shook her head. 'What we need to do is contact the IARC. The FBI. Somebody. Anybody. And let them know what's happening.'

'And what precisely would you tell the authorities?' he countered. 'That a murder occurred at the Hopkins Museum for which there is no body? Or perhaps we could regale the local constabulary with the tale of the fabled Stones of Fire? Given that the relic disappeared several millennia ago, I somehow doubt the police will believe that the relic was stolen from the aforementioned non-existent corpse. In fact, if not for the dead man at the zoo, whose murder they will most assuredly accuse you of having committed, the police would label you a lunatic.'

'I could take a lie-detector test.'

'And if your heart rate accelerated but a notch, your fate would be sealed.'

Edie unfolded her arms, the wind dying in her sails. 'You could go to the –'

'If I come forward with my suspicions regarding the Stones of Fire or the Ark of the Covenant, my motives would immediately be suspect, the chaps at the FBI no doubt believing it a publicity stunt to increase my book sales.'

'So, what are you saying – that our hands are tied?'

'Most certainly not. We know that Colonel MacFarlane and his men are searching for the Ark of the Covenant. Furthermore, we have reason to believe that they'll be searching for it in England.'

'Oh, you have got to be kidding!' Edie exclaimed, realization dawning. 'You're not really suggesting that we go to England and track down Stanford MacFarlane and his goons.'

'Rest assured, I do not expect you to come.'

'Ouch! That hurts,' she retorted, taking offence where none was intended. 'Going to England in pursuit of the Ark of the Covenant is big. Huge. You've given this – what? – about thirty seconds of thought before making a decision.'

'If you're accusing me of being rash, nothing could be further from the truth.'

'Then how's this for rash? Have you thought about how you're going to pay for this little junket? As soon as you whip out a credit card, MacFarlane will be on to you like ugly on an alligator.'

'I agree that electronic transactions can easily be traced.' He cleared his throat. Knowing there was but one way to clear the hurdle, he charged forward. 'Which is why I thought to ask you for a loan.' When Edie looked at him askance, he added, 'I'm good for it, as you Yanks are wont to say.'

'Well, here's another phrase we Yanks are wont to say – "My way or the highway." Meaning you take me with you or you don't see a dime of my money.'

No sooner was the ultimatum delivered than an invisible Maginot Line loomed between them. Ignoring him, Edie reached into the now wet Starbucks bag and removed a hazelnut biscotti. Behaving as though he didn't exist, she loudly bit into it.

'Why the sudden interest in pursuing my "crazy" theory?' he asked, if for no other reason than to break the unnerving silence.

'I have my reasons. Look, I'm good with details. And let's not forget the old adage about two heads being better than just the one.'

'Honestly, Edie, I don't think that –'

'I can be your research assistant,' she interjected, unwavering in her persistence.

'I don't need a research assistant. Once I arrive in England, I have connections that –'

'Yeah, speaking of "connections", you told Eliot Hopkins that you could contact Interpol, making me wonder just what kind of shadowy connections you have.'

Not seeing the sense in keeping it from her, he said, 'I used to be an intelligence officer with MI5 – the Security Service.'

Her eyes opened wide. 'You mean like James Bond?'

'Hardly. During my tenure at MI5 I spent most of my time in an office and very little time chasing nefarious characters. Certainly none with an outland-ish moniker.'

'Well, that explains your street smarts,' she re-marked, seeming to take his confession in her stride. 'Yesterday I was truly stumped as to how a book-worm could so easily keep his cool when the bullets started to fly. In fact, there were a couple of times at the National Gallery when you looked like you were in seventh heaven.'

'Trust me, that wasn't the case,' he countered, not about to let her think otherwise.

'Whether you enjoy that kind of action or not, I still want to go with you.'

Something in Edie Miller's brown eyes – a defiant expression – seized hold of him and refused to let go. He was well aware that even if they paid for their air tickets with cash, it wouldn't prevent MacFarlane from discovering their destination. If MacFarlane could get hold of airline passenger manifests, he would soon discover they'd flown into Heathrow. Whereupon they would find themselves, once again, in dangerous straits.

He raised his face heavenwards. 'It's raining feathers,' he remarked conversationally, the hail hav-ing softened into light snow. 'Admittedly, it's not an original thought. Herodotus coined the phrase some twenty-four hundred years ago.'

'I've got one for you: "It's raining men." The Weathergirls at the height of the disco era.'

Cædmon sighed, thinking them an odd pair.

'It would appear that our destinies are linked,' he said, capitulating. For several long seconds he stared at her. He glimpsed a wariness in her eyes. The wariness at odds with her usual defiance, he intuited that Edie Miller's tough facade was akin to gold leaf. Solid to the glance, but gossamer thin.

'You know, Cædmon, I'm a little uncertain about the agenda. Are you planning to stop MacFarlane from finding the Ark or are you hoping to beat him to the punch?'

He ignored the second part of her question: 'For now, we must concentrate our efforts on stopping MacFarlane finding the Ark.'

'I agree. If the Ark is, as you claim, a weapon of mass destruction, it doesn't bode well that an ex-military man is after it.'

He acknowledged Edie's spot-on observation with a brusque nod. 'Just as worrisome, I suspect that MacFarlane is well funded, his cash translating into a highly developed communications and logistics network.'

'So, in other words, it's going to be a whole lot like David going up against Goliath.'

Cædmon kept silent, not about to point out that David at least had had a catapult.

31

'I will take revenge on my hateful enemies. I will sharpen my sword and let it flash like lightning.'

Being a military man, Stan MacFarlane knew that another battle loomed on the horizon. Yet another chance to vanquish the enemy.

A lesson well learned in Panama, Bosnia, Operation Desert Storm.

And, of course, Beirut.

Some said that's where he found religion. He preferred to think that's where his relationship with the Almighty began.

He still had vivid nightmares of that deadly October day when two hundred and forty-one marines were taken out by a suicide bomber driving a water truck packed with explosives ... the sickening stench of sulphur and burnt flesh ... the cacophony of pain and outrage ... the frenzied rush to rescue the injured ... the grievous task of finding the dead.

Amazingly, he'd survived the blast, his bunk mate not so lucky.

In retrospect, able to see with a survivor's clarity, he knew the attack had been the first sign that the End Times were near.

His wife, the treacherous Helen, left him within a year of his conversion, claiming spousal abuse. In the nine years of their marriage he'd never laid a violent hand on the woman – although he'd been tempted to wring her scraggy neck with his bare hands during the divorce proceedings.

The judge, a pussy-whipped liberal, had given Helen custody of their son Custis, Stan only able to see his son at the weekends. Afraid Custis would turn into a mummy's boy, he'd made sure his son joined the Reserve Officers' Training Corps while still in high school. Pulling a few strings, he'd been able to secure Custis a berth at Annapolis. Helen claimed that he'd bullied Custis into joining the marines, but he knew he'd done right by his son, the Corps making a man of him.

Who or what had turned him into a weak-kneed coward was to this day a deep, dark mystery. The official account claimed that after one deployment to Afghanistan and two to Iraq, Custis had been suffering from PTSD. Stan knew it wasn't post-traumatic stress disorder that had caused his son to put the barrel of a loaded M16 rifle into his mouth. Stan knew it was the barbarous infidels of Babylon who had caused his only son to heed Satan's siren call. Men of God had a duty to battle the godless among them. Custis had shirked his duty.

And would burn in the pits of hell because of it.

Soon after his son's death, he had founded the Warriors of God, convinced it was his duty to lead the army of the righteous, that duty akin to King David leading the Israelite army to victory over the Jebusites and Philistines, or Godfroi of Bouillon heading the crusaders as they battled Muslim infidels in the streets of Jerusalem. And, of course, there was his personal hero, Thomas 'Stonewall' Jackson, a deeply religious military man who had refused to fight on Sunday and had led his men in prayer before each battle.

Today, despite his fervent prayers, the battle had yet to be won.

Part of his contingency plan had been to send in a sniper in case the old man lost his nerve. No need to worry about the scion of one of America's great industrial families being gunned down in the middle of the National Zoo; the police would jump to the conclusion that a copycat killer was replicating the sniping spree that had paralyzed the nation's capital during the autumn of 2002.

No doubt the funeral eulogies would wax poetic about Eliot Hopkins' generosity and philanthropy, making no mention of the many stolen items featured in his collection. The tributes would also not cite Hopkins' secret passion, the Ark of the Covenant. Because of Stan's thorough planning, the biblical scholars and archaeology watchdogs would continue to snore, unaware of any goings-on.

When all the pieces were in place, only then would the world know of Stan's divinely inspired mission. At the moment the world was following his timetable.

It was early, too early to reveal God's great plan. Although if the unbelievers had but eyes to see they too would know that global events manifested an urgent call to arms from the Almighty.

Anxious about the upcoming mission, the colonel hit the intercom button on his phone console. 'Any word on the flight plan?'

'I've just received the official approval, sir. You're wings up at thirteen hundred hours.'

'Excellent,' Stan said to his chief of staff before disconnecting.

Despite the fact that English food rivalled mess-tent slop, he looked forward to greeting the new day in London. The Miller woman had set the schedule back a full twenty-four hours, and while frustrated by the snafu, he felt curiously uplifted, ready, willing and able for the task he was about to undertake. Besides, in the larger scheme of things, Edie Miller and her consort were insignificant, minor players in a drama penned by the Almighty twenty-six centuries ago.

He glanced at his watch. He had enough time to post his daily blog.

Seating himself at the desk, he used his two index fingers to type his opening Bible passage, a favourite from Psalm 11.

'He will send fiery coals and flaming sulfur down on the wicked . . .'

32

'At this juncture I should probably mention that I'm not an adventurous person. I like stability. I'm predictable. I watch the same TV programme every Monday night. The only things in my life that change on a regular basis are the light bulbs.'

Cædmon glanced away from the Oxfordshire scenery passing in a blur on the other side of the oversized coach window. Having touched down at Heathrow two hours ago, they were en route to Oxford.

'How curious. You strike me as a most intrepid woman.'

'Appearances can be deceiving.'

'Indeed?' He pointedly glanced at her attire.

Their clothes having taken a shabby turn for the worse in yesterday's cross-country race, they'd each purchased a new set at the airport. He'd selected tweeds, wool and a beige anorak. Opting for more colourful plumage, Edie had chosen a yellow knitted hat, a red military-style jacket, complete with epaulettes, and knee-high riding boots into which she'd tucked jeans. While he resembled one half of a stodgy English couple in town for the day, she looked like a Mondrian painting come to life. He would have preferred her in earth tones, colours that faded into the winter scenery. Should an RIRA operative happen to catch sight of him, he would suddenly have two enemies to contend with rather than one.

'Do you think MacFarlane and his goons will actually find the Ark of the Covenant?'

'It's an outside wager at best,' he replied. 'Over the centuries many have searched – all in vain. Although if found, the Ark of the Covenant would be the most astounding discovery in the history of mankind.'

Edie closed the Bible they'd purchased in the gift shop at Dulles airport. 'It's been a while since I last read the Old Testament, being what you might call a New Testament kind of gal.' She stuffed the King James edition into the Virgin Airlines shoulder bag that they were now using for their meagre belongings. 'Somehow I'd conveniently forgotten about all the death and mayhem associated with the Ark. Just now I was reading about the battle of Ebenezer.'

'If my memory serves me correctly, Ebenezer was where the Philistines not only defeated the Israelites but also managed to steal the Ark of the Covenant.'

'And wasn't that a big mistake? Within hours of installing the Ark inside the Temple of Dagon, the Philistines discovered the statue of their deity smashed to smithereens. But of course that was nothing compared to the plague of boils that suddenly afflicted the entire city of Ashdod. In the ensuing panic the Philistine king wisely decided to return his ill-gotten booty to the Israelites.'

'At which point the Philistines loaded the Ark of the Covenant onto a cart and took it to the Hebrew town of Bethshemesh.'

'Where, as you mentioned yesterday, fifty thousand residents were slaughtered because of a curious few who dared to peek inside the Ark.' Edie's brow furrowed. 'You know, I'm trying hard, but I just can't get a handle on an all-loving, all-forgiving God doing that kind of thing.'

'I, for one, don't believe that God had anything to do with the Ark's devastating powers.' Cædmon leaned back in his coach seat, crossing his legs. 'Rather I believe that the Ark's power was entirely man made. To comprehend its supposedly supernatural power, one must understand how the Ark was constructed.'

'You said that an Egyptian bark was more than likely the prototype used by Moses.'

He nodded. 'I'm certain of it. First, consider the materials used. Both bark and Ark were manufactured from gold. An enormous quantity of gold.'

'Well, gold is one of the most valuable metals known to man.'

'More importantly, gold is an extremely dense metal and chemically non-reactive. Although it can't be proved, there are some biblical scholars who believe that the gold used on the Ark was nine inches thick.'

'You're kidding! That would make for a *huge* hunk of gold.'

'Indeed.' Rifling through the bag, he removed pen and paper. Calling to mind the descriptions given in the Old Testament, he managed to produce a fairly detailed sketch of the Ark of the Covenant.

'As you can see, the gold box was covered with a lid. This was known as the Mercy Seat.'

Edie chuckled. 'Not the hot seat?'

Cædmon smiled at his companion's remark. 'The Mercy Seat was adorned with a matched pair of gold cherubim. These weren't the adorable putti that clutter the paintings of Peter Paul Rubens. The cherubim who stood sentry atop the Ark were fierce, otherworldly creatures, not unlike the winged figures of Isis and Nephthys that adorned many an Egyptian bark.'

'Underneath all that gold, the Ark was made of wood, wasn't it?'

'Acacia wood, to be precise, a tree native to the Sinai Desert. In ancient times this wood was thought to be incorruptible. Additionally, it would have acted as an insulator.'

Her brown eyes opened wide, a realization having

just dawned. 'And gold is an excellent conductor. Since the acacia box was lined, inside and out, with gold –' using her hands, she made a sandwich, leaving several inches of air in between her two palms '– the Ark would have been an incredibly powerful condenser. And given all the dry desert air in the Sinai, I bet the darned thing would have packed a very potent electrical punch.'

Despite her quirkiness, Edie Miller possessed a nimble mind.

'Touching the Ark with bare hands would have resulted in instant death,' he said, confirming her theory. 'Moreover, the Old Testament is rife with tales of the Ark producing skin lesions on people who came into close proximity. Interestingly enough, recent research has verified that skin cancer is an occupational hazard of working near high-tension power lines.'

'So how did the Israelites protect themselves?'

'The high priest wore special ritual clothing when handling the Ark, the Stones of Fire part of his protective outfit. Because the Ark built up an electric charge due to all the shaking while in transport, it was carefully wrapped in leather and cloth.'

'Which acted as a protective barrier so that the guys stuck with carrying it wouldn't be tossed on their keisters,' she astutely, if not irreverently, remarked.

'Not that calamities didn't occur. Despite the precautions taken, there are accounts of Ark bearers being tossed bodily through the air and a few being killed outright.' Cædmon pointed to the drawing. 'Now imagine that the wings on the two cherubim were hinged with leather and bitumen, enabling them to flap back and forth. The accumulated electric charge would not only have created visible sparks, it would have emitted strong electromagnetic pulses similar to Hertzian radio waves. Once charged, the Ark would have picked up strikes of lightning. That in turn would have created audible static.'

'Like the crackling sound you get in between AM radio stations, right?'

'Precisely. And to the ears of the ancient Israelites that crackling would have sounded like the voice of God. A careful reading of the Old Testament proves that the Ark of the Covenant is most definitely *not* a *deux ex machina*. Rather it was envisioned and executed by Moses.'

Edie stared at his sketch as though seeing the Ark of the Covenant in a new, and slightly disturbing, light. 'Yeah, well, there's a whole legion of true believers who would disagree with you on that one.'

Knowing she spoke the truth, Cædmon wearily nodded, having more than a passing acquaintance with fanatics. A few feet away from where they sat, the coach's windscreen wipers swung hypnotically to and fro. Blinking, he fought off a wave of tiredness, having only had a quick nap on the flight.

In the distance he could see the honey-coloured villages and rolling sheep pastures of Oxfordshire.

From those pastures, limestone had been quarried and carted to Oxford, where it had been used to construct some of the most stunning architecture in England. As the countryside passed in a wet blur, so too did his memories. He'd journeyed to Oxford by coach as a gangly lad of eighteen, his father too busy to accompany him. As the coach neared the city limits, he'd been in a tumult, his emotions ranging from anxiety and excitement to shame on account of his father's indifference. Then, quite suddenly, those emotions had been superseded by a burst of exhilaration, his younger self staggered to be arriving in the most famous university city in the world – 'that sweet city with her dreaming spires'.

'You mentioned that you went to Oxford,' Edie remarked, making him wonder if she might not be a mind reader. 'This will be like a homecoming for you, huh?'

'Hardly,' he murmured, disinclined to reveal his tainted academic past. Particularly since she would find out soon enough.

As with most postgraduate students, he had spent two years doing field research. After which he had confined himself to his Oxford digs and commenced writing his dissertation. 'The Manifesto', as he'd jokingly taken to calling it, had been an exhaustive examination of the influence of Egyptian mysticism upon the Knights Templar. But to his horror the head of the history department at Queen's College had denounced his dissertation, claiming it was a 'hare-brained' notion that could only have been opium-induced. Not unlike the poetry of William Blake.

Such criticism amounted to the kiss of death. Finished as an academic, he left Oxford with his tail between his legs.

What an irony that he was once again en route to the fabled city of his youth. The gods must be chortling, gleefully rubbing their hands in anticipation.

He wondered what Edie would say if he were to inform her that Moses and the Templars had been initiated into the same Egyptian mystery cult. He bit back an amused smile, certain his assertions would be met with a raised eyebrow and a witty response. Truth be told, he enjoyed their verbal jousts. While she could punch hard, hers was an open mind.

He hoped that Sir Kenneth Campbell-Brown would be equally open-minded. If not, they would have journeyed to Oxford in vain.

As Edie peered through the coach window, he in turn peered at her. The straight brows gave his companion a decidedly serious mien wholly at odds with her exuberant personality. Then there was the softness of her lips and the pale Victorian smoothness of her skin. When he first met Edie Miller, he'd thought her an unusual mix of Pre-Raphaelite beauty and quirky modernity.

Unthinkingly he raised a hand, cupping her chin between his fingers. Slowly he turned her face in his direction. Startled, her eyes and mouth opened wide. *Perfect*, he thought as he leaned into her, about to ascertain if those lips were as soft as they appeared.

Amazingly, they were.

Not having asked permission, he barely grazed his lips across her mouth, concerned she might baulk at his presumption. For several seconds he played the gentleman, softly applying pressure, deepening the kiss in small increments. Until she murmured something against his lips. What, he had no idea; he only knew the incoherent utterance sounded incredibly sexy. The male biological response not unlike a trigger mechanism, he shoved his tongue into her mouth. Then he clamped his hand to the back of her neck, effectively imprisoning her. Open-mouthed, he kissed her wetly and deeply, doing all that he could to wed his lips to hers.

For several long moments he went at her like a mad man, his hand moving from her neck to her back, pulling her that much closer to him, not stopping until her breasts were crushed against his chest.

Not stopping until he heard a gasp from across the aisle.

Abruptly, and somewhat awkwardly, he ended the kiss. Hoping she didn't notice the visible lump between his hips, he cleared his throat.

'That was unplanned and . . . Forgive me if I acted inappropriately.' His cheeks warmed at the butchered apology.

Wet lips curved into a fetching smile. 'The only

thing you did wrong was to end that kiss *way* too soon.' Edie glanced out the window. 'Looks like we just pulled into Oxford.'

33

Hoping she didn't appear too awestruck, Edie discreetly checked out the buildings that fronted High Street.

Everywhere she looked there were hints, some subtle, some in your face, of Oxford's medieval past. Battlements. Gate towers. Oriel windows. And stone. Lots and lots of stone. Varying in shade from pale silver to deep gold. All of it combining in a wondrous sort of sensory overload.

'Where's the university?' she enquired, scrunching her shoulders to avoid hitting a group of midday shoppers who had just emerged from a clothes shop. She and Cædmon were en route to some pub called the Isis Room, where Cædmon seemed to think they would find Sir Kenneth Campbell-Brown.

Cædmon slowed his step as he gestured to either side of the busy thoroughfare. 'Oxford University is everywhere and nowhere. Since leaving the bus station, we've already passed Jesus, Exeter and Lincoln colleges.'

'*We did?*' Edie swivelled her head, wondering how she could have missed three college campuses. She knew that Oxford University was made up of several dozen colleges spread throughout the town.

Having attended a downtown college herself, she assumed there would be signs identifying the various buildings. Clearly, she'd been working under a false assumption.

'Look for the gateways,' Cædmon said, pointing to an imposing iron portal wedged in a stone wall. 'They often lead to a quadrangle, most of the colleges built to the standard medieval pattern of chapel and hall flanked by residential ranges.'

Edie peered through the iron bars. Beyond the gatehouse, she glimpsed an arched portico on either side of a quadrangle.

'That's a formidable entrance. Guess it's meant to keep the little people out, huh?'

'Having spent an inordinate amount of time on the other side of those "formidable" gateways, I always thought they were intended to keep the students from leaving – the college's way of cultivating a slavish devotion to one's alma mater.' Edie wasn't certain, but she thought she detected a hint of sarcasm in his voice.

'Sounds like an academic Never-Never Land.'

'Indeed, it was.'

'So, where are the Lost Boys?'

His copper-coloured brows briefly furrowed. 'Ah, the students. Michaelmas Term ended last week, so the vast majority of students have gone home for the holidays.'

'Well that would certainly explain all the riderless bicycles,' she said, nodding towards a mass of bikes parked in front of a stucco wall. Above the tidy lines of chained bicycles, old posters flapped in the breeze, hawking an array of student activities. Debating societies. Drama societies. Choral societies.

Cædmon's gaze momentarily softened. 'By their bicycles you shall know them,' he murmured, his sarcasm replaced with something more akin to nostalgia.

Surprised by his sudden shift in mood, Edie surreptitiously checked out her companion, her gaze moving from the top of his thick thatch of red hair to the tips of his black leather brogues. She was beginning to realize that Cædmon Aisquith was a complicated man. Or maybe she was just dense when it came to men. He'd certainly taken her by surprise with the killer kiss. For some idiotic reason, she'd assumed that because he was such a brainiac he lived a monkish existence. *Wasn't that a stupid assumption?* Given the passionate smooch on the bus, he'd make a lousy monk. *Wonder what kind of lover he'd make?*

Giving the question several moments' thought, she decided it was impossible to tell, the cultured accent acting like a smokescreen. Although the unexpected kiss most definitely hinted at a deeper passion.

Oblivious to the fact that he was being ogled, Cædmon turned his head as they passed an ATM.

'Though sorely tempted to use the cashpoint, it would undoubtedly lead Stanford MacFarlane right to us.'

'Don't worry. As keeper of the vault, I can assure

you that there are enough funds to keep us afloat. At least for a little while.' The airline tickets and new clothes had set them back a bit, but at the last count she had nearly three thousand dollars.

'Being a kept man doesn't sit well with me. Bruised ego and all that.'

She affected a stunned expression. 'You're kidding, right? We've spent three days together and only *now* am I learning that you object to being my sex slave?' Playing the part for all it was worth, she theatrically sighed. 'Here I thought you were having the time of your life.'

To her surprise, Cædmon blushed, his cheeks as red as holly berries. Raising a balled hand to his mouth, he cleared his throat.

'*Hel-lo*. I'm teasing. You're hardly a kept man,' she assured him, amused by his embarrassment.

'Then how about spotting me two quid for a pint?' Taking her by the elbow, Cædmon ushered her to a panelled wooden door. Above the door a brightly painted sign emblazoned with the pub's name swung from a metal bracket.

'Be my pleasure, luv,' she replied in an attempt at a cockney accent.

Not expecting the interior to be so dim, it took several seconds of squinting before her pupils adjusted, the room bathed in soft amber light. All in all, the joint was pretty much as she had envisioned an English pub – wood-panelled walls, wood-beamed ceiling and wooden tables and chairs scattered about.

Framed lithographs of sea battles hung on the cream-coloured walls, a limp bouquet of mistletoe tacked above the Battle of Trafalgar.

Her eyes zeroed in on the easel where a black-board listed the day's menu: HOME-MADE LENTIL SOUP, TWO-CHEESE QUICHE, SEAFOOD SALAD. She placed a hand over her abdomen, having long since digested the rubbery chicken cordon bleu she'd been served on the transatlantic flight.

'Any idea what this Sir Kenneth character looks like?' she asked over a very unladylike stomach growl.

'Ruddy cheeks, aquiline nose and a pewter-coloured mop of curly hair. Looks like a sheep before the spring shearing. You can't miss him.'

Edie scanned the crowded pub. 'How about we divide and conquer? You take that side of the room and I'll take the other.'

'Right.'

A few seconds later, seeing a man of middling height with curly grey hair standing at the bar, Edie headed in that direction. Raising her hand to catch Cædmon's attention, she pointed to her suspect. For several seconds Cædmon stared at the man's back, drilling the proverbial hole right through the older man's head. She wasn't certain but she thought Cædmon straightened his shoulders before heading towards the bar.

Reaching the target a few seconds ahead of Cædmon, she lightly tapped the grey-haired man on the shoulder.

'Excuse me. You wouldn't happen to be Sir Kenneth Campbell-Brown?'

The grey-haired man slowly turned towards her. Although decked out in a brown leather bomber jacket, a red cashmere scarf jauntily wrapped around his neck, he resembled nothing so much as a woolly ram, Cædmon's description right on the mark.

'Well, I'm not the bloody Prince of Wales.'

'Ah! Still the amiable Oxford don much beloved by students and fellows alike,' Cædmon said, having overheard the exchange.

Slightly bug-eyed by nature, Sir Kenneth became even more so as he turned in the direction of Cædmon's voice. 'Good God! I thought you crawled into a hole and died! What the bloody hell are you doing in Oxford? I didn't think the Boar's Head Gaudy was your cup of tea.'

'You're quite right. In the thirteen years since I left, I've yet to attend the Christmas dinner.'

The older man snickered. 'I suspect that's because your soft-hearted sympathies go out to the apple-stuffed swine. So, tell me, young Aisquith, if the pig is not your purpose, what bringeth you to "the high shore of this world"?'

'As fate would have it, you're the reason I'm in Oxford.' Outwardly calm – maybe too calm given the older man's condescension – Cædmon redirected his gaze in Edie's direction. 'Excuse me. I've been remiss. Edie Miller, may I present Professor Sir Kenneth Campbell-Brown, senior fellow at Queen's College.'

Sir Kenneth acknowledged the introduction with a slight nod of his woolly head. 'I am also the head of the history department, secretary of the tutorial committee, defender of the realm and protector of women and small children,' he informed her, speaking in beautifully precise pear-shaped tones. 'I am in addition the man responsible for booting your swain out of Oxford.'

34

'Mind you, that was years ago,' Sir Kenneth added, still addressing his remarks to Edie. Then, turning to Cædmon, 'Water under the Magdalen Bridge, eh?'

Refusing to be drawn into that particular conversation – one could drown in a shallow puddle if led there by this don – Cædmon jutted his chin towards the far side of the pub. 'Shall we adjourn to the vacant booth in the corner?'

'An excellent suggestion.' Smiling, Sir Kenneth placed a hand on Edie's elbow. 'And what is your pleasure, my dear?'

'Oh, I'll just have a glass of water. It's a little early for kicking back the brewskies.'

'Righto. An Adam's ale for the lady and a King-fisher for the gent. I won't be but a second.' Turning round, Sir Kenneth placed the order with a barmaid.

As he steered Edie towards the booth, Cædmon wondered how, after so many years, his estranged mentor still remembered his preferred lager. *The old bastard always did have a mind like a steel trap.*

Which meant he'd have to be on his guard to keep from ending up in the poacher's sack.

As they sidestepped a jovial group arguing the merits of the new PM, Edie elbowed him in the ribs.

'You didn't tell me that you knew Sir Kenneth.'

'Forgive the omission,' he replied, failing to mention that the oversight had been quite intentional.

'You also didn't tell me that you were "booted" out of Oxford. Gees, what else are you hiding from me? You're not wanted by the police or anything like that, are you?'

'The police? No.' *The RIRA, yes.* Knowing he'd only frighten her if he disclosed that titbit, Cædmon kept mum.

'So, what happened? Were you "sent down", as the highbrows on Masterpiece Theater are wont to say?'

'No. I left of my own accord after it was made painfully clear to me by Sir Kenneth that my doctorate would not be conferred.'

She glanced at the curly-haired don. 'I'm guessing there's bad blood between the two of you, huh?'

'Of a sort. Although in England we conduct our feuds in a chillingly polite manner,' he replied, relieved when she didn't pry further. He'd been a cocky bastard in his student days, supremely confident of his intellectual prowess. He'd had his comeuppance. And preferred not to talk about it.

He assisted Edie in removing her red coat, hanging it on a brass hook on the side of the booth. That done, he removed his anorak and hung it on another hook. He then motioned her to the circular table in the high-backed booth.

'Do you mind grabbing that bag of crackers on the next table?' Edie asked as she seated herself, not in the booth but in the Windsor chair opposite.

Cædmon complied, commandeering an unopened bag of crisps left by a previous patron. Handing the crisps to Edie, he seated himself in a vacant chair just as Sir Kenneth, juggling a small tray, approached the table.

'Nothing like malt, hops and yeast to usher in a spirit of fraternal concord, eh?' A man of mercurial moods, Sir Kenneth had forsaken his earlier condescension for a show of bluff good humour. Drinks passed out, he seated himself in the booth. Surrounded on three sides by dark wood, he looked like a Saxon king holding court.

Edie lifted her water glass. 'I assume that I'm included in all that brotherly love.'

'Most certainly, my dear.' As Edie bent her head, Sir Kenneth slyly winked at him, Cædmon wanting very badly to bash him on the nose.

Although he hailed from the upper echelons of British society, Sir Kenneth wasn't averse to mucking in with the common man. Or woman, Sir Kenneth being particularly fond of the fairer sex. The man had a voracious sexual appetite, an appetite that had evidently not diminished with age. According to rumour, the provost had once remarked that Oxford might do well to return to the days of celibate fellows, if for no other reason than to keep marauding dons like Sir Kenneth under control.

'So, tell me, young Aisquith, to what do I owe the pleasure of this most unexpected visit?'

'We'd like to ask you about a thirteenth-century knight named Galen of Godmersham.'

'How curious. I had an appointment yesterday with a chap from Harvard, a professor of medieval literature interested in Galen of Godmersham's poetic endeavours.'

Curious indeed. Cædmon immediately wondered if the 'chap from Harvard' was working for Colonel Stanford MacFarlane. Or was it mere coincidence that an American scholar had been inquiring about an obscure English knight? Since Sir Kenneth Campbell-Brown was the foremost authority on English crusaders, it could be pure chance. Although Cædmon had his doubts.

'What's this about poetry?' Edie piped up. 'Are we talking about the same knight?'

His tutorial style having always been to answer a question with a question, Sir Kenneth did just that. 'How familiar are you with Galen of Godmersham?'

Plucking several crisps out of the bag, Edie replied, 'I know him by name only. Oh, and the fact that he discovered a gold chest while crusading in the Holy Land.'

'Ah ... the fabled gold chest.' His eyes narrowing, Sir Kenneth directed his gaze at Cædmon. 'I should have known this was about that nonsense.'

'I assume the American professor expressed a similar interest in Galen's treasure trove,' Cædmon countered, ignoring the jibe.

'If you must know, he never mentioned Galen's

gold chest. The chap's field of expertise was thirteenth- and fourteenth-century English poetry. Recited reams of archaic verse. I almost nodded off.'

'Time out,' Edie exclaimed, holding her hands in a T shape. 'I'm totally confused. We're talking about a gold chest and you're talking about poetry. Is it just me or did we lose the connection?'

Sir Kenneth smiled, the question smoothing the old cock's ruffled feathers. 'Because you are such a lovely girl, with your raven elf locks and skin so fair, I shall tell you all that I know of Galen of Godmersham. After which you will tell me why you are chasing after dead knights.'

'Okay, fair enough,' Edie replied, returning the smile.

Not wanting Sir Kenneth to know the full story, Cædmon decided to intervene when the time came to tell him the reasons for their interest. If mishandled, such knowledge could get one killed.

'As your swain may or may not have told you, during the medieval period the entire Middle East, including the Holy Land, was under Muslim control. Given that this was the land of the biblical patriarchs and the birthplace of Christ, the Christian Europeans believed that the Holy Land should be under their control. The centuries-long bloodbath that ensued has come to be known as the Crusades.'

'No sooner was Jerusalem conquered by the crusading armies than the Church moved in, organizing religious militias to oversee its new empire. The two best-known militias were the Knights Templar and the Hospitaller Knights of St John, the rivalry between the two orders legendary,' Cædmon interjected, keeping his voice as neutral as possible. The Templars had been a point of bitter contention between him and his former mentor.

'And it should be noted that the men who swelled the ranks of the Templars and the Hospitallers were anything but holy brothers,' Sir Kenneth remarked right on his coat-tails. 'These were trained soldiers who fought, and fought mercilessly, in the name of God. One might even go so far as to liken the two orders of warrior monks to mercenary shock troops.'

On that point, Cædmon and Sir Kenneth greatly differed. But they were there to learn about Galen of Godmersham, not to rekindle an ancient dispute.

'As the crusading knights soon discovered, the Holy Land was rich in religious artefacts, relics being sent back to Europe by the shipload,' Sir Kenneth continued, folding his arms over his chest, an Oxford don in his element.

'Holy relics were a big fad during the Middle Ages, weren't they?'

'More like an obsession, many a pilgrimage made to view the bones or petrified appendage of a holy man or woman. St Basil's shrivelled bollocks. St Crispin's arse bone. Such oddities abounded.'

Beside him, Cædmon felt Edie's shoulders shake with silent laughter, his companion obviously amused by Sir Kenneth's bawdiness.

'Christians in the Middle Ages were convinced that holy relics were imbued with a divine power capable of healing the sick and dying while protecting the living from the malevolent clutches of the demon world.'

'Sounds like a lot of superstitious hooey.' Indictment issued, Edie popped another crisp into her mouth.

Sir Kenneth pruriently observed the passage of crisp to lip before replying, 'While superstition did exist, the medieval fascination with relics was more than mere cultish devotion. Given that we live in a disposable society with no thought for the past and little for the future, it is difficult to comprehend the medieval mindset.'

'Guess you could call us the here and now generation,' Edie remarked, seemingly unaware of the effect she was having on the Oxford don.

'Indeed. But the generation that set out for the Holy Land, clad in mail and armed with sword, full-heartedly believed that the land of their biblical forebears was their birthright. To these stalwart knights, biblical relics were a tangible link between the past, the present and the unforeseen future. Thus the obsession with uncovering the treasures of the Bible.'

'The most sought-after prize being the Ark of the Covenant,' Cædmon pointed out, deciding to broach the subject in a roundabout manner. 'No less a thinker than Thomas Aquinas declared, "God himself was signified by the Ark." Other Church fathers likened the Ark to the Virgin, the mother of Christ.'

'Ah, yes ... *Faederis Arca*.'

Edie tugged at his sleeve. 'Translation, please.'

Secretly pleased that Edie had turned to him, Cædmon replied, 'It's the feminine form for the Ark of the Covenant. *Faederis Arca* was used to convey the religious belief that just as the original Ark had contained the Ten Commandments, the Virgin Mary had contained within her womb the saviour of the world.'

'So where does Galen of Godmersham fit into all of this?' Edie asked, proving herself an attentive student.

'As with many younger sons with not a prayer of inheriting the family estate, Galen of Godmersham decided to earn his fortune the old-fashioned way, in this case pillaging the infidels in the Holy Land.'

'Rape and ruin – the stuff of English history,' Cædmon mordantly remarked.

Grinning, Sir Kenneth banged his palm against the table, causing their half-empty glasses to rattle. 'Ah! Those were the days, were they not?' Then, his voice noticeably subdued, 'Both the Knights Templar and the Hospitallers were actively engaged in seeking the Ark of the Covenant. As a Hospitaller, Galen of God-mersham would have joined the hunt. Ultimately, the knights' hunt proved the wildest goose chase known to history, but this is where our story takes an intriguing turn.' Leaning forward, giving every appearance of a man taking a woman into his confidence, Sir Kenneth said in a lowered voice, 'While Galen of Godmersham did not uncover the goose, the lucky lad did happen upon a very fat gold-plated egg.'

In like manner, Edie also leaned forward. 'You're talking about the gold chest, right?'

Sir Kenneth nodded. 'In 1289, while patrolling the region between Palestine and Egypt, Galen of Godmersham was leading a small contingent of Hospitaller knights through the Plain of Esdraelon. There, in a village called Megiddo, he –'

'Discovered a gold chest,' Edie interjected. 'But this is what I don't get.' She paused, a puzzled expression on her face. 'If no one has seen this gold chest in nearly seven hundred years, how do you know the darned thing ever existed?'

'My dear, you are as mentally nimble as you are beautiful. I know because the local Kent records from the years 1292 to 1344 tell me so.'

'Of course ... the Feet of Fines,' Cædmon murmured. When Edie turned to him, a questioning glance on her face, he elaborated: 'The Feet of Fines was the medieval record of all land and property owned in England.'

'And the Feet of Fines clearly indicates that Galen of Godmersham had within his possession a gold chest measuring one and a half by two cubits. The Feet of Fines also indicates that the gold chest was kept in Galen's personal chapel in the grounds of his estate. In addition to the gold chest, Galen owned a king's ransom in miscellaneous gold objects. *"Objets sacrés"*, as they are listed in the official records.'

'So when Galen of Godmersham discovered the gold chest, he went from rags to riches, huh?'

The Oxford don nodded. 'Like many a crusader, Galen of Godmersham profited from his sojourn in the Holy Land. Although he seems to have had a generous streak. In 1340 he bequeathed to St Lawrence the Martyr church several *"vestiges d'ancien Testament"*.'

'Old Testament relics,' Cædmon said in a quick aside to Edie. Then, to his former mentor, 'Bound by his vows of celibacy, Galen would have had no legal offspring. Who inherited the gold chest and all the *objets sacrés* when Galen died?'

'While it's true that Galen of Godmersham had neither son nor daughter, it wasn't for lack of trying. No sooner did he return to England than Galen left the Hospitallers, taking up worldly pleasures with a vengeance.'

'So who inherited the gold chest?' Edie enquired, playing the wide-eyed ingénue to perfection.

'That, my dear, is a mystery, a mystery that has confounded historian and treasure seeker alike. Bear in mind that when the plague struck in the middle of the fourteenth century, its effects were devastating, one third of England's population succumbing. As you can well imagine, chaos ensued, record keeping thrown into a state of complete disarray. It has been suggested that Galen, who was nearing his eighty-fifth year when the bubonic plague reached English shores, took the precaution of removing his precious gold chest from the family chapel in order to safe-guard it from the looting that followed in the plague's wake. Generations of treasure hunters have focused on Galen of Godmersham's deathbed burst of creative inspiration, the wily old knight having composed several poetic quatrains just prior to his death in 1348.'

'Oh, I get it!' Edie exclaimed, nearly falling off her chair in her excitement. 'The clues to the where-abouts of the gold chest are contained within the poetic quatrains.'

'Possibly,' Sir Kenneth replied, refusing to commit himself. 'Although Galen's verse is cryptic in nature, there is reference in the quatrains to an *arca*.'

'*Arca* being the Latin word for chest,' Cædmon said, taking a moment to consider all that Sir Kenneth had divulged. If clues to the gold chest's whereabouts were contained within the quatrains, it would explain why a Harvard scholar had expressed an interest in those very lines of verse. And if the scholar was in Stanford MacFarlane's employ, it meant the bastard had a twenty-four-hour head start in solving the centuries-old mystery.

'Is there any chance that the gold chest discovered by Galen of Godmersham was the Ark of the Covenant?' Edie enquired abruptly.

No sooner was the question posed than Sir Kenneth's woolly head swivelled in Cædmon's direction. 'Is that your purpose in grilling me, so that you can chase after a myth?'

Cædmon opened his mouth to speak, but Edie beat him to the punch.

'We thought there might be a *slim* possibility that Galen of Godmersham had discovered the Ark of the Covenant.'

'A fool's errand, my dear. The Holy Land fair brimmed with golden gewgaws, more than one impoverished knight returning to England a wealthy man.'

Undeterred, Edie said, 'If Galen didn't discover the Ark of the Covenant then –'

'I didn't say he didn't.'

'But you just said –'

'I said that Galen of Godmersham discovered a gold chest. It has yet to be proved whether the gold chest is the much-ballyhooed Ark of the Covenant. I am a scholar not a conspiracy theorist, and as such, I deal in fact not innuendo,' the older man brusquely stated. As he spoke, he locked gazes with Cædmon. Then, his expression softening, he returned his attention to Edie, 'Did you know there's an old Irish legend which claims that not only did a band of intrepid Hebrews take refuge on the Emerald Isle, but that they brought with them the Ark of the Covenant. Supposedly they buried the blasted thing under a hill in Ulster. Nearly as preposterous a tale as that of Galen of Godmersham discovering the Ark on the Plain of Esdraelon.'

Just then the door of the pub opened, a gaggle of giggling women crossing the threshold, a birthday cake held aloft.

'It would appear that the lacy-frock brigade has taken the field,' Sir Kenneth dryly remarked. 'Shall we continue the conversation at Rose Chapel?'

Not bothering to wait for a reply – it being more of a summons than an invitation – Sir Kenneth rose to his feet.

Leaning towards him, Edie whispered in Cædmon's ear, 'He wants to go to *church*?'

'Not in the sense that you mean. Sir Kenneth resides at Rose Chapel.'

'Just like a medieval monk, huh?'

Cædmon watched as Sir Kenneth appraised the cake bearer's backside.

'Hardly.'

35

Leading the way through the twisting labyrinth of narrow streets, Sir Kenneth came to a halt in front of a fan-vaulted entryway. 'After you, Miss Miller.'

Edie pushed open a wrought-iron gate. At hearing the spine-jangling squeak, she said, 'A little WD-40 will fix that right up.'

'My dear, I have no idea what you just said, but it sounded utterly delightful.'

She forced her lips into a tight smile. *God save me from horny college professors.*

Discovering that they had entered an ancient cemetery, a good many of the weathered headstones tilted at drunken inclines, Edie unthinkingly leaned into Cædmon.

'Very creepy,' she murmured, not wanting to disturb the dead.

'The scenery improves on the other side,' he assured her, gently squeezing her hand.

A few moments later she breathed a sigh of relief at finding herself in a medieval knot garden. Taking the lead, his red cashmere scarf jauntily flapping in the breeze, Sir Kenneth guided them through the clipped boxes. Imagining the older man manoeuvring through the maze after a night at the pub, Edie bit back a smile.

The knot garden navigated, they strolled through a copse of cedar trees and copper beeches.

Peering through the tree limbs, Edie's breath caught in her throat.

Lovely to behold, even dressed in winter's stark garb, Rose Chapel was constructed of rubbled stone beautifully punctuated with arched stained-glass windows. Adjacent to the chapel was a three-storey Norman tower that seemed out of place with its plain facade and arrow slits, tower married to chapel like a masculine–feminine yin yang.

Stepping through an irreverently painted canary-yellow door, Sir Kenneth led them into a lobby. He removed his red scarf with a theatrical flourish, draping it round a marble bust of a bald-headed, beaked-nosed man.

'Who's that?' Edie mouthed.

'Pope Clement V,' Cædmon mouthed back.

An older woman in a plain navy-blue dress – Edie placed her around fifty – scurried into the lobby. Any notion of the woman being Mrs Campbell-Brown was instantly dispelled when she obsequiously bobbed her head and said, 'Good day, Sir Kenneth.'

Acknowledging the greeting with little more than a brusque nod, Sir Kenneth removed his leather bomber jacket and shoved it at the woman. With a distracted wave of his hand, he indicated that Edie and Cædmon should do likewise.

'Soon after you left, sir, the Norway spruce was delivered,' the housekeeper politely informed the master of the castle, her arms now laden with three sets of outerwear.

Sir Kenneth glanced at a beautiful, but bare, Christmas tree that had been set up at the other end of the room.

'Mrs Janus has an annoying habit of stating the obvious.' He gestured to the stacked boxes on the console table. 'Please overlook the Christmas fripperies. Mrs Janus also has an annoying habit of decking Rose Chapel with boughs of holly and streams of satin ribbon.'

Not liking Sir Kenneth's lofty tone, Edie walked over to the table and carefully lifted a glass angel out of its nest of tissue paper. As she held it aloft, its gilt-edged wings caught the wintry light. 'These are lovely ornaments,' she said to Mrs Janus, smiling.

'That is from Poland.'

Without being told, Edie sensed that the Christmas holidays were particularly difficult for Mrs Janus. Like many emigrants, she no doubt longed for the traditions of her native land. Taking care, she replaced the fragile angel in its box. 'I'm sure it'll be a beautiful tree.'

'The Christmas season is one of joy and remembrance,' the housekeeper replied, casting a quick glance in her employer's direction.

'And hot mulled wine,' Sir Kenneth loudly barked.

'And bring us some of those little tarts I saw you pop into the Aga.'

Orders issued, Sir Kenneth led Edie and Cædmon down a hall. Playing the baronial lord, he swung open a panelled door and strode into a large, high-ceilinged room. About to follow him, Edie hesitated, taken aback by the stone grotesques that flanked the doorway.

'Is it my imagination or did one of those butt-ugly creatures just move its lips?'

'It's the play of light and shadow,' Cædmon informed her. 'Sir Kenneth's way of instilling fear into the hearts of all those who enter his *sanctum santorum*.' Given what was clearly a grudge match between the two men, Edie wasn't surprised by Cædmon's sarcastic tone.

At a glance, she could see that the *sanctum santorum* had originally been the actual chapel, the massive arched ceiling, stone floor and a stained-glass three-light window being dead giveaways. Put all together, it made for an impressive sight. Assuming one ignored the half-dozen cats snoozing in various places throughout the room. A feline with chewed ears perched on top of a bookcase drowsily lifted its head, the rest of the tribe taking no notice of the intrusion.

Trying not to gawk, she checked out the room. Some things, like the medieval torchères, looked right at home. Other things, like the modern shelving unit jam-packed with vinyl records sheathed in clear plastic looked conspicuously out of place in the medieval setting.

'I dare say that you are looking at the best collection of 1950s American rock 'n' roll in the entire UK,' Sir Kenneth remarked, having noticed the direction of her gaze. 'The music of my youth, as you have undoubtedly deduced.'

Edie also deduced that music wasn't the don's only passion. On the wall nearest to where she stood there hung a black-and-white poster of the 1930s movie siren Mae West, her curvaceous figure swathed in a satin evening gown. Beside the poster a large animal horn hung from a bright blue tassel, the hideous thing banded with engraved silver. All too easily, she could visualize Sir Kenneth, decked out in his red cashmere scarf and brown bomber jacket, swigging gin and tonics out of the cup like tap water.

'My dear, before you depart, you must have a look at my collection of incunabula,' Sir Kenneth said, gesturing to a bookcase bursting with leather-bound volumes.

Not having the least idea what he was talking about, Edie gave the bookcase a cursory glance, recalling a philosophy professor who'd once invited her to his house to look at his collection of Chagall prints. She sidled closer to Cædmon.

Sir Kenneth motioned to a pair of upholstered chairs positioned in front of a paper-laden desk, one stack of papers weighed down with a rusty astrolabe, another with a snow dome of the Empire State

Building. Behind the desk, beautifully framed in gilt, hung a reproduction of Trumbull's painting depicting the signing of the Declaration of Independence.

'Sir Kenneth has a love of all things American,' Cædmon whispered in her ear as he dislodged a dozing cat from his chair. 'Be on your guard.'

'That's why you're here, Big Red,' she whispered back at him.

Walking over to them, Sir Kenneth jovially slapped Cædmon on the back. 'Middle age becomes you, Aisquith.' Then, turning his attention to Edie, 'When he first arrived at Oxford, he was a gangly-limbed lad with a thatch of unruly red hair.'

Grinning, Edie gave Cædmon the once over. 'Hmm. Sounds cute.'

'Ah! The lady has a penchant for red-headed lads.' As Sir Kenneth took his seat behind the desk, Edie heard him mutter, 'Lucky bastard.'

36

At finding himself seated in Sir Kenneth's study, inundated with the twin scents of damp wool and musty leather, Cædmon experienced an unexpected burst of painful nostalgia. Striving for an appearance of calm, he glanced at the stained-glass window that dominated the room. A beautiful piece of medieval artistry, the three lights depicted that most famous of cautionary tales, the Temptation in the Garden.

Overtly phallic snake. Bright red juicy apple. Hands shamefully placed over fig-leafed genitals.

For some inexplicable reason it reminded him of his student days at Oxford – perhaps because he too had dared to eat the fruit from the Tree of Knowledge. And if he was the hapless Adam, Sir Kenneth Campbell-Brown could only be the conniving Lucifer, although in his impressionable youth, he'd cast his mentor in a far more exalted role.

A brilliant scholar, rigid taskmaster and at times capriciously cruel bastard, Sir Kenneth demanded unswerving fidelity from his students. In return, he gave his charges an unforgettable academic journey. Ever mindful that Oxford had started out with groups of young scholars gathered around the most illustrious teachers of the day, Sir Kenneth maintained the tradition, hosting weekly tutorials within the stone confines of Rose Chapel.

For nearly eight years, he and Sir Kenneth had maintained a close relationship. Not unlike a father and son.

Initially, Sir Kenneth had approved his dissertation topic, intrigued by the notion that the Knights Templar may have explored the tombs and temples of Egypt during their time in the Holy Land. But when he dared to suggest that the Templars had turned their backs on Catholicism and become devotees of the Isis mystery cult, Sir Kenneth not only refused to countenance the notion, he took the rejection one step further, publicly ridiculing him for having 'embraced rumours and passing them off as the truth'.

It was as if he'd been mugged in the middle of a dark and rainy night.

Thirteen years later he turned misfortune to advantage, his derided dissertation paper becoming the cornerstone for *Isis Revealed*.

Shoving aside old memories, Cædmon cleared his throat, ready to embark on what would undoubtedly be a bumpy ride.

'Let us consider whether Galen of Godmersham did discover the Ark of the Covenant while on reconnaissance in Esdraelon,' he carefully began, mindful that Sir Kenneth dealt in 'fact not innuendo'. 'Is there any evidence to support this notion?'

Leaning back in his leather wingback, blue-veined fingers laced over his chest, Sir Kenneth's gaze narrowed, the old man undoubtedly deciding whether or not to reply. With a noticeable lack of enthusiasm, he finally said, 'There are a few shreds of historical data to support your theory.'

'Like what?' Edie piped up, subtlety not her strong suit.

'As you undoubtedly know, theories have waxed and waned as to how and why the Ark disappeared. However, if one carefully sifts through centuries of biblical silence, the Ark's disappearance might possibly be laid at the sandalled foot of the Egyptian pharaoh Shishak, who conquered the holy city of Jerusalem in the year 926 BC.'

As his former mentor began to speak, Cædmon was reminded of the fact that Sir Kenneth never prepared for his tutorials, always speaking extemporaneously. And brilliantly. Most who flew by the seat of their pants eventually crash-landed. Never Sir Kenneth Campbell-Brown, his lectures also legendary.

Cædmon turned to Edie. Filling in the gaps, he said, 'Shishak's invasion occurred not long after Solomon's son Rehoboam inherited the crown of Israel. Because the northern tribes had recently broken away during a power struggle, the kingdom of Israel was vulnerable.'

'In other words, the opportunistic Egyptians swept down like vultures on roadkill.'

Sir Kenneth laughed aloud, clearly amused. 'Well put, my dear! Well put indeed.'

On the far side of the room, the study door suddenly swung open. Without uttering a word, Mrs Janus, bearing a tray laden with Wedgwood and pewter, walked over to the tea table. Still silent as the grave, she handed each of them a tankard of mulled wine and a dainty plate with two small tarts. Watching the housekeeper depart, Cædmon thought he recognized the woman, unable to fathom why any domestic would willingly suffer Sir Kenneth's mercurial ways for so many years. Clearly, the woman possessed the patience of Job.

'The blasted Aga has been running full throttle since the first of December. If I'm not careful, I'll put on a stone before Twelfth Night.'

Forgoing a beautifully incised dessert fork, Edie plucked a miniature tart off the plate with her fingers. 'You were about to regale us with the story of Shishak's invasion of Israel.'

'So I was.' Choosing wine over pastry, Sir Kenneth cradled his tankard between his hands. 'According to the Book of Kings, in the fifth year of Rehoboam's reign "Shishak king of Egypt came up against Jerusalem: And he took away the treasures of the house of the Lord, and the treasures of the king's house; he even took away all."'

'Meaning that the pharaoh stole the Ark of the Covenant!' When her exclamation met with silence, Edie's brows puckered in the middle. 'Well, what else could it mean?'

'The Old Testament makes no mention of Shishak seizing the Ark. It merely records that the pharaoh managed to come away with five hundred shields of beaten gold.'

'Solomon's famous shields,' Cædmon murmured.

'There are some biblical historians who have theorized that King Rehoboam willingly handed over the five hundred gold shields to repay a debt of honour. Years earlier the pharaoh had granted the wayward Hebrew prince asylum when his father ordered his assassination. All that internecine rivalry between family members is what makes the Bible such a jolly good read,' Sir Kenneth said in an aside, broadly winking at Edie.

'Are there any historical records aside from the Old Testament that mention Shishak's invasion of Israel?' Cædmon asked, wishing the other man would keep to the point.

'The only other account is an inscription at Luxor inside the Temple of Amun-Ra. According to this, after he attacked Jerusalem, Shishak apparently stopped on the Plain of Esdraelon, where he had a commemorative stela erected. The custom of the time mandated that Shishak show his gratitude to the gods by leaving behind a sizeable offering. As with the taxman, one must always appease one's god. And to answer your next question, there is no record of what Shishak did with his ill-gotten gains once he returned to his capital city of Tanis.'

'I thought the Ark was placed in Shishak's tomb. At least that's the theory put forth in *Raiders of the Lost Ark*,' Edie conversationally remarked.

To Cædmon's surprise, rather than berate Edie for introducing a fictional movie plot into the discussion, Sir Kenneth smiled. 'You are absolutely charming, my dear. But you have jumped to an erroneous conclusion regarding Shishak and the Ark of the Covenant. As I earlier mentioned, there is no evidence that Shishak took the Ark.'

'It stands to reason that if the pharaoh's army took Jerusalem, Shishak would have looted Solomon's Temple,' Caedmon argued. 'After all, the sole purpose of invading Israel was to come away with as much treasure as they could pocket.'

'And what proof do you have that Shishak actually laid his greedy hands upon the coveted prize?'

'As you have already stated, there's no direct biblical evidence. However, it stands to reason that –'

'Rubbish! It does not stand to reason!' Sir Kenneth loudly exclaimed, punctuating his rebuttal with a fist on the arm of his chair. 'Your assumptions are unwarranted. You would be well advised, young Aisquith, to refrain from fantastical deductions.'

Warning issued, the woolly-headed don surged to his feet and strode over to a nearby window. Despite the December temperatures, he threw open the window, letting in a burst of wintry air. The centuries-old glass caught the midday sun, cloaking the older man in a silvery-grey nimbus.

'*Reginae erunt nutrices tuae!*' he yelled to the bare trees that bordered the chapel yard.

Edie's jaw nearly came unhinged, so great was her astonishment.

Having witnessed the performance many times before, Cædmon rose to his feet, walked over to the tea table and took two pecan tarts from a Wedgwood plate. He handed one of the tarts to Edie. '"Queens shall be thy nursing mothers,"' he translated. 'Taken from the Book of Isaiah, it is the Queen's College motto.'

Munching on his tart, Cædmon gazed beyond the woolly head at the window, espying the small stone terrace that overlooked the knot garden. In the blossoming profusion of Trinity Term, Sir Kenneth liked to gather his favourites on the terrace. For some inexplicable reason, the memory of those lush spring days was especially poignant. And especially painful.

Edie put in, 'I know Sir Kenneth will jump all over me if I suggest this, but what if Shishak dumped the Ark of the Covenant at Esdraelon just like the Philistines dumped the Ark at Bethshemesh? Shishak might have done that if his soldiers started to complain of tumours and lesions. Or, better yet, what if the pharaoh witnessed one or two of his soldiers tossed in the air because of the electric current produced by the Ark? I'd think that'd be reason enough to hide the Ark, say a prayer, and get the heck out of Esdraelon as quick as possible.'

Thinking this a likely scenario, Cædmon reseated himself, the maudlin mood instantly lifted. 'You are a woman after my own heart.'

He also thought it probable that Shishak's offering was, centuries later, happened upon by an English crusader, the dimensions listed in the Feet of Fines for Galen's gold chest an exact match for the dimensions given in the Old Testament for the Ark of the Covenant. And Esdraelon, the site where Galen of Godmersham had discovered his gold chest, was where the commemorative stela had been erected by Shishak.

'Sir Kenneth said something about Galen being the proud owner of a number of *objets sacrés*. Are you thinking what I'm thinking, that Galen also happened upon a few of Solomon's shields?'

'It's not outside the realms of possibility that Shishak left a number of shields as a peace offering to the gods. Although I wouldn't broach the notion with our host.'

'Gotcha.'

Closing the window, Sir Kenneth strode back to his desk.

'Nothing like a full-throated bellow to clear one's mind, eh? You should try it, my dear. I suspect you have a healthy pair of lungs.' Pronouncement issued, he turned to Cædmon. 'While this has been a most entertaining discussion, young Aisquith, your original supposition is not unlike a fart in a wind tunnel. Ephemeral at best.'

'And thus "A terrible beauty is born,"' Cædmon drolly murmured.

'You were always fond of a literary flourish. Had you studied medieval literature rather than history, you might have gone far.'

'Um, speaking of literary endeavours, I'm curious about the poems that Galen wrote prior to his death,' Edie interjected, taking upon herself the thankless job of referee.

'Yes, I thought the two of you would be interested in Galen's poetry. The originals are kept at Duke Humphrey's Library and do not circulate. But luckily for you, my dear, I've got a copy right here.'

Still standing, he shuffled through a pile of papers on his desk. When he didn't find what he was looking for, he impatiently rifled through the next pile. And then another, all the while muttering under his breath.

'This is unconscionable!' he angrily exclaimed, slapping a palm on the last pile. 'Someone has pinched the blasted quatrains!'

37

As she did each and every year, Marta Janus carefully removed the tissue-wrapped ornaments from the box. First she unwrapped the six hand-blown glass angels from her native Poland. Next she got out the tartan-clad Santas. As always, she found the green-and-blue-plaid porcelain figures slightly grotesque, but Sir Kenneth was inordinately proud of his Scottish forebears, and so each year she hung the gaudy ornaments upon the tree. One plaid Santa for each crystal angel. Sir Kenneth always complained about the dressing of the tree, claiming it a strange ritual for a woman who professed to be a devout Catholic. Marta simply turned a deaf ear. After twenty-seven years in Sir Kenneth's employ, she was no longer affected by his condescension. She'd built a wall around her heart, brick by brick, the mortar so thick as to be impenetrable.

At first she had believed Sir Kenneth Campbell-Brown was a kind and generous man. While many intellectuals had professed sympathy for the Polish dissident movement, few were willing to take in a refugee who barely spoke English. Sir Kenneth had no such qualms. He pointed; she cleaned. For the first year they had no verbal communication whatsoever. And then one day she awoke to find handwritten signs taped to nearly every piece of furniture. Her grace period having abruptly expired, the lord of Rose Chapel expected her to master the English language. At first, it had been nothing more than a silly game of butchered phrases and garbled sentences, then it went from game to something deeper, more complex, Marta determined to prove her worth to the man who had plucked her from the ashes of fear and uncertainty.

She was one of the lucky few who had managed to escape, paying an exorbitant fee to a 'guide' who smuggled her out of Gdansk in the hold of a fishing vessel. Her husband Witold had not been so fortunate. Caught in the communist crackdown, he'd been sent to prison for crimes against the state. A bricklayer by trade, his only crime had been to dream of a free Poland. Sentenced to ten years' hard labour, he lasted three. Marta did not receive word of his death until he'd already been dead and buried sixteen months. She spoke of his death to no one, not even Sir Kenneth, obeying an unspoken rule in Rose Chapel: never speak of matters of the heart.

She supposed the rule had come about because Sir Kenneth did not possess a heart. Or if he did, it was rarely in evidence. In twenty-seven years there had been only two occasions when Sir Kenneth Campbell-Brown had exhibited any sort of tenderness. The first was when, having read of her plight in a local newspaper, he rang up the Catholic charity that had sponsored her when she first arrived in England, informing them that he would provide gainful employment for her. Nearly ten years would pass before the second.

Although there were countless incidents in between, incidents that spoke of a decadent and depraved existence. Many nights Sir Kenneth did not return to Rose Chapel. Many nights were spent in drunken revelry. One such night she happened upon two naked, giggling girls in the kitchen smearing butter on each other's breasts. Another night she went to turn down the bed only to discover Sir Kenneth and a muscular black man committing an unspeakable act. Some nights she thought him the devil incarnate. Other nights, a beautiful Bacchus.

He'd certainly been beautiful that long-ago December eve, attired in a crisply tailored black tuxedo, his grey curls gleaming like polished pewter. He'd returned early from a party, claiming it had been a 'ghastly bore'. Marta offered him a cup of mulled wine and asked if he would like to help dress the Christmas tree. He laughed at the invitation but loosened his bow tie and helped nonetheless. He'd even steadied a chair so she could place a twinkling star atop the tree. But the chair wobbled and she accidentally fell into his arms. Before she knew it, they were rolling together on the recently vacuumed carpet, pulling at each other's garments like two crazed animals. She had not lain with a man in the ten years since she left her native Poland. In that impassioned instant Sir Kenneth ceased to be the master of Rose Chapel; he was simply a man. Forceful. Hard. Commanding. She'd cried out, the pain so exquisite she thought she would be torn asunder.

The next morning silence returned to Rose Chapel. Not unlike the first year of her tenure, Sir Kenneth did little but point and mutter. She did nothing but sweep and vacuum. No mention was made of the previous night's passion. Had it not been for the crystal angel smashed beneath the tree and Sir Kenneth's bow tie entangled in the tree, she could almost believe it had never happened. The broken angel went into the dustbin, the satin tie into her keepsake box.

One week later, on Boxing Day, when masters traditionally gave gifts to their servants, a small box wrapped in plain brown paper mysteriously appeared on her dresser. Inside was a hand-blown crystal angel. There was no card. Each year the mystery angel was the first to be unwrapped. And each year, despite his protests and complaints, Marta dressed a Christmas tree, forcing the master of Rose Chapel to remember their night of passion.

She'd long since given up any hope that Sir Kenneth's soul could be saved. For to have a soul, one must first have a heart. Heartless man that he was, she feared the day would come when she would be replaced with a younger woman, a woman whose hair had not turned grey, whose body had not sagged.

Marta feared what would become of her if she was made to face the wolves, penniless and pensionless.

But there was now a way to avoid the wolves. An American angel had come to deliver her from that which she most feared. She could now leave Rose Chapel on her own terms, her grey head held high. It required just one phone call.

Reaching into her apron pocket, Marta removed the scrap of paper with the scrawled mobile phone number. For two days she'd carried the slip of paper in her pocket. Staring at the number, she hesitated. Uncertain. Assailed with memories of that long-ago December eve. Like a woman lost in a blizzard, Marta turned her gaze to the neat line of Christmas ornaments waiting to be placed on the tree. In the kitchen a timer pealed.

Time to take the buns out of the oven.

Marta turned away from the ornaments. As she did, her hip jogged the table. One hideous blue-and-green Santa rolled to the edge, falling to the stone floor.

Marta stared at the broken bits of porcelain.

No longer uncertain.

38

'Are you thinking what I'm thinking,' Edie said in a low voice, 'that the Harvard "chap" stole the quatrains from Sir Kenneth?'

'Indeed,' Cædmon replied, the missing poems seeming proof that Stanford MacFarlane believed Galen of Godmersham had uncovered the Ark of the Covenant. It also strongly suggested that MacFarlane believed clues to the Ark's whereabouts were contained within the lines of those verses. A poetic treasure map as it were. He and Edie had to move quickly.

'Sir Kenneth, did you say that Galen's poetry is housed at the Bod?'

Still shuffling through the piles of paper on his desk, Sir Kenneth glanced up. 'What's that? Er, yes. The original copy of the quatrains is kept at Duke Humphrey's Library.'

Duke Humphrey's Library was one of fourteen libraries in the Bodleian. Unless things had greatly changed, only matriculated students and researchers who'd obtained written permission could gain entry to Duke Humphrey's Library, the premises strictly off limits to visitors. To circumvent the restrictions,

MacFarlane's man had stolen a copy from Sir Kenneth.

'Is there any possibility that I might be able to examine the original quatrains?'

Sir Kenneth stopped in mid-shuffle. For several long seconds the older man stared at Cædmon from across the paper-strewn desk. Making him feel like a child awaiting a parent's decision about attending an upcoming football match. Except Sir Kenneth wasn't his father. Although he had once been a father figure. Long years ago.

'I could call the head librarian and ask that the two of you be granted a special dispensation to view the library's collection. But I warn you, Galen's quatrains are a linguistic puzzle tied with an encrypted knot.'

Having assumed no less, Cædmon respectfully bowed his head. 'I am in your debt, Sir Kenneth.'

'Did you know, my dear, that young Aisquith graduated with a first?' Sir Kenneth remarked, abruptly changing the subject.

About to raise her tankard to her lips, Edie stopped in mid-motion. 'Um, no. Guess that makes Cædmon a really smart cookie, huh?'

'Indeed, it does. The smart cookie then went on to write a brilliant master's thesis on St Bernard of Clairvaux and the founding of the Knights Templar. Later, when he went off to Jerusalem to conduct his dissertation research, I had every expectation that he would submit an equally brilliant dissertation.'

The knot in Cædmon's belly painfully tightened.

Bloody hell. This was the old man's price for granting the favour, to stuff his entrails with red hot coals.

'As you have no doubt guessed, I was not up to the challenge. I did not meet Sir Kenneth's high standards,' he confessed, refusing to let his estranged mentor deliver the coup de grâce. Better a self-inflicted wound than to be led meekly to the scaffold.

'It didn't have to be that way. If you had come to me and discussed your plans before going off half-cocked, I could have –'

'Is that what angered you, that I failed to obtain your esteemed academic opinion?' *Or were you angered that the son had rejected the father?*

Seeing the sparks about to catch fire, Edie jumped to her feet. 'We've sort of veered a little off track, don't you think?' Then, acting as though nothing untoward had occurred, she calmly walked over to the tray and helped herself to a tart. 'Now, let me make sure I've got this straight, Sir Kenneth. You said that Galen of Godmersham had no children.'

'That is correct.'

'But since he left the Hospitallers when he returned to England, I assume that he was married.' Holding the tart between thumb and forefinger, she waved it to and fro as she spoke.

'Galen went to the altar not once but thrice. No sooner did each spouse shuffle off her mortal coil than Galen found himself a young replacement. His last bride, Philippa Whitcombe, was the daughter of the justice of the peace for Canterbury. When Galen died, Philippa promptly joined a cloistered order of nuns. One can assume that she did not take to the married state.'

About to take a bite, Edie lowered the tart. 'So who inherited the gold chest?'

'Ah! An excellent question, my dear.' Walking over to the tray, Sir Kenneth plucked a mince tart from the near-empty plate. 'Since the gold chest does not appear in any Feet of Fines record after 1348, one can infer that it was never found. Not altogether surprising given that not a single inhabitant of god-forsaken Godmersham survived the plague.'

'Meaning no one was left who had any recollection of ever seeing Galen's treasures,' Cædmon murmured. For all intents and purposes, it was as though Galen's gold chest had never existed once the plague struck. With no Feet of Fines record for the intervening centuries, the mystery would be that much more difficult to solve.

'Okay, but what about the quatrains? How did they come to be discovered?' Edie asked, clearly as determined as he to glean information.

'Galen's estates remained in a state of ruin until the reign of Queen Elizabeth. The new owner, a wealthy wine merchant by the name of Tynsdale, had the chapel demolished to make way for a hammer-beamed monstrosity. It was during demolition that the quatrains were discovered beneath the altar stone. Sir Walter Raleigh, a close acquaintance of the merchant, was the first to conjecture that the *arca* mentioned in Galen's poetry might refer to the Ark of the Covenant. He and Tynsdale scoured every inch of the property. To no avail, I might add. Not a century passes that some addle-brained treasure hunter hasn't attempted to find –' Catching sight of his housekeeper poking her head through the study door, he stopped in mid-flow. 'Yes, what is it?'

'A call, sir. From the provost's office.'

Clearly annoyed by the intrusion, he waved her away. 'That blasted relic's not working,' he said by way of explanation, gesturing to an antique black telephone on his desk. 'There's a telephone in the lobby. I won't be a moment.'

Cædmon rose to his feet. 'We must go.'

He wasn't certain, but he thought he detected a disappointed glimmer in the older man's eyes. Suddenly uncomfortable, he glanced at his wristwatch. 'Duke Humphrey's Library is open until seven. If you could call ahead and make the necessary arrangements, we would be most appreciative.'

'Yes, of course. My pleasure.' As he spoke, Sir Kenneth escorted them to the lobby.

Out of the corner of his eye, Cædmon caught a flash of colour. Turning his head, he saw that the once-bare Norway spruce now sparkled, richly tinted glass ornaments glowing jewel-like among the dark foliage.

'Did you know that it was Queen Victoria's husband, the bewhiskered Albert, who introduced the Christmas tree to these shores? He had them all done up with edible fruit and little wax fairies.' Sir Kenneth fingered a glossy green limb, a wistful look in his eye. 'I told her to get a pine not a spruce. Blasted woman.'

'I think it's absolutely gorgeous,' Edie remarked.

'Yes, it always is.' Turning his back on the tree, Sir Kenneth cleared his throat. 'The Choral Society is singing Handel's *Messiah* at seven thirty this evening. Perhaps you and Miss Miller would care to join me? There is nothing that compares to the sound of crystal voices lifted to the heavens. Quite moving. Even if one does not believe in the Christmas myth spoon-fed to us by power-hungry Church fathers, eh?'

Having obtained all he needed from his old mentor, Cædmon shook his head. He'd had enough of him for one day. 'Thank you, Sir Kenneth. Unfortunately, we –'

'Yes, yes, I understand.' Then, his right index finger pointing heavenwards, like a man struck with an inspired idea, he said, 'I've got just the thing. It arrived only this morning.' Turning his back, he searched the boxes piled high on the console table. 'Where is the blasted – Ah! There it is!' Reaching into a wooden crate, he removed a bottle.

'Merry Christmas, young Aisquith.'

Cædmon hesitated a moment, instantly recognizing the label on the bottle of Queen's College port that the older man offered to him. *COLLEGII REGINAE*. He well recalled the port decanter being passed between the senior fellow and his small band of favourites long years ago. Those were fond memories unsullied by the later rupture.

With a brusque nod, he accepted the bottle. 'And a merry Christmas to you, Sir Kenneth.'

The other man patted his stomach. 'I don't know about "merry", but it shall be filling. Mrs Janus is certain to stuff me with Christmas pudding and mince pies.'

Uncomfortable with the pleasantries, knowing they hid the bitter feelings that had earlier bubbled to the surface, Cædmon took Edie by the elbow. 'We must be on our way.'

To his surprise, she disengaged herself from his grasp, stepped over to Sir Kenneth and kissed him on his right cheek. 'I hope you have a very merry Christmas!'

Grinning like a besotted fool, Sir Kenneth followed them to the door. 'And, in turn, I hope that you and young Aisquith uncover Galen's blasted box. If the gold chest is to be found, you are the man to find it.' This last remark was directed to Cædmon.

Caught off guard by this unexpected support, Cædmon said the first thing that came to mind.

'Thank you, sir. That means a great deal to me.'

39

Enraged, Stan MacFarlane snapped shut his mobile.

Aisquith and the woman were in Oxford.

Why was plainly evident. They had managed to find out that Galen of Godmersham had uncovered the Ark of the Covenant while on crusade in the Holy Land. Eliot Hopkins must have told them before his death.

'Do you want me to take care of it, sir?'

Stan glanced over his shoulder. He knew that former Gunnery Sergeant Boyd Braxton was anxious to make amends for the débacle in Washington.

'Sometimes it's in one's best interest to be merciful.'

It took a few moments for the other man's befuddled expression to morph into an amused grin. 'Oh, I get it, Colonel. Like Tony Soprano, you want to keep your friends close and your enemies even closer.'

That being as good an answer as any, Stan tersely nodded. 'Tell Sanchez to put a tail on Aisquith. I want to know the Brit's every move.'

Turning on his heel, he strode down the low-ceilinged hall, his booted footfalls muffled by a well-worn Persian runner. On either side of him hung gilt-framed landscape paintings. 'A tastefully appointed house for the discriminating traveller.' When he had leased the house from the Internet website, he hadn't given a rat's ass about the decor. He only cared that the manor house was located midway between London and Oxford at the end of a half-mile oak-lined driveway. He needed a base camp to set up operations. Oakdale Manor fitted the bill.

Nodding brusquely, he acknowledged the armed sentry standing ramrod straight beside an upholstered chair. The Heckler & Koch MP5 clutched to the man's chest came courtesy of a sergeant major in the Royal Marines who routinely supplemented his pension with illegal small-arms sales.

Passing the age-blackened doors that led to the formal dining room, he glanced in, verifying that his highly paid contract worker was busy deciphering Galen of Godmersham's archaic poetry. A postgraduate student enrolled in Harvard's medieval studies programme, the scraggly-haired twenty-nine-year-old had jumped at the chance to pay off the nearly seventy thousand dollars in student loans that hung over him like a well-honed axe blade. Softly spoken and effeminate, the man put Stan in mind of a loose bowel movement. If not for the fact that he possessed the rare skills necessary to decipher the fourteenth-century quatrains, Stan would have disposed of the stoop-shouldered pencil dick after yesterday's meeting with the Oxford highbrow. For the moment, however, he served a purpose.

Satisfied to see the bespectacled scholar staring intently at his laptop, an eight-hundred-year-old map of England spread out on the table beside him, Stan continued down the hall to the kitchen.

For some reason the stone-floored room put him in mind of his grandmother's kitchen back home in Boone, North Carolina. Maybe it was the green-mottled crocks that lined the open shelves. Or the scarred wooden table that dominated the centre of the room. Whatever the reason, he could almost see his aproned grandmother standing at the oversized gas stove frying up some freshly laid eggs with big slabs of salted ham.

Reduced to eating English slop, he cut himself a thick slice of bread from the loaf on the table. Slathering it with plum jam, he carried it over to the casement window that overlooked the garden. Through the gnarled branches of dead wisteria that framed the outside of the window, he could see a fine-looking white horse frolicking in a distant field.

How much does Aisquith know? Probably not much. That's why he's in Oxford consulting the foremost expert on English crusaders. Strange the two men are acquainted. The intelligence dossier on Aisquith makes no mention of the relationship.

Luckily, he'd had the foresight to recruit the professor's housekeeper. Still it was troubling to discover that Aisquith knew about the quatrains. Although, given he possessed the sole copy of the quatrains outside Duke Humphrey's Library and given that the library was only open to Oxford faculty and students, the Brit didn't have a prayer of examining the original codex. Without the quatrains, Aisquith was just pissing in a gusty wind.

He glanced at his watch.

13:31 local time.

He'd hoped to have the quatrains deciphered by now, his excitement mounting with each passing hour. No doubt this was how Moses felt when he crafted the Ark of the Covenant, placing inside it the two stones inscribed with the Ten Commandments. With the creation of the Ark, Moses had ushered in a new world order. The hinge of history had swung upon the Ark. And it would soon swing again.

Praise be to the Almighty! For the battle is the Lord's.

Although Stan knew he had a tough fight ahead of him, he took solace from the knowledge that he would have at the ready the best weapon a soldier could have. For twenty-five years he'd been readying himself. Love of God. Purity of Heart. Cleanliness of mind and body. Those were the qualities of the Ark Guardian.

Harliss, a burly ex-marine, now a 'consultant' with Rosemont Security, poked his head into the kitchen. 'Sir, he's got something for you.'

Knowing that 'he' referred to the Harvard scholar, Stan headed for the dining room.

'What do you have?' he barked without preamble as he entered the room.

The chairs had all been pushed against one wall,

enabling free movement around the large oval table. Several framed paintings were also propped against the same wall. The scholar walked over and dimmed the chandelier. A PowerPoint slide appeared on the pictureless wall. Stan found himself staring at the four quatrains that Galen of Godmersham had composed just prior to his death.

The despitous Zephirus rood forth from Salomon's cite jubilant they sang
But a goost forney followed as a tempest of deeth
Repentaunt for his sins the shiten shepherd yeve penaunce
Thanne homeward he him spedde the ill-got treasure on holy stronders

From Jerusalem a companye of Knights in hethenesse they ryden out
Ech of hem made other for to winne on the heeth of Esdraelon
They bataille ther to the deeth the Vertuous knight the feeld he wonne
And ther-with-al chivalrye he kepte wel the holy covenaunt

This ilke worthy knight from sondry londes to Engelond he wende
Arca and gold ful shene he carried to the toun he was born
With open yë he now did see the blake pestilence he wrought
And whan this wrecche knight saugh it was so his deeth ful well deserved

Sore weep the goos on whom he truste for oon of hem were deed
I couthe not how the world be served by swich adversitee
But if a manne with ful devout corage seken the holy blissful martir
In the veyl bitwixen worlds tweye ther the hidden trouthe be fond

'Just as you thought, this word *arca* is the key to deciphering the quatrains.' Using a pointer, the younger man indicated the second line of the third quatrain. '*Arca,* of course, is the Latin word for chest.'

Since the bespectacled idiot hadn't told him anything he didn't already know, Stan made no reply. While he'd provided his mercenary scholar with a high-speed Internet connection enabling him to hook into the world's best libraries, he'd briefed him carefully, ensuring the man had no clue as to the purpose of his research.

'By those who come near me I will be treated as holy.'

Not one to disobey God's dictates, Stan intended to do all in his power to make sure that the unholy did not cast their gaze upon the Ark. The scholar had merely been told that Stan and his men represented a consortium of art collectors trying to track down a medieval chest believed to have been buried in the mid-fourteenth century somewhere in England. If the Harvard-educated boy wonder wondered at the trio of armed guards, he'd been wise enough to keep his own counsel. Unbridled greed has a way of making a man turn a blind eye.

When no reply to his brief exposition was forth-coming, the pasty-faced scholar nervously rubbed his hands together. 'Slowly but surely, it's all coming together. I've got the first three quatrains more or less figured out, but I'm still trying to pin down number four. Don't you guys worry. I'm guessing that I'll have this baby cracked in the next couple of hours.'

'You've been deciphering the verses since late yesterday. I had expected some tangible results by now.' Stan made no attempt to hide his annoyance, the scholar unaware that he was working to a carefully crafted timetable.

'Hey, you can't rush these things. Although I can tell you that the four quatrains form a rectilinear allegory.'

'What the hell does that mean?' Boyd Braxton muttered, staring at the scholar as though he were a turd on the bottom of his boot heel.

Smirking, the turd replied, 'For those of us who never took geometry, I am referring to the four-sided geometric configuration known as a square.'

40

More slowly this time, Cædmon reread Galen of Godmersham's poetry.

This wasn't the first time he'd been ensconced in the wood-panelled reading room of Duke Humphrey's Library, muddling his way through a thorny conundrum. In his student days he'd spent countless hours in this very room seated at the very same table, medieval texts piled around him.

Believing that a tidy work area elicited a similar tidiness in one's thinking, he organized the miscellaneous items on the reading table. The librarian, no doubt prompted by Sir Kenneth Campbell-Brown's advance call, had been most solicitous in delivering the requested materials to their table. In addition to the leather-bound codex that contained a selection of fourteenth-century poetry, including Galen's quatrains, she had produced a slim volume that contained the Godmersham Feet of Fines records for the years 1300 to 1350. Paper, pencils and cotton gloves had also been provided.

An exasperated frown on her face, Edie pointed a gloved index finger at the open codex. 'Just look at this, will ya. It's written in Old English. Which is a whole lot like saying it's written in a dead language.'

Noticing that several other library patrons were glowering irritably, Cædmon raised a finger to his lips, reminding Edie that silence reigned supreme within the walls of Duke Humphrey's Library. If one must speak, a muffled whisper was the preferred mode of communication.

'Actually, the quatrains are written in Middle English rather than the more remote Old English, enabling me to produce a fairly accurate interlinear translation.'

'You're talking about a line-by-line translation, right?' Her voice was noticeably lower. 'When I was a graduate student, I wrote a research paper on the Wife of Bath. You know, from *The Canterbury Tales*. The paper was for a seminar class on women in the Middle Ages and it darned near did me in.'

Hoping to bolster her spirits, he patted her hand. 'Don't worry. I'm certain that you'll survive the ordeal.' Then, not wanting to dwell on the fact an ordeal was by its very nature a trying endeavour, he reached for a pencil and a sheet of blank paper.

While it had been a number of years since he last translated Middle English, he managed to quickly work his way through the archaic spelling and phraseology with only a few missteps.

'Hopefully, this will make for more coherent verse,' he said, pushing the sheet of paper in his companion's direction.

Lifting the handwritten sheet off the table, Edie

held it at arm's length. Lips moving, she read the translation silently.

The merciless west wind rode forth from Solomon's city jubilantly singing
But a ghost fire followed like a deadly tempest
Repentant for his sins, the befouled shepherd did penance
Then homeward he sped, the ill-gotten treasure left on holy shores

From Jerusalem, a company of knights rode out in heathen lands
Each of them tried to profit from the other on the field of Esdraelon
They battled to the death, the virtuous knight winning the field
And with his show of valour, he kept the holy covenant

This same worthy knight went from sundry lands to England
He carried a chest and bright gold to the town where he was born
With open eyes he now saw the black plague that he wrought
And when the wretched knight saw this, his death was well deserved

The trusted goose sorely wept for all of them were dead
I know not how the world be served by such adversity
But if a man with a fully devout heart seek the blessed martyr
There in the veil between two worlds, the hidden truth be found

As she wordlessly lowered the sheet of paper to the table, Cædmon guessed from Edie's frown that she was as befuddled by the translation as she had been by the original text.

'I suggest that we take the allegorical and symbolic references in turn. Phrases such as "the merciless west wind", the "befouled shepherd" and "the veil between two worlds" should be thought of as pieces of code which have been strategically placed within the quatrains. The key to solving the riddle will hinge on how we decode the symbols contained within each line of verse.'

'And what if Galen loaded his word puzzle with a bunch of mixed signals?' she asked, still frowning.

'Oh, I have no doubt that Galen deliberately inserted semiotic decoys into the quatrains. The medieval mind was quite nimble when it came to inserting secret messages into seemingly innocuous text.'

Edie stared at the verse. 'Something tells me that we're gonna need a CIA code breaker.'

'Here, take this, for instance,' he said, pointing to the first line of text. '"The merciless west wind rode forth from Solomon's city jubilantly singing." I detect a bit of linguistic legerdemain at work. Clearly, this refers to Shishak leaving Jerusalem after successfully pillaging Solomon's Temple. Death then followed in the Egyptians' wake, the first quatrain ending with Shishak leaving the pilfered treasure behind as he and his army scurried back to Egypt.'

Edie's eyes suspiciously narrowed. 'Unless I'm greatly mistaken, you're actually enjoying yourself.'

'Who doesn't enjoy the intricacies of a well-constructed word puzzle?'

'Well, me, for starters,' his companion groused. 'I'm more of a Sudoku person. You know, the only reason we're sitting here in Duke Humphrey's

Library is because we *assume* that when Galen of God-mersham composed his quatrains, he was actually leaving clues as to where he hid the gold chest.'

'That is our basic assumption,' he said with a nod.

'Then I guess it's already crossed your mind that someone may have deciphered the quatrains and recovered the treasure years ago.'

'Since the cart has yet to pull the horse, we shall deal with that if and when it presents itself.'

Edie smiled, a teasing glint in her eyes. 'I think this is where I'm supposed to make a rude comparison between you and the back end of a horse.'

Unable to help himself, he stared into those lively brown eyes. Since the kiss on the coach, the air between them had become more sexually charged. He wondered if the storm would pass or if they would be caught in driving rain.

'Shall we continue?' Tapping the pencil on the quatrains, he refocused her attention.

Catching him by surprise, Edie snatched the pencil out of his hand. 'This is just a guess, mind you, but I think Galen's puzzle is configured like a square.'

41

'In early-fourteenth-century art a chest or box of any sort was always depicted as a flat, two-dimensional square.' Making no attempt to hide his condescension, the bespectacled scholar glanced at Boyd Braxton. 'Once perspective was introduced into the artist's grab bag during the Renaissance, all of that changed, of course.'

Arrogant little piss ant, Stan silently fumed as he stared at the archaic verses projected onto the dining-room wall. Had the lank-haired weasel been under his military command, he would have kicked his scrawny ass between his narrow shoulders. At the moment, however, he needed the scholar's expertise. And cooperation. Although he suspected it would take a full measure and a half of self-control to keep his temper in check.

'To Galen of Godmersham's mind a flat two-dimensional square would have been no different than the three-dimensional medieval chest your consortium is hoping to uncover. You guys following?'

Stan thought of how the Ark of the Covenant would have been illustrated in a church or cathedral during the fourteenth century. The weasel was right:

more than likely, it would have been depicted as a plain four-sided square.

'Carry on,' he ordered, not about to reply to the other man's question. Nor did any of his men say so much as a word. He'd told them point blank that he'd shaft each and every one of them with a steel reinforcing rod if just one let the words 'Ark of the Covenant' pass his lips.

'Now I think the phrase in the first quatrain "Salomon's cite" refers to Galen being in Jerusalem on Crusade. And in case you guys haven't figured it out yet, the first quatrain is also the first side of our metaphorical square.'

Again Stan remained silent. In truth, he didn't give a rat's ass about the first quatrain, assuming it referred to Shishak not Galen of Godmersham. That part of the story he was well acquainted with, since it was written in the Old Testament, Kings I, Verse 14 that Shishak 'came up against Jerusalem' and that he then 'took away the treasures of the house of the Lord'. What he was interested in were the cryptic messages contained within the next three quatrains. Somewhere in those archaic verses Galen of Godmersham revealed where he hid the Ark, the sacred chest that enabled God to dwell among men. And from which God would lead his holy army against the infidels in the last days.

Feeling his excitement rise, Stan glanced at the watch strapped to his left wrist.

Four days, nine hours and twenty-six minutes until the start of Eid al-Adha, the Muslim holy day.

Which meant he had four days, nine hours and twenty-six minutes to find the Ark of the Covenant.

42

'Ah yes. A square. Spot on,' Cædmon enthused, smiling. 'A quatrain is, after all, a poem with four lines.'

'And Galen composed *four* quatrains,' Edie added, the number four having been the giveaway.

'Not to mention that the Ark of the Covenant was usually depicted in medieval art as a four-sided square.' Still smiling, Cædmon winked at her. 'You must excel at Sudoku. Now, what about this metaphorical square?'

Pleased that Cædmon wanted her input, she gave it her best shot. 'I think Galen was trying to compose a chain of custody for the Ark of the Covenant. And he begins the chain right here in the first quatrain with Pharaoh Shishak taking the Ark from Solomon's Temple. From what Sir Kenneth told us earlier today, we know that the pharaoh left an offering – the Ark – on the Plain of Esdraelon.'

'Where it was happened upon some twenty-two centuries later by a roving band of Hospitaller knights led by Galen of Godmersham.' He pointed to the second quatrain. 'It would appear that the knights fought one another to the death over the treasure, Galen the lone man left standing on the field after the mêlée.'

Lips pursed, Edie stared at the last line of the quatrain in question. 'What does this mean, "And with his show of valour, he kept the holy covenant"?'

'It probably means that Galen of Godmersham became the self-appointed guardian of the Ark.'

'So, we're definitely on the right track, huh?'

'I believe so.'

In all honesty Edie didn't know how she felt about that. While excited that they were working their way through the verses, she was at the same time uneasy about the whole thing. A little voice inside her head kept saying, *Leave it be*. Over and over.

'And it's clear from the third quatrain that Galen took the Ark to England, specifically to the place of his birth, Godmersham,' Cædmon continued, oblivious to her unease. 'Correlating precisely with the information listed in the Feet of Fines property records. Now, *this* I find rather interesting,' he said, pointing to the third line of the third quatrain. '"With open eyes he now saw the black plague that he wrought."'

'It could be that Galen believed the Ark was responsible for the plague that hit England in 1348.'

'He had ample reason to think so, the pustules that erupted on faces and bodies during the plague uncannily similar to the lesions and boils that befell the Philistines. God's punishment for the theft of the Ark.'

Cædmon's last remark made Edie wonder at the punishment for *finding* the Ark of the Covenant.

Normally, she wasn't one to believe in curses or hexes, but the evidence was damning. Literally. The Old Testament Bible stories and Galen's quatrains both came stamped with DANGER in big, bold, threatening type. Skull and crossbones included.

'Perhaps Galen hid the darned thing in the hope that it would bring an end to the plague. Too bad he didn't have the Stones of Fire to protect himself.'

Too bad they *didn't have the Stones of Fire*, Edie silently added, her unease now laced with fear, the type of fear that made one double-check all the doors and sleep with a nightlight.

'The last line of the third quatrain was probably composed while Galen was on his deathbed,' Cædmon blithely continued, unintentionally throwing fuel onto the fire.

Knowing that the only way to combat fear was to take decisive action, Edie grabbed a sheet of blank paper.

'Okay, let's take our square analogy.' Pencil in hand, she carefully drew a square. 'And fill in the Ark's chain of custody as detailed by Galen in the quatrains.'

'That's excellent.' Clearly accustomed to being in a library, Cædmon managed to keep his enthusiasm to a hushed whisper. 'You know, you were absolutely right. Galen *did* use his four quatrains as a poetic cryptogam. The Ark's current whereabouts must be encoded in the lines of the fourth quatrain.'

She stared at the enigmatic fourth quatrain.

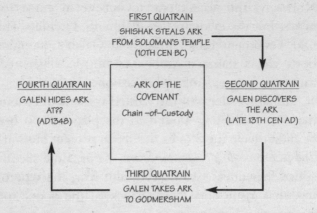

FIRST QUATRAIN
SHISHAK STEALS ARK
FROM SOLOMAN'S TEMPLE
(10TH CEN BC)

FOURTH QUATRAIN
GALEN HIDES ARK
AT??
(AD1348)

ARK OF THE
COVENANT
Chain –of–Custody

SECOND QUATRAIN
GALEN DISCOVERS
THE ARK
(LATE 13TH CEN AD)

THIRD QUATRAIN
GALEN TAKES ARK
TO GODMERSHAM

A trusted goose. A man with a fully devout heart. And the veil between two worlds.

'This would be a whole heck of a lot easier if Galen had simply drawn an X-marks-the-spot treasure map,' she muttered.

'Had he done that, the Ark would have been unearthed centuries ago. Sir Kenneth mentioned that the encrypted quatrains have stumped more than one treasure hunter.'

'While we're on the topic, this might be a good time to mention that I'm starting to worry about Colonel MacFarlane having the Stones of Fire in his possession. You said it yourself: not only was the breastplate a protective shield, it was also used as a divination tool, enabling the wearer to communicate with God. Like a two-way radio. If MacFarlane finds the Ark of the Covenant, he'll not only have the best intelligence device known to mankind – the Stones of Fire – he'll also have an enormously powerful weapon. You can't deny that makes for a deadly duo.'

For several long seconds, Cædmon held her gaze. 'Then we'll do all in our power to ensure that doesn't happen.' Although the words were quietly spoken, he had about him an air of fierce determination. For one brief, blurry second, she saw him decked out in chain mail, fighting to the death on the Plain of Esdraelon.

Returning his attention to the Edie's diagram, Cædmon tapped his finger on the fourth side of the square. 'This is where we get into really murky water.'

'Actually, this is where we need to call it quits,' she matter-of-factly announced, unable to keep the jet lag at bay one second longer.

Cædmon patted her on the back. 'Come now. Time to brainstorm. Group dynamics and all that.'

She dolefully shook her head. 'I need to refuel. How about we get grab some pub grub? If I remember correctly, they're serving seafood salad and lentil soup at the Isis Room.'

'Er, right. An excellent suggestion.'

Not for one second was Edie fooled, able to see the disappointment in Cædmon's blue eyes. He might be able to manage an all-nighter, but there was no way she could tackle the fourth quatrain without some much-needed food. Followed by some much-needed sleep.

While Cædmon returned the leather-bound

volumes and cotton gloves to the stern-faced librarian, Edie stuffed the pencils and notepaper into their flight bag.

A few minutes later, Cædmon's protective arm around her shoulders, they made their way along the crowded pavement. Locals, heads ducked against the cold wet wind, scurried along. Casting a quick sideways glance down a shadowed alleyway, Edie had the sudden feeling that something malevolent, even deadly, lurked nearby.

'. . . at which time Galen of Godmersham succumbed to the Black Death, the great plague of 1348.'

With his pointer Marshall Mendolson underlined the last line of the third quatrain. He had given in and begun deciphering the verses. These guys were a tough crowd, the older dude with the buzz cut the scariest of them all. He wanted the goods, no two ways about it. Marshall doubted the guy even knew his name. Earlier he had overheard one of his steroid-enhanced bodyguards refer to him as 'the lil Harvard prick'.

'And the fourth quatrain, what of it?' his benefactor pressed, making no attempt to hide his impatience.

Marshall struck a thoughtful pose, doing a fair imitation of one of his favourite Harvard professors. 'Hmm . . . good question.' And one he had no intention of truthfully answering.

Did these Neanderthals really think they could outsmart a Harvard graduate?

It had taken only a cursory reading of Galen's verses for him to figure out that the *arca* in the third quatrain was an oblique reference to the Ark of the

Covenant. *Not* the medieval chest the head dude had hired him to find. These guys wanted him to hunt down the Ark of the Covenant so they could cash in on it, his cut being a paltry seventy thousand dollars. After he paid off his student loans, there wouldn't be enough left for a Happy Meal at McDonald's.

Yeah, well, think again.

Jesus. The freaking Ark of the Covenant. According to the Bible, the Ark could raze fortified cities, part seas and kick some serious ass. And if you believed *that*, he had some mountain property in Florida to sell you. Although you didn't have to be a Bible thumper to know that the Ark of the Covenant was a treasure of immeasurable worth. As in more money than he could ever count.

Hello, Tahiti and a life of indolent leisure surrounded by bare-breasted island beauties.

Given that his mother had once sued the Fairfax County school board over the 'one nation under God' phrase in the pledge of allegiance – the groundswell of religious fervour nearly swallowing Adele Mendolson whole – his finding the Ark of the Covenant would be ironic, to say the least.

This one's for you, Mother.

'The "goos" reference in the fourth quatrain is pretty straightforward,' he answered after a long drawn-out pause, figuring some straight talk in order, every good lie cloaked in the truth.

'You're talking about the goose that laid the golden egg, right?' This from the brawny bruiser named

Boyd, the man straddling an expensive Sheraton chair like a lap dancer straddling a paying crotch.

'Very good, Sir Rambo. Go to the head of the class.' A measured half-beat later, he mockingly exclaimed, '*Not!*' At that moment he wanted nothing more than to smash the muscled behemoth's face into the floorboards. As had been done to him by countless bullies in years gone by.

Knowing he could go only so far, he switched gears, once more the erudite Harvard grad. 'In the medieval lexicon, the goose represented vigilance. And given the fact that Galen composed his quatrains just prior to his death, it specifically means vigilance *in* death.'

Liking the sound of that, Marshall smiled, having just figured out how he could outmanoeuvre his benefactor. 'Line two of the last quatrain is simply a "Woe is me" commentary on the plague,' he continued, barely able to suppress an excited grin. 'That takes us to line three, which is an offhand reference to Saint —'

'I want to know where Galen hid his chest,' the older dude hissed, his eyes narrowing as he stared him down.

'Well, now, that *is* the sixty-four-thousand-dollar question, isn't it?' Or a thousand times that amount.

It was all he could do not to break into song. Like the bearded Tevye in *Fiddler on the Roof*. Except he really would be a rich man. No if about it.

Stepping over to his laptop, Marshall clicked

several keys, projecting the next slide – a page from a nearly-seven-hundred-year-old document – onto the wall. 'From the Feet of Fines record I discovered that Galen donated a hefty number of golden objects to –' he snatched his handwritten notes from the table '– St Lawrence the Martyr church in Godmersham. That being the "holy blissful martir" of the fourth quatrain. Like most medieval men, Galen no doubt believed that he could buy his way into heaven.' *Or bribe his way into heaven, depending on your point of view.* 'Put it all together and my guess is that Galen, quite literally, took the *arca* to his grave.'

The older dude chewed on that for a few seconds. Then, obviously an anal sort who liked to verify the facts, he said, 'Are you saying that the gold chest is buried in Galen of Godmersham's tomb at St Lawrence the Martyr church?'

'Yup. That's as good a hypothesis as any.' Seeing a flash of annoyance on his benefactor's face, he hastily added, 'It was the custom of the time to wrap a corpse in linen, that being the "veyl bitwixen worlds tweye". Aka the veil between two worlds.'

Marshall inwardly breathed a sigh of relief. Although crafted on the fly, the lie had the ring of truth about it. Actually, when the Ark had been housed in Solomon's Temple, inside the Holy of Holies, a veil had been hung in front of it to keep it hidden, the "veyl" in Galen's last quatrain referring to the Ark not a medieval death shroud.

While the quatrains provided scant clues, he

figured the Ark was really hidden inside the church under a statue of the martyred St Lawrence. Or maybe behind a plaque or wall carving. Which is why he intended to steer the old dude and his three big bad bears away from the church itself, focusing instead on the adjacent cemetery. Then, once his benefactor had given up the search, he would return on the sly to St Lawrence the Martyr and lay claim to the prize.

A drum roll, please ...

'Galen of Godmersham's tomb – you're completely certain of this?'

'Certain enough,' he retorted, not liking the way he was being hauled over the coals.

A man clearly accustomed to giving orders, the older dude brusquely gestured to the paper-laden table. 'Pack it up. We leave in ten minutes.'

44

'I don't know about you, but I'm not a big fan of dark and dreary weather,' Edie grumbled. For the last few minutes she'd been standing guard at their hotel window, closely monitoring the courtyard below, relieved they weren't in a ground-floor room.

Relieved because her sixth sense told her that they were being watched.

Although, given that she had zilch in the way of psychic ability, she couldn't rule out the possibility that her intuition was nothing more than irrational fear.

Busying himself with placing pencils and paper on the small circular table tucked into the oriel window on the other side of the room, Cædmon glanced over at her. 'Small wonder we English are such a gloomy lot.'

'The Mahler doesn't help.' Turning her head from the window, Edie pointedly glanced at the small radio on the bedside table. The incessant sound of rain striking cobblestones competed with the ponderous strains of the Sixth Symphony in A minor.

'Ah, but it doesn't hurt.' Cædmon had earlier informed her that the drippy classical music helped him to think. Something about musical notes and higher maths.

Preferring rhythm and blues, Macy Gray her favourite singer, Edie let it go. There were worse faults than questionable taste in music.

With a quick tug, she pulled the damask curtains across the window. That done, she glanced around the small hotel room. As had repeatedly happened since they checked in, her gaze landed on the king-sized bed under its red-striped coverlet. Evidently a hotel room with two doubles was unheard of in England, the receptionist staring at her as though she were bonkers when she made the request.

She averted her gaze.

If she overlooked the bed – and it was darned difficult – the room had a warm, inviting feel to it. Ivory-coloured walls punctuated with dark wood beams and lots of pleated floral fabric. In a nod to the season, a ribbon-strewn garland hung above the door.

Again she glanced at the bed.

'Yes, I know,' Cædmon said, seeing the direction of her gaze. 'Rather imposing, isn't it?'

'It's just that we're not ... You know.' She fought the urge to look away, the unspoken topic of sex rearing its tempting head.

Cædmon held her gaze a second too long. Although her dating skills were rusty, she had the distinct impression that he was silently asking. When no answer was forthcoming, he strode over to the foot of the bed. His jaw tight, he placed a palm on either side of the mattress and . . .

. . . separated the double into two single beds.

'Not certain what we should do about the bedding.' He gestured to the red coverlet sagging between the beds.

Acting on a hunch, Edie walked over to the wardrobe, opened it and removed two sets of single sheets. 'We're in luck. There's sheets stowed away for this very emergency.' She tossed the folded sheets onto the bed. 'Don't worry. I'll take care of it later.'

If he was disappointed, he hid it well.

'Afraid we'll have to share the loo. My powers don't extend beyond dividing the bed.' Turning away from the coverlet, he reached for the bottle of port. 'For some reason, I feel oddly buoyed by our progress today. Like a medieval monk who's completed his duties and can now sit down to a jug of wine in the full knowledge that he has earned his simple pleasure.' As he spoke, Cædmon inserted a corkscrew into the top of the bottle, having procured the implement from reception.

A wet *plunk!* ensued as the cork slid from the bottle. He poured.

Holding a glass in each hand, he walked over to where she stood. 'I apologize that the port isn't decanted. Since we're slumming it, we must make do.' Then, smiling, 'Careful. This stuff is dangerously gluggable.'

Edie took the proffered glass. Returning his smile,

she took a sip of the ruby-coloured wine. 'Yum. This stuff *is* gluggable.'

Cædmon laughed, the sound deep, rich, inviting. A lot like the port wine, it made her smile.

'Now, to the task at hand.' He motioned to the oriel window and the small circular table. 'Hopefully, we'll be able to yoke together the last four lines of verse.'

Not sure how much help she would be, her brain working in slo-mo due to the jet lag, Edie seated herself in one of the two wingback chairs wedged into the projecting window. Having a funny feeling that the port wine wasn't going to help, she stared at the last four lines of translated text.

The trusted goose sorely wept for all of them were dead
I know not how the world be served by such adversity
But if a man with a fully devout heart seek the blessed martyr
There in the veil between two worlds, the hidden truth be found

Using her index finger as a pointer, she underscored the first line. 'Undoubtedly, a thinly disguised reference to Mother Goose.' Tongue literally in cheek, she winked at him.

All business, Cædmon circled 'goose' with a pencil. 'The words "goose" and "swan" were interchangeable in the medieval lexicon, the goose symbolic of vigilance. In the light of all that we know, that makes complete and utter sense.'

'It does? Sorry, but I'm not following.'

'Remember that Galen took upon himself the role of Ark guardian, vigilance *the* most important attribute of a sentinel.'

'And let's not forget that the quatrains were also Galen's swansong.'

Cædmon glanced at her glass as if to enquire, *Just how much of that stuff have you had?*

Edie pushed her glass aside. 'Sir Kenneth mentioned that everyone in Godmersham except for Galen's wife succumbed to the plague. So, I'm guessing that's the gist of line two.'

'That looks to be a correct assumption. As for the third line —' lifting his glass, Cædmon took a measured sip '— it's the typical admonition one finds in any medieval tale.'

'Only the knight who is pure of heart can seek the Holy Grail, right?'

'Mmmm, quite.'

Slowly, he drummed his fingers on the table, lost in thought.

A few moments later the tapping increased to a rapid *rat-a-tat-tat*.

'I take it that's a good sign.'

'So good it makes my bollocks tingle,' he replied bawdily, slapping his palm on the tabletop. 'Unless I'm mistaken, the bloody "blessed martyr" is none other than St Lawrence the Martyr.'

Edie searched her memory banks, the name vaguely familiar. It took a second for her to access the correct data file, the one about Galen donating a slew of 'sacred relics' to the local church. 'Ohmygosh! Galen hid the Ark at —'

'St Lawrence the Martyr church!' they exclaimed in unison, grinning at each other.

'According to the Old Testament accounts,' Cædmon excitedly continued, underlining the last line of the quatrain with his finger, 'when the Ark of the Covenant was placed inside Solomon's Temple, in the Holy of Holies, a veil was placed over the entrance to shield that most sacred place. The expression "beyond the veil" was thus coined because no one, not even the priests, could enter that sacred space.'

'Which means that the last line is a direct reference to the Ark.' When he nodded, she switched gears entirely. 'Okay, when do leave?'

'We don't have a coach timetable. However, I suspect we can be in Godmersham by early tomorrow afternoon. Sooner if we hire a car.'

'Gee, I'm surprised you don't want to leave tonight. It's only pouring down rain out there,' she teased.

'While I refuse to entertain the notion that MacFarlane may yet steal the prize, we need our rest.'

On that point they were in complete agreement.

'Do you think the church is still standing?'

'Difficult to say. Any number of churches and monasteries were destroyed during the Reformation and the Civil War. Tomorrow will be soon enough to ascertain if St Lawrence the Martyr is intact.'

'Even if it's still there, we have no idea *where* in or around the church the Ark is hidden.'

'I never said this would be an easy venture.' Pushing back his chair, Cædmon rose to his feet. As he walked over to the divided bed, one of Bach's melancholy cello suites droned from the radio. Edie thought it sounded like a funeral march.

Ignoring the music, she surreptitiously watched as Cædmon took a packet of biscuits from the bedside table. No doubt about it, Cædmon Aisquith was very much his own man, his quirky intellectualism strangely appealing. As he headed back to the oriel, biscuits in hand, Edie could see that something was wrong, his expression not nearly as ebullient as it had been seconds before.

'Uh oh. What happened? You're no longer in a John Philip Sousa mood.'

Cædmon handed her the packet of chocolate-covered biscuits. 'Here, tuck in.'

'You're not going to have one?'

Waving them away, he reseated himself at the table. 'Something about the solution is too neat and tidy. Too bloody obvious.'

'Maybe Galen wanted the solution to be obvious.'

'Had that been his intention, he would never have gone to the trouble of writing the quatrains.'

Her sweet tooth having also gone south, she put the biscuits aside.

'Yeah, I see your point.' She stared at the quatrain.

'Maybe a not-so-neat solution will come to you in the morning.'

'Or to you. Your chain-of-custody box showed a marked talent for analytical reasoning.'

Edie smiled. 'You liked that, huh?'

'It's one of many things that I like about you.'

Cædmon's reply made her instantly regret the parting of the red bed.

'Well, what do you know? I like you too.' A great deal, in fact. Maybe more than she should, given that she knew so little about him. Other than he had once attended Oxford, had worked for MI5 and recently wrote a book, she knew nothing about Cædmon Aisquith. A man of mystery was one thing. A man without a past was something else entirely.

But then she'd not been very forthcoming herself.

'Cædmon, there's something I've been meaning to tell you,' she blurted without preamble.

His blue eyes locked on to hers.

Edie took a deep breath, bracing herself for the backlash.

'I lied to you.'

45

'Nothing here but a bunch of old bones.'

Stan MacFarlane shone his Maglite into the open grave, in which his man stood chest deep. Scattered at Braxton's booted feet were the mortal remains of Galen of Godmersham. And a whole lot of mud, the grave quickly filling with water. Earlier the night sky had opened up, the rain coming down in buckets.

Stan next shone his torch into the face of the Harvard scholar, who stood shivering on the other side of the grave, the beam casting a golden light onto the driving rain.

'You told me it would be here.'

'Based on the quatrains, I thought there was a good possibility that the gold chest would be found in Galen's grave.' His paid medieval expert, beginning to look like a wet rat, shrugged. 'What can I say? We played the odds and lost.'

'Could you have misinterpreted the quatrains?'

The scholar rubbed the back of his neck. 'Hmm . . . it's possible, but . . . I really thought I correctly deciphered them. That's the tricky thing about Middle English, it's all about layered meaning. Hey, do you guys mind if I sit inside the Range Rover? I'm gonna catch my death if I stand out here much longer.'

Tuning out the man's whiny-ass complaints, Stan carefully considered his next move, knowing it was a move twenty-five years in the making. For it was twenty-five years ago that the archangels Michael and Gabriel had appeared to him soon after the blast in Beirut. Sent by God to pull him from the rubble.

The terror attack on the marine barracks had been the first of the signs that the End Times were near.

Saved in body, and more importantly in spirit, he had given his life over to God's work. Not once had he shirked his duty, commissioned with the task of building God's holy army here on earth. What had begun as an informal prayer group in the First Gulf War had become a twenty-thousand-strong faith-based force by the time the tanks rolled into Baghdad eleven years later.

Twenty-five years had come and gone, yet his mission was still incomplete.

God had something great and glorious intended for him.

But *only* if he uncovered the Ark.

The Ark was the key that would unlock the gates of the Millennial Kingdom.

The Ark was the weapon that would destroy the Muslim infidels.

Just as it had destroyed the Canaanites, and the Hittites, and the Jebusites.

'You know, I'm as stumped as you.' The scholar had apparently decided not to go back to the Range Rover.

His train of thought interrupted, Stan realized that the remark didn't ring true, the other man too pat. Too well rehearsed. As though it were a gun aimed at point-blank range, Stan shone the Maglite at the scrawny man's face. Pupils quickly contracted into black dots. 'Why do I suddenly not believe you?'

'You're kidding, right?' The other man affected a theatrical look of stunned disbelief. 'What reason would I have to lie? I need the cash to pay off my loans.'

'I can think of any number of reasons why you might lie to me.' Stan continued to shine the light at the other man's face. As though he were boring a hole right through the middle of his forehead.

'Look, I thought for certain the Ark would be – I mean the gold chest would be buried with Galen.'

'What did you just say?' The beam of light drilled that much deeper.

'*Arca*. I said *arca*. As in "Arca and gold ful shene he carried to the toun he was born." Remember the third quatrain?'

The truth revealed, Stan stared at the scholar, contempt washing over him in waves.

Sensing the winds had suddenly shifted, the Harvard scholar nervously glanced at the car. No doubt trying to remember if the keys had been left in the ignition.

'You can't outrun a bullet,' Boyd Braxton jeered, having climbed out of the grave.

Judge and jury, Stan pointed an accusing finger.

'"And then shall the wicked be revealed, whom the Lord shall consume with the spirit of his mouth, and shall destroy with the brightness of his coming."'

Surprisingly belligerent, the other man pointed a finger right back at him. 'You're a fucking lunatic, that's what you are!'

'Unkind words for the man who holds your fate in his hands.'

The Harvard scholar glanced at the Israeli-made Desert Eagle automatic pistol negligently held in the gunnery sergeant's right hand, belligerence now replaced with fear. Cowardly, snivelling fear.

'You're right, dude. Heat of the moment. Sorry. And just to prove that I'm still part of the team, I think I know where the Ark is hidden.' The scholar jutted his chin towards the small church nestled on the other side of the cemetery. 'When you guys did your earlier security check in the church, I caught sight of a *very* large marble plaque depicting the martyrdom of St Lawrence.' Spreading his arms, the other man indicated an expanse of some four feet. 'I'm guessing that if we pry that mother off the wall, we'll find the Ark hidden behind it.'

'Pray that we do.'

46

'Back in DC,' Edie clarified, not wanting Cædmon to think she'd lied to him recently.

'A lie would certainly explain your embarrassment.'

'Actually, you've got it all wrong. I'm not the least bit embarrassed that I lied; I'm thoroughly ashamed.' And, as he undoubtedly knew, shame was embarrassment on steroids.

'Did you lie about Padge's murder?'

'What!' Edie vehemently shook her head, the image of Dr Padgham's sprawled, lifeless body flashing across her mind's eye. 'No, of course not. I lied about my, um, family background.'

Crossing his legs at the knee, Cædmon sat silent, waiting for her to fill in the blanks. If he was upset or disappointed by the fact he'd been lied to, he gave no indication of it.

'Remember how I told you that my parents were killed in a boating accident off the coast of Florida? Well that story was ... well, it was a flat-out lie. I can't speak for my father, but my mother never stepped in anything that ever floated on the water.'

She snatched a mandarin orange from the bowl on the table. Hands shaking, she began to peel it, if for no other reason than to give her suddenly sweaty fingers something to do. *God, I feel lousy.* Unbelievably, she'd just told Cædmon Aisquith more about her childhood than she'd ever told another living soul.

'Did you lie to elicit my sympathy?'

Edie stopped peeling.

'No! Absolutely not!'

Knowing why she had told the lie, but not altogether certain why she suddenly wanted to tell the truth, Edie abandoned the orange and got up from the table. Maybe she was sick and tired of going to bed with men under false pretences. Slowly, trying to collect her thoughts, she paced back and forth in front of the divided twin mattresses. Out of the corner of her eye, she noticed Cædmon finishing his glass of port.

She stopped. Turning towards him, she said, 'Were they still alive, there's not a single member of my family that I would be proud to introduce to you. I just . . . I just wanted a normal, sane, loving family. Was that so wrong?'

Cædmon shook his head. 'It is what we all long for.'

'Yeah, it is, isn't it? But those weren't the cards I was given.' Realizing how clichéd and melodramatic that sounded, she decided to just stick to the facts. No emotion. No drama queen theatrics.

'Okay, here it is. The unedited version of the story is that my mother Melissa was addicted to heroin, and bad men, and playing the state lottery. And just so you don't jump to the conclusion that she was a horrible person, it wasn't completely her fault. She grew up in a very repressive evangelical household. Unfortunately, she fell in love with a Jewish boy in her geometry class. Pops didn't approve. So he kicked her out of the house. She was sixteen years old.'

'I take it the ill-fated lover was your father?'

Edie derisively snorted. 'Hmph! Don't I wish?' *Maybe things would have turned out different if Jacob Steiner had been my father.*

'According to my mother, there was a freak car accident. A strong gust of wind caused the vehicle to swerve into a tree. Jacob died, she survived.'

'Is that when your mother turned to drugs?'

Edie nodded. 'The grief nearly did her in. At least that's the excuse she gave for not being able to pull it together. Oh, every now and again she'd clean up her act. In fact, she cleaned up real good. But then –' Edie snapped her fingers '– just like that, she'd start to reek of stale beer and vomit.'

Which was about the same time that strange men started to show up, the thin walls of the trailer doing little to muffle the grunts and groans.

'I suppose I should mention at this juncture that my mother had no idea who fathered me. She thought it might have been "the guy with the Harley".' Using her fingers, Edie made a pair of air quotes. 'But that's mere speculation.'

Having just confessed to being illegitimate, Edie

stared at the worn carpet beneath her feet. She could only imagine what Cædmon thought of her. He probably hailed from a snooty English household. Something straight out of *The Forsyte Saga*.

'It sounds as though your mother had a tragic life,' he quietly remarked.

'Try tragically flawed. Anyway, it wasn't a long life. She overdosed on her twenty-eighth birthday. I found her on the floor of our trailer, the Allman Brothers song "Sweet Melissa" playing on a second-hand tape recorder. They say that only the good die young, but . . .' She waved away the thought. 'Never mind. I'm not really sure where I was going with that.' She sat down on the edge of the bed, suddenly very tired.

'How old were you when your mother died?'

'Hmm?' She belatedly realized that Cædmon had asked a question. 'Oh, eleven.' *Eleven going on forty.*

'If you don't mind my asking, what happened to you when your mother died?'

Gnawing on her lower lip, Edie debated whether or not to tell him. But like a runaway train that couldn't put on the brakes, she went ahead and answered the question put to her.

'I was put into a foster home. There were five of us. Some older, some younger. The older ones knew the drill, the younger ones were clueless.'

Cædmon's brow furrowed. 'What drill? You've lost me.'

'Lonny Wilkerson, my foster father, the man who

signed a contract with the state of Florida agreeing to furnish me with a safe, clean and healthy home, had a fondness for young girls.'

'Bloody bastard! Don't tell me that he —'

'I have to tell you,' she interjected. *Please, Cædmon. Let me tell my story. Let me give birth to this hideous memory. In the hopes that I can finally be free of it.*

'One night Lonny came into the room that I shared with the two older kids and he ... he put his hand over my mouth, he pulled down my panties and he ... he raped me.' As she spoke, she kept her eyes downcast. She didn't want Cædmon's sympathy. She didn't want his outrage. She just wanted a witness. 'To this day I can't recall any of the details. It was too much to process. All I can remember is that it was painful, it was quick, and I was afraid I would suffocate.'

Taking a deep breath, she glanced up at him. Just as she had guessed, his expression was equal parts anger and sorrow.

'That's all I remember,' she said with a shrug. 'That and the fact it happened once a week for the next two months. When Lonny moved on to a new girl, she told the social worker what was happening, and we were all moved to different homes.'

Edie paused, battling the old recriminations.

'I should have been the one to expose that monster but —' she laughed caustically, '— I was afraid of being abandoned. Of having to make a new start.' *Yet again.*

'You were a child,' Cædmon insisted.

She shook her head, unwilling to discuss the point. 'Anyway, to make a long story not nearly so long, a few years later a social worker took pity and tracked down my maternal grandparents. I stayed with them until I was eighteen years of age.' And then, like her mother before her, she took a Greyhound bus out of Cheraw. Never to return.

Getting up from the table, Cædmon walked over to where she sat on the edge of the bed. Wordlessly, he sat down beside her, his hip brushing against hers.

'Don't get me wrong or anything. I'm not some emotionally scarred person who can't cope with the real world,' she matter-of-factly informed him. 'I cope just fine.'

'Yes, I know. But memories have a way of creeping up when you least expect them.'

Something in his voice made Edie think he spoke from experience. Maybe his childhood hadn't been Masterpiece Theater wonderful after all.

'You looked into hell at a tender age, but somehow, out of your pain, you found a way to survive.' As he spoke, Cædmon took her hand. 'You are a remarkable woman, Edie Miller.'

'Remarkable enough that you want to go to bed with me?' Turning her head, Edie looked him straight in the eye. 'You see, that's why I came clean. Every relationship I've ever had has been wrapped in a lie. This time I wanted a clean slate.'

Cædmon let go of her hand. 'Are you sure that's

what you want, for the two of us to sleep together?'

Edie watched the conflicting emotions on Cædmon's face. At times, and this was one of them, he could be too much the gentleman.

'I came very close to climbing into bed with you the other night. And just so you know, this isn't a puzzle that you can reason your way through. It's just sex, okay?'

Seeing the uncertainty in his eyes replaced with desire, Edie rose to her feet and stepped towards the bedside table.

Cædmon grabbed her by the wrist, stopping her in mid-step.

'Where are you going?' There was a decided huskiness in his normally cultured voice.

'I thought I'd switch off the lamp.'

He pulled her onto his lap.

'Leave the light on.'

47

Having verified that the gaping hole in the church wall was indeed empty, Stan sat down wearily on the nearest pew. The powerful Maglite cast an otherworldly glow over the small parish church. Looking down from the windows, stained-glass saints silently castigated him. His two men, one holding a sledgehammer, the other a pickaxe, stood at the ready, waiting for orders.

For the first time in twenty-five years Stan was worried that he might not be able to fulfil his obligations to God. With the Ark in his possession, he could change the destiny of the world according to God's holy plan. But first he had to find it.

I have to find the Ark.

Those six words reverberated in his head like an emergency message playing on a continuous loop.

He pushed himself off the pew. A soldier of God would not, could not, surrender.

As he stepped towards his men, he kicked aside several pieces of broken marble, the centuries-old bas-relief detailing the life of St Lawrence destroyed. The thick Saxon wall had not given up without a fight, nearly an hour of labour required to expose the glaringly empty cavity.

Stan straightened his shoulders, ready to fight the next battle. His rest would come when the mission was completed.

'Looks like we've hit another dead end, huh?'

Stan turned his attention to the Harvard scholar. Stoop-shouldered and shivering, he stood next to the pile of shattered stone.

'Yes, my thoughts exactly.'

Suddenly realizing that all was not right in the world, the scholar's gaze furtively moved from man to man. If it had not occurred to him before, it did now. He was outnumbered three to one.

'Hey, fellas! Why so grim? The clues are there, embedded in the quatrains. We just need to go back to the drawing board.' When he received no reply, the scholar held his arms out, motioning to each of them in turn. 'All for one and one for all, right?' When that received no reply, he tried a different tack. 'I say we talk this over. All those in favour of peace talks, raise your hand.'

Stan wordlessly stared at the scholar. The snivelling pansy wanted to shake hands, forget their differences and begin again.

'There is nothing more to be said.'

Intuiting that his death sentence had just been issued, the scholar turned on his heel. Like a church mouse scurrying in the shadows, he ran towards the porch doors at the end of the nave.

'You lil fuckwad!' Dropping the pickaxe, Boyd

Braxton reached for the .357 Desert Eagle secured in the holster under his arm.

Stan slapped a hand on the gunny's raised forearm. 'Not in the house of God,' he ordered sternly.

'Yes, sir!'

Their weapons drawn, his men raced from the church in pursuit of the scholar who had betrayed them.

In no particular hurry, knowing the prey would soon be cornered, Stan headed for the double doors at the back of the church. Tomorrow morning the denizens of the small hamlet of Godmersham would wonder at the jumbled pile of stone. Teenage vandals would be blamed. No doubt an endless series of jumble sales would be held to pay for the damage.

Stuffing his Maglite under his arm, he reached into his trouser pocket and removed a gold money clip. He quickly unpeeled three hundred-dollar Franklins and shoved them into the wooden slit of the collection box.

Amends made, he stepped outside, pleased to note that the rain had finally faded to a manageable drizzle. In the adjacent cemetery he saw a bobbing pinpoint of red light, the laser beam from the gunny's pistol. He headed in that direction.

Trapped en route to the Range Rover, the scholar now stood before Galen of Godmersham's open grave, his arms raised in surrender.

'"God swiftly traps the wicked,"' Stan murmured.

Boyd Braxton placed the muzzle of his Desert Eagle against the other man's temple. 'I think we're gonna have to rename him Mister Twinkletoes.'

'Do you guys have any idea of the sentence for murder?' the scholar wheezed, his arms wavering in mid-air. Like bed sheets flapping in the breeze.

'I answer only to God's law,' Stan replied. Then, giving the scholar an opportunity to atone for his depraved existence, '"Except ye repent, ye shall die in your sins."'

'Hey, I didn't do anything wrong! You're the guys sneaking around, breaking into churches, carrying guns. I'm just a debt-ridden grad student trying to make an honest –'

'Man up! For you are soon to meet your maker.'

'Christ! Don't do this! I'm begging you to –' The soliloquy was cut short by a mewling whimper.

'Whew! Somebody needs a diaper,' Boyd Braxton muttered, the scholar having lost control of his bowels.

Disgusted, Stan nodded at the former gunnery sergeant. 'Kill him. He is an abomination unto the Lord.'

A single shot reverberated in the night.

Like the tolling of a church bell.

'Now *that's* convenient,' the gunny remarked, gesturing with his gun barrel to the near-headless body crumpled in the bottom of the grave. Stuffing the powerful pistol into his holster, he bent at the waist and retrieved a shovel. 'All in a day's work, huh, sir?'

'God derives no pleasure from the death of the wicked. Neither should you.'

His faith renewed, Stan knew that Eid al-Adha was four days and counting. Time enough to find the Ark. Like the good marine that he was, he had a contingency plan.

'Has Sanchez checked in yet?' Sanchez was the man tasked with surveillance in Oxford.

'About three hours ago, sir. Aisquith and the woman are holed up in a hotel. Sanchez snagged the room next to theirs. Since there's an adjoining door between the two rooms, he's keeping an eye on the pair with a peephole video camera.'

'Relieve Sanchez,' he said to Braxton. 'I want hourly status reports. If the Brit so much as sneezes into a snot rag, I want to know about it.'

48

'Leave the light on.'

His request, not hers.

Believing sex an act of give and take, she'd wordlessly complied.

The golden glow from the bedside lamp illuminating their every move, they had undressed one another, fingers and hands slightly trembling. Both of them succumbing to a nervous hesitancy. A bashful sort of voyeurism as more and more flesh was revealed. *Torso. Breast. Pelvis. Thigh.* Until they finally faced one another, completely and disarmingly naked. Edie was acutely aware of her own body. Her breasts brushing against her inner arm. Her puckered nipples. The slight quiver in her knees. It'd been three years since her last lover. She wondered if she measured up.

'You are lovely.'

Pleased with the compliment, Edie stepped forward. Needing to make contact, she ran her hands over his chest, surprised to discover that he had the lean, tight build of a younger man. Moving closer, she pressed her mouth against the pulse at the base of his throat. Able to feel the blood course through him with each rapid beat of his heart.

He was nervous.

For some strange reason that excited her.

Bending her head, she brushed his nipple with her tongue. Teetering slightly, Cædmon moaned her name, the cultured accent nowhere in evidence. She bit into his pectoral muscle.

'I just put my mark on you,' she murmured, tilting her head to one side as she admired her handiwork.

'Two can play at that game.' Warning issued, he slid his hand between her legs, possessively cupping her mons. A moment later, he smiled. She was already wet.

Maybe not so nervous after all.

Feeling an insistent nudge against her abdomen, Edie glanced down. For several seconds she stared brazenly. *Now who was smiling?* With his fully erect penis and ginger curls, he put her in mind of a lusty Viking.

A lusty Viking who liked Beethoven, the strains of a piano concerto drifting across the room from the clock radio. Thinking she needed to introduce Cædmon to R & B, she placed her hands on his shoulders. Taking the lead, she slowly backed him to the divided bed. When the backs of his knees hit a mattress, she shoved him to a seated position. She then straddled his hips.

Caedmon's hands glided along the tops of her thighs, up the sides of her ribcage, before finally stopping at her breasts. A nipple popped between the V of his fingers. It was a strangely beautiful sight. She was glad they had left the light on.

Intuiting what she wanted, his hands slid back to her waist. His eyes having turned an iridescent shade of blue, he helped her to find the right angle.

'Ready?'

'Set, go,' she replied, wrapping a guiding hand around him.

Taking her time, she seated herself, biting back a yelp as her body stretched and widened. The slow, steady expansion bordered on pain.

'Lie back on the bed,' she ordered. A second later, her hands on his chest, she started to move. Gripping her thighs, Cædmon groaned, the guttural sound competing with the strident piano chords in the background.

Edie clenched her muscles. Then released. The movement merited another groan. Cædmon's grip tightened. *Go faster.*

Heeding the silent request, she picked up the pace, her buttocks slamming against his crotch with each downward stroke. She started to pant, sight and sound coalescing into a synchronized blur. *Bouncing breasts. Bunched muscles. Pulsating veins on the backs of his hands.* All of it accompanied by a frenzied piano crescendo.

Her fingers dug into his shoulders. The achy fullness between her legs tightened.

Until . . .

She came. Quickly. Powerfully. Cædmon held her gaze, silently pleading with her to keep moving. Reaching behind her, she touched him. Then watched as he shuddered, his eyes rolling to the back of his head.

The crisis passed, Edie fell forward, crash-landing on his torso. Tears in her eyes, she struggled to catch her breath. Her damp cheek nestled against his, she laughed softly.

'I don't know about you, but I now have a whole new appreciation for classical music.'

49

Cædmon raised a hand to his mouth, stifling a yawn.

'Sorry. I'm a bit knackered. Last night was ...'
He laughed softly. 'No need to tell you. You were
there.'

Walking alongside him as they made their way
down High Street, Edie nudged him in the ribs. 'Was
I ever.'

Their paltry belongings stuffed into the Virgin
shoulder bag, they had checked out of the hotel
immediately after breakfast. The plan being to take a
coach to Heathrow and there hire a car for the drive
to Godmersham, they were presently en route to
Gloucester Green. The receptionist had informed
them that the airport coaches left every twenty
minutes. Cædmon and Edie were nevertheless agreed
that St Lawrence the Martyr church might well prove
a false lead.

He glanced at his watch. Half past seven. It explained why High Street was nearly deserted. Smiling,
Edie pressed closer. Returning the smile, like most
men in the initial throes of lust he wondered if he
fancied Edie a bit *too* much, his thoughts frequently
settling upon her.

The events of the previous evening had unfurled

so quickly, he could only call them to mind in flashes. The quiet hum of rain pounding against the window-panes. The not so quiet guttural moans and lusty sighs. Round one had ended in an exhausted tangle. Round two had been more subtle, more seductive. They'd eaten mandarin oranges in bed, Edie squirting the juice onto his lower abdomen then lapping it up with her tongue, a mass of curly hair falling to either side of his hips. Unable to control himself, he'd grabbed her head and pushed her lower. The pleasure that ensued had been near unbearable.

'You're smiling. Broadly, I might add. Just what the heck are you thinking about?'

'Hmm?' He glanced at his companion, seeing breasts like smooth melons, legs falling open to expose an overripe fig. 'I am contemplating the most erotic fruit bowl imaginable,' he replied.

Edie laughed, no prude. 'I hear tell you guys have one of those thoughts every ten seconds. Amazing that you ever get anything accomplished.'

'A pencilled list helps greatly.'

She laughed all the harder.

As he'd already discovered, understanding Edie Miller was one thing, sorting her out another thing altogether. Her early life had been one of abuse and betrayal. And unfathomable pain. Yet somehow she had persevered.

Simply put, he was awed by her strength.

'What if we actually find the Ark of the Covenant hidden at the church?' Edie asked out of the proverbial blue. 'Have you given any thought as to what we would do with it?'

In truth, he'd given this scant consideration, focusing instead on deciphering the quatrains.

'I mean do we hand it over to a museum? Or do we give it to a church or synagogue?'

'Perhaps we should wait until we find the Ark,' he answered evasively.

'Or maybe you intend to keep it for yourself,' she pressed, refusing to let the matter drop. 'Fodder for your next book.'

'Bloody hell! I must have talked in my sleep.'

'I'm serious, Cædmon. So far, you've refused to give me any answer as to why we're on this insane quest.'

'I believe you've just hit the nail square on the head. It's a quest, is it not? Like a knight of old, I seek knowledge and enlightenment.'

'Oh, puh-*lease*.' Her voice fair dripped with derision. 'Henceforth, Sir Gawain, I would appreciate it if you gave me a straight answer rather than a sound bite.'

Cædmon inwardly cringed at the comparison. In later Grail legends, Sir Gawain, possessed of a singular arrogance, failed to grasp the holiness of the quest. He suspected that Edie had purposely plucked the name from the Round Table cast.

'All I'm saying is that we need to give this a little forethought before rushing off like a pair of fools into the great unknown. And what about MacFarlane and his holy warriors?' She stared at him, clearly apprehensive. 'What happens if we run into them while wandering around in Godmersham?'

Although most fringe groups were all mouth and no trousers, he knew MacFarlane's group to be the exception to the rule.

'Rather than succumbing to fearful imaginings, let's concentrate on finding the blasted Ark.'

A pronounced silence ensued. Uncomfortable, he feigned an interest in the passing shop windows.

'We can always go to the police,' Edie suggested, the first to break the unnerving quiet.

'And promptly be accused of two murders we didn't commit?' He forcefully shook his head. 'We can't go to the authorities unless the situation absolutely demands it.'

'And who gets to make that call, you or me?'

'We're a team, are we not?' As he spoke, he slung an arm round her shoulders, marrying trunks, hips and thighs, one to the other. '"She winters and keeps warm her note,"' he murmured into her ear, reciting the lyric from an old English song.

Edie wrapped an arm around his waist. Turning her face up, she smiled. 'Yeah, I'm with you. I much prefer to make love than war.'

50

Oh man, he wanted to fuck her.

So bad his dick had been standing on end for the last couple of hours. Ever since, peephole video camera shoved against the adjoining door, he'd had a front-row seat on what had turned out to be an unbelievable fuck fest.

At first Boyd had been pissed off he'd been given the surveillance shift. Small wonder Sanchez had been grinning when Braxton relieved him. Who the hell would have thought the curly-haired bitch had the moves of an experienced whore? It'd been all he could do not to jerk himself off against the door like a raghead in an Islamabad alleyway.

The colonel was fond of saying, 'When lust hath conceived, it bringeth forth sin. And sin, when it is finished, bringeth forth death.' The Bible verse helped to keep his lusts in check. Usually.

Placing a hand over his crotch, Boyd Braxton rearranged his equipment.

A shop assistant manhandling a bucket of flowers behind a plate-glass window glared at him. He glared right back. And continued on his merry way, Aisquith and the woman one block ahead of him. The streets practically empty of pedestrian traffic, shadowing them was a piece of cake. Besides, the red-headed Brit was too intent on whispering sweet nothing into the bitch's ear to even realize he had a tail.

On account of the audio surveillance, he knew they were headed to the local bus depot. His job was to head them off at the pass, grateful for the chance to redeem himself after the fuck-up four days ago in DC.

He adjusted his stride, quickening the pace.

As he did, his heart excitedly pounded against his breastbone.

He couldn't wait for the take-down. Knowing it would happen in ten, nine, eight . . .

51

Craning her neck to examine a shop window display, Edie caught a sudden flash of movement reflected in the plate glass.

She turned her head. First stunned, then shocked.

It was Dr Padgham's killer. No more than twenty feet behind them.

Without thinking, she pivoted on her booted heel, placed both hands on Cædmon's shoulder and shoved him as hard as possible off the pavement.

'Cædmon, run!' she screamed at the top of her lungs, realizing too late that she'd pushed him directly in front of an oncoming vehicle.

Car horns blared. Tyres screeched.

Deciding that Cædmon would be safer in the road than in the line of fire, she ran, sparing a quick glance over her shoulder.

As she had hoped, the killer, forced to choose between the two of them, decided to pursue her rather than Cædmon.

Up ahead, Edie caught sight of an aproned man pushing a trolley loaded with cardboard boxes. A second later, he disappeared into a building. Without thinking she followed, surprised to discover the entry led to an indoor shopping arcade, narrow corridors snaking out in several directions. Like he'd vanished into a big black hole, the delivery man was nowhere in sight.

Not so Padgham's killer, the behemoth having followed her into the arcade.

Edie willed her legs to move that much faster as she veered down a deserted corridor. All of the shops were closed, their darkened windows decked with Christmas greenery. *Pet supplies. Home accessories. Jewellery. Leather goods.* It all passed in a blurry flash.

Hearing a heavy footfall directly behind her, Edie, frantic, grabbed a display stand wedged into the doorway of a closed gift shop. With a yank, she hurled it to the ground. Roadblock erected, she kept on running.

A second later she heard a muttered curse. Then a crash. Evidently her pursuer had encountered the stand.

Good. She hoped the bastard broke his neck.

Catching sight of plucked and trussed birds hanging from a wall, she ran in that direction. The course adjustment took her down a different corridor, this one well lit. Several shops – a greengrocer's, a coffee emporium and a butcher's – were actually open for business, although customers were few and far between. And the ones that were afoot took no notice of the harried woman running past.

On the periphery of her senses, she became aware of an almost nauseating swirl of fused scents – Stilton cheese, ground coffee, fresh meat. As though a hundred years of smells had coalesced into one uniquely weird odour. She opened her mouth and gulped down a breath of air.

Which is when she ran headlong into a pimply-faced tattooed youth carrying a wooden box of iced fish.

'Silly cow!' the teen bellowed as iridescent fish and white blobs of crushed ice arced through the air, pelting him on the head and shoulders. A scatologically detailed rant immediately ensued.

Managing to stay upright, Edie muttered an apology as she sprinted off. Her energy flagging, her leg muscles now protested each and every forward stride. And she didn't have to turn her head to know that her pursuer was fast closing on her, the collision with the fishmonger almost wiping out her lead.

No more than ten yards away, Edie saw what looked like an exit, the bar across the steel door meaning it was for emergency use only. Fast running out of options, she raced for it. Slamming her palms onto the metal bar, she pushed for all she was worth.

The door swung open.

A heartbeat later she emerged into a narrow alley-way. At a glance she could see that there wasn't a soul in sight, only a cluster of parked delivery vans.

'Don't even think about it, bitch!'

Edie spun round. The moment she opened her mouth to scream, her assailant slapped a hand over her mouth, grabbed a fistful of hair and yanked her towards him. Slamming into his chest, Edie tried to jerk free. Anticipating the move, he let go of her hair and clamped a hand round her wrists. Smiling maliciously, he yanked her arms above her head, pulling her onto her toes. With few options left to her, Edie tried to bite the hand that covered her mouth. Smile widening, her assailant mashed her lips against her teeth. Blood gushed into her mouth. Still grinning, he shoved her between two parked vans, ramming her against a stone wall. Completely out of sight.

Unable to use her hands, Edie tried to knee him, but discovered she couldn't move her lower body, her assailant's hips and thighs pressed hard against her own. She was completely immobilized against the wall.

Oh God!

'I've got a little gift for you,' the behemoth hissed as he crudely and repeatedly shoved himself against her pelvic bone. 'Nice isn't it?'

Edie stared into his face – seeing the heavy shadow of stubble, the flared nostrils, the thick lips – noticing everything and anything in a desperate attempt to block out what he was doing to her.

Still thrusting his hips, he licked her face, his tongue moving from her jaw to her temple. 'Baby girl, I'm gonna split ya right in two.'

Like salt on a wound, old memories flashed in front of her eyes.

Terror turned to rage. This time she'd fight back.

No way in hell would she let this animal rape her. Writhing, squirming, Edie did everything she could to free herself.

'You want it bad, don't you, bitch?'

Belatedly realizing that her struggles were exciting him, Edie went still.

Within seconds the dry humping ceased.

'Fucking cock tease!' Criss-crossed veins bulged on either side of his head. Ready to blow.

Able to feel that he'd gone soft, Edie contemptuously snorted against his hand. Her would-be rapist removed his palm from her mouth. Fist balled, he pulled back his arm.

Closing her eyes, Edie braced herself for what she figured would be a bone-crushing blow.

It never came.

Instead her assailant grunted loudly as he rolled away from her. Edie opened her eyes, surprised to see blood pouring down the side of his face, gushing from those criss-crossed vessels. She was even more surprised to see Cædmon standing a few feet away, a broken bottle gripped in his right hand. Lurching forward, she ran to his side.

The stand-off lasted only a few seconds. Then, like the coward he was, the bloodied behemoth scurried away down the alley, what looked like a gun protruding from his waistband.

Edie and Cædmon stood silent, watching him depart. When he reached the end of the alleyway, he vanished.

'Did you see that? He had a gun! Why didn't he use it?'

'He may yet.' Cædmon tossed aside the broken bottle. Edie could see that he was furious.

'How did you find me?'

'I simply followed the trail of destruction.' As he spoke, Cædmon glanced up and down the alleyway, his eyes settling on a delivery man who had just emerged from the market.

'The box of fish was an accident.'

'Tell that to the fishmonger. Come on! We're wasting time.' Grabbing her by the elbow, he steered her towards a black van, *MORTON & SONS* emblazoned on the side panel in fancy Edwardian script. Exhaust fumes snaked from the silencer.

Cædmon reached for the handle on the back door.

'Get in!' he brusquely ordered. 'Before he goes!'

Edie glanced inside, surprised to see a row of trussed fowls swinging from a metal rod.

'You're kidding, right? There's no way I'm hitching a ride with a bunch of dead birds.'

'Don't make me put my boot to your arse.'

Having been manhandled enough for one day, Edie wordlessly climbed into the back of the van.

52

Positioning himself near the rear of the van, Cædmon wedged his foot against one of the double doors, ensuring they wouldn't be locked inside the refrigerated vehicle. As the van moved off, the door bounced gently against the sole of his shoe.

'How long do we have to stay cooped up in the chickenmobile?' Edie grumped, head and shoulders hunched to avoid being sideswiped by the swinging fowl overhead. She held his wadded handkerchief to her mouth, blotting the blood from a cut lip.

'We remain in the van as long as I deem it necessary. And the birds in question are geese.' Bound for Christmas tables all across the shire.

He spared Edie a quick glance, still furious about her foolhardy sprint through the arcade, the woman having more blasted moves than the Bolshoi Ballet.

Bloody hell. She nearly got herself killed. Had I not arrived in time . . .

'I figured he'd take you out first,' Edie explained. 'That's why I pushed you into the street. To cause a diversion.'

And to ensure that the goon chased after her not him.

I should throttle her.

'You're quick on your feet, but that doesn't mean that you made a wise decision,' he chastised, not in a forgiving mood. Then, dreading what her answer might be, 'Did he harm you in any way?'

'I wouldn't go so far as to say he violated my person, but he did take a few liberties.'

'Bloody bastard!'

'It was nothing. Trust me. Other than a cut lip, I'm fine.'

Cædmon stared into Edie Miller's brown eyes, able to see the scared, vulnerable child she once had been. He fought the urge to pull her to him, worried that he might say something utterly asinine.

Evidently suffering from no such qualms, Edie crawled towards him, nearly losing her balance when the van made a sudden left turn. He grabbed the bottom of the door with his hand, preventing it from swinging wide open. Despite the anger, he stretched out his free arm, cradling her face in his hand.

'It's cold in here,' she complained, nestling beside him.

Cædmon gently rubbed his thumb over her swollen lip. 'Thank God you're all right.'

'What now?'

'Taking any form of public transport is out of the question as MacFarlane's men will undoubtedly be monitoring the coach and train stations. So we'll remain in the van until we've safely departed Oxford. Hopefully, we'll be able to find a sympathetic motorist willing to take us to London.'

'Maybe we should notify the authorities.'

'It's not as though we can have the villain brought to book. And given your rampage in the market, should you contact the police, you'd probably end up an overnight guest of the Thames Valley Constabulary.'

'So where does that leave us?'

'Floundering about like two —'

'Geese,' she interjected, staring at the birds swinging overhead.

'I was about to say two landed mackerel, but I suppose a pair of frightened geese would do.'

'No. I'm talking about the first line of the fourth quatrain.' Snatching the airline bag, she unzipped it, removing the folded sheet of paper with the translated quatrains. 'Here it is,' she said, underlining the line with her finger as she read aloud. '"The trusted goose sorely wept for all of them were dead." Do you remember I told you that I once wrote a research paper on the Wife of Bath from Chaucer's *Canterbury Tales*?'

He nodded, wondering where this particular projectile would land.

'Well, these geese reminded me of a line from the prologue to that particular tale. Mind you, it's been more than ten years, so I'm paraphrasing big time, but Chaucer wrote, "Nor does any grey goose swim there in the lake that, as you see, will be without a mate." In fact, the whole premise of my paper was that women in the Middle Ages *had* to wed. Or join a nunnery. Those were the only two options available.'

Admittedly baffled, he raised a brow. 'Your point?'

'I just remembered that in medieval literature "goose" *always* refers to the good housewife. Yesterday, you said that the goose was a symbol for vigilance. And you're right. Who in the medieval world was more vigilant than the good housewife? I suspect no one ever considered the possibility that the quatrains were written by *Mrs* Galen of Godmersham, Philippa being the "trusted goose".' She folded her arms over her chest, theatrically rolling her eyes. 'Male chauvinism at its academic best.'

'I admit that your theory has possibilities. However –'

'Think about it, Cædmon. How could an eighty-five-year-old man hide a heavy gold chest? What do you want to bet that Galen's dying wish to his much younger wife was to hide his precious *arca* from the looters rampaging through the countryside during the plague? Sir Kenneth told us that everyone in Godmersham perished from the plague.'

'Save Philippa,' he murmured, Edie's theory beginning to ring with perfect pitch. 'And once her husband was dead, Philippa hid the gold *arca* somewhere in the grounds of St Lawrence the Martyr church.'

'Actually, I've got a theory about that too,' Edie countered, surprising him yet again.

'Brains *and* beauty. I am totally bewitched.'

Edie playfully hit him in the arm. 'Hey, you forgot to mention the brawn.' Then, her tone more serious, she said, 'I'm beginning to think we got the martyr part of the quatrains all wrong.'

'I take it you're referring to the third line of the last quatrain?'

'Correct. "But if a man with a fully devout heart seek the blessed martyr" does *not* refer to St Lawrence the Martyr. At least I don't think it does. I'm thinking it refers right back to the goose.'

'I don't follow.' Unhindered by ego, he didn't care who exposed the truth, only that it was found.

'Okay, we now know that the goose refers to Philippa, the good housewife,' Edie said, ticking off her first point on her little finger. She next moved to her ring finger. 'According to Sir Kenneth, Philippa was the daughter of the justice of the peace for Canterbury.' Going on to her middle finger, she then declared, 'And Canterbury, as you know from having read Chaucer, is where medieval pilgrims journeyed –'

'To see the site where St Thomas à Becket was killed in 1170 by Henry II's henchmen,' Cædmon finished, well acquainted with the incident, the murdered archbishop a victim of the conflict between Church and state. 'Within weeks of the murder, wild rumours began to circulate throughout England, those who came into contact with the bloodied vestments of the dead archbishop attesting to all sorts of astonishing miracles. Soon after, the Catholic

Church canonized Thomas à Becket as a *martyred* saint.'

'And thus the cult of St Thomas was born.'

With perfect clarity, Cædmon knew that Edie was absolutely correct. When they deciphered the fourth quatrain, they had misread the clue. As Philippa no doubt intended.

Edie leaned against the side of the van, a satisfied smile on her lips. 'It makes perfect sense, doesn't it? Philippa, entrusted with hiding the Ark, takes it to the only place other than Godmersham that she knows, the town of her birth, Canterbury.'

'Mmmm.' He mulled it over, still sifting through the pieces. 'We don't know that Philippa actually hid the Ark in Canterbury,' he said, well aware that Edie had a tendency to hurl herself at a conclusion.

'Of course we know that Philippa hid the Ark at Canterbury. It's right there in the quatrains. "There in the veil between two worlds –"'

'The truth will be found. The truth, not the *arca*,' he quietly emphasized. 'Which may be an encrypted way of saying that we'll find our next clue at Canterbury.'

Clearly disgruntled, Edie sighed. 'And here I thought this was going to be easy. Okay, any ideas where in Canterbury we should look?'

More accepting of this latest challenge, he didn't waste his time on peevish complaints, having assumed from the onset that they would follow a crooked path.

'Thomas à Becket was murdered inside the cathedral. I suggest that as a starting point.' As he spoke, the van slowed to a stop.

Cædmon peered out the rear door, able to see that the driver had pulled into the car park of a roadside café. Hopefully, they would be able to hitch a ride to London from one of the dozen or so motorists parked in the lot.

'I believe this is our stop.'

53

'You might be interested to know that these medieval walls were built on Roman foundations. The original settlement was called Durovernum Cantiacorum.'

As they strolled along the ancient stone battlements that ringed the town of Canterbury, Edie was relieved that she and Cædmon had reverted to their earlier camaraderie. She wasn't altogether certain, the male beast a difficult one to decipher, but she thought Cædmon had been angry in the alley because he hadn't been able to protect her from MacFarlane's goon.

The goon had a gun, why hadn't he used it?

Seeing in her mind's eye those massive shoulders, the scary buzz cut and the rivulet of blood zigzagging down a throbbing temple, Edie shuddered.

'Cold?' Cædmon asked solicitously, draping an arm over her shoulder.

Shoving the frightening image aside, she wordlessly snuggled closer to him. Although she couldn't be one-hundred-per-cent certain, she didn't think they were being followed. Having hitched a ride to London, they had caught a train at Victoria station, the trip to Canterbury taking only ninety minutes.

The station being on the outskirts of town, they were now en route to the cathedral.

A damp breeze chilling her back, Edie flipped up the collar on her coat. Overhead the clouds hung low in the sky, casting a dreary pall over the town.

Taking a quick peek at the map they'd picked up at the station, Cædmon ushered her to the left, past the remains of an old tower that she guessed had once been attached to an equally old church.

'All that remains of St George's Church,' he remarked, 'the tower having somehow weathered the travails of history.'

'Although it looks like most of the town fared pretty well.' She gestured to the neat line of half-timbered structures that fronted the narrow street. 'I feel like I'm walking through a medieval living-history museum.'

'Indeed. Much of Canterbury is little changed from the days of Chaucer.'

Like Oxford, the town was dressed in its Christmas finery, fairy lights twinkling merrily behind shop windows. Although Canterbury had about it a magical air that the staid Oxford lacked. Probably on account of its fairy-tale appearance.

As they walked along Mercery Lane, the pavement teemed with tourists, the modern-day pilgrims undeterred by the chilly weather. With each stride Edie was very much aware that she walked in another woman's footsteps, that woman none other than Philippa of Canterbury. Like most medieval women,

Philippa's life story had been written at birth. A man's life in the fourteenth century was recorded on vellum, enabling changes to be made, but a woman's life was carved in stone. Unchangeable.

Nearing the city centre, the thorny spires of the cathedral filled more and more of the skyline. To Edie's surprise, she began to experience a sense of agitation. Cædmon evidently felt it too, taking her by the hand as they approached a massive three-storey gatehouse. Bedecked with tiers of carved shields and a contingent of stone angels, the Saviour stood front centre, welcoming saint and sinner alike.

Cædmon led her through the arched portal. 'Christ Church Gate, the physical divide between the secular and the sacred.'

Emerging, Edie caught her first real sight of Canterbury cathedral. 'Wow,' she murmured, the cathedral so immense as to be downright daunting. One of those soaring Gothic structures purposefully constructed for maximum impact, everywhere she looked, there were towers and spires and statues. 'Wow,' she murmured again, yet to emerge from her awestruck state.

Cædmon remarked, 'Of course, the magnificence of Canterbury is not surprising, this being the mother cathedral of the Church of England.'

'More like the mother ship,' Edie muttered, still overwhelmed by the sheer size of the place. 'This is gonna take days. Particularly since we don't even know what we're looking for.'

'But we know that whatever it is, it's located inside the cathedral. And I suspect the clue has something to do with the Ark of the Covenant.'

'But the clue could be anything. A piece of sculpture, a painting, a carving. *Anything*. It could even have something to do with Thomas à Becket,' she added. 'After all, he is the "blessed martyr", right?'

'I think Thomas is a peripheral character, little more than a reference to direct us to Canterbury. For it's this colossus of stone and glass –' raising his arm, Cædmon motioned to the cathedral '– that played a pivotal role in Philippa's daily life before she left for Godmersham. Moreover, she –'

Cædmon stopped in mid-sentence and mid-step. Wordlessly, he stared at the façade of the cathedral. Like a man transfixed.

'What's the matter?' she asked, grabbing him by the upper arm.

He turned to her, a beatific smile upon his lips. 'The clue is contained in glass. Stained glass, to be precise. One of the greatest artistic achievements of the medieval world, it was the first modern medium of mass communication.' His smile broadened. 'Not to mention that stained glass forms a "veil between the two worlds".'

Edie stared at the windows in the southern façade of the cathedral.

'Stained glass was intended as a barrier between the secular world of the city streets,' Cædmon continued, 'and the sacred world contained within the cathedral. Illuminated by light, the first of God's creations, stained glass can literally come to life before one's eyes.'

As though an affirmation from on high, a bell tolled sonorously.

'Come, Miss Miller. Destiny beckons,' Cædmon said portentously, ushering her towards the entrance.

Following on the tail of an American tour group, they entered the elaborately carved doors at the western end of the cathedral. Immediately they were assaulted by the twin scents of incense and flowers and the twin sounds of clicking cameras and a Midwestern twang.

'Above you, in what is known as the West Window, you will see a brilliant example of medieval stained glass,' the American tour guide expounded in what was obviously a canned speech. 'The sixty-three glass panels, which depict various saints, prophets and kings, is just a drop in the ocean compared to what you're gonna see on the tour, the cathedral boasting hundreds of glass panels. Make no mistake, folks, *this* is one of the cultural treasures of Europe.'

Along with everyone else in the group, Edie peered up.

'Oh God,' she groaned, stunned. 'It's gonna be like finding a holy needle in a sacred haystack.'

Taking her by the elbow, Cædmon led her away from the group. 'Admittedly, we have a daunting task ahead of us.'

Edie craned her neck, taking another gander at the sixty-three glass panels of the West Window.

'You think?'

54

Neck inclined at an awkward angle, Cædmon stared at the top of the stained-glass panel, the blaze of colour dazzling, casting what could only be described as psychedelic patterns of light onto the gloomy walls of the Gothic interior.

Les belles-verrières, he mused silently. Certainly more beautiful glass than one man and one woman could reasonably absorb in a single day. But mindful of the possibility that MacFarlane had correctly deciphered the quatrains, he and Edie forged on.

Some two hours into their search, they stood in the Corona, the semicircular chapel originally built to house the relics of St Thomas à Becket. Despite the fact that they had methodically examined dozens of stained-glass panels created before the mid-fourteenth century, thus far they'd seen no images or references to the Ark of the Covenant.

Swaying slightly on his feet, the coloured light almost hypnotic, several lines of Bible verse came to mind. '"I will lay thy stones with fair colours, and lay their foundations with sapphires. And I will make thy windows of agates, and thy gates of –"'

Edie raised a hand, cutting him off in mid-sentence. 'Enough already. I am totally and completely Bibled out. Trying to decipher these windows is an awful lot like learning a foreign language. Except we don't have the Berlitz tapes. And you spouting verses from the good book does not help matters.'

'Understood,' he contritely replied.

Although Cædmon had studied medieval iconography while at Oxford, to any modern observer the symbolism contained within the Canterbury windows was not unlike a foreign language. But this language had been well understood eight hundred years ago. Illiteracy the norm during the Middle Ages, stained glass had enabled the faithful to learn the stories of the Bible through pictures.

Ignoring the painful crick in his neck, Cædmon continued to study the panels, forcing himself to examine only those images specific to the Old Testament. *Moses consecrating Aaron. The ascent of Elijah. Samson and Delilah.*

As they continued to the next group of panels, he caught sight of a leather-clad figure in the corner of his eye. The size and shape of the figure similar to those of their assailant in Oxford, he slowed his step. Almost instantly, his heartbeat escalated, goose pimples prickling his skin. He knew this feeling, had had it any number of times when he worked for MI5. Something in Denmark most definitely stank to high heaven.

Muscles tightening, he slowly turned to face the enemy.

It took only an instant to verify that the man was

simply a tourist. While the robust physique was similar, the facial features were completely different.

Bloody hell.

'Is something the matter?' his companion asked. 'All of a sudden, you're looking awfully tight around the jaw.'

'No, no, nothing is the matter,' he assured her, taking her by the elbow and steering her towards the aisle of the cathedral choir. To one side of them, massive columns supported incised stone arches; on the other side, stained-glass windows gleamed beautifully.

'Ah! The famed Typology Windows,' he announced, effectively changing the subject. Knowing that the Typology Windows had been created prior to the thirteenth century, he angled his head to examine the upper panes of glass, ignoring the bolt of pain that travelled from the nape of his neck to the base of his spine.

Edie elbowed him in the ribs. 'Explanation, please. In case you've forgotten, I'm a novice at this.'

'Typology was a tool often used in the Middle Ages to confirm the legitimacy of the New Testament using stories taken from the Old,' he explained. 'A typical example is the tale of Jonah and the whale. According to the Old Testament, Jonah remained within the whale's belly for three days and three nights.'

'Prefiguring Jesus being entombed for the same length of time,' she astutely commented.

'Precisely. Usually the stories were paired, thus reinforcing a particular theological point through the manipulation of biblical imagery.'

'Thought control at its very best.'

He winked at her. 'How else does one control the masses?'

'Hey, look, it's Noah and the Ark!' she exclaimed, pointing to a half-roundel. Placing a hand to her mouth, she stifled a snicker. 'Yeah, I know, wrong ark. Although at this point I'm happy to see *any* ark.'

Not nearly so amused, Cædmon led the way to the next panel. Again, he began the slow process of identifying each and every biblical figure, his gaze systematically beginning at the top and moving down. A monumental window, the panel was divided into seven horizontal sections, each section containing three separate scenes. When he came to the fifth section, he did a double take.

'Bloody hell! I think I've found it.'

Edie's eyes slowly scanned the length of the window, opening wide when they hit the telltale image. 'Ohmygosh! It's a four-sided gold box.'

'Actually, it's *the* four-sided gold box. None other than the Ark of the Covenant.' Barely able to contain his excitement, he had the overwhelming urge to laugh aloud, to raise his voice to the heavens and whoop with joy. Instead, he pulled Edie into his arms, hugging her close. 'We've found it,' he whispered in her ear. 'We've actually found the bloody thing.'

Disengaging her right arm, Edie excitedly pointed

to the window in question. 'Did you notice the two baby geese in the basket?'

He nodded, certain they'd found the very panel that Philippa had intended them to find. The scene, the presentation of Christ, depicted the well-known New Testament story of Mary and Joseph presenting the infant Jesus to the high priest in the Temple at Jerusalem. Two seemingly innocuous items within the scene screamed at him: Joseph carrying a basket that contained two goslings, and Mary, holding the baby Jesus aloft, standing before the Ark of the Covenant.

'Yesterday you and Sir Kenneth were rambling on about the medieval comparisons between Mary and the Ark of the Covenant. Is this what you were talking about?'

Deciding not to take issue with the 'rambling' charge, he nodded. 'It was a religious concept known as *Faederis Arca*. No less a theologian than St Bernard of Clairvaux explicitly compared the womb of Mary to the Ark of the Covenant, for, as the Ark contained the Ten Commandments, so Mary carried Christ within her womb.'

'The symbolism of the Old Testament reinforcing the New Testament.'

'Precisely.'

Clearly excited, Edie yanked the Virgin bag off her shoulder. Unzipping it, she hurriedly rifled through its contents, removing her digital camera.

Excitement was soon replaced with a crestfallen

expression. 'It's a dead dog,' she muttered, showing him the darkened display. 'The digital camera has yet to be invented that will run on a drained battery.' She glanced at the exit located on the far side of the nave. 'I could run out and buy some new batteries at one of the souvenir shops.'

Cædmon checked his watch. 'I don't know if you'll have enough time. The cathedral closes in twenty minutes. The photo will have to wait until the morning.'

'Do you *really* want to wait that long? Yeah, we found the window, but now we have to figure out what it means. And to do that, we need a picture.'

'I agree. However –'

She put a hand on his chest. 'Don't move. I'll be right back.'

He watched as Edie rushed towards the northwest transept. When she disappeared from sight, he returned his gaze to the stained-glass panel. As he stared, spellbound, the distinctive scent of incense wafted through the chill air. It suddenly occurred to him that here, within the confines of one of the world's great cathedrals, where man-made bread daily became God's flesh, anything was possible.

Turning away from the panel, he watched as Edie returned with a bespectacled, long-haired young man in tow. 'This is William. He's agreed to do a quick line drawing of the window.'

A man of few words, William removed an artist's sketch pad from his satchel. Ignoring them, he negligently leaned against a nine-hundred-year-old column and began to draw.

'I earlier noticed him sketching the St Thomas memorial inside the transept,' Edie explained.

'A budding artist then.'

'More like a budding con artist,' she replied, lowering her voice to a whisper. 'He refused to put pencil to paper for less than fifty bucks. Since we need an image in order to decipher the window, I agreed.'

The silent seconds ticked past. Cædmon anxiously checked his watch, hoping the young artist completed his masterpiece before the attendants herded them out.

'What happens if we actually find the Ark?' Edie asked, staring at the four-sided gold box in the glass panel.

That question again.

And still he didn't have an answer. Only a mounting sense of excitement.

The Ark of the Covenant.

Truly the stuff of dreams.

Having yet to utter a word, the artist ripped the sheet from his pad. Paper in hand, he walked over to where they stood and silently handed Edie the drawing he'd made. She in turn handed him a small wad of American bills. Transaction concluded, she politely thanked him for his services.

'This better be worth fifty dollars,' she muttered under her breath as William wordlessly took his leave.

Cædmon examined the drawing, pleased with the

result. 'I'd say it's bang on.' Thrilled that all was going so well, he unthinkingly said the first thing that came into his mind. 'Fancy a quick bonk?'

Her eyes opened wide. 'What? Here? In the middle of Canterbury cathedral?'

'We passed a dimly lit niche on the other side of the choir earlier on.'

'Are you crazy? In case you haven't noticed, O horny one, we're in a church.'

This being the stuff of fantasies, he smiled. 'Nothing the Almighty hasn't seen countless times before. Come on, Edie. Surely you can spare me a moment of your time?'

'Not with all the angels and saints watching from on high, I can't.' She glanced pointedly at a haloed figure in a nearby stained-glass panel. 'But just so you don't think me a complete killjoy, I might be amenable to a bonk in a hotel room.'

Cædmon grabbed her by the hand and dragged her towards the nearest exit. 'We passed a guest house on Mercery Lane. If we hurry, we can be between the sheets within the half-hour.'

55

'It's not the Savoy. But then again it's not the alms-house,' he'd remarked drolly, surveying the modest accommodation.

Edie glanced at the iron bedstead. 'What now?'

'A drink, I think. No, let's skip the pleasantries and get right down to it, shall we? In the prone or upright position? Your choice, love.'

After a moment's thought, she picked the latter . . .

Trousers refastened, Cædmon bent down and retrieved a pair of lacy knickers from the threadbare carpet. Somewhat sheepishly, he handed them to Edie. His embarrassment stemming from a decided lack of finesse, he glanced at the undisturbed bed.

He could do better. He *would* do better.

He'd always considered himself a considerate lover, but for some inexplicable reason he'd acted on his animal urges, behaving like a testosterone-driven oaf.

'I just need to, um, you know, freshen up.' Her cheeks flushed, Edie pointed to the adjoining bathroom.

'Er, right.'

A few moments later there was the sound of a

running tap, followed by a muttered complaint about the lack of hot water. Unable to find a vacant room at an accredited B & B, they'd been forced to take a room at a small guest house, the only available one an attic. In an attempt to add some charm to the claustrophobic space, the walls and the steeply pitched ceiling had been papered with prancing maids in farthingales and sad-faced Pierrots straight out of a Watteau canvas.

'Shall we have a go at the stained-glass window?' he enquired when Edie returned.

'Sounds like a plan. Since there's no table, how about we pull that pine bench over to the side of the bed?'

Cædmon obediently fetched the bench in question, the two of them sitting side by side on the mattress, their shoulders lightly touching. In front of them, spread across the bench, Edie placed the sketch of the window, the handwritten copy of Philippa's quatrains, a blank sheet of paper and two sharpened pencils.

'When deciphering code, no stone unturned is the best rule of thumb,' he instructed. 'Prisons are full of thieves and murderers.'

'No kidding. Your point?'

He smiled at what was fast becoming a familiar refrain. 'Look for the obvious. Every link in the chain is somehow relevant.'

'Well the geese in the basket are pretty obvious, don't you think?'

'Indeed. But what is the significance of the pair? We know that one of the geese represents the good housewife Philippa. But what about the other?'

Edie shrugged. 'I have no idea. But the fact that Philippa has led us to Canterbury makes me think she may have given the Ark to the cathedral. The scene in question does show the Holy Family inside the Temple of Jerusalem.'

For several seconds he pondered the notion. While the idea had merit, something about it didn't ring true.

'"I know not how the world be served by such adversity,"' he said, reading aloud from the fourth quatrain. 'It's clear that Philippa attributed the plague to her husband's ill-gotten treasure. Good Catholic woman that she was, Philippa would not have burdened the Church with that same adversity.'

Getting up from the bed, Edie walked over and retrieved the Virgin bag from the room's one and only chair, a lumpy reproduction antique upholstered in the same pattern as the wallpaper. She removed a metal nail file from the zippered pocket and sat down.

'I broke a nail.'

Realizing that she was in no mood to decipher the drawing, Cædmon stared moodily at the pine bench. In truth, he wasn't at all surprised by her lack of enthusiasm, the day's events having no doubt taken a heavy toll on her.

'Will you be spending Christmas with your family?'

Cædmon's head jerked, caught off guard by Edie's unexpected query. Although he knew she'd eventually ask about his private life, he'd foolishly hoped it wouldn't happen soon.

'My father died some years ago. But even when he was alive, we were never big on family events, Christmas falling by the wayside when I was young. My mother died in childbirth,' he added, anticipating her next question.

'This is the first time you've mentioned your family.'

'My father and I had what you might call a strained relationship. He was strict and had no time for frivolity.'

'He sounds like a real hard-ass.'

'Actually, he was a solicitor.'

Edie laughed aloud. 'Sorry. It's just the way it came out. It sounded . . .'

'Absurd?' The old wounds not nearly as painful as they'd once been, he managed a half-smile. 'Yes, there was a certain absurdity to our relationship.'

'Absurdity aside, I bet your father was proud of you. Going to Oxford and everything.'

Cædmon snorted. 'Maybe. Certainly when I left Oxford, the shame killed him.'

'Don't you think you're exaggerating just a *weensy* bit?' With thumb and index finger, she mimed 'weensy'.

Shoving the bench aside, he rose to his feet. There being little room to pace, he walked over to the

357

fireplace. The act of confession an uncomfortable one, he turned his back to her.

'Within days of my Oxford débacle, I was summoned to a hospital where my father was undergoing tests for an intestinal complaint.' Able to see the sterile white room in his mind's eye, he frowned, the vividness of the recollection unnerving. 'My father was wearing a light blue hospital gown. It was the first time I'd ever seen him in clothes that hadn't been properly pressed.' He glanced over his shoulder at her. 'A very dignified man, my father.'

Although she made no reply, he could see that he had a captive audience, Edie leaning forward in the chair.

'The morning sun was shining through the window by my father's bed. He looked like a kindly old gentleman. An aged putto, I irreverently thought at the time.'

'So what happened?'

'Something that had been years in the making.' He turned and faced his confessor. 'At this juncture I should mention that I spent the first thirteen years of my life fearing the bastard and the next thirteen loathing him because of that fear.'

'Did he physically abuse you?'

He tersely shook his head. 'No. In fact he never laid a hand on me, not in anger nor affection. It was emotional abuse, a systematic shutting-out that left little doubt he rued the day I had been born. On those few occasions he did take notice of me, it was always to criticize.'

'I'm guessing it all came to a head when you went to visit him in the hospital.'

Cædmon nodded. 'No sooner did I arrive than he told me precisely how much it had cost him to support me at Oxford. He then point blank said that he expected me to pay it back. With interest.'

'You're kidding, right?' Her stunned expression was almost comical.

'I told the old bastard to bugger off and left, perversely pleased with myself for finally standing up to him. Twelve hours later the hospital rang to tell me that my father had unexpectedly died from an embolism.'

'How did you feel about that?'

The question was so typically American, he should have anticipated it. Should have, but didn't.

'If you're asking if I felt complicit in my father's death, I did not. Although I've spent an inordinate amount of time trying to understand his motives.' He shrugged, indicating this had been a futile endeavour. 'All I know is that my father lacked the ability to love.'

Good God! Did I really just say that?

Horrified, he self-consciously cleared his throat, refusing to meet Edie's disarmingly direct gaze.

'Maybe he did love you; he just didn't know how to express it.'

'To know the man was to know better.'

Getting up from her chair, Edie walked towards him. 'I think your father was an idiot for wasting his life the way he did. It's what Herman Melville referred to as the "horror of the half-lived life". So, what about the rest of your life? Have you ever been married? Do you have any kids?'

Cædmon stared at the threadbare carpet, the conversation having veered into uncomfortable territory. The ghost of his dead lover was close. If he told Edie about Juliana, he'd also have to tell her about his murderous revenge in the streets of Belfast.

Arms crossed over his chest, he listened as the mantel clock relentlessly ticked off each passing second with an air of funereal inevitability.

Edie placed a hand on his forearm. 'Look, whatever it is that you're afraid to tell me, I'll understand. Really, I will.'

Angry at being cornered, he moved away from her. 'You'll understand? Correct me if I'm wrong, but we first met four days ago. Barely enough time to know how I take my tea, let alone understand me.' He snatched his anorak from the nearby hook. 'There's a curry house down the road. I'm going to get a takeaway.'

56

Edie yanked the black turtleneck over her head and threw it onto the wooden toilet lid. Reaching her hand into the claw-footed bathtub, she swirled the sudsy water, testing to make sure she had the right mix of hot and cold. Evidently, it had yet to occur to the Brits that a single spout was a whole heck of a lot better than duelling taps. But as she was quickly learning, the Brits were a curious lot.

She unhooked her bra and let it drop onto the linoleum floor. Seeing the small mark next to her nipple, she smiled. Cædmon had surprised her with his passion, morphing into a lusty alpha male the moment he removed his woollens and tweeds. A lot of things about Cædmon surprised her. The way he would dunk a cookie in his coffee then immediately apologize as though he'd committed the gravest of sins. His almost boyish exuberance when it came to anything even remotely esoteric. His insistence on opening doors and preceding her down steps. His sweetness. His tenderness. His unrelenting resolve when it came to the Ark.

God, but he could be a hard-ass. She suspected that he took after his father more than he realized. Yeah, she'd pushed him. But he'd pushed back even harder.

Short of killing a man in cold blood, she'd understand whatever deep, dark secret he kept under lock and key. She was certainly no saint.

What she needed to do was back off. When he was ready, when he felt more comfortable with the relationship, he would open up.

Clothes removed, she walked over and turned off the taps. Tentatively, she stuck a big toe into the water. Then, a hand braced on either side of the claw-footed bath, she slowly sank into the frothy water, having found a half-used bottle of lemon-scented bubble bath.

'Perfect,' she crooned, her tense muscles finally relaxing. She stared at the pitched ceiling, the light from the adjoining room turning the surface a pretty shade of candy-floss pink.

She reached for the flannel she'd earlier draped over the curved lip of the tub.

'Deck the halls with boughs of holly, fa-la-la-la, la-la-la-la-la.'

Realizing it was one of those songs that sounded better after a couple of drinks, she switched tunes, instead humming 'The Little Drummer Boy' as she soaped up the flannel.

Raising her right leg out of the water, she washed it from toe to knee.

Again, her thoughts turned to Cædmon. Christmas had to be a difficult time of year for him given that his father –

'Getting all cleaned up to do the dirty, huh?'

Hearing the deep-throated voice, Edie swung her head towards the open bathroom door.

O, God. It was him.

57

Stunned to find her Oxford assailant negligently leaning against the door jamb, Edie thought her heart would explode. Overcome with fear, she helplessly gripped the sides of the tub.

'And in case you got any notions about screaming or hollering or complaining to the management, you might want to reconsider,' the intruder drawled, slowly pulling a gun from the waistband of his military-style cargo pants. 'The two of us are gonna do this nice and quiet.'

Edie stared at the dark lump of steel clutched in his meaty hand. She didn't know much about firearms, but she knew a silencer when she saw one. He could kill her in cold blood and no one in the guest house would be the wiser. Just like he had killed Dr Padgham at the museum. Just like he'd probably killed God knows how many people.

Gun in hand, he strolled over and retrieved her bra from the floor. As he did, Edie noticed the surgical tape on the side of his head. Evidently, he'd had to have stitches after Cædmon hit him with the bottle. Like he wasn't scary enough already, the little pieces of white tape made him look like a turbocharged Frankenstein.

Holding her bra up to his face, the behemoth read the inside tag. 'Thirty-four C. *Nice*. They ought to fit my hands just perfect.'

Edie wanted to puke.

'H-how d-did you find me?' she stammered, hoping that if she changed the subject, she could somehow change his intentions.

Grinning, he dropped the bra. 'Amazing how you can hunt down a person anywhere in the world with a microdot tracking device and a PalmPilot. And the beauty of it? It don't cost more than two hundred dollars. That's the good thing about them Chinks and how they mass-produce everything on God's green planet. Keeps down the cost of surveillance.'

'You attacked me in Oxford, so you could plant a tracking device?'

'Aren't you the clever bitch?' His gaze slowly moved down her soap-covered body, stopping at her quivering breasts.

Edie sank deeper into the bubbles, her head the only thing that remained above water. If she could, she would have squeezed herself right down the drain.

'He's going to be back. Any minute now. So you better leave while you still have the chance.' She glanced pointedly at his sutured skull, hoping to drive home her point.

'Ooh, I'm quaking in my boots. Besides, I've got my doubts about your red-headed honey returning any time soon. Last I saw, he was sitting at the corner bar, downing a cold one. So, it looks like it's gonna be just me and you, sweet tits. But after what I saw last night, I think you can handle it.' He winked lewdly at her. 'I got last night's fuck fest on video. Hot. Real, real hot.' Reaching down, he cupped his crotch with his free hand, pursing his thick lips in an exaggerated air kiss.

'I'm going to be sick,' Edie moaned, leaning over the side of the tub, gagging.

'The fuck you are!'

Charging forward, her would-be rapist grabbed her by the hair. Lemon-scented water splashed onto the floor as he yanked her up and out of the tub. Arms flailing, Edie reflexively slammed her fist into the wound on the side of his head.

'Fucking shit!' he bellowed, instantly releasing his hold.

Edie seized her chance, running into the bedroom.

A weapon. She had to find a weapon.

Her eyes darted from the standard lamp to the bed to the lumpy chair.

The nail file.

Oblivious to the fact that she was stark naked, she lunged towards the chair.

That's where I was sitting when I was filing down my nail.

From behind her, she heard the *thud* of his boots.

Where the hell was the nail file?

She shoved her hand down the side of the seat cushion, her search coming to an abrupt end when a muscled arm snaked around her waist, yanking her away from the chair. Frantic, she tried to twist free, but it was as though she had a giant vice clamped around her midsection.

'Think again, cunt,' he snarled, lifting her bodily off the ground. Pivoting, he tossed her onto the bed, the iron frame clanging against the wall. Edie immediately rolled to her right but, anticipating the move, he grabbed her by the ankle, pulling her back to the middle of the bed.

'Don't move,' he ordered, pointing the gun at her heart. 'Or there won't be anything left of your left titty.'

Not so much as twitching, Edie braced herself, certain a bullet would slam into her chest at any moment.

When it didn't happen, she released a pent-up breath, wordlessly watching as her would-be rapist clicked the safety catch on his weapon. That done, he placed it on the mantel. Completely out of reach.

Cracking his knuckles, he walked towards the bed. 'In case you're wondering, I can kill you with my bare hands as easily as I can shoot you.'

Edie didn't doubt for one second that he spoke the truth.

Intently staring at her, he placed a knee on the foot of the bed. The next instant, he had her pinned beneath him. His harsh breath hit her full in the face. Edie figured he had a good hundred pounds on her.

Unable to move, barely able to breathe, she stared mutely at her assailant.

She had only two choices: submit or fight. Either way, when all was said and done, she figured she'd end up dead. At that thought, Edie heard a buzzing in her ears and the rapist-cum-murderer's unshaven face blurred at the edges.

Submit, Edie.

Submit and you might live.

If you live, you might be able to get to his gun.

If you get the gun, you can blow him away.

Mind made up, Edie clenched her jaw and stared at the ceiling.

Pushing his hand between their hips, the monster unbuttoned his trousers. In the same instant his mobile vibrated, Edie able to feel the pulse against her bare hip.

'Fucking shit.'

Removing his hand from between their two bodies, he reached for the phone clipped to his waistband. 'Not a word,' he warned, supporting himself on his elbows.

Relieved to have some of his weight removed, Edie nodded obediently.

'Braxton. Yes, sir, I got her.' He frowned, his brows drawing together in the middle. 'No, sir, she's all right ... Yes, sir ... I'll have her there in fifteen minutes.'

Disconnecting the call, he snapped his mobile shut and clipped it back on his waistband. Muttering some of the most foul-mouthed profanities she'd ever heard, he pushed himself to his knees, clamping a hand around her upper arm as he did so. With no explanation as to what he was doing, or why he was doing it, he pulled her off the bed.

Edie had no idea who had been on the other end of the line. And she didn't much care. She only knew that she'd been given a reprieve.

Hand still wrapped round her upper arm, he dragged her over to the mantel, retrieving his gun, then shoved her through the open bathroom door.

'Get dressed,' he ordered, gesturing to the pile of clothes on the toilet seat.

Bending at the waist, Edie picked up her discarded bra. 'Can I at least dry off? I'm still wet.'

'Bitch, do I look like I care?'

58

Cædmon, without a doubt, you've been a pompous ass.

Ashamed of himself, Cædmon hoped that a heart-felt apology would smooth things over. If it didn't, he would woo Edie with lamb jalfrezi and cardamom pudding. He glanced at the brown takeaway bag clutched in his hand, hoping the peace offering would lead to improved relations. And that improved relations would lead to something decidedly more intimate. More romantic.

As he climbed the well-worn treads that led to their garret room, he wondered if the day would ever come when he could make a full confession. When he could freely and openly tell Edie about the pain of love lost, of vengeance sought and claimed, of his eventual emergence from an alcohol-induced fog. He thought that because of her own travails she would understand. Maybe even accept.

'And a warm fuzzy hug would be nice too,' he said aloud, chortling.

Still laughing as he reached the top of the stairs, the chuckle caught in his throat.

The door to their room was ajar.

Afraid of what he would find on the other side, he slowly pushed the door all the way open and entered the room. At a glance, he could see that some sort of commotion had taken place. Almost immediately his gaze landed on the large dark patch that stained the tousled coverlet. Setting the brown bag on the dresser, he walked over to the bed. His heart painfully thudding against his chest, he placed his hand upon the wet spot. He breathed a sigh of relief. It wasn't blood.

Edie was still alive.

Maybe not as well as she might be, but definitely alive.

Thank God.

Out of the corner of his eye, he spotted the Virgin bag on the floor next to the bed, upended, emptied of its contents. He next scanned the room, searching for a ransom note. There wasn't one, although he didn't need a scrawled scrap of paper to know Edie had been kidnapped because they wanted him.

Stunned by the abduction, he went into the bathroom, heading straight for the sink. Turning on the cold-water tap, he rinsed his face.

He knew the drill: wait for further instructions. Eventually he would be contacted. If their plan had been to kill Edie, they would have left her corpse behind as a warning to him. But there was no sprawled, blood-splattered body. Her abduction was simply a means to an end.

He reached for the neatly folded bath towel and dried his face.

Taking deep, measured breaths, he walked back

into the bedroom. Again, he checked the room, searching for anything that could be used as a weapon. When the time came to confront his enemies, he didn't want to stand before them defenceless. His gaze alighted on the upholstered chair. The chair where Edie had sat earlier, filing a broken nail.

Having no recollection of her returning the file to the shoulder bag, he walked over to the chair. The file not being in view, he slid his hand around the chair cushion. Coming up empty-handed, he removed the cushion from the chair.

There, between two squashed crisps and a boiled sweet, dully gleaming in the lamplight, was the nail file. While hardly a honed broadsword, it would have to do.

He replaced the cushion.

Bloody hell, but he wanted a drink. Needed a drink to –

Not on your life. You need your wits about you. She's yours and she needs you.

Lowering himself into the lumpy chair, he inhaled the exotic scents of cardamom and cumin mingled with the more prosaic smell of lemon-scented bath-water.

Wait.

59

'I mean you no harm,' Stanford MacFarlane said as he ushered her into the room.

Edie snorted, the memory of her near rape all too vivid. 'Yeah, and British beef is safe to eat. Guess you're unaware of the fact that your henchman sexually assaulted me.'

MacFarlane stared at her. She guessed him to be in his mid- to late-fifties, the sharply defined widow's peak in the greying buzz cut being the giveaway. At one time he had probably been handsome, but years spent in the sun had turned age lines into deeply incised creases, giving him a stern gnome-like visage. A man of medium height, he had an erect military posture and an air of command that bordered on the egomaniacal.

'You lie,' he said dismissively.

'I should have known you'd stand by your man.'

'I will always stand by a man of God.'

So much for sowing the seeds of dissent.

Shot down, Edie glanced around her, taking in what appeared to be an old mill, the metal cogs and wheels of the original machinery still in place on the other side of the room. Able to hear water running beneath the floorboards, she figured the mill was located on a stream or river.

She turned her gaze back to the man standing across from her. 'Just answer me this: what are you going to do if you actually get your hands on the Ark?'

'That's between me and the Almighty,' Mac-Farlane replied.

'What if the Ark of the Covenant turns out to be nothing more than a gold-plated box?'

MacFarlane smiled. 'And God said to Moses, "Let them make me a sanctuary, that I may dwell among them."'

Clearly he considered the Ark some kind of God box, so Edie decided to try a different approach. 'There's no question in my mind that you're a God-fearing man. Which means that we have a lot in common. You may not know this, but I go to church every Sunday and ... well, I don't have to tell you what the Bible says about mercy and compassion. "Blessed are those who are pure in heart: for they shall see God,"' she recited, tossing out a Bible verse of her own, figuring the only way to fight fire was with more of the same.

MacFarlane's gaze narrowed. 'Like many of your ilk, you've hijacked the Bible in order to advance your left-wing, feel-good agenda. According to people like you, the carjacker will not steal your vehicle if you show some compassion, nor will the killer pull the trigger as he is an intrinsically good man.'

Turning away from her, MacFarlane walked over to the kitchen counter, the stone-walled room a big open space with matching sofas on one side, a dining table in the middle and a kitchen area at the far end. She watched as he took down two mugs from a shelf. He opened two packets of instant cocoa. That done, he added hot water from an electric kettle.

Even as he handed her one of the mugs, he glared at her. A dark, impassioned glare that sent a chill down her spine. She didn't dare refuse the cocoa.

'I know you and your kind, Miss Miller. You think that by putting your carcass in a pew every Sunday, God will look kindly upon you, perfect church attendance equalling a free pass to salvation.'

'You've got me mixed up with some other person. Personally, I think it's important for –' she searched for the right word '– the *betterment* of one's soul to engage in good works. Christian charity being the touchstone of –'

'Spare me the secular sermon. As if volunteering at some inner-city soup kitchen will gain you entry into heaven. Faith, not deeds, will secure you a place among the righteous.'

'Don't you mean the self-righteous?' she retorted.

'You and your kind are anathema unto the Lord.'

'Then we clearly worship two different gods.'

'At last, something we can agree upon.'

And as Edie knew full well, it was an agreement based on a bitter divide.

Truth be told, she was taken aback at how much Stanford MacFarlane reminded her of Pops, her maternal grandfather having held to a very conservative interpretation of the Bible. At the time she'd thought it a stifling interpretation. But when espoused by a man like MacFarlane, it went from stifling to scary. Put a black robe on him and Stanford MacFarlane would have made the perfect Spanish inquisitor.

'Speaking of entry into heaven, if you think finding the Ark is your stamped ticket, think again,' she said, refusing to go quietly to the stake.

About to raise his mug to his lips, MacFarlane lowered it. For several seconds – seconds that conjured up images of burning bodies – he stared at her.

'Unlike you, I will die and rise with the Old Testament saints.' Then, as though he'd simply made a passing comment about the weather, he calmly took a sip of his cocoa.

Edie was silent.

There's no way you can argue with a zealot. The years spent with Pops had taught her that, the memory still weighing heavy. Like a giant millstone on her heart.

Out of the corner of her eye, she caught sight of a gossamer strand of cobweb dangling from the wood-beamed ceiling. Staring at it, she suddenly felt very much like the fly ensnared in the deceptively beautiful trap.

But unlike the ensnared fly, she had an out.
Cædmon.

She knew he would come. If not to rescue her,
then to find the Ark.

60

Hearing a knock, Cædmon turned in his chair. The guest-house proprietor, a florid-faced Welshman, stood in the doorway, no doubt wondering why the door had been left open. Simply put, he had not seen the need to close it.

'You've got a call,' the man announced, clearly annoyed at having had to climb four sets of stairs to convey the message. 'You can take it downstairs.' Announcement made, he departed.

Cædmon rose to his feet. As he walked towards the door, he glimpsed the sketch of the Canterbury window and the handwritten translation of the quatrains on the wooden bench. Stark and painful reminders that Edie's abduction had everything to do with the Ark of the Covenant. Knowing he would have need of both, he retrieved the two sheets of paper, slipping them into his anorak pocket, these being the only things of value in the room. He followed the proprietor, closing the door behind him.

A few moments later, standing at the rough-hewn counter that masqueraded as a reception desk, Cædmon lifted the heavy handset of an old-fashioned telephone. 'Go ahead. I'm listening,' he said, refusing to engage in the hypocrisy of a civil greeting.

'I do hope you're having a pleasant evening,' an American male on the other end said smoothly and sarcastically.

'Sod off! Is she still alive?'

'You know that she is.'

'I know no such thing. If we are to continue this conversation, I require some proof.'

'You're hardly in a position to make demands.'

'I am not demanding,' Cædmon countered in a calmer tone, reining in his emotions. 'I am requesting, as a show of good faith, that you give me proof that Miss Miller is your captive.'

Cædmon was able to detect a muffled command being issued, then, a few seconds later, 'It's me, Cædmon. I'm . . . I'm all right.'

She was alive.

'Have they harmed you in any way?'

'No, they –'

'Satisfied?' her captor snarled into the phone.

'Yes, I'm satisfied. What do I have to do to ensure her safe return?'

The other man chuckled, obviously amused by the question. 'Find me the Ark of the Covenant, of course.'

Cædmon fell silent.

Hearing the deal so clearly and bluntly spelled out made him acutely aware that MacFarlane might well be asking the impossible. For nearly three thousand

379

years the Ark had remained hidden. Nothing more than a legend. Many before him had failed to find it. Somehow, against impossible odds, he had to succeed.

His stomach muscles cramped painfully. Knowing the negotiations could come to a rapid end if he sounded anything less than totally confident, he strove for a calmness he didn't feel. 'Do I have your word that when I find the Ark Edie Miller's life will be spared?'

'You do. And my word is my bond,' the other man promptly replied. 'As soon as we hang up, I want you to leave that rat hole of a hotel and head three blocks south. Turn left at the telephone booth on the corner. There's an alley halfway down the street. My men will be there waiting for you. Don't try anything foolish. If you do, the woman dies. And, trust me, it won't be a pleasant death.'

Instructions issued, the call was unceremoniously ended.

For several long seconds Cædmon stared at the telephone, events moving at a faster pace than he would have liked.

He brought his palm down hard on the silver bell on the counter. When the Welshman appeared, Cædmon slid his hand inside his coat pocket, removing his wallet. 'I would like to check out.'

The proprietor stared suspiciously at him. 'Where's the missus?'

'She has gone ahead without me.'

Bill paid in full, he left the guest house and headed south as directed.

He passed a pub on his right, yellow light spilling onto the pavement. Earlier in the evening he'd sat glumly in that same pub, staring at a pint of lager. Knowing alcohol would do nothing to resolve the unsettled business with Edie, he'd handed the untasted glass to an inebriated local before wordlessly slinking out. Had he not succumbed to a moment's weakness, he might have been able to thwart the abduction.

Cædmon shoved the thought aside. He couldn't change the past; he could only affect the here and now. If used correctly, the metal nail file hidden beneath the leather insole of his right shoe could be a deadly weapon. He'd killed before; he could do so again. He rehearsed the plan in his mind's eye. *A jab to the eye. A deep puncture to the neck.*

Approaching a red telephone box, he turned left as he had been instructed. When he came to the alleyway, he made another left. At the end of the deserted lane, he sighted two men leaning against a parked Range Rover.

MacFarlane's bully boys.

While he could not be sure, Cædmon assumed that MacFarlane recruited his mercenaries straight out of the US military. Special forces more than likely.

'Good evening, gentlemen,' he said, touching his fingers to an imaginary hat brim.

Neither man acknowledged the greeting, although

one of them pushed himself away from the vehicle and stepped towards him. Without being asked, Cædmon raised his arms, grasping the back of his head with his clasped hands. The man impersonally patted him down, searching every crevice where a weapon might be concealed.

Search concluded, Cædmon slowly lowered his arms.

'Take off your clothes.'

'I beg your pardon?'

'You heard me, take off your clothes.' To ensure that the order was obeyed, the man opened his jacket, revealing a holstered gun.

Bang goes the smarty-pants plan with the nail file. He had not planned for a strip search.

There being nothing he could do but comply, Cædmon removed his anorak, dropping it onto the ground. Then, giving every indication that he was a man with nothing to hide, he levered off his right shoe, purposely kicking it in his escort's direction. The subterfuge worked, his shoe warranting little more than a uninterested glance.

As quickly as possible, he divested himself of the rest of his clothes.

Naked, he stood before his captors. He couldn't think of a time when he'd felt more vulnerable. 'I know. I should probably be more diligent about my exercise regime.'

Neither man responded, although the one with the holstered weapon did reach inside his jacket pocket.

Removing a dark length of fabric, he tossed it at Cædmon's bare chest.

'Put on the blindfold.'

'That's a bit draconian, don't you think?'

Evidently not draconian enough, the man's response quick and ruthless. Pulling his gun from its holster, he stepped forward and smashed the revolver butt into Cædmon's face.

Myriad splashes of colour, like a Jackson Pollock abstract, instantly flashed behind his eyes. An instant later, the colours bled together, turning a deep, dark inky black.

61

Lucidity still beyond his grasp, Cædmon shuffled into the room. He heard himself nattering on about something. George Eliot and *The Mill on the Floss*. Or some such nonsense.

He tried to focus but couldn't contain his flyaway thoughts. Couldn't stop the ringing in his ears.

Bloody hell, my head hurts.

'Cædmon! Are you all right?'

He turned, his vision still blurred.

'I'm fine,' he lied, uncertain to whom he spoke.

He blinked several times, willing vague shapes to come into focus. They came in bits and bobs. *Two parallel worry lines between two equally worried brown eyes. Long curly hair. A red bruise on a pale cheek.*

'Edie ... Thank God. Are you all right?' He immediately realized that it was an asinine question; he could see that she wasn't.

'I'm fine.'

His vision clearing, he looked about. All around him he saw solid eighteenth-century construction. Shuttered windows. Wooden floor. Thick stone walls. It was a prison from which there would be no escape, even if he could somehow disable his captors, of which he counted four. He wondered which of the quartet had been responsible for the bruise on Edie's cheek; any one of the brutes appeared capable of hitting a defenceless woman.

'Cædmon, what did they do to you?' Edie cried, prevented from approaching him by an older man who had a hand clamped around her upper arm.

As though he were caught in one of those bizarre dreams in which he was naked and everyone else fully clothed, he belatedly realized that while he was wearing his trousers, shirt and shoes, he held in his hands jumper, pants and socks. Mercifully, his trousers were zipped, although his shirt was completely unbuttoned.

'I was subjected to a somewhat thorough body search. Needless to say, I feel a bit violated.'

'I hope my men weren't too rough,' the older man remarked, smiling mirthlessly. 'I ordered them to go easy on you.'

Assuming the grey-haired man to be none other than Stanford MacFarlane, Cædmon summoned up an equally humourless smile. He wiped his hand under his bloodied nostrils, his escorts having come damn close to breaking his nose. 'I shall live to fight another day.'

'As you can well imagine, I have several questions that I'm hoping you can answer for me.'

'I believe this is where I'm supposed to say, "I want my solicitor."'

Ignoring Cædmon's sally, MacFarlane asked quietly, 'First and foremost, where is the Ark of the Covenant?'

Knowing that Edie's life was at stake, he replied as sincerely as he could, 'I have no idea. Although I'm certain that if we put on our thinking caps, we can uncover its location.'

'That's what the last scholar said to me ... right before his death.'

Out of the corner of his eye, Cædmon saw Edie put a hand to her mouth. In truth, he felt a bit queasy himself.

'I'm not a bloody psychic; I'm an academic. And as such, I must insist that you give logic a chance. In my anorak pocket you'll find a sketch which I believe may be of some interest.'

MacFarlane walked over to the thug holding his anorak. Removing two sheets of folded paper from the front pocket, he first examined the translated quatrains, then the sketched drawing of the presentation of Christ.

'Before I get to the drawing, I should tell you what we've learned to date. We now believe that the quatrains were not written by Galen of Godmersham.' MacFarlane's head jerked round, the man clearly thunderstruck. 'Rather they were written by Galen's third wife, Philippa of Canterbury.'

'You're certain of this?'

'There is no doubt in my mind.'

MacFarlane chewed on this morsel for several

seconds. 'And what about St Lawrence the Martyr?'

'A red herring,' Cædmon replied, suspecting the 'last scholar's' fate had been sealed with that particular misinterpretation. 'The "blessed martyr" in question is Thomas à Becket. Which led us to Canterbury cathedral, where we discovered a stained-glass window.'

MacFarlane stared at the sketch like an addict staring at a full needle.

'As to the specifics of the window, one must bear in mind that it was created by an artisan with a very different set of cultural references. From a semiotic standpoint, deciphering the window is akin to peering through a dark lens. Complex theological tenets, historical fact and archaic linguistic structures are all jumbled together in that one seemingly innocuous drawing. It will take time to sort out the various strands.' Seeing the frown on MacFarlane's face, he hastily added, 'However, we have reason to believe that the two geese in the basket are significant.'

'What makes you think that?'

'Because one of the geese represents Philippa herself, in the medieval guise of the good housewife. Unfortunately, we have yet to decipher the meaning of the second goose.'

'When will you have it deciphered?'

'Not until I have recovered.' Cædmon stood his ground, knowing that if he didn't, there was no hope. Then, gesturing to Edie, he said, 'We both need food and rest.'

The caveat was more for Edie's sake then his own. He could see by her strained expression that she was utterly exhausted. If an opportunity arose to escape, she would need to be sufficiently rested to turn that opportunity to advantage.

MacFarlane impatiently tapped his watch. 'If the Ark of the Covenant is not in my hands in sixteen hours, I'll kill the woman.'

Although the proceedings had so far proved civilized, Cædmon recalled the old proverb advising the unsuspecting diner to use a long spoon when supping with the devil.

'I will do all in my power to find the Ark,' he assured his adversary.

MacFarlane locked gazes with him, a barely contained malevolence lurking beneath his controlled expression. 'Behave like a guest and you'll continue to be treated as such. Am I making myself clear?'

'As a bell.'

62

'I don't know about you, but I've had enough chips for one day,' Cædmon grumbled.

'And guys with big guns and things that go bump in the night.' Edie squinted, there being only a glimmer of light shining under the locked door. MacFarlane's idea of food and rest was a cupboard and a couple of bags of soggy fried potatoes.

'But on a bright note, we shall be lulled to sleep by the babbling brook that runs beneath the mill.'

Edie made no reply, a damp chill oozing up through the floorboards on account of that same babbling brook. Already she could feel the ache in her joints.

'By the by, I've got your metal nail file hidden under the insole of my shoe.'

'I can top that. I've got a thousand dollars stuffed inside my boot. After the attack in Oxford, I was worried someone might steal the Virgin bag.' She abruptly changed gear. 'There's something I need to tell you: I have intimate knowledge of Stanford MacFarlane.'

'Indeed?'

'Not biblical knowledge,' Edie quickly amended. 'But I do know the heart of Stanford MacFarlane.'

'And how is that?' There was no mistaking the interest in his voice.

'My maternal grandfather was something of a religious zealot. If not from the same bolt of cloth as MacFarlane, Pops was certainly cut from a similar one.' She laughed caustically, the memory an unpleasant one. 'My grandfather believed that freedom of religion extended only to other evangelical Christians.'

'Being a young girl, I'm surprised that you weren't, er . . .'

'Indoctrinated? Having been raised by a mother who repeatedly told me she would clean up her act and who repeatedly failed made me a hard sell. Deep-seated trust issues, I suppose.' She readjusted her legs, the dark space a tight fit for the two of them. 'Having sat through all those Sunday sermons, I know that men like Pops and Stanford MacFarlane lie awake at night consumed with visions of a global theocracy.'

She paused a moment, recalling her conversation with MacFarlane. 'Although I get the feeling that, unlike Pops, MacFarlane thinks of himself as some sort of Old Testament patriarch.'

'One of those bastards who prays before the bloodletting, hmm?'

Edie shuddered. 'He's probably praying as we speak.'

Putting an arm round her shoulder, Cædmon pulled her close. 'As long as there's a chance of finding the Ark, you're safe. MacFarlane knows that if he harms you in any way, I'll refuse to comply with his demands.'

'You don't actually trust him to keep his word, do you?'

It being too dark in the closet for her to discern Cædmon's features, she sensed rather than saw his sardonic smile.

'In my experience, deciding how much to trust one's enemy is a fine art.'

In the same way that she had sensed the smile, Edie intuited its disappearance.

'It's my fault you got dragged into this mess. I should never have agreed to –'

Edie put a hand over his mouth, hushing him. 'Since meeting you at the National Gallery of Art, everything I've done, and I mean *everything* – from coming to England, to making love, to riding in the back of that refrigerated truck – I've done of my own free will. We're in this together, Cædmon. And don't for one second think that we're not. There was no way either of us could have known that MacFarlane's goon had planted a tracking device on me.'

'Are you saying the punch-up in the alley was a blind? Bloody hell. From the outset MacFarlane has been one step ahead of me.'

Hearing the self-recrimination in his voice, she thought a change of subject in order. 'We've got sixteen hours to figure out the meaning of those two geese in the basket. All we know is that one of them represents Philippa.' She sighed, sixteen hours suddenly a very brief amount of time. 'I wish we knew more about Philippa. Other than the fact that she married Galen and joined a nunnery, we've got precious few clues.'

'The nunnery ... The *nunnery*! That's it! You, Edie Miller, are bloody beautiful!'

Cædmon began to bang on the cupboard door with his fist.

'What the hell's goin' on in there?'

'Tell MacFarlane that I know where the Ark is hidden.'

63

Onward, Christian soldiers, Cædmon mused silently, noticing that each of the four armed men gathered around the table wore a Jerusalem cross ring on his right hand.

'And you're absolutely certain that the two geese depicted in the stained-glass window will lead us to the Ark of the Covenant?' MacFarlane gestured to the drawing on the tabletop.

Seated in front of a laptop computer, Cædmon stopped typing, taking a moment to glance at his adversary. He knew that for this man he served but one purpose. Once he had fulfilled that purpose, he would no longer be in a position to safeguard Edie.

Surreptitiously, he glanced at the locked cupboard door on the far side of the room.

Somehow he had to devise a suitable enticement, a bargaining chip, that he could use to gain Edie's freedom. Until then he would reveal enough to whet MacFarlane's voracious appetite but not so much that he lessened his worth. Stanford MacFarlane had to continue to believe that without him he would never find the Ark.

'As I earlier mentioned, one of the geese symbolizes Philippa in her role as the good housewife to her husband Galen of Godmersham. After Galen's death, Philippa joined a nunnery, where she lived out her remaining days. With that in mind, I believe that the second goose also represents Philippa, nuns often referred to as brides of Christ. So Philippa was the good housewife of Christ, as it were.'

MacFarlane took a moment to digest the crumb tossed to him. 'What does Galen's widow being a nun have to do with anything?' he asked, his eyes narrowing with suspicion. He'd already been led down a false path by one man. Clearly, he was not about to proceed without a clear map.

'It's possible that Philippa took the Ark with her to the nunnery.' Cædmon jutted his chin at the Oxford University search engine he'd brought up on the internet. 'Hopefully, I'll be able to find out which order Philippa joined, although it may take some time as there were scores of now-defunct religious orders active in the fourteenth century.'

'Time is the one thing we've got in short supply.'

As he waited for the search results, Cædmon couldn't help but wonder at MacFarlane's impatience. It made him think that the Warriors of God were working to some sort of deadline. *But a deadline for what?* Although tantalized by an ancient mystery that had beguiled such luminaries as Newton and Freud, Cædmon was keenly aware that lives had been ruthlessly taken, MacFarlane's obsession with the Ark clearly knowing no bounds.

'Ah! We have a hit,' he announced, pointing to the

computer screen. 'According to a fourteenth-century document called the *Regestrum Archiepiscopi* –'

'Can the Latin,' MacFarlane snarled.

'Right.' Cædmon decided to dumb down. 'What you are looking at is the Archbishop of Canterbury's register of nunneries compiled in the year 1350. That being two years after the plague, I suspect the archbishop was very keen to have a head count. Since most folk in the Middle Ages rarely travelled more than thirty miles from the place of their birth, I'll first search for Philippa in the Kent listings.'

As he scrolled through the register, Cædmon knew that he was operating on nothing more than a strong hunch. A hunch that if proved wrong could have tragic results.

'There she is,' he murmured. 'Philippa, widowed wife of Galen of Godmersham, is listed as a member of the Priory of the Blessed Virgin Mary. According to the entry, she entered the nunnery with a dowry worth approximately –'

'Just tell me where the priory is located,' MacFarlane interrupted.

'It is located in the hamlet of Swanley, south-east of London.'

MacFarlane turned to the behemoth with the sutured head. 'Pull it up on the GPS system.'

Using a stylus that looked ridiculous in his oversized hand, the brute began pecking away at a hand-held device.

'I've got it. It's at the intersection of highways M20

and M25,' he announced, passing the apparatus to his superior.

MacFarlane studied the computer-generated map. 'You were right. Swanley is exactly thirty miles from Canterbury. Which means we can be there within the hour.'

Cædmon shook his head and calmly pointed out the obvious. 'If we traipse around a medieval priory in the middle of the night, we might very well be confronted by the local constabulary, particularly if the nunnery is a National Trust property. Given the importance of the task, we would be better off waiting for daylight.'

MacFarlane stared at him, long and hard.

'We hit the road at first light,' he said at last. Then, his gaze boring into Cædmon, he hissed, 'If you're thinking about sidestepping me like that Harvard pencil dick, you think again, boy.'

Although he took exception to being called a 'boy', Cædmon kept himself in check. 'Bear in mind that Swanley may simply be where we find the next clue.'

'What are you saying, that this is going to turn into some sort of scavenger hunt?'

'If you wish to hide a tree, put it in a forest. We won't know if the Priory of the Blessed Virgin Mary is the forest until we can properly examine the site.'

'Well, you better hope to God that it is the right forest.'

Cædmon wondered what would happen should they not find the Ark. He guessed slit throats and bodies buried at low-water mark featured somewhere.

64

Dawn arrived, damp and grey, the passenger windows on the Range Rover still ice-rimmed. The cold went right through Edie, causing her teeth to chatter loudly. Although she suspected that fear had more to do with her rattling teeth than the outside temperature.

Rudely awakened only a short time earlier, she and Cædmon had been bundled into the back seat of the waiting vehicle. Seated in front of them was the driver, Sanchez, a sullen man given to muttering in Spanish, and his co-pilot Harliss, a southerner with an accent so thick he might as well have been speaking in Spanish. Both men were armed. And both had made it very clear that they would not hesitate to use their weapons.

Leading the pack in a second Range Rover were Stanford MacFarlane and his right-hand man Boyd Braxton. To Edie's relief, she'd had little to no contact with the hulking brute since the attempted rape. Knowing that Cædmon had enough on his plate, she'd made no mention of the near miss.

'Didn't you say something about swans and geese being interchangeable in the medieval lexicon?'

'Hmm?' Clearly lost in thought, Cædmon tore his

gaze away from the window. 'Er, yes, I did say that.'

'Making it all the more likely that this place Swanley is where we'll find the Ark.'

'I have no idea if the Ark is hidden at the nunnery. The Priory of the Blessed Virgin Mary may simply be where we find the next clue.'

Enviously she watched as Harliss passed a cup filled from a Thermos of hot coffee to Sanchez.

'My feet feel like two blocks of ice,' she complained in a low voice, pointedly glancing at the pair of green wellies she'd been issued with.

Cædmon, decked out in an identical pair of boots, commiserated. 'The English wellington was designed to keep the foot dry not warm. Although we'll be glad of them should we have to tramp through a damp field.'

Edie didn't bother to point out that a sprint through that same damp field would be next to impossible in the clunky rubber boots.

They had been driving through the post-dawn gloom about twenty minutes when Edie sighted the first road sign for Swanley. Approaching the town limits, she was surprised to see that Swanley looked a lot like any American residential suburb, its outskirts littered with car dealerships and fast-food eateries.

How are we going to find the Ark in the middle of this suburban sprawl?

'The priory is located in the countryside,' Cædmon remarked, guessing her thoughts.

As if on cue, Sanchez took the next exit off the

main road, veering onto a narrow country lane. Peering out the window, she'd forgotten how simple things – trees in the distance, pastures, farm fences – could create a stark cinematic beauty, the contrast between the countryside and the nearby town like midnight and high noon.

Up ahead, MacFarlane's Range Rover slowed and then stopped at the side of the road. Sanchez pulled in a few feet behind.

'Is this the place?' she asked, not seeing anything in the rural landscape that even remotely resembled a medieval nunnery.

'I believe so,' Cædmon replied. 'MacFarlane plotted the course on a satellite navigation system. Although we'll probably have to trek across a field or two to reach it.'

Harliss opened the rear door. 'Get out.' Gun in hand, he ushered them towards the other vehicle while Sanchez unloaded several large bulky canvas packs from the Range Rover's boot.

Edie and Cædmon were ordered to keep their distance while MacFarlane briefed his men. She managed to see that Harliss had a hand-held GPS receiver which all four men studied intently. Although she tried to listen in, she could only catch a few snippets of what was said – 'avenues of approach ... terrain features ... obstacles ... reconnaissance'.

'They're treating this like some sort of military operation,' she whispered to Cædmon.

'Apparently so.'

'Making us the enemy, huh?'

Too busy scanning the surrounding area, Cædmon made no reply.

'Move 'em out,' MacFarlane ordered gruffly.

Sandwiched between two pairs of armed men, she and Cædmon moved off in a north-easterly direction. In front of them about two hundred yards in the distance was a dense grove of trees. As they trudged across the field, Edie wondered if Philippa of Canterbury had had any notion of the deadly train of events she would someday trigger with her quatrains.

More than likely she had guessed. Why else would the noblewoman-cum-nun have gone to such lengths to hide her dead husband's gold *arca*? Philippa had survived the horror of the plague and no doubt blamed the Ark for the deadly pestilence that had swept across England.

Last night Cædmon told her that Philippa had belonged to the Gilbertines, an order of nuns founded in England. In the span of only six years, Philippa had risen through the ranks, eventually becoming the priory cellaress, a position in which she oversaw all of the food production. A capable woman with a flair for management, she could have easily arranged for the Ark of the Covenant to have been brought to Swanley. Maybe she let her fellow nuns in on the secret. Since they lived a life devoted to worship and contemplative prayer, there was little fear that the secret would be revealed to nosy outsiders.

The GPS receiver held in his right hand, Harliss led them through the grove of trees, the gnarled leaf-less limbs like so many arthritic hands.

Just beyond the bare boughs, Edie glimpsed a stone wall.

'I see it!' she exclaimed, raising her right hand and pointing, inexplicably excited. 'It's over there.'

'Roger that,' Harliss responded, leading them towards to the right.

A few moments later they entered a clearing.

Edie glanced from side to side.

'Oh God . . . It's been destroyed.'

65

Stunned, the six of them stood rooted in place.

'What the fuck happened?' Braxton muttered, expressing what everyone in the group was no doubt thinking, all that remained of the Priory of the Blessed Virgin Mary being three stone walls punctuated with arched windows, tangled strands of dead ivy cascading from the glassless openings.

'It looks like it was hit by mortar fire.' This from MacFarlane, his leathery cheeks flushed with what Edie assumed to be barely contained rage.

'My guess is that the priory was destroyed during the Reformation,' Cædmon stated quietly. 'In 1538, Parliament, at the behest of Henry VIII, issued an edict known as the Dissolution of the Monasteries. The law enabled Henry to confiscate all property owned by the monastic orders. Aided by many in the general population, who hoped that Church riches would stick to their greedy hands, many monastic buildings were demolished and the stone reused for secular building projects.'

Edie stared at the eerie remains: the gouged Gothic shell open to the heavens, the sheaves of ice-laden grass shimmering jewel-like. Perhaps it was the early-morning mist, but she could have sworn that a ghostly hint of incense and candles and chanted prayers still lingered.

She turned and glanced at Cædmon, asking the silent question: *What if the next clue was contained in a piece of stained glass that had been smashed to smithereens centuries ago?* With an almost imperceptible shake of the head, he warned her against voicing her query. He then pointedly glanced at Stanford MacFarlane. Edie got the message loud and clear. If MacFarlane thought the game was up, she and Cædmon would be killed on the spot. No matter what, they had to maintain the pretext that it was still game on.

Startled by a screech, Edie turned.

Perched on the branch of a leafless tree was a raven.

Although not a superstitious person by nature, she considered the raven a *very* bad omen.

66

'Not to worry,' Cædmon announced, affecting a tone of bluff good cheer. 'The fact that the priory has been destroyed will not impede our progress in the least. In fact, it should make the task far easier.'

'Do you think I suddenly went loco? There's nothing here,' MacFarlane argued, gesturing to the empty space within the three stone walls.

'Ah! "They have eyes, but they do not see."'

'And what does King David have to do with anything?'

Knowing that he needed to produce a rabbit from his hat, Cædmon replied, 'The king's observation is most appropriate. For while the untrained eye sees nothing but overgrown grass and three stone walls, the trained eye sees the nunnery as it once stood.'

Several seconds passed in silence.

'Go ahead. I'm listening,' MacFarlane said, rather grudgingly.

Relieved that he passed the initial audition, Cædmon cast Edie a quick, reassuring glance.

Don't worry, love. I can do this. I can buy us the time we need.

He gestured to the meadow adjacent to the walls.

405

'If you care to join me, I would like to take what the archaeologists call a field walk. Since we don't have the benefit of an aerial photograph, by slowly walking the site we should be able to detect slight fluctuations and anomalies in the ground surface. These fluctuations and anomalies will enable us to reconstruct the plan of the original nunnery. Once we've done that, we'll be in a much better position to know where to begin the search.'

Although MacFarlane nodded his assent, a silent addendum was included – *You better come up with something fast.*

Cædmon commenced the tour. 'First, a quick primer in monastic layout. The majority of medieval priories followed a standard prototype of three buildings, usually two storeys in height, arranged in a U shape. This U-shaped configuration would have abutted a church.' He gestured to the three stone walls. 'As you can see, the demolished church is all that remains of the Priory of the Blessed Virgin Mary.'

'So, if I'm imaging this correctly, the church and the U-shaped buildings would have enclosed some sort of courtyard,' Edie remarked.

'Quite correct. The garth, or cloister as it is more commonly called, was the large open space within the enclosed buildings. The cloister was primarily used for gardening and the interment of the dead.'

A definite spark of interest in his eyes, MacFarlane clearly recognized the possibilities that the cloister presented. 'I'm guessing that no one would have thought twice about a deep hole being dug in the courtyard.'

'Precisely. Furthermore, only nuns and novices were permitted inside the cloister, thus making it the perfect place for Philippa to bury the Ark of the Covenant.' Arms spread wide, Cædmon gestured to the open meadow that moments ago MacFarlane had been so quick to dismiss. 'Here, Philippa could have secreted the Ark from the outside world and at the same time kept an eye on it. Shall we begin our stroll around the cloister?'

Taking the lead, he walked to the other side of the small meadow, MacFarlane on his heels, Edie and the rest in tow.

'This, I believe, is where the refectory would have been situated,' he said, gesturing to an area of over-grown weeds and tangled grass. 'The refectory was, as you undoubtedly know, the hall where all meals were taken.'

'Aka the penguins' mess tent,' one of MacFarlane's henchmen snickered.

Ignoring this contribution, Cædmon marched forward approximately fifteen yards. 'And this would have been the *lavatorium*.'

'The wash area, right?'

He nodded at Edie. 'That's correct.' He then walked another fifteen yards. 'Here would have stood the kitchen area.'

'And just how is it you know all this?' MacFarlane

asked suspiciously, glancing back and forth between the last two areas delineated.

Cædmon smiled knowingly, about to divulge how he had pulled a rabbit out of thin air. 'If you look carefully, you'll see a slightly raised area.' He pointed to the ground. 'That is what's known as a kitchen midden. Or what the layman might refer to as a rubbish heap. And if you were to search the *lavatorium*, you would see a depression rather than a raised area.'

'Caused by centuries of running water,' Edie correctly deduced.

'Satisfied?' He directed the question to the man who held their fate in his hands.

Again, MacFarlane glanced back and forth between the 'kitchen' and the '*lavatorium*'. Appeased, he jutted his head at the small meadow. 'Keep walking.'

Cædmon continued with the tour. 'Across from us, on the other side of the cloister, would have been the nuns' dormitory. And directly opposite the church would have been the chapter house and abbess's quarters.' Raising his arm, he motioned in four directions. 'With each of the nunnery buildings accounted for, we can now extrapolate the cloister boundaries.'

MacFarlane surveyed the area in question. 'And you're certain that the Ark would have been buried somewhere within the cloister?'

Cædmon hesitated. 'There are strong reasons to

believe that Philippa would have deemed the cloister the safest place to hide the Ark. Although where in the cloister, I couldn't begin to speculate.'

To his surprise, this admission was greeted with an unconcerned shrug. Turning to his men, MacFarlane commenced to give orders.

'Sanchez, I want you on the metal detector. Gunnery Sergeant, you've got the GPR. And Harliss, you're on guard duty.' The orders met with a deferential chorus.

His input no longer needed, Cædmon was ordered to stand beside Edie, the two of them placed under the watchful eye of the unintelligible southerner. A man prone to toothy grins that conveyed a dark malevolence, Harliss let it be known that he had disabled the safety mechanism on his MP5 sub-machine gun. 'Meanin' I can shoot y'all all the sooner,' as he had so obligingly informed them.

Scanning the landscape, Cædmon could see no avenue of escape, no farmhouse that he and Edie could run to, the Priory of the Blessed Virgin Mary situated in a remote spot. If they could somehow make their way to the country lane where the Range Rovers were parked, they might be able to flag down a passing motorist. But getting there amidst a hail of bullets was a remote possibility at best. Which left only one viable option: he had to disarm one of MacFarlane's men – no easy feat given that all three were sturdily constructed and clearly knew how to handle themselves.

'What's going on?' Edie asked, nudging him with her elbow. Sanchez's sweep of the cloister already underway, the ground was littered with several small flags.

'Each time his metal detector finds any buried metal, it beeps. The spot is marked with a flag. I'm guessing the colour of the flag indicates the type of metal detected.'

'Oh, I get it. So ... grey is for silver, orange for bronze, black for lead and yellow for gold?'

He nodded. ' I should think so. Since a metal detector can't tell what a buried object actually is, Braxton will use his ground-penetrating radar to survey all the areas that show gold. The assumption being that the Ark of the Covenant was indeed made of pure gold.'

Edie raised a quizzical brow. 'Radar? You mean like they use at airports?'

'Not exactly. Rather than sending radio waves through the air, these waves are directed into the ground. The electronic signals then bounce back to a receiver.' He nodded towards the laptop computer that Braxton had set up on top of the GPR receiver. 'A computerized map will be generated based on the density and position of the returned signals. It should enable them to determine the size and depth of any buried object.'

'Normally, I'd say, "Way cool," but I've got a funny feeling this ground-penetrating radar is going to make or break us.'

Cædmon made no reply, having reached the same conclusion. He stared wordlessly at Edie. At the curls covered in a bridal veil of morning mist. At the mottled purple bruise on her right cheek. He thought she resembled nothing so much as a bedraggled street urchin. Something straight out of Dickens. Brave and vulnerable in the face of danger.

'I've got something!' Braxton suddenly yelled.

Hearing that, Cædmon inwardly breathed a sigh of relief. 'I'd say we're bang on target.' Then, his interest getting the better of him, he called out, 'May I have a look?'

When MacFarlane nodded his assent, Harliss escorted them over to the laptop, prodding them forward with his sub-machine gun.

'I'm getting a whole bunch of small objects,' Braxton said, pointing to the computer screen.

Cædmon studied the monitor, the computer-generated image resembling nothing so much as a black-and-white photograph of the moon. And the dark side of the moon at that.

He tapped several small spots on the computer screen. 'These are probably stones scattered when the nunnery was destroyed. But this looks promising,' he said, pointing to what appeared to be a large, solid object buried some two yards below the surface.

'Whatever it is, it's a big mother. Sir, you want me to dig it up?'

A definite gleam in his eyes, MacFarlane nodded.

Moments later, pickaxe in hand, the behemoth began swinging like a brigand in search of gold doubloons, no thought whatsoever given to properly excavating the site, of carefully slicing away section by section in order to recover any historic artefacts that might be nestled in the soil. For these men, there was only *one* artefact of any import.

While Braxton attacked with his pickaxe, Sanchez assisted with a shovel, the two men making fast work of it. Donning a pair of knee pads, MacFarlane perched himself on the edge of the hole. His gaze intent, he peered into the deepening chasm, putting Cædmon in mind of a large bird of prey about to swoop upon its quarry.

Overhead the clouds fused together to release a cold drizzle on their uncovered heads. The light rain soaked MacFarlane's grey hair, the spiky tufts clinging to his head like a skullcap. Seen in profile, he resembled a fierce Celtic warrior come to life.

'Yeah, boy! We got it!' Braxton shouted jubilantly.

Sanchez heaved himself out of the hole and rushed over to one of the canvas equipment bags, retrieving some rope. He tossed the coiled length at his digging partner.

Edie slipped her hand into Cædmon's. 'I can't believe it . . . They actually found it,' she whispered.

As Sanchez and Braxton pulled their find to the surface, Cædmon held his breath, about to set his eyes on the most sought-after relic in the history of mankind.

It could have been mine, he thought jealously, *had I played the game differently.*

After several loud grunts and a muttered curse, a box was hauled out of the hole.

Its appearance met with a stunned silence.

'I don't think it's made of gold,' Edie said at last, the remark provoking a glare from Stanford MacFarlane.

'No, it isn't gold,' Cædmon agreed. 'A lesser metal. Bronze perhaps. Difficult to say, under all the grime.' The box was secured on the outside with a large lock.

Braxton ran the back of his hand over his dirt-smudged brow, still panting from his labours. 'Maybe the Ark is inside.'

'Open it,' MacFarlane ordered.

With one strong-armed swing of the pickaxe, the behemoth broke the lock.

His jaw tightly clenched, his gaze resolute, MacFarlane threw back the lid. Everyone stared wide-eyed at the uncovered treasure.

Everyone save Stanford MacFarlane.

'What are *those*?' MacFarlane pointed an accusing finger at the golden objects that filled the box.

Extending a hand, Cædmon lifted a finely wrought candlestick from the chest. Next, he examined a jewelled gold chalice.

'These are the altar vessels from the destroyed church,' he said, running his hand over an exquisitely fashioned paten. 'No doubt the nuns had advance warning that the king's men were en route to the priory. I imagine they hid them so they wouldn't be confiscated.' He gestured to the gold objects. 'Not exactly a king's ransom, I admit, but still valuable. You should have no problem finding a buyer for –'

'I'm not interested in earthly profit,' MacFarlane interjected. 'My reward will come in the next life.' Turning his head, he looked pointedly at Edie. Then, like an Old Testament patriarch, he very quietly and calmly said, 'Kill her.'

The behemoth raised his pickaxe.

Cædmon lurched forward but, anticipating the move, Harliss and Sanchez seized hold of him.

'No!' he shouted, violently struggling to free himself.

Not like this! God in heaven, not like this!

67

'Last night you gave me sixteen hours to find the Ark of the Covenant! I have forty minutes left!' Cædmon yelled, twisting and straining to free himself from his captors.

MacFarlane stared at him as he considered his appeal, Michelangelo's stern-faced Moses come to life.

'Colonel MacFarlane, I know you to be a man of your word,' Edie croaked, her eyes flooded with tears, every limb in her body quivering with fright. 'Please give Cædmon a chance. Without him, you'll never find the Ark.'

Pondering it later, Cædmon decided that this last throw by Edie had swung it. MacFarlane nodded curtly. 'You have exactly forty minutes. If you don't want to see Miss Miller's head split open like a Fourth of July watermelon, you *will* find the Ark of the Covenant.' He glanced dismissively at the gleaming altar vessels in the still-open trunk. 'I'm not interested in digging up any more golden trinkets.'

Stay of execution issued, Braxton lowered the pickaxe. Glancing at Edie, Cædmon battled the strong desire to bend over and retch.

It had been close. With one swing, the behemoth

would have punched a gaping hole right through her skull.

'I'll find your bloody gold box,' he muttered, glancing at his watch, the countdown already begun.

Christ. Forty minutes to find something buried centuries ago.

The clock ticking, he ignored the stricken expression still plastered on Edie's face. They had to stay focused on the task at hand. To that end, he slowly turned, studying the wintry landscape that surrounded the cloister. Leafless trees. Dead grass. The shattered walls of the church.

There was something here that he wasn't seeing. But what?

In the distance he heard a loud honking sound. A swan searching for its mate.

Bloody hell.

'Swans and geese,' he murmured, wondering if the answer to Philippa's riddle could really be so simple. He turned to MacFarlane. 'In the medieval lexicon, the two words are interchangeable, one and the same. And if you'll recall, there were two geese depicted in the Canterbury window, symbolizing the fact that swans and geese mate for life.'

The older man's brow furrowed. 'I'm not following.'

'The name of this place is Swanley. In the Middle English of the fourteenth century, a ley was a meadow.'

'I got the clue!' Edie exclaimed, realizing the

significance of the place name. '"Swanley" would translate as "swan meadow". Meaning that we need to start searching for a meadow. Or some swans. Or maybe even both.'

The furrow in MacFarlane's forehead deepened. 'What kind of bullshit are you trying to pull? Swans swim on the water; they don't flap around on a grassy field.' He gestured to the surrounding dell.

'I'm the first to admit it's a nonsensical word combination. But that doesn't detract from the fact that it is highly significant. In the quatrains Philippa referred to herself as the "trusted goose". At Canterbury we discovered a stained-glass window in which the Ark of the Covenant was depicted along with two geese in a basket. Now we find ourselves here at Swanley. Trust me. It *does* mean something.' He turned to Harliss, the keeper of the GPS navigation device. 'Is there a lake or pond in the vicinity?'

Given the go-ahead by his commander, the muscle-bound lackey consulted his hand-held device. 'Yeah, I got a body of water about two hundred yards east of here.'

'Then I suggest we proceed there with all haste.'

When no objection was raised, he motioned to Harliss to lead the way. Sanchez remained behind at the cloister to pack up the equipment. Braxton, the pickaxe jauntily swung over his left shoulder, a powerful Desert Eagle pistol clutched in his right hand, brought up the rear.

As they trooped off towards the new destination,

bare branches rustled in the damp breeze. Whispering. Warning.

'Please tell me that I've got more than thirty-some minutes to live,' Edie said in a lowered voice, glancing furtively at MacFarlane.

'Hold up,' Cædmon answered in an equally hushed tone, not wanting her to dwell on the time. He knew from experience that it was best to deal with those variables one could control rather than to obsess on something beyond one's grasp.

'Yeah, yeah, I know. I need to stand tall. Or stand my ground. Or some silly cliché.' While she appeared composed, Cædmon detected a note of panic in her voice.

He reached over and squeezed her hand. 'An opening will present itself. It always does. And when that happens, we must seize the moment. No time for hesitation, right?'

She nodded, a vengeful gleam in her brown eyes. Cædmon suspected that she entertained a gruesome fantasy that involved a certain behemoth and a very sharp pickaxe.

A few moments later they arrived at a fish pond that he estimated to be a good ten acres. Towards the centre of the pond there was a small island. *The swan meadow.* In the middle of the isle a simple stone cross had been erected. It appeared to have taken root centuries ago.

'This is looking really, *really* good,' Edie said, clearly relieved at seeing the rough-hewn cross. 'As the priory cellaress, the fish pond would certainly have been Philippa's domain. Do you think she had the cross placed in the middle of the island as a sign?'

Cædmon shook his head. 'I suspect the cross was erected before the construction of the priory. However, Philippa would certainly have recognized its significance. As with the Ark of the Covenant, the cross is a point of direct communication between heaven and earth.' He cast a quick sideways glance at MacFarlane, the older man staring intently at the lone cross. As though it were some sort of mystical beacon.

He'd made his case. *Thank God.*

'It could very well be that even before the priory was built, this was a religious site,' he continued. Then, gesturing to the surprisingly clear, glassy surface of the pond, 'Undoubtedly the pond is fed by a natural spring. Such springs were often dedicated to a local saint.'

'Making this a holy place, right?'

Cædmon nodded. 'And that would have made the isle a fitting place for Philippa of Canterbury to hide the most sacred relic in all Christendom.' He gestured to a quartet of small rowing dinghies moored to the nearby bank. 'I doubt if the local anglers will mind if we make use of their boats.'

MacFarlane walked over and inspected the boats bobbing on the water. 'Gunnery Sergeant, I want you to row across with the woman. Harliss, you wait for Sanchez to arrive with the equipment. Aisquith and

I will take the lead.' Orders given, he untied one of the boats, brusquely gesturing for Cædmon to precede him into the vessel.

'Hopefully she's still seaworthy,' Cædmon muttered as he took hold of the oars and began the laborious business of rowing towards the isle.

MacFarlane made no reply, his unblinking gaze set upon the limestone Lorelei that stood sentry in the middle of the isle.

For the next several minutes the only sounds were the creak and groan of oars repeatedly slicing through the chill water and the occasional honking of the resident swans. The rain having stopped, wispy tendrils of white vapour hovered over the surface of the water, wrapping the pond in a cloying embrace.

No sooner did the prow of the boat ground against the small isle than MacFarlane disembarked, the older man hurriedly sloshing through the calf-high water that lapped the grassy shoreline. Clearly impatient, he motioned for Cædmon to secure the boat to a clump of nearby bushes. A few moments later, Edie and the behemoth docked beside them. Together the four of them made their way to the cross.

Well aware that he only had eighteen minutes left on the clock, Cædmon fingered the worn stone. If a clue had been carved into the cross, the rain gods and wind zephyrs had long since made certain of its erasure.

Undeterred, he walked around to the back of the

cross. Treading on something hard, he sank to his knees, shoving aside the long grass.

'What are you doing?' MacFarlane hissed, hunkering down beside him.

'There's something embedded in the ground. I think it's a ... yes, a plaque of some sort. Do you have a handkerchief or something? I need to wipe the surface.'

MacFarlane gestured to the behemoth, wordlessly ordering him to remove the black knitted hat he wore on his head.

Cap in hand, Cædmon began to rub vigorously at what looked like a bronze plaque some ten inches square, years of dirt having accumulated on its incised surface. As he worked, a shadow fell over him. Glancing up, he saw Edie hovering over his right shoulder, an anxious look on her face. She knew that her life hung in the balance, that whether she lived or died could very well hinge upon this bronze plaque. Fear a powerful motivator, Cædmon rubbed that much harder.

It took several minutes of determined polishing to reveal a single line of Latin script.

Staring at the plaque, Cædmon's heart thudded against his breastbone, utterly staggered by that solitary line of Latin. Like a man who'd just seen a ghost flit past.

'*Hic amicitur archa cederis,*' he murmured as though it were a magical·incantation.

'What does it mean?' MacFarlane demanded,

shouldering him out of the way to examine the plaque.

Cædmon took several deep breaths, collecting himself. 'It reads, "Here is hidden the Ark of the Covenant."'

68

'The corpus delecti is about to be uncovered. But not by me,' Cædmon murmured, standing so close to Edie that she could feel his body heat.

She sidled even closer, a cold breeze setting her teeth chattering.

They were standing a few feet from where Braxton and Sanchez swung and shovelled in unison, the excavation already well underway, the stone cross upended in the frenzy that had ensued after Cædmon translated the bronze plaque. Believing the inscribed plaque to be no different to a giant X inscribed on a treasure map, MacFarlane hadn't bothered with a ground scan, clearly convinced the Ark of the Covenant was buried beneath the stone cross.

'Incredible to think that it's been nearly seven hundred years since someone last set eyes on the Ark,' she remarked, if for no other reason than to keep her terror at bay. According to her watch, there were six minutes left. 'I now know how Galen of Godmersham felt when he found the Ark on the Plain of Esdraelon.'

'If you recall, he had to fight to the death for possession of the relic.' Like her, Cædmon stared intently at the deepening hole. 'However, if it means coming away with our lives, I'll gladly forfeit all claim to the prize.'

'Somehow, I don't think you'll have much say in it. Which still leaves the matter of battling MacFarlane and the terrible trio.' Having had to endure several minutes of threats while Braxton rowed her over to the isle, the man a blunt instrument in search of a victim, she was acutely aware of the fact that they were outgunned and outnumbered. 'I'm not much of a military tactician, but I'm guessing that being out here, literally, in the middle of nowhere, is not to our advantage. Even if we could sneak over and untie a boat, there's no way we can row to shore fast enough.' At least not fast enough to elude the bullets.

'Like you, I fear Philippa's fish pond will become a watery grave should we attempt to escape.'

'So, where does that leave us?'

'In very dire straits,' Cædmon quietly replied, not one for sugar-coating the truth.

Out of the corner of her eye Edie noticed that MacFarlane had carefully removed several items from the canvas equipment bag that Sanchez had brought over to the isle. Unzipping what appeared to be a waterproof garment bag, he took out a long white robe and some sort of striped apron. Unconcerned that he had two avid onlookers, he unbuttoned and removed his waterproof. Raising his arms, he pulled the robe over the top of his cargo pants and military-style sweater. Over that, he donned the apron, belting it at the waist.

Attired in the strange-looking garb, he next opened a padded container from which he removed a gem-studded item that Edie instantly recognized.

She nudged Cædmon in the ribs. 'Look, it's the Stones of Fire.'

With an air of rehearsed solemnity, Stanford MacFarlane donned the gold breastplate.

'What in the world is he doing?' she whispered out of the corner of her mouth, suddenly wondering if, in addition to being dangerous, their adversary might well be deranged.

'Unless I'm greatly mistaken, he's preparing to view the Ark of the Covenant. Which is why he's attired in the garb traditionally worn by a Hebrew high priest.'

Edie squinted, the breastplate not quite as she remembered it. 'It looks as though MacFarlane had the twelve stones reset. Maybe it won't work and he'll get blasted to the fire pits of hell. Just like the Nazis in *Raiders of the Lost Ark*.'

'According to the Bible, it was the twelve stones, not the gold breastplate, that gave the high priest the necessary protection to interact with the Ark.'

MacFarlane, wearing what could only be called a patronizing sneer, approached them.

'Steadfast faith and the Stones of Fire will ensure my safety,' he announced, evidently having overheard Cædmon's last remark. 'For just as the Ark was constructed according to God's specific instructions to Moses, so too was the breastplate. As you undoubtedly know, the twelve stones were God's gift to Moses, the first guardian of the Ark.'

'Implying that you have appointed yourself the new guardian of the Ark,' Cædmon replied.

'I am the *ordained* guardian of the Ark.'

'How interesting.' Folding his arms over his chest, Cædmon smiled mirthlessly, Edie sensing that he was about to use the only weapon left to him, his superior intellect. 'Were you aware of the fact that the Stones of Fire once belonged to Lucifer?'

MacFarlane's eyes narrowed, his angry expression near-comical.

'Ah! I can see that you are familiar with the tale,' Cædmon blithely continued. 'Then you undoubtedly know that contained within the pages of the Apocrypha – those being the twelve books omitted from the Protestant Bible – the story is recounted of how God presented to his favourite, the beautiful and arrogant Lucifer, the Stones of Fire. Proudly Lucifer wore the breastplate as a symbol of his elevated status amongst the heavenly host.' Tilting his head to one side, Cædmon examined the gem-studded relic. 'Curious to think the same breastplate that you now wear once adorned the Prince of Darkness.'

In unison, MacFarlane's three subordinates glanced at the Stones of Fire. Edie could see that Cædmon's remarks were unnerving more than one man among them.

If they could flip one of them, they might have a shot at escaping with their lives.

While Braxton was loyal to a fault, she thought Harliss or Sanchez might be persuaded to swap teams. Assuming she and Cædmon could push the right buttons.

Hoping the relic's infamous lineage would create some dissension in the ranks, Edie asked the obvious. 'What happened to the Stones of Fire when Lucifer was cast out of heaven?' As she spoke, she noticed that all three of MacFarlane's henchmen cocked an attentive ear.

'The Stones of Fire then passed to the archangels Michael and Gabriel. Not only did they have joint custody of the breastplate, but it is their two images that supposedly adorn the lid of the Ark.' Picking up Edie's intention, Cædmon glanced pointedly at Braxton, Harliss and Sanchez before turning his attention to MacFarlane. 'Do you think it's safe for your lads to be in such close proximity to the Ark? Unlike you, they have no protection should an accident occur.'

'Yeah, I hear tell that skin cancer can be difficult to treat,' Edie piped up. 'And as far as I know, there's no cure for the plague.' Seeing Sanchez's slack-jawed expression, she decided to push the fear button for all it was worth. 'Oh, and let's not forget about those poor guys at Bethshemesh. Not a pretty story, let me tell ya.'

Craning his head, Cædmon peered into what was now a five-foot-deep hole, directing his comments to Braxton and Sanchez. 'Did your commander mention that the Ark of the Covenant is, in fact, a weapon of mass destruction, once used to slaughter the enemies of Israel? My own theory is that the Ten Commandments were inscribed upon pieces of radioactive –'

'Lies! Every last word of it!' MacFarlane bellowed, his face having turned a distinctly unhealthy shade of madder red.

Nervously gripping his shovel, Sanchez came to a standstill. 'But, sir, what if –'

'Keep digging!'

'Yes, sir!' Sanchez replied, applying spade to dirt with a renewed vigour.

Realizing the momentum had just swung the other way, Edie's shoulders slumped. 'So much for converting one of the faithful.'

'There is a reason why they are called true believers,' Cædmon replied. While he didn't show it, she knew that he too was dismayed by her near win.

At hearing a loud metallic *clunk!*, MacFarlane rushed over to the hole.

'Sir, we just hit some sort of metal box,' Braxton declared excitedly.

Edie swallowed a nugget-sized lump of fear.

'I think they may have actually found the bloody Ark of the Covenant.' Like a man possessed, Cædmon stared intently into the hole.

Repeating the procedure from the cloister, Sanchez fetched the coiled rope. After a little more digging he and Braxton were able to secure it around the buried object.

MacFarlane, smiling indulgently, turned his attention to Cædmon. 'Do you by any chance know the meaning of the words "apocalypse" and "tribulation"?'

If Cædmon thought the question odd, he gave no indication. 'Apocalypse is taken from the Greek word *apokalupsis*, meaning revelation. And tribulation is from the Greek *thlipsis*, meaning affliction. Did I pass?'

MacFarlane's smile broadened. 'No, you did not. Because like most, you have no concept of the *power* that is inherent in those two words, the prophetic *truth* that those two words reveal. Most people think of Judgement Day as a fairy tale that can never come to pass.'

'I take it you think differently?'

'"And I will plead against him with pestilence and with blood; and I will rain upon him, and upon his bands, and upon the many people that are with him, an overflowing rain, and great hailstones, fire, and brimstone."'

Listening to the verbal sparring, Edie started to get a very bad feeling in the pit of her painfully cramped stomach.

Apocalypse. Tribulation. Judgement Day.

She'd heard those words before. Many years ago when she'd been made to sit silent while her grandfather nightly read aloud from the dog-eared family Bible.

End Times prophecies.

The Bible, both Old and New Testaments, was full of them. As a young girl, those stories of disease, famine and global warfare had terrified her.

But what did End Times prophecies have to do with the Ark of the Covenant?

69

'I know that Bible verse ... It's from the Book of Ezekiel,' Edie murmured.

Knowing that Edie had been force-fed a biblical diet during her teenage years, Cædmon turned to her. At a glance he could see that she was distressed by MacFarlane's recitation.

'I didn't take you for a woman versed in the prophecies,' MacFarlane replied dismissively.

Edie shrugged. 'My grandfather held to the same End Times belief, absolutely certain that Ezekiel's war, as he called it, loomed on the horizon.'

'Then you undoubtedly know that the ancient prophecies are a gift from God. A light in the midst of the spiritual malaise that is so prevalent in our day and age. Many centuries ago the prophet Ezekiel clearly spelled out God's battle plan to save mankind from the forces of evil.' MacFarlane spoke with a proprietary air. As though imparting a great and wondrous secret.

'Which merely proves what I've thought all along – that biblical prophecy is too often used to justify the hate-filled agendas of warmongers like yourself.' Edie's normally pale cheeks were flushed with vivid colour, Cædmon aware that for her this argument had

a personal dimension. 'There are many fundamental-
ist Christians who believe that contained within the
verses of Ezekiel there's a detailed plan for the
invasion of Israel by an alliance of foreign countries,'
she continued, addressing her comments directly
to him. 'It's what's known as the Battle of Gog and
Magog. Furthermore, they believe that this battle will
be fought during the last days.'

The last days.

By that he supposed that Edie referred to the
much-ballyhooed apocalypse. The end of life as we
know it. As in get down on your knees and kiss the
world goodbye.

Was MacFarlane's obsession with the Ark of the
Covenant somehow intertwined with an apocalyptic
vision? God help them if it was, history full of men
who had proclaimed that the end of the world was
at hand. In almost every instance such prophets had
left only pain and misery in their wake.

'I'm curious about this Battle of Gog and Magog.'
If he'd learned anything during his spell with MI5, it
was that information was a form of power, sometimes the only power one had over one's enemies.
'Where precisely will the conflict take place?'

'The great battle will be fought in the mountains
of Israel,' MacFarlane replied.

'I see.' Cædmon mulled the disclosure, his curiosity piqued. 'And who will be involved?'

Smiling, his nemesis answered, 'The prophet
Ezekiel writes of an alliance of nations from remote

parts of the north known as "the land of Gog". This alliance will fight under the leadership of the ruler of Gog –'

'Aka Magog,' Edie interjected.

'– and will include the princes of Rosh, Meshech and Tubal.'

Cædmon pondered what, to the uninitiated ear, was so much gibberish. 'I assume that Rosh refers to the tribe of Ros, an ancient group of people believed to have inhabited the region of modern-day Ukraine and Russia.' When MacFarlane nodded, he next said, 'So, presumably this northern alliance will comprise countries formerly part of the Soviet Union.'

'Many of which, such as Kazakhstan and Tajikistan are Islamic nations,' Edie pointed out.

Islamic nations fighting a cataclysmic battle within the borders of Israel.

The plot had considerably thickened.

'According to Ezekiel, Magog's army will be supported by the nations of Persia, Cush and Put.' This also from Edie, who was fast proving herself a fount of biblical information.

'Iran, Sudan and Libya, if my ancient history serves me correctly.' Cædmon took a moment to mull over what he'd been told thus far. Then, finding a glaring inconsistency in the prophesied scenario, he said, 'Let's assume for argument's sake that the Ezekiel prophecy does foretell of a Russian-led invasion of Israel, what possible reason would Russia have for initiating such a war?'

MacFarlane stared at him as though he'd asked a simpleton's question. 'Economic and political instability are reason enough, don't you think? Israel is, after all, the Silicon Valley of the Middle East.'

'And don't forget the wealth of minerals to be mined around the Dead Sea, as well as the untapped oil reserves within Israel's borders,' Edie chipped in, her remarks leaving Cædmon unsure of whether or not she believed the apocalyptic tale. 'Given that both Russia and Israel have nuclear weapons, the end result would be catastrophic.'

'I must confess it's not a totally improbable scenario, the Middle East being so volatile,' Cædmon admitted in response to Edie's last remark. 'Although if that particular conflict ever came about, it would be started by man not God. The world's thirst for oil is unquenchable and Russia is undoubtedly concerned that the US has secured a foothold in the Arab world. The Iron Curtain may be gone, but the rivalry lingers.'

'The prophet Ezekiel describes the battle to come in clear, concise terms,' MacFarlane said with a manic gleam in his eyes. 'One has only to read the daily newspaper to know that the prophesied Battle of Gog and Magog can come at any time.'

'I'm curious as to who you think will be the victor if this conflagration were to occur.'

'Why Israel, of course. And that victory will assure Jews and Christians alike that God is still in their midst, as he was in the days of old, when he dwelt among them during the forty-year trek through the wilderness. With victory, a new temple will be erected in Jerusalem. Once it is constructed, the Ark of the Covenant will be restored to its rightful place.'

The Ark of the Covenant. Finally, they had come full circle.

Cædmon glanced at the trio of men engaged in hauling the treasure out of the hole. Time was not on his and Edie's side. And it was certainly against them if the excavation turned up anything other than the sought-after prize.

'Why are you telling me all this? Aren't you letting the cat out of the biblical bag?'

MacFarlane took a step in his direction, Cædmon surprised to see a look of entreaty on his face.

'I have a reason for sharing the prophecy with you – I want you to join us in our holy cause. The Lord always has need of good, stalwart men ready to fight his battles.'

70

'As with Paul on the road to Damascus, you have a chance to redeem yourself. Read the prophecies for yourself and you will see that I speak the truth.'

Astonished that the offer had even been made, Cædmon stood silent for several seconds. That is until cynicism got the better of him.

'Ah, yes, "the sure word of prophecy",' he remarked drolly, quoting another Church father, St Peter.

'I know you to be a man searching for meaning in his own life and in the world around him.'

'While that may be true, I'm not a malleable soul ready to latch on to the first bloke who offers a ready-made cure for life's travails.' He held MacFarlane at bay, knowing that if he committed too soon, he would show his hand.

'Your words imply a deep-seated fear. I can take that fear from you.' MacFarlane expansively gestured to the three men working industriously. 'My Warriors of God know no fear.'

'He's feeding you a load,' Edie exclaimed, grabbing Cædmon by the arm as though she feared he might step across the imaginary line that had been drawn between them and their nemesis. 'I've read the

Ezekiel prophecies, and do you know what I think? I think Ezekiel was a madman, a doomsday prophet who would have been on lithium and a very short leash had he lived in the twenty-first century. One of his so-called visions tells of how he came upon a pile of dry bones in the desert and breathed life into those same bones, creating a mighty army. Maybe I'm the crazy one here, but that sounds like the kind of delusional prophecy that would be spouted by some homeless guy pushing a shopping cart.'

Eyes narrowing, Stanford MacFarlane glared contemptuously at Edie.

Hoping to smooth the waters, Cædmon cleared his throat. 'While I won't go so far as to speculate on Ezekiel's mental state, I know that many of the Old Testament authors wrote metaphorically, never intending their verses to be interpreted literally by later generations.'

'This I know above all else,' MacFarlane countered in an acid tone. 'Not only will the divine revelation given to Ezekiel come to fruition, but the Battle of Gog and Magog *will* be fought. Only those who put their trust in the Almighty will escape the coming doom. And those who take up arms against the soldiers of Magog will be doubly blessed. When the battle is fought and won, the Ark of the Covenant will be restored to its rightful place within the new temple. Repent and you will live eternally. Turn your back on the Lord and you will be damned.'

'But why ask me to join you? It's been years since I last stepped foot in a church.'

'We can use a man with your specialized talents.'

Something in the offhand compliment gave Cædmon pause, leaving him with the distinct impression that MacFarlane knew about his time with MI5. His skills would be useful to a man like MacFarlane. Although he had a small army at his disposal, there was a world of difference between a soldier and a trained intelligence officer.

'Very well. I would be happy to join you. However, there is a condition – you must free Miss –'

'Don't do it, Cædmon!' Edie screeched.

'– Miller. Needless to say, this is not negotiable,' he added, hoping to check Stanford MacFarlane. And to check Edie as well. He glanced at her, wordlessly imploring her to keep quiet.

'The woman knows too much. She can't be trusted,' the colonel replied.

'I trust her implicitly. Is that not enough?'

'She is a degenerate vessel, unworthy of your consideration. My offer does not include the woman.' Visibly rigid with the force of his contempt, MacFarlane glared at Edie. Loathing incarnate.

Caedmon reflected that throughout history men such as Stanford MacFarlane had repeatedly and passionately blamed women for the ills of the world. He'd always thought their hate stemmed from a deep-seated fear of woman's innate wisdom. Knowing that such monsters by their very nature were devoid of mercy, he said, 'Your offer puts me in mind of a medieval inquisitor attempting to convert a heretic. Regardless of whether or not the heretic repented, it usually ended badly. For the heretic, that is.'

'I can see that your eyes are jaded. That you aren't fit to gaze upon God's glory.' His contempt mutating into stern-faced rage, MacFarlane turned to his men. 'Harliss, prepare the tabernacle!'

'Yes, sir.' Like a marionette on a string, Harliss unzipped one of the oversized equipment bags.

Unable to look Edie in the eye, mortified that he had failed to save her life, Cædmon was surprised when she leaned her head against his shoulder.

'When the end comes, at least we'll be together,' she whispered.

'Yes . . . we will be at that.'

'Any idea what they're up to?' She jutted her chin at the folded stacks of material that Harliss had removed from the zippered bag.

'A badger skin, a length of blue cloth and a tightly woven veil were traditionally wrapped around the Ark whenever it was in transit. I suspect the three layers created a primitive form of non-conducting insulation. Clearly, MacFarlane intends to play by the book.'

'That being the good book, huh?'

'Indeed. Although the scriptures have a way of becoming distorted beyond recognition when spouted by a man like MacFarlane.'

Curiosity overcoming his dread, Cædmon watched

as the other two members of the trio finally dragged a large metal box out of the hole. A quick mental calculation proved that the box was large enough to house the Ark of the Covenant. As he'd done at the cloister, Braxton smashed the lock with a mighty swing of his pickaxe.

His movements slow and reverential, Stanford MacFarlane opened the lid.

Although he craned his neck, Cædmon could see nothing more than the dull glimmer of gold. A gold *what*, he couldn't say. What he could see, however, was the awestruck expression affixed to the face of each of the four men gathered around the open box. As though they'd just wandered into Aladdin's cave.

'"And there was seen in his temple the ark of his testament and there were lightnings, and voices, and thunderings, and an earthquake, and great hail,"' Stanford MacFarlane loudly intoned.

'Don't forget the drizzle,' Edie muttered under her breath. 'And the fog,' she added a moment later when Harliss set off a smoke bomb, completely obscuring the proceedings from their view.

'The Hebrew priests used to shroud the Ark in a thick blanket of incense to keep it hidden from curious onlookers.' As he spoke, Cædmon squinted and strained, but the smoke was impenetrable.

A few seconds later Harliss emerged from the smoke. Two sets of plastic handcuffs dangled from his fingers. 'I've got a restraining order for you two.'

'Will you at least tell us if it is the Ark of the Covenant?' Cædmon asked.

'Oh yeah,' the other man slowly replied, the bedazzled expression returning to his unshaved, raw-boned features. 'The two angels on top of the gold box were the giveaway.'

Hearing that was like hearing an unexpected boom of thunder, Cædmon swaying slightly on his feet.

They have actually found the Ark of the Covenant.

Knowing it was futile to resist, he stood motionless as Harliss cuffed his hands, his mind unable to comprehend the enormity of the find.

Softly humming a jaunty tune, Harliss ripped a piece of duct tape from a roll. 'Wouldn't want to disturb the neighbours,' he said with a mean-spirited cackle as he slapped the length of tape across Cædmon's mouth. That done, he bound and gagged Edie in a similar fashion.

'We got orders to row you two to shore and take you to a remote location. The colonel says it wouldn't be right to kill you in the same place where we found the Ark.'

71

For the second time that morning the spectre of death hovered at Edie's shoulder. But this time, unlike those petrified moments when she'd stood shaking beneath Braxton's pickaxe, she had time to prepare for her death. Harliss and Sanchez had loaded them into the Range Rover and headed east – somewhere towards the sea, Edie beginning to discern the tang of salt in the air.

In the distance she heard the outraged screech of a gull. The faint roar of a jet engine. Familiar sounds. Probably the last sounds she would hear.

At least she'd lived longer than her mother.

She turned and glanced at Cædmon, who, duct tape over his mouth, hands cuffed in front of him, stoically stared at the passing scenery. She wondered if he too had used the time to take stock of his life. He could have saved himself back on the isle. But he hadn't. Instead, he had tried to gain her freedom. From a madman, no less. Although furious with him for passing up his one and only chance, she thought she might just love the brave, quixotic Englishman.

Harliss, again relegated to co-pilot, peered over the headrest. 'Soon you two will be sleepin' with the angels. The colonel is fond of sayin', "The judge-ments of the Lord are true and righteous altogether. More to be desired are they than gold . . . sweeter also than honey and the honeycomb."'

Oh yeah. A bullet to the back of the head. How sweet is that?

Still leaning over the back of his seat, Harliss reached into his jacket pocket and removed a pack of filterless Camels. 'I'd offer you one but . . .' Chortling, he shook a cigarette free. He then flipped open a silver lighter. Taking a drag, he blew a perfect smoke ring into her face.

Forced to inhale the smoke through her nostrils, Edie gagged. Beside her, Cædmon twitched, his muffled protest sounding as though he were attempting to speak underwater.

Sanchez steered the SUV onto what looked like a farm road, the Range Rover lurching from side to side as they drove slowly down the rutted lane. They'd gone approximately a half mile when Sanchez put on the brakes and cut the engine.

Edie and Cædmon simultaneously turned and looked at one another.

I'm sorry, Cædmon.

Craning from side to side, Harliss gave an approving nod. 'This looks as good a place as any. Don't know that anyone's been down this road in a good long while.' He turned to his partner. 'What do ya think?'

'I think I gotta take a crap,' Sanchez blurted, releasing his seat belt.

'Jesus! A body could tell time by your bowel movements.'

'Shut up and get me the wipes out of the glove compartment.'

A few seconds later, packet in hand, Sanchez was ambling towards a clump of trees. Harliss, another half-smoked Camel sticking out of the corner of his mouth, opened the passenger door and got out of the Range Rover. Slamming the door shut, he stretched then walked round to the front of the vehicle. Leaning against the bonnet, his back to them, he proceeded to finish his cigarette.

No sooner were they alone than Cædmon urgently nudged her with his elbow. Having got her attention, he nodded towards his anorak pocket before shooting her a meaningful glance.

The nail file.

When they'd been given the wellington boots earlier that morning, Cædmon had managed to remove the file from his shoe and put in his coat pocket. Since he'd already been subjected to a thorough body search, he had assumed they wouldn't search him a second time. With his hands cuffed in front of him, he wasn't be able to retrieve the file. But her hands, although similarly bound, were much smaller.

Quickly she flipped open the flap on his pocket, shoving her fingers into the opening. It took only an instant for her to remove the file from Cædmon's pocket.

Now what? she asked with her eyes.

Cædmon indicated that he wanted the file.

A few seconds later, the metal file tightly grasped between his interlocked fingers, he motioned for her to saw her plastic cuffs back and forth across it.

It took several moments of frantic sawing before the plastic gave way.

Her hands freed, she immediately reached up to remove the strip of duct tape from her mouth. Beside her, Cædmon tersely shook his head. Uncertain why he wanted her to keep the tape in place, she grabbed the file out of his hands; they had a narrow window and she wasn't about to waste any time second-guessing him.

Gripping the file between her clenched fists, she held steady while Cædmon sawed through his cuffs, freeing himself at the exact moment that Harliss flicked aside the end of his cigarette. Cædmon snatched the file from her. Then, his hands lying inert in his lap, he stared straight ahead. Now understanding his reason for not removing the tape, Edie struck a similar pose. With the tape in place, they created the illusion of still being bound.

Harliss, humming softly to himself, walked round the front of the Range Rover. With one hand he retrieved the gun shoved into the back of his waistband while with the other he reached for Cædmon's door handle.

Edie tensed. Completely in the dark as to what Cædmon intended to do, her heart beat a painful tattoo.

An instant later, Cædmon's door swung open.

'Okay, boys and girls. Time to say hello to the hang –'

Edie saw Cædmon smash his shoulder against Harliss's right hand, slamming the southerner's wrist against the door frame, the unexpected motion causing Harliss to drop his gun.

'Fucking shit! I'm gonna –'

Nail file in his hand, Cædmon raised his right arm. A split second later blood splattered onto the passenger window. A thick, red Rorschach blotch. Then a blood-curdling scream of agony.

Harliss fell to the ground, his legs twitching convulsively. Once. Twice. Before he went eerily still, his booted feet splayed awkwardly.

Cædmon ripped the piece of duct tape off his mouth. 'Don't look!'

The caution came an instant too late.

Horrified at the metal nail file protruding from the sprawled man's eye socket, Edie yanked the tape from her mouth, spraying the back of the front seat with yellow stomach bile.

'Quick! Get out of the car!' Cædmon ordered. 'Sanchez will be here any second.'

Operating on autopilot, Edie reached for the door knob, stumbling out of the SUV in an ungainly heap. Turning her head, she saw that Cædmon had got out on his side and was hunched on the ground, searching for Harliss's weapon.

Just then, a salvo of bullets peppered the Range Rover.

Edie screamed, instinctively throwing herself to the ground. Peering under the vehicle, she saw Sanchez slam an ammunition clip into his weapon as he charged towards them. She also saw Cædmon grab Harliss by his shoulders, using the lifeless man as a shield.

Another *rat-a-tat-tat* of gunfire rang out.

Edie slammed a balled fist into her mouth, hoping, praying that Cædmon –

Reaching her side of the Range Rover, Cædmon immediately released his hold on the bullet-riddled corpse, the human shield having no doubt saved his life. Crouched beside the bonnet, he began firing Harliss's retrieved weapon.

'Search his pockets for an ammo clip!'

Edie crawled over to the dead southerner. Forcing herself not to look at the nail file protruding from his eye socket, she shoved her hand into Harliss's jacket pocket.

'All I've got is the GPS receiver and a cigarette lighter!' she hissed at Cædmon, frantically wondering how long he could keep Sanchez at bay. A quick peek over the bonnet verified that the other man had taken up a firing position behind the tumbled remnants of a brick wall.

'Damn! I'm out of ammunition,' Cædmon muttered, tossing the gun aside.

Suddenly catching a whiff of a very familiar scent, Edie glanced down to see liquid pooling at her feet. 'Oh God! He hit the gas tank! We've got to get out of here!'

Snatching the GPS receiver and cigarette lighter out of her hand, Cædmon shoved them into his anorak pocket.

'Keep low!' he whispered, grabbing her elbow. 'We don't want Sanchez to know that we're on the move. Hopefully, he'll maintain his position long enough for us to escape.'

But to where? Edie wondered, seeing nothing but overgrown fields in every direction.

They'd gone no more than twenty yards when Sanchez resumed firing. Placing a hand on her shoulder, Cædmon shoved her to the ground.

'On your belly,' he ordered, flinging himself beside her.

Side by side, they lay hidden in the tall grass.

Every limb in her body shaking as though palsied, Edie watched as Cædmon removed the piece of duct tape that had been stuck over his mouth from his coat pocket. Along with Harliss's silver cigarette lighter.

'What are you planning to —'

'Shhh!'

Terrified, Edie watched as Cædmon flicked on the lighter, the blue flame jauntily waving to and fro. He then wrapped the salvaged strip of duct tape around the lighter trigger so the flame wouldn't go out. Edie noticed USMC engraved on the side of the lighter.

Putting a finger to his mouth, Cædmon wordlessly warned her to be silent, the admonition totally unnecessary, fear rendering her speechless.

Narrowing her gaze, she watched as Sanchez crept away from the wall. Bent at the waist, his gun held between his hands, he slowly approached the Range Rover.

Edie held her breath, suddenly realizing what Cædmon intended to do.

In no apparent hurry, Cædmon waited until Sanchez was within a few feet of the SUV. His expression steadfast, he then rose to his knees, cocked his arm back and hurled the lighter towards the Range Rover.

An instant later, a ball of fire engulfed the car.

Jubilant, Edie clutched Cædmon's knees. 'Oh God! Do you think we're actually gonna get away?'

Cædmon smiled crookedly. 'To paraphrase that American chap, we're not done for until the fat lady sings.'

'I've never been able to sit through a Wagner opera.'

'Nor I. But on the off chance that Sanchez survived, we need to find safe haven.'

More concerned with speed than stealth, they hurried off through the dry stalks of winter grass.

72

They'd gone nearly a mile when they came upon an abandoned farmhouse. From its derelict appearance, the house had been vacated years before, there being more than a few missing panes of window glass.

'Now what?' Edie asked, glancing around the farmyard, seeing only a jumble of weeds and tall grass.

Cædmon surveyed the area. 'Search the house for weapons. Knives, scissors, anything you can lay your hands on. I'll search the outbuildings for a vehicle.'

'You actually know how to hot-wire a car?'

'In theory. Assuming I can find one.'

Rising on tiptoe, Edie leaned over and kissed him on the cheek, then, having her orders, rushed towards the front porch. The door being warped, it took some joggling of the knob and a very determined shoulder to coerce it open. Ignoring the dust mites, cobwebs and a heavy odour of mildew, she scanned the hall, her gaze alighting on a solitary golf club protruding from a tall metal milk jug. Thinking it as good a weapon as any, she grabbed the eight iron.

She then felt her way down the dark hallway, the light switch producing nothing but a dull click, and soon found herself in a primitive kitchen. The grimy window above the dry sink shed enough light for her see that vermin had had the run of the place. More than one cupboard door was ajar, containers of boxed food having been ripped open. A bag of sugar and a box of salt had been torn asunder on the kitchen counter.

She hurriedly began opening drawers, hoping to find a kitchen knife. To her dismay, the search turned up nothing more deadly than an ice-cream scoop and a rusty can opener.

Seeing an old-fashioned telephone mounted on the wall, she rushed over and grabbed the heavy handset.

Damn. Dead air.

As she hung up the phone, the floorboards near the doorway creaked.

'You didn't really think that someone would abandon the house but leave the phone connected?'

Hearing that accented voice, Edie spun on her heel, the golf club slipping through her fingers, clattering onto the wood floor.

Her heart caught in her throat.

Standing across from her, holding a gun aimed at her chest, was Sanchez. Not only were his face and clothes blackened with soot, but blood poured freely from a jagged wound on his cheek, the skin flayed in the car blast.

Edie stood unmoving. Like a frog in a warming cauldron.

'Hope springs eternal,' she told the unsmiling

gunman, striving for a calm she didn't feel. To keep her hands from shaking, she reached behind her, gripping the edge of the worktop.

'Where's your red-headed lover boy?'

'We got separated after the blast,' Edie lied, knowing Sanchez would be out for vengeance, eye for an eye taking on a whole new meaning.

The sound of a car door being slammed echoed across the farmyard.

Sanchez cocked his ear, then shrugged. 'Can't start a car with a dead battery. What a bitch, huh?'

As he spoke, Edie inched her hand towards the salt that she'd earlier seen on the counter. 'Yeah, what a bitch,' she retorted, tossing a handful of salt at the gaping wound on his face.

Sanchez bellowed loudly, his head and body twisting in different directions.

Pushing herself away from the counter, Edie charged down the hall towards the open front door.

No sooner did she clear the doorway than she ran headlong into Cædmon. In his right hand he held a small axe, in his left he had what looked like a long-handled garden rake.

'Sanchez is in the kitchen!' she breathlessly exclaimed. 'And he's got a gun!'

She saw the muscles in Cædmon's jaw clench and unclench, saw the feral gleam in his eyes. This was a man who had mercilessly taken out a foe by jamming a nail file into his skull.

Wordlessly, he shoved the axe into his anorak

pocket then wrapped his free hand around her upper arm and ran, Edie barely able to keep pace with his long-legged stride.

They'd gone no more than a hundred yards when shots rang out, half a dozen in rapid succession. Cædmon dodged towards a large outbuilding. Kicking open a wood-planked door, he shoved her inside.

Edie squinted at a huge chain with an ominous hook at the end of it dangling from a ceiling beam.

'It looks like some kind of torture chamber.'

'Close enough,' Cædmon muttered, dragging her across the dimly lit space. 'It's an old abattoir.'

'What's an abattoir?'

'A slaughterhouse.'

73

The place does have a decided charnel-house feel to it, Cædmon thought as he hurried Edie across the abattoir.

Hopefully not a harbinger of things to come.

Shouldering open a rickety door, he motioned Edie through. A second later they emerged into another dimly lit space, this one with a high-pitched ceiling and an arched window set into the gable. More heavy chains dangled from rafters, more hooks on the walls. Elaborate cobwebs adorned all four corners. Overhead, a pair of sparrows flew out through the broken window. The menacing space would have made a black-robed inquisitor feel right at home.

Quickly, knowing he had only a few moments to set the trap, he shoved Edie towards a rusty metal cart, the only object of any size in the room.

'Get yourself behind the cart. And for God's sake, don't move.'

Satisfied that she was out of sight, he placed the rake on the floor near the door, the prongs pointing up in what he hoped would be Sanchez's direct path. Then, removing the axe from his pocket, he positioned himself in a dark cobweb-strewn corner.

Knowing he would have just one chance with the dull axe, he waited.

A few moments passed in tense silence. Then, as though scripted, the door to the cavernous room creaked open.

Sanchez, looking like a battered chimney sweep, slowly entered the room, pistol gripped in his right hand. A powerful weapon, it could blow a man's head clean off his shoulders. Two steps into the room, Sanchez came to a standstill, scanning for the slightest hint of movement.

Don't move, Edie. For the love of God, don't even think about moving.

Cædmon held his breath, hoping that the other man didn't glance down, the rake some six feet from his booted right foot.

Tightening his grip on the axe handle, he mentally pictured the attack. A practice run. Having bowled many an over while at Oxford, he first imagined hurling the axe using a straight-armed delivery. Thinking he wouldn't get the desired height, he replayed the scenario in his mind's eye, this time with bent elbow.

He spared a quick sideways glance at the cart, relieved to see that Edie had faded into the shadows. His gaze then ricocheted back to Sanchez, who had taken a tentative step forward.

He calculated the other man to be three steps from the upturned prongs of the rake.

Then two steps.

One step.

As planned, the instant that Sanchez's booted foot landed on the prongs, the rake handle flew up, hitting him square in the face. Like a child's top, Sanchez wobbled. The element of surprise now on his side, Cædmon stepped out of the shadows and hurled the axe towards the other man's chest.

A dust-laden beam of light from the window glinted off the spinning blade.

Instinctively Sanchez twisted, his arm shielding his heart, parrying the blow as best he could.

The dull blade caught him on the right bicep, slicing deep. But not deep enough. Sanchez grunted as he grasped the axe by its handle, yanking the blade out of his arm. His eyes glazed but still alert, he searched the room, gun in one hand, the bloody axe in the other.

Seeing Cædmon standing in the corner, his gaze narrowed.

Slowly, in no apparent hurry to kill his quarry, Sanchez aimed the powerful pistol at a point somewhere in the middle of Cædmon's head.

There being nothing he could do to stop the bullet, Cædmon defiantly stood his ground.

Smiling, Sanchez pulled the trigger.

There was a dull click.

The smile vanishing from his lips, Sanchez pulled the trigger a second time. Again, the only sound was the hollow click of the firing pin.

He was out of ammunition.

With a muttered oath, Sanchez dropped the gun. Then, in a blur, he was on Cædmon, swinging his arm, the axe blade aimed at his belly, the man clearly of a mind to eviscerate him. Cædmon leapt sideways, the blade missing him by a scant inch.

Out of the corner of his eye, Cædmon saw Edie lurch to her feet.

'You bastard!' she screamed. Wild-eyed, she grabbed a chain from a nearby wall hook and began swinging it over her head like a medieval mace.

Endowed with enviably quick reflexes, Sanchez pivoted in Edie's direction.

Which is when Cædmon lifted his left foot off the ground, ramming his welly into Sanchez's kidneys. The well-aimed kick propelled the other man several feet, his head smashing into the wall. The axe slipped through his fingers, falling to the floor. Not giving his foe time to recover, Cædmon rushed forward. Placing one hand at the back of Sanchez's skull and the other against his spine, he rammed the brute's head against the metal cart.

The walls of the abattoir shook with the impact.

Sanchez, a stunned, owl-like expression on his face, rolled into a fetal ball. A moment later, he opened his lips. To speak or scream, Cædmon knew not. The only thing emitted from his gaping mouth was a bright red trickle of blood. A second later his body shook with a mighty spasm, his feet jerking convulsively. Cædmon suspected that the man's brain battled on, still sending flight-or-fight messages to his limbs, refusing to accept the inevitable, refusing to lie down and die.

Edie turned her head, unable to watch Sanchez in his death throes.

A few seconds later Cædmon placed a comforting hand on her shoulder.

'He's gone. Where to, I can't say. Although I suspect he will be refused entry to heaven.'

Edie glanced at the sprawled corpse. Deprived of that animating spirit called the soul, bulging muscles were flaccid, eyes open wide in a ghoulish stare.

'I need to get out of here.' Pushing him aside, Edie staggered towards the door.

Going down on his knee, Cædmon quickly searched Sanchez's pockets then followed Edie out of the abattoir.

Silently they stared at the wrecked farm. On the wet breeze Cædmon smelt rotted wood. In the distance a dilapidated shutter rattled against an equally dilapidated window frame.

'Now what?'

'No idea,' he told her.

'Couldn't you have come up with something more positive?'

'Sorry. My brain is a bit mashed.' He showed her the mobile he had discovered in Sanchez's coat pocket.

'Do you think MacFarlane will give chase?'

Cædmon thought about this for only a second before shaking his head. 'He has the Ark. That's all he cares about.'

74

'*Surely in that day there shall be a great earthquake in the land of Israel, so that the fish of the sea, the birds of the heavens, the beasts of the field, all creeping things that creep on the earth, and all men who are on the face of the earth shall shake at my presence. The mountains shall be thrown down, the steep places shall fall, and every wall shall fall to the ground.*'

Opening the storage compartment in the middle of the Range Rover's dashboard, Stanford MacFarlane stowed away his well-worn Bible, the words of the prophet Ezekiel never ceasing to inspire him.

Beside him, in the driver's seat, his gunnery sergeant muttered under his breath, complaining yet again about having to drive on the left side of the road. Stan ignored him. They would be in Margate soon enough. A small fishing boat docked at the harbour would enable them to bypass British customs.

Again, he craned his neck to look at the well-padded crate in the back of the Range Rover.

The Ark of the Covenant.

It had taken more than twenty years for him to find the most sacred of relics. During this search ordained by God he had followed every lead, every rumour, every crackpot theory, his quest taking him to the distant corners of the globe. *Ethiopia. Iraq. France.* One by one, each theory had been discredited, leaving only the quatrains of Galen of Godmersham.

Again, he glanced at the crate, experiencing a tingling sensation. As though his entire body was enveloped in a static electric field.

The Lord was near at hand! He could feel it!

For it was at the Ark that God, made manifest, had appeared to Moses. The Ark not only embodied the Almighty, it was the symbol of God's promise to his chosen people. Nothing had changed. It was now as it had been then. Adorned with the Stones of Fire, he would be able to speak with the Almighty. Just as Moses had conversed with God in the wilderness. With that heady thought in his mind, Stan was able to hear the blast of trumpets and the clash of cymbals, the shouts and cheers, the joyful hosannas. As though thirty-five hundred years had come and gone in the blink of an eye.

All praise to God the Almighty!

He knew full well that God's plan for mankind had been formulated in the Garden of Eden and that it would end with a new paradise where those worthy of his blessings would enjoy a thousand years of peace and prosperity. Finally, their rest well deserved, the warriors would put aside their bloody weapons and lie side-by-side with the meek and gentle lamb.

With astounding clarity, the prophet Ezekiel had seen the crimson future that would precede this golden dawn. Stan did not doubt that Ezekiel's prophecy would soon unfold, taking an unprepared world by storm. The future was already written, prophecy the gift that God gave to quell man's fear in the face of the dark and violent nights that were to come. And when Ezekiel's prophesied war came, sinful man would have no doubt as to God's existence.

Those would be dark days. Days that would push man to the limit of his endurance. But those who refused to traffic with the enemy would be reborn in the new world to come. A time of rest for the people of God. When the deserts of the earth would be made fertile and when the Dead Sea would no longer be dead. Ezekiel had foretold how those waters would be stocked with the very fish that would feed the new kingdom of God.

A thousand of years of peace. Time for an old warhorse to at long last take his rest.

Reaching into his pocket, Stan removed his BlackBerry and rapidly keyed in a numeric code with his thumbs. Double-checking each digit, he sent the message, knowing it would simultaneously reach the Warriors of God stationed in Europe and the Middle East. Battle orders issued, he returned the device to his pocket.

As they approached the outskirts of Margate, Stan thought of the Englishman and his harlot. Their execution well-deserved, he felt no pity. Instead, a wave of hatred washed over him. Hate was good.

Cleansing even. Hate enabled a man to slay the
infidel and slaughter the sinner.

He would put his hate to good use in the days to
come.

75

'I know this is going to sound crazy, but I'm actually sad,' Edie confessed, taking the proffered coffee cup from Cædmon's outstretched hand. 'Angry, but sad. I mean those two guys were a couple of homophobic misanthropes in dire need of some sensitivity training. But watching them die was . . .' She broke off and stared at the narrow road in front of the public bench.

Coffee cup in hand, Cædmon seated himself beside her. He, too, gloomily stared at the main thoroughfare that ran through the middle of the small seaside port of Gilchrist.

Knowing the local constabulary would be drawn to the plumes of black smoke produced by the Range Rover explosion, and that in turn would lead them to at least one dead body, he'd used the pilfered GPS receiver to plot a course in the opposite direction from the charred ruins. Although exhausted, they'd tramped through deserted fields, eventually arriving at their present location. Unwelcoming in the way that some small towns tend to be, Gilchrist had about it the distinct scent of salt and dead fish, the town's only saving grace being its coach station.

Assuming one could call a metal bench in a shelter beside the road a coach station.

Raising the paper cup to his lips, Cædmon took a sip of the horrible-tasting brew he'd purchased at the fish and chip shop across the way. According to the reticent fellow behind the counter, the afternoon coach to London was due to arrive in forty minutes.

'It's never easy to watch the end of a life,' he replied, also haunted by the deaths of Harliss and Sanchez. 'Try as you might to erase the memory, it leaves an imprint on your soul.'

'Not for MacFarlane or his men.' Raising the plastic lid of her cup, Edie took several swallows. Only to grimace a few seconds later from the bitter aftertaste. 'They believe that when they pull the trigger, they're doing God's work.'

'Somehow I doubt whether MacFarlane's God would have much truck with those who long for peace.'

Sighing, Edie wrapped her free arm around his waist and leaned her head on his shoulder. 'I don't know about you, but I'm in desperate need of a group hug.'

As am I, love. As am I.

He hoped the day's atrocities would quickly recede from Edie's memory and she could forgive what she'd seen him do. As soon as they reached London, he intended to call in a favour from an old chum at MI5 and get her into an out-of-the way safe house.

Some place where Stanford MacFarlane and his assassins could never find her.

Edie lifted her head from his shoulder. 'What do you think MacFarlane plans to do now that he has the Ark?'

'The first thing is to get it out of Britain. If he's discovered with the Ark on English soil, not only will the bloody thing be confiscated, it will be sent direct to the British Museum.' Where it would draw larger crowds than the Rosetta Stone, the Elgin Marbles and the Sutton Hoo treasure combined.

He removed the GPS receiver from his anorak pocket. 'It'll take a few moments to initialize,' he informed her as he hit the 'Power' button. He held the receiver aloft to get a satellite fix on their position. A few seconds later, glancing at the small display screen, he said with a teasing smile, 'Ah, we are exactly where we should be.'

Edie half-heartedly returned the smile. 'Since I have yet to correctly programme the TV remote, I'll have to trust you on that one. But isn't the GPS a bit superfluous? I mean, we're here already and we know where here is.'

'On the contrary. This is a hand-held computer with satellite capabilities and untold stored information.' Using the 'Nav' key, he accessed a database file of saved maps. 'Now, isn't this interesting? A number of maps have recently been downloaded. There are maps for Oxford, Oxfordshire, Godmersham, Swanley and . . .' He stared at the list.

'Come on, Cædmon. I can only hold my bated breath for so long.'

'And Malta,' he replied, turning the receiver in her direction.

'Malta?' Tapping her pursed lips, she stared at the screen. 'Although world geography isn't one of my strong suits, I seem to recall that Malta is a spit of an island located in the Mediterranean Sea. Do you think that's where MacFarlane is headed?'

'Given that the list of maps perfectly corresponds to MacFarlane's known movements in the last seventy-two hours, we must assume that Malta is his destination.' How ironic, given that the diminutive isle had once been home to the Knights of St John, the same order of warrior monks of which Galen of Godmersham had been an initiated member.

'Isn't Malta where St Paul was shipwrecked en route to Rome?'

'Hmm? Er, yes,' he answered, interrupted from his reveries. 'As a crossroads between Africa and Europe, the island has been visited by many famous and infamous people.'

'But why would MacFarlane take the Ark to Malta?'

Cædmon shrugged, at a loss. 'The dreams of a madman are difficult to decipher.'

'I'm guessing that getting the Ark out of England is going to be difficult, what with airport security being so tight.'

'Which is why Stanford MacFarlane will no doubt

use a boat. An innocuous trawler leaving port in the dead of night sounds about right.' As he spoke, the mobile phone in his pocket began to beep.

'What's that?'

Cædmon shoved his hand into his anorak pocket and removed the mobile he'd taken from Sanchez. He glanced at the display.

'Unless I'm greatly mistaken, we've just been given Stanford MacFarlane's next move,' he said, showing her the message: '105-13-95-39-17-35-90-63-123-51-20-98-34-27-43-110-87-71-41-9-54-2-120'.

'Will ya look at that? It's some sort of text message from Rosemont Security Consultants. Although I don't know that I would call it a text message *per se* since it's nothing more than a list of numbers.'

'A *coded* list, I dare say.' Cædmon suspected that Stanford MacFarlane maintained contact with his men using flash messages sent via mobile phones, a brilliant means of communication in the satellite age, enabling MacFarlane to issue simultaneous orders across the globe.

'If only we had the encryption key,' he murmured.

'Do you think it has anything to do with the map of Malta on the GPS receiver?'

'Mmmm ... difficult to say.' His gaze ricocheted between the receiver and the mobile. 'Probably not – Harliss was the only one of MacFarlane's men to carry a satellite receiver. I suspect that MacFarlane moves his chess pieces very carefully across the board, the master plan revealed in dribs and drabs.'

'Where do we begin the hunt?'

'In Malta. However, from this point forward, there is no more "we".'

Edie's brown eyes gleamed furiously. 'So you're planning to dump me and chase after MacFarlane on your own.'

'I intend to retrieve the Ark, yes.' Getting up from the bench, he walked over to a bin and dropped in his coffee cup.

He had no delusions as to the difficulty of the task he'd set himself. Tracking down MacFarlane and securing the Ark of the Covenant would more than likely prove an impossible, if not deadly, undertaking. But try he must. The GPS receiver had proved a godsend. Now at least he knew where to hunt for his nemesis.

Grabbing him by the wrist, Edie dragged him back down onto the bench. 'I know you're worried about me, but going after the Ark isn't a one-man job. You're going to need all the help you can get with MacFarlane and his Warriors of –'

'I can't take you with me.'

'Why not?'

'Because I don't have time to potty-train you.'

'You arrogant bastard!' She leapt to her feet. 'I'm not some Bond girl along for the ride; I'm your partner. And in case you didn't get the memo, I am a full and equal partner.'

Cædmon stared at her, unable to take his eyes off the long corkscrew curls that blew about her flushed face. Also unable to erase the memory of her standing beneath an upraised pickaxe.

'"In the world you *will* have tribulation,"' she continued. 'John sixteen. A Bible verse that Stanford MacFarlane no doubt holds near and dear.'

'A frightening prospect.'

'Yes, it is frightening. Which is why I'm going with you to Malta. Unlike you, I completely understand MacFarlane and his beliefs. For five years I was fed a steady diet of Ezekiel and End Times prophecy.'

'After today's primer in apocalyptic beliefs, I should be able to manage.'

'What you heard was just the tip of the iceberg. Think of me as your very own expert in Christian fundamentalism. Besides, we're a team. We have been from the very beginning. So, short of knocking me unconscious, there's nothing you can do to stop me.'

'Very well,' he murmured.

If she wondered at his easy acquiescence, she gave no indication. 'Okay, now that we've got that settled, what's the game plan?'

'Simply put, to grab MacFarlane by the Old Testament and squeeze very, *very* hard.'

76

Cædmon took a deep breath, the sea air invigorating. Bracing his hands on the railing, he stared at the rolling blue Mediterranean waves that danced in the lemony light of early morning. It was the same sea that Odysseus had sailed on his way to battle the Trojans.

Standing beside him, cheeks tinted red from the breeze, Edie also inhaled deeply. 'Other than a Potomac River dinner cruise, this is the first time I've ever been on a big boat. I think I like being on the open sea.' A mischievous smile playing about her lips, she winked at him. 'Could be because I was a lady pirate in a past life, what do you think?'

'I think I'd rather be in a plane high *above* the sea,' he grumbled. 'Too many of these ferry boats have sunk in recent years. Not to mention that travelling by sea is a damn slow way to get from point A to point B.' Point A being Naples and B their final destination, Malta.

'Yeah, but in the dead of winter flights into Malta are few and far between. This will actually get us there six hours sooner than if we'd waited for the next available flight. Which you would know if you'd ever watched *The Amazing Race*. So stop griping.'

'I have been doing a bit of that, haven't I?'

'Understandable. You're under a lot of stress.'

Truly an understatement. Already, the old paranoia had set it. The niggling fear that an unseen enemy would lurch from the shadows. Danger and treachery but a heartbeat away. If allowed to run rampant, fear could quickly become a man's worst enemy. More dangerous than an assailant with a gun.

Because of his intelligence training, he knew the drill – always pay with cash, never use your real name and never, ever, sleep in the same bed two nights in a row. Simple enough, but Edie's Pre-Raphaelite beauty attracted attention wherever she went.

'Short of knocking me unconscious, there's nothing you can do to stop me.'

'You've got two very big creases in the middle of your brow. Care to share your worries?'

'I was thinking about the Ark and the poor blokes at Bethshemesh,' he lied.

'And you're concerned that when we get the Ark from MacFarlane, it may gobble us whole.'

'Mock me if you must, but the Ark *was* once used as a supercharged weapon of mass destruction,' he said, still hoping she would have a change of heart.

'Aeons ago. Which means there's nobody around who knows how to activate the ancient electromagnetic technology that once powered it. To operate a piece of machinery, you need an instruction manual. And that manual, whether it was written down or passed verbally from father to son, has long since vanished. In other words, the Ark has lost its oompah-pah. So, no need to worry about it exploding in our faces, or anything like that.'

'That's not what I fear. The Ark could be used to convince millions of God-fearing people that the End Times are truly upon us.'

Her eyes focused on the sprightly waves in the distance, Edie sighed. 'Yeah, that has me worried as well,' she conceded. 'While God may not be fooled by MacFarlane's false piety, a whole lot of good, well-intentioned people will eat up his ramblings. But enough said on that topic, huh?'

Edie turned away from the water. Leaning against the railing, her arms folded across her chest, she stared at him. Brazenly. Although they were surrounded by other travellers, there was something intimate about the wind, the water, the warmth that radiated from their two bodies that countered the cool satin chill of the winter's day.

Cædmon sidled closer.

After Jules he'd had a few casual relationships, unwilling to get too close. Which is why it made no sense, with the Ark hanging over his head like the Sword of Damocles, to now want the very thing he'd studiously avoided.

Bloody hell. He was daft to think they could make a go of it. They didn't even live on the same continent.

Torn asunder by Apollonian reason and Dionysian desire, the age-old conflict between head and heart, he simply did not know what to do.

In truth, he didn't know how he felt about Edie Miller. He'd not had time to analyze his feelings. He only knew it was like coming out of a Tube station and suddenly finding himself in an unfamiliar location.

'Christ! I need a map,' he muttered.

'I beg your pardon.'

'Nothing.' He waved away the thought. 'A bit of nonsense.'

And it was nonsense. He was forty. Middle-aged. He'd long since put happy ever after behind him. *And yet . . .*

Edie slid her hand behind his head, pulling him close. 'You know what? I'm in the mood for a no-nonsense kiss,' she announced, rising up on tiptoe, giving him no time to say yea or nay.

It took only a second for the unexpected kiss to turn decidedly passionate, Edie sucking his tongue with erotic abandon as she mashed her pelvis against his crotch. Growling, Cædmon framed her face between his hands, angling her head to deepen the contact, suddenly consumed with the overriding urge to slake his lust on her. Like one of his wild Scottish forebears. Civility be damned.

Unbelievably arousing, the kiss, when it finally ended, left both of them panting.

'Chins will wag,' he rasped, resting his forehead against hers as he took several deep restorative breaths.

'I certainly hope so.' Smiling, Edie caressed his stubbled cheek, making him wish he'd had the time to use the disposable razor he'd purchased in Naples. 'Being a well-travelled man, you've undoubtedly heard of the mile-high club.' As she spoke, she traced the outline of his lips with the tip of her finger.

'Er, yes. Although, alas, I'm not a member.'

'How would you, instead, like to become a bona fide, card-carrying member of the high-seas club?'

He held her stare, silently communicating a wicked and slightly outrageous fantasy. One that involved her sweetly rounded arse and the upholstered bench he'd earlier spied in their cabin.

'I believe I would enjoy that greatly,' he replied.

'And, of course, it goes without saying that membership has its perks.' She winked at him. Just before she reached down and brazenly cupped his testicles.

Afraid she might have taken public indecency too far, he furtively glanced over his shoulder, relieved to see that they were now alone on deck.

'How fast do you think we can get to our cabin?'

'Not fast enough,' he muttered, smoothing his palm across the front of his corduroy trousers, rearranging himself as best he could.

Taking her by the arm, he strode down the gang-way, Edie having to jog to keep up with him. It took only a few moments for them to reach their cabin, his hand shaking as he inserted the key into the lock. He wasted no time dragging her inside, slamming the door shut behind them.

Neither spoke, the only sound being their harshly

drawn breaths. A shaft of orange light emanated from the small WC on the other side of the room. While hardly romantic, it did cast a warm glow.

Aching from the want of her, Cædmon stood with his fists tightly clenched at his sides, afraid that he might overwhelm her with the intensity of his passion.

He wanted to go slowly. To be considerate. To savour each and every moment.

He feared it might not be possible.

'You've bewitched me,' he murmured hoarsely, reaching for her, unable to restrain himself another second.

Splaying his hands on her bottom, he lifted her onto her toes and nestled her against his straining cock. He rocked back and forth, burying his face in the luxurious mass of brown curls. He couldn't recall the last time he'd felt so strongly about a woman. It had been years. Decades even. This had the feel and urgency of his youth.

Worried he might start growling like an animal in rut, he sought her lips, kissing her deeply, fusing his mouth to hers.

It was Edie who finally pulled away, laughing as she did so. 'Clothes off this time, okay?'

'Right.'

Guiltily aware that she was referring to the stand-up quickie in Canterbury, Cædmon released his hold on her bottom and immediately started kicking off his shoes and unfastening buttons.

Still chuckling, Edie did likewise, removing her jacket and tossing it onto the upholstered bench. Her jeans and turtleneck jumper soon followed. Then, proving herself a confident woman, she pulled off her bra and wound it over her head like a lasso before slinging it across the room. Seeing the small bumblebee tattooed on the ball of her right shoulder, he smiled.

'An impulsive moment of youthful indiscretion, I'll wager.'

Craning her neck, Edie glanced at the whimsy. 'I'll have you know that for a good many years I took every opportunity to show off my tat. How about you, any skeletons in the closet?'

'If you're asking if I ever sported a green Mohawk or a pair of trousers made from a tattered Union Jack, the answer is no.'

'It's never too late,' she retorted, barely able to stifle a giggle. As she spoke, she slid her hands under the waistband of his pants and slipped them off his hips. She then grasped him, moving her hand up and down the throbbing length of him. He thought it best not to mention that bees were the age-old symbol of chaste womanhood.

'You're liable to cause an explosion if you keep that up,' he groaned, entranced by the sight of her hand brazenly fondling his organ.

'Oh dear. The British are coming! The British are coming!'

Snatching her hand, he pulled her towards him,

crushing her bare breasts against his chest as he backed her towards the bed. Gently he nudged Edie down onto the edge of the mattress and knelt before her. Prying her legs apart, he kissed his way up her inner thigh, rubbing his unshaved face against her warm soft skin. Then, bracketing his thumbs on either side of her genitalia, he gently pulled aside the plump folds. As he did, the blood rushed from his heart to his cock in painful surges.

'The stuff of dreams,' he whispered, mesmerized by her lush beauty.

He didn't know what tomorrow would bring. *But for now you're mine.* He pressed his mouth to her, laving her with his tongue.

'Umm ... you just hit the sweet spot,' Edie crooned, leaning back on her hands, her hips coming several inches off the bed. Again proving the bumblebee a poor choice for a tattoo. A few moments later she pulled away from him. 'That's *way* more than I can handle. Too much more and I'll fall overboard.'

Not about to let her escape, he clambered onto the bed. Covering her body with his, he took a swollen nipple into his mouth and suckled. As he did, he thrust into her. Deeply. Forcefully. Their two bodies melded into one.

Who possessed whom in that instant, he couldn't say.

Levering his torso away from her breasts, Cædmon raised himself onto his forearms. Edie unabashedly stared at the in-and-out movement of his sex.

'Now *that* is what I call a Kodak moment,' she said with a husky laugh.

'If you pull out a bloody camera, I'm leaving.'

'I wouldn't have taken you for the modest type,' again she laughed, 'Big Red.'

Sliding a proprietary hand beneath her hips, he angled her up. 'I can't take credit for the colour and the size is entirely your fault.'

'Oh, God, that feels —'

'Better,' he grunted, pressing her thighs to her chest, increasing the friction.

'Umm … just like that … *perfect*.' Smiling, she grasped him by the shoulders. 'Is this totally crazy or what?'

His climax fast approaching, he somehow found the wherewithal to say, 'Actually, this is the one sane act in a world gone mad.'

77

It was a moment of quiet intimacy. Of murmured endearments. Life slowed down to its simplest, most lovely, facet.

In the midst of the quietude, Edie felt a spark. She snuggled closer to Cædmon, burrowing her head into the crook of his bare shoulder. This not being the first time she'd felt the spark, she wondered if anything would come of it.

Could anything come of it?

On paper she gave their relationship the shelf life of a carton of milk. If that. They were simply two sexually healthy people caught up in the excitement of the moment. Although, glancing at the small clock mounted on the wall, she could see that the excitement had lasted quite a few hours.

'You do know that this . . . this attraction is nothing more than a primitive urge,' she said, propping her head on his chest.

'Perhaps it must be primitive in order for us to forget our preconceived notions of what should and shouldn't be.'

Hmm . . . it sounded as though he'd given their relationship more than a passing thought.

'And maybe Freud was right – about there being

no such thing as pure unadulterated love. Maybe there's sexual need and nothing else,' she countered, testing him.

'I suspect Freud was an impotent bugger who wouldn't have known love if it had slapped him in his bearded face. Let's not analyze it; let's just accept it, whatever it is, as a beginning. Tentative and tenuous perhaps, but a beginning nonetheless.'

She smiled, Cædmon having passed the test with flying colours.

'Agreed. But if you think I'm one of those women who'd settle for a man just because he puts down the toilet seat, think again.'

'Point taken. Although I hope I get several bonus points for being considerate.'

'Change of subject,' she announced. 'I'm curious as to what would have happened if you had stayed at Oxford and received your doctorate?'

'You mean how my life would have unfolded?' When she nodded, he said, 'In a very conventional way, no doubt. I would have got a college post, most likely at Queen's. At which point my life would have become a steady stream of tutorials, committee meetings and university functions.'

'You know, I'm one of those people who believe that things happen for a reason. Personally, I don't think you were meant to live a sheltered life. Just look at Sir Kenneth Campbell-Brown. Okay, the man is brilliant, but he's also a confirmed alcoholic bachelor. You were meant for a better life.'

Smiling, Cædmon brushed his lips against hers. 'At the mention of the path not taken, I feel strangely glad.'

'Me too.'

'Bloody hell,' he abruptly exclaimed a half-second later. 'How do terrorists communicate with one another?'

Surprised by the unexpected question, she lifted a shoulder. 'Beats me. Although I suspect the answer is not carrier pigeons.'

'Correct. They communicate via the internet,' he informed her, his blue eyes shining. 'Which enables them to pass messages to cells and operatives all over the globe. Perhaps MacFarlane and his Warriors of God are no different.'

'Okay, suppose that's true. How does the message on Sanchez's cell phone fit in? I thought *that* was how MacFarlane was communicating with his men.'

'When we first received the flash message, I thought that a communiqué had been encoded into the numbers and that an encryption key would be needed to decipher the message. But what if the list of numbers *is* the encryption key?'

'Sorry, I'm not following.' Edie propped her head on her hand.

'Knowing he can't be too careful about sending messages across the globe, MacFarlane might have devised a two-part mode of communication. The first part being the numeric list that was sent to Sanchez's mobile phone.'

'And the second?'

'Mind you, this is mere speculation, but the second piece of the puzzle might be the Warriors of God website.'

'You're talking about the website we checked out back in DC, right?'

Cædmon shrugged. 'As I said, it's only a theory.'

'So, let me make sure I've got this straight,' she said, still uncertain how all the pieces fitted together. 'You think there might be a message encoded in the Warriors of God web page and that this message can only be *decoded* using the numeric list from the text message.'

'There's only one way to find out. Unless I'm mistaken, this boat is equipped with Inmarsat.'

'What's that?'

'A mobile communications system that enables internet access while at sea.'

Throwing back the sheet, Edie swung her feet to the floor. 'Well, what are we waiting for?'

78

'Doom and gloom of the worst sort, eh?'

Sitting side by side in front of the ship's computer monitor, Edie and Cædmon stared at the Warriors of God home page.

Unnerved by its apocalyptic content, Edie shuddered. 'You don't really think there's a secret message buried somewhere, do ya?'

Leaning back in his chair, Cædmon tapped his index finger against his chin. Several seconds passed in contemplative silence before he finally said, 'My guess is that MacFarlane has used a simple alpha-numeric substitution cipher. Since his flash message was intended for mass consumption, I doubt if he would employ too elaborate a code.'

'The old KISS rule, huh?' Seeing Cædmon's quizzical expression, she smiled. 'As in "Keep it simple, stupid."'

Cædmon chuckled. 'Let's hope we're right. Employing the KISS rule, I suggest we consecutively number each letter and punctuation mark in MacFarlane's diatribe.'

Using a pencil, he carefully wrote out the 'The Warrior's Diary' text on a sheet of paper. He then sequentially numbered each letter and punctuation mark.

While Cædmon busied himself with the cipher, Edie glanced nervously around, the ship's internet computer set up in the very public club room. A few tables away a middle-aged quartet played cards. From the cigarette butts overflowing the table's only ashtray, she guessed that they had been playing for some time. About twenty feet away, a well-dressed older man and his much younger male companion were huddled together in front of a soft-drink machine. And on the other side of the club room a harried mother openly breastfed her infant.

'I'll have you know that this is the same cipher that won you Yanks your independence, the words "revolution" and "patriot" being dead giveaways.'

Her eyes opened wide. 'You're kidding, right?'

'Not in the least. Created by Benjamin Franklin, this particular alphanumeric cipher was used to code messages between the Continental Congress and sympathetic French diplomats. Would you like to do the honours?' Cædmon offered her the pencil.

Taking the implement, Edie first glanced at the alphanumeric chart that he had created from MacFarlane's web page.

W	H	E	N	T	H	E	W	A	R	R	I	O	R	'	S	O	F	G	O	D	B	A	T	T
1	2	3	4	5	6	7	8	9	10	11	12	13	14	15	16	17	18	19	20	21	22	23	24	25
L	E	T	H	E	D	A	R	K	F	O	R	C	E	S	_	W	I	L	L	Y	O	U	B	E
26	27	28	29	30	31	32	33	34	35	36	37	38	39	40	41	42	43	44	45	46	47	48	49	50
R	E	A	D	Y	F	O	R	T	H	I	S	H	O	L	Y	R	E	V	O	L	U	T	I	O
51	52	53	54	55	56	57	58	59	60	61	62	63	64	65	66	67	68	69	70	71	72	73	74	75
N	?	W	I	L	L	Y	O	U	B	E	A	P	A	T	R	I	O	T	M	A	R	C	H	I
76	77	78	79	80	81	82	83	84	85	86	87	88	89	90	91	92	93	94	95	96	97	98	99	100
N	G	U	N	D	E	R	G	O	D	'	S	G	O	L	D	E	N	B	A	N	N	E	R	?
101	102	103	104	105	106	107	108	109	110	111	112	113	114	115	116	117	118	119	120	121	122	123	124	125

Then she glanced at the list of numbers from the text message: 105-13-95-39-17-35-90-63-123-51-20-98-34-27-43-110-87-71-41-9-54-2-120.

'Wish me luck.'

Cædmon having done all the work, it only took a few moments for her to write out the deciphered message: *dome of the rock eid al-adha*.

Neither of them said anything, Edie not altogether sure what, if anything, the message meant.

'The Dome of the Rock is the big gold-leafed Islamic shrine that sits on top of the Temple Mount, right?'

'The most famous silhouette on the Jerusalem skyline,' he confirmed, Edie able to detect a husky catch in his voice.

'MacFarlane's message means something to you, doesn't it?'

Still staring at the decoded message, Cædmon nodded slowly. 'I now know why Stanford Mac-Farlane and all of his men wear the Jerusalem cross ring. As you no doubt recall, the Jerusalem cross was the symbol adopted by the medieval crusaders when they conquered the Holy City in 1099.' The entire time he spoke, he stared at the decoded message.

'And why do you think that's significant?' she prodded, not altogether certain she wanted to know the answer.

'Because Jerusalem was theirs for less than a hundred years, the Muslims under Saladin retaking the city in 1187.' Suddenly resembling a sad-faced crusader from a medieval woodcut, Cædmon turned his head and looked at her. 'I think MacFarlane has taken up the crusaders' cause.'

'What cause?'

'Like the medieval crusaders, MacFarlane and his men intend to conquer the Holy City, and their first target is the Dome of the Rock.'

Edie's jaw dropped. 'When? How?'

'I have no idea as to how. As to when, it seems they intend to attack on the Islamic holy day of Eid al-Adha. Which this year, unless I'm greatly mistaken, falls on December the eighth.'

'But that's only two and a half days away.'

79

'Giving us very little time.'

As he spoke, Cædmon was acutely, painfully, aware of the play of opposites. Good and evil. Love and hate. Life and death.

'So are you saying that MacFarlane intends to destroy the Dome of the Rock on December the eighth?'

'It does fit in with all his apocalyptic posturing. And there's a certain irony in his selection of the day, Eid al-Adha being the Muslim day of sacrifice, commemorating the day when Abraham intended to sacrifice his beloved son Ishmael to prove his love to Allah. The Dome of the Rock marks the precise location of where the sacrifice was to have taken place. It is also the spot where the Prophet Muhammad ascended to heaven. Making the Dome of the Rock the third-holiest site in all of Islam.'

'Right behind Mecca and Medina.'

He nodded, staggered by MacFarlane's dark vision. *Eid al-Adha. The Day of Sacrifice. Muslim worshippers would be packed onto the Temple Mount. Thousands of them.*

'Maybe we need to pull back a bit. I mean, the encrypted message doesn't specifically mention anything about *destroying* the Dome of the Rock,' Edie pointed out, playing devil's advocate.

'But MacFarlane did unequivocally state that he intends to install the Ark of the Covenant in the newly constructed temple,' he countered. 'And it's surely no coincidence that the Dome of the Rock sits on the very spot where Solomon's Temple once stood.'

'Solomon's Temple?' Edie gave him a long wordless stare, her pupils contracting into microdots. 'Oh God ... I didn't know,' she murmured. 'That changes everything.'

'The terrible thing about the truth is that sometimes you find it. Since the Temple Mount is a holy site for the three major religions of the world, over the centuries it has been one of the most fought-over pieces of land anywhere.' The history of the Temple Mount was a fantastical tale almost too violent to be believed.

'I know that in 1967, during the Six Day War, the Israelis captured the Temple Mount.'

'That's right. Although in an attempt to placate the Muslims, the Israelis permitted a *waqf*, an Islamic trust, to continue to act as the official administrators of the site.'

'So while the Israelis have sovereignty over it, the Muslims retain control.'

'And, as you undoubtedly know, this arrangement has been a source of contention for several generations.' A heaviness in his heart inspired him to say,

'I have often wondered if the world would have been a better place had Solomon's Temple never been constructed. It's one of the most volatile spots on the planet.'

Slumping in her chair, Edie stared at the innocuous sheet of lined notepaper in front of her.

Cædmon also gazed at the deciphered message. 'And now a madman has arrived on the scene, intent on destroying the Dome of the Rock so he can build a third temple. With the Ark in his arsenal and a well-trained force at his disposal, he could easily bring about events that mimic those foretold in the Old Testament. Thus fulfilling Ezekiel's prophecy.'

'We can't let that happen,' Edie whispered, her body rigid with the strength of her emotion. 'I don't know if you're aware of this, but for some time now there's been a growing alliance between Jewish and Christian fundamentalists.'

'Birds of the same dark feather.'

'They both believe in the Old Testament prophecies, which means that MacFarlane might have allies inside Israel who would be willing to help him destroy the Dome of the Rock.'

Cædmon shook his head, the scenario becoming more and more frightening.

'Fanatical Christians working with fanatical Jews to attack Muslims. Incite any of the three and you have global instability. Incite all three and you have the makings of the next world war.'

Cædmon turned his head and stared at the

churning water visible through the picture window on the other side of the club room.

We can't get to Malta soon enough.

80

Cædmon glanced up from the map spread before him on the bar counter.

A vacancy having come up at the last minute, he and Edie were seated at the Dragonara Hotel bar waiting for the maid to finish cleaning their suite. To his surprise, Valletta, the capital of Malta, was quite a convention centre, their seaside hotel currently hosting a large gathering of British plastic surgeons. Since Malta had at one time been part of the British empire, it was a popular destination with his countrymen. He'd purposefully selected the Dragonara in order to fade into the crowd. If a receptionist or bellboy was asked whether an Englishmen had checked into the hotel, he would say, 'Yes, the hotel currently has two hundred English guests.'

Before returning his attention to the map, Cædmon surreptitiously glanced at the mirrored wall behind the bar, resorting to old tricks, scanning each and every bar patron, running scenarios in his head, trying to decide who among them might be hostile. He would have preferred an inconspicuous table at the back of the room, but the horde of plastic surgeons swilling pre-dinner drinkies had forced them to take two stools at the bar.

'You know, I've been meaning to ask, is there really a big rock inside the Dome of the Rock?'

Cædmon nodded. 'The rock, known in Hebrew as the *shetiyah,* is believed to be the foundation stone of the world. Before it was stolen by Shishak, the Ark of the Covenant rested on top of the *shetiyah.*'

The barman, a swarthy fellow with an amiable disposition, placed a tonic water and a cola in front of them. Then, with a practised flourish, he presented Edie with a plate of fried squid and a small dish of quartered lemons.

'*Grazzi,*' she replied in Malti, having memorized a few key phrases from the guidebook they had picked up in the hotel lobby. The response earned her a toothy grin.

Out of the corner of his eye Cædmon watched as Edie squeezed lemon, not on her squid but into her cola. He continued to watch as she pursed her lips around the end of a fuchsia-coloured straw. He well recalled how her lips had clamped around him earlier in the day.

Calm down. Now is not the time for prurient thoughts and adolescent longings.

With renewed focus, he stared at the GPS receiver, continuing the business of transferring the coordinates that he had discovered in the database file onto a local topographical map. In the event of the GPS batteries dying a sudden death, he wanted a hard-copy backup.

'From where I'm sitting, Malta doesn't look like that big an island.'

'Approximate three hundred square miles. About the size of the Isle of Wight.' He plotted the last set of coordinates. 'Ah! I think I've got a location.' Excited to have made such fast work of it, he pointed to a small promontory on the south-west coast.

Edie peered at the map. 'Calypso's Point,' she read aloud. 'Gees, it's no bigger than my front yard. What do these wavy lines mean?' She pointed to the contour lines that distinguished a topographical map from the run-of-the-mill tourist map.

'It means we'll have to scale a cliff. Although there's a road leading to the point, we must assume MacFarlane will have that guarded.'

He signalled to the barman. When the young man approached, Cædmon swivelled the map round. 'Are you by any chance familiar with a place called Calypso's Point?'

The barman barely glanced at the map. '*Iva*, I know it well. It used to be a hideout for the Barbary pirates until the knights defeated them. But –' he shrugged '– why do you want to go there? There's nothing. Only seabirds and the ruins of St Paul's *torri*.'

An abandoned tower … how interesting. No doubt a signal tower once used by the Knights of St John.

'Actually, it's the birds I want to see,' he lied glibly, turning the map back round. 'I am something of a birdwatcher. Would you happen to know anyone who would be willing to take us to the point by boat?'

'My brother-in-law has a fishing vessel. I am sure he could be persuaded to take you there. Assuming the price is right.'

'He has but to name it, but I would like to depart later this evening.'

If the young man thought it odd that someone would go birdwatching in the dead of night, he gave no indication, scribbling his brother-in-law's phone number onto a paper napkin.

Their business concluded, the barman turned to a portly surgeon, who was raving about the 'jolly good pasties'.

Relieved that the logistics were taken care of, Cædmon folded the map. That done he slid it into his anorak pocket. There being one more task to attend to, he glanced through the glass doors of the bar, across the lobby into the so-called 'business centre'. One of the hotel amenities was free use of a desktop computer, fax machine and colour copier. For the last twenty minutes the computer had been occupied.

'Is he still there?'

'If you're asking if I can still see his bald head, the answer is yes.'

'Why do you need a PC anyway? We got everything we needed from the ferry computer. Or at least I thought we did.'

'I need a computer because I want to put together a dossier for the British consulate. If by tomorrow morning we haven't returned to the hotel, the dossier will be sent to the consulate here in Valletta. From there it will be forwarded to British intelligence. Hopefully, the lads at Thames House will be able to succeed if we fail.'

'You're talking about your old buddies at MI5, right?'

He nodded. 'One doesn't need an oracle to know that Stanford MacFarlane won't relinquish the Ark without a fight.'

'A deadly fight,' Edie murmured. Cædmon could see that she was still distressed by the message they had deciphered. For several seconds she stared into her cola glass, the only sound being a dull *clink-clink* as she continued to swirl her straw.

Abruptly she stopped.

'I keep thinking about that proverb "Everything has an end." And I can't help wondering, is this the beginning of the end?'

His thoughts running on a similar course, Cædmon glanced through the second set of French doors. These opened onto a terrace, the hotel set on a scenic point overlooking the water. The sun had already begun its descent into the sea, creating a glorious explosion of tangerine and magenta so beautiful it was almost painful to watch. To his right, the baroque city of Sliema, a burnished maze of stone façades, rose as if spawned from the sea.

How did I get myself into this? More importantly, how had he got Edie so deeply involved?

At first it had been simple academic curiosity. The

Ark of the Covenant. If he could find it, if he could lay his hands on it, he could prove himself to the man who had ended his academic career. And prove to his long-dead father that –

'I'm afraid,' Edie said, her tremulous voice breaking into his thoughts. 'What if we can't stop him? We couldn't stop him taking the Ark.'

Turning his head, he peered into Edie's sad brown eyes. 'While MacFarlane may beat us, knowledge has a power all its own.'

'It's the guns and bullets that have me worried.'

'They can only kill you. But knowledge lives on.'

Placing a hand on his knee, she leaned towards him. 'So does this,' she whispered, brushing her lips against his.

81

Like a miser counting pennies, the crescent moon stingily cast a jaundiced light upon the choppy sea. Its lantern extinguished, the small fishing vessel steadily made its way towards the barren chunk of limestone in the distance. Calypso's Point. The captain, a wizened salt who spoke no English, stood at the helm. Amply compensated for his services, he cared nothing about the peculiarities of the voyage.

Cædmon glanced at Edie, only the pale oval of her face visible in the inky darkness, both of them garbed in diving suits with matching black hoods.

'You know, maybe we *should* let British intelligence handle this,' Edie said in a hushed voice. 'It's not too late.'

Seated across from her, he leaned forward, resting his elbows on the top of his thighs. 'Until MacFarlane actually steps foot inside Jerusalem, there's little that anyone can do to stop him. While the intelligence agencies will do all in their power to prevent a terrorist act from occurring on the Temple Mount, they won't be able to act until they have material proof that MacFarlane intends to commit the unthinkable. I am no longer bound by such dictates.'

'Yeah, but short of killing Mac –' She slapped a hand over her mouth. A second later, she lowered it. 'That's what you're intending to do, isn't it?'

'In order to destroy a snake, one must decapitate it.'

'But what if the snake turns around and bites you?'

Rather than answer the question, he said, 'I think you should return to Valletta with the captain.'

'I told you already, you'll have to knock me unconscious to stop me from going with you to Calypso's – What's happening?' she hissed, clearly startled.

'No need for alarm. The captain has just cut the engine.'

'So this is our stop, huh?' She stared at the forbidding promontory that loomed above the small vessel.

Cædmon peered up. The limestone cliff rose approximately six hundred feet from the sea. 'Yes, I know. It has a Gothic aspect.' He stepped over to the side of the boat, his neoprene booties smacking softly against the deck. Edie followed in his wake, dashing any hope he had that she'd had a change of heart.

'Right. Let's get on with it,' he said, swinging his leg over the side. A second later, he plunged into the cold sea, grateful they had only a short distance to swim.

Treading water, he watched as Edie joined him, proving herself an able swimmer.

A few minutes later, shivering from the cold and breathing heavily from their exertions, they emerged onto a spindly strip of beach strewn with chunks of rock fallen from the cliff face. Cædmon could see that the fishing vessel had already begun its homeward voyage, the captain not bothering to confirm whether or not they had landed safely.

Removing her hood, Edie jutted her chin at the imposing cliff. 'Without climbing gear, I don't know how we're going to get up that sucker.'

'I have it on good authority that there's a narrow trail not far from here.' That authority being none other than the hotel barman, who claimed to have ascended the cliff on many a youthful outing. Something of a local rite of passage.

Cædmon swung a rubberized rucksack off his shoulder. Opening it, he removed yet another watertight bag, from which he removed a coil of wire, a sheathed diving knife, a green laser light, two torches, the GPS receiver, the map and two pairs of trainers. Inventory verified and double-checked, he unzipped and removed his diving suit. Like Edie, he wore black hiking gear beneath his suit.

'Guess it's time for the final reckoning, huh?' Although Edie attempted a brave smile, she fell woefully shy of the mark.

'Yes, I'm afraid the time has come.'

Pulling back his arm, his right hand balled in a fist, he delivered a quick, precise blow to the side of Edie's head.

Instantly, her eyes rolled back in her head, Cædmon catching her as she pitched forward in an unconscious heap. KO'd by the ghost fist that she never saw coming.

Very gently he laid her on some saltwort, using the empty rucksack as a pillow for her head. He then placed a torch in her limp hand. If he didn't return before she came to, or if he didn't return at all, she would be able signal for help.

Still on his knees, he leaned forward and softly kissed her on the lips.

'I'm sorry, love. You gave me no choice.'

82

Unable to stop what had become almost compulsive behaviour, Stan MacFarlane again glanced at the innocuous-looking shipping container on the other side of the tower room.

Before permitting the Ark to be packed for transport, he'd spent hours gazing upon it. Awestruck. For someone accustomed to the severe austerity of a Baptist church, the Ark had about it an almost pagan beauty. From the fierce pair of winged cherubim mounted on the gold lid to the strange and incomprehensible symbols incised on all four sides, it spoke of an ancient and holy heritage. A time when Moses led the Hebrew children to the land promised to them by God.

Anxious, he pushed his folding chair away from the camp table and reached for the pair of night vision goggles. He walked over to the opening on the other side of the circular room. The tower had once been used by the Knights of St John to monitor sea traffic. Tonight it served the same purpose, Stan watching for the luxury yacht that had set sail from Israel earlier in the week. Owned by Moshe Reznick, Knesset member and co-founder of the Jerusalem-based Third

Temple Movement, the yacht would briefly anchor in the bay, pick up its precious cargo then return to Haifa. From there, the Ark would be transported to Jerusalem. Stan and Gunnery Sergeant Boyd Braxton would accompany the Ark on its sea voyage. The rest of his men would fly into David Ben-Gurion Airport, Christian tourists making the pilgrimage to Jerusalem.

The yacht was due to arrive within the hour.

There were many who would argue that the re-discovered Ark should be placed in a museum, but there was only one place for it, the place ordained by God, the yet-to-be-built third temple in Jerusalem. Once constructed, this would stand for a thousand years. As foretold by the prophet Ezekiel. Stan's allies, the Third Temple Movement, were Jews who fervently believed in the prophecies of Ezekiel, certain that from the ashes of the great Battle of Gog and Magog, a new Messiah would emerge.

While some Christians despised the Jews for having killed Christ, Stan knew that Jesus had himself been a Jew. As had been his parents. And all his forebears. Each and every member of the original Church had been a Jew. The Jews were the Chosen People, the custodians of the first and second temples, the original guardians of the Ark of the Covenant. And in the great battle to come, the Jews would prevail, fulfilling the destiny envisioned for them by Ezekiel.

Hearing a high-pitched chime emanate from his

laptop, Stan lowered the night vision goggles and walked back to the table.

Praise be. The much-anticipated email from his comrades at the Third Temple Movement.

Seating himself in front of the laptop, he quickly pulled up the message and opened the attachment.

'It's beautiful,' he whispered, examining the architectural blueprint for the third temple forwarded to him. 'Absolutely beautiful.'

Based on the precise description given by the prophet Ezekiel – cubits converted to feet and inches – the temple would be constructed on the same parcel of sacred land where the first and second temples once stood. When completed, it would rival the beauty of even Solomon's fabled marvel.

Only two more days.

Two days until Eid al-Adha. The Muslim day of sacrifice. There would be two million Muslims gathered at Mecca. And when those two million infidels learned that the Dome of the Rock in Jerusalem had been destroyed, they would take up arms against Christians and Jews. To become the fierce and bloodthirsty army of Gog. As foretold by the prophet Ezekiel.

A battle between good and evil would ensue.

But this time the crusaders will be victorious.

With the destruction of the gaudy and heathenish Dome of the Rock, the children of God would finally be delivered from Islamic tyranny, the gold-plated shrine built on the exact site where Solomon's

Temple once stood. For the first time in eight hundred years the Temple Mount would again be a place of holy worship.

Obliterating the Dome of the Rock from the Jerusalem skyline had been planned to the last detail, the Muslims having actually simplified the task. For years now the Islamic caretakers of the Temple Mount had turned a blind eye to a two-hundred-yard-long bulge in its southern wall. With the help of a few carefully placed IEDs, the ancient wall would come tumblin' down, bringing with it the newly built al-Marawani Mosque constructed on the southern end of the Temple Mount. In the ensuing chaos his demolition experts would be able to set a ring of high-explosive charges around the exterior perimeter of the usually closely guarded Dome of the Rock.

The infidels will never know what hit them.

With the second explosion, the path would literally be cleared for the construction of the third temple.

Only then could the Ark of the Covenant be returned to its appointed place within the Holy of Holies. Only then could the Ark become the vehicle through which heaven and earth become one. And only then could a new covenant be made between man and God, paving the way for a holy kingdom that would prosper for a thousand years. A true theocracy where non-believers would be judged swiftly and harshly. One Christian nation under God.

'Sir, the sentries just made their rounds and have given the all-clear.'

Stan glanced at Gunnery Sergeant Boyd Braxton, who stood in the doorway. The sitrep did little to allay his fears. So far the lanky Englishman had proved a worthy adversary, somehow managing to kill two of his best men. While certain that Aisquith had no way of knowing the Ark had been brought to Malta, he couldn't forget that the man had done what many before him had tried and failed to do – he had found the Ark of the Covenant.

'Keep me posted.'

Snatching the night vision goggles, Stan walked over to the window. Elbows braced on the limestone sill, he returned his gaze to the sea.

One if by land, two if by sea.

He chuckled, amused by the thought. Like Paul Revere, he was about to launch a revolution. One of biblical proportions.

83

Cædmon made his way up the treacherous path cut into the side of the limestone cliff, grateful for the faint light shed by the stars overhead. He couldn't risk using the torch, at least not until he had reached the summit and surveyed the area. MacFarlane would undoubtedly have sentries posted. Men who would not hesitate to shoot at a suspicious light.

His forty-year-old knees aching from the ascent, he was very much aware of the fact that he did not have the resources or influence of the British government behind him. He was on his own. *A lone and hungry wolf.*

He snorted, amused by the thought.

In sheep's clothing.

Puffing slightly, he reached the top; the top being a treeless, rocky plateau. About two hundred yards to the north-west he could make out the outline of St Paul's Tower, the only visible landmark on the barren escarpment. Wishing he had a pair of night vision goggles, he thought he spied what looked like a large military truck parked beside the tower.

MacFarlane might have the Ark stored inside the tower. Out of sight of prying eyes. Or it could be in the truck, ready for transport.

Motionless, he scanned the terrain, searching for the slightest sound or a suggestion of motion. Something to indicate that he was not alone. That others lurked in the shadows.

A good two minutes passed before he saw a faint flicker, little more than a pinprick of light.

A burning cigarette.

The target sighted, he set off.

As he navigated his way across the bramble-strewn plateau, his thoughts turned to the Knights of St John, who for nearly three centuries had patrolled those same craggy heights, safeguarding their domain from Turkish corsairs. During the great siege of 1565, sixty stalwart knights had defended the fort at St Elmo against a Turkish force numbering eight thousand. Perhaps this night history would repeat itself.

Lord, I hope so.

The thought that he might never again set his gaze upon Edie Miller's face left him bereft.

Shoving this thought aside, he turned his attention to the man negligently leaning against a large slab of limestone, a lit cigarette dangling from the corner of his mouth. And a MP5 sub-machine gun cradled against his chest. Though it was impossible to see in the darkness, Cædmon assumed the man's finger was on the trigger and the safety catch was off.

Keeping to the shadow cast by the limestone outcrop, he slid the five-inch diving knife from its sheath. The hilt securely grasped in his right hand, he inched forward, hoping the sentry didn't suddenly turn, praying he didn't inadvertently kick a loose stone. To his dismay, he saw that the man had a communication device protruding from the side of his head.

If the sentry as much as whimpered, the game would be over before it even began.

Cædmon slowed his breathing. An age-old trick to calm one's nerves.

Then, coming within two feet of the sentry, he lunged forward.

In one smooth, sure-footed motion, the movement ingrained from his distant training, he grasped the other man from the rear, clasping a hand over his mouth as he yanked his head back, exposing the jugular vein and carotid artery. First he slashed. Then he ripped.

Warm blood gushed from the opened artery.

A silent kill.

As the sentry dropped to the ground, Cædmon shoved his finger into the weapon's trigger guard, yanking the MP5 out of the dying man's grasp, knowing that a shot would be his undoing. Sliding his arm through the gun's shoulder strap, he crouched beside the now-dead sentry, relieving him of the radio equipment, the device both a blessing and a beast. While he'd be able to monitor sentry movement in and around the tower, when the man failed to report in, MacFarlane and his henchmen would know they had an enemy in their midst.

84

Edie sat up and hacked, the frigid sea air scouring her lungs.

Damn Cædmon Aisquith.

Her head ached. Her body ached. And, not un-expectedly, her heart ached, Cædmon not having trusted her to pull her weight. *So what did he do?* He cut her adrift. No warning. No discussion. Just wham, bam, thank you, ma'am.

Rolling onto all fours, she awkwardly pushed herself to her feet. She glanced at her left wrist. *No watch.* Since the cheapo Timex wasn't waterproof, she'd left it behind at the hotel.

She wondered how long she'd been out. Hopefully not too long.

With a groan, she bent down and picked up the torch.

'How considerate,' she muttered, wishing her AWOL partner had instead left her a bottle of aspirin.

Knowing her anger wouldn't get her off the strip of beach, Edie tilted her head back and peered up, the cliff like an impregnable fortress wall. One that she intended to ascend. Just a few months ago she'd mastered the rock wall at one of DC's largest sporting goods stores.

So, I'm good to go.

She searched the rocky shoreline, recalling that Cædmon had said something about a path. Switching on the torch, she followed the footprints that he'd left in the sand, tracking them about forty feet.

Right to the foot of the path.

Afraid the torch might attract attention, she switched it off, securing it to one of the elasticized loops on the waistband of her trousers. Hands free, she carefully began the steep climb up the incised stone steps. She wondered whether Barbary pirates or the Knights of St John had undertaken the task of carving what amounted to a staircase into the cliff. No doubt Cædmon would have been able to pull that particular factoid out of his hat. Had he been there.

Damn him, anyway. The man actually thought that he could take on the doomsday prophet all by himself. MacFarlane would fight him tooth and nail. And his loyal followers would use far deadlier weapons.

That thought spurring her on, Edie glanced behind her, able to see that she was only at the halfway mark. Her breathing noticeably laboured, she struggled to keep on climbing, realizing she was pitifully out of shape.

Finally, sheer willpower taking over, her leg muscles having long since turned to rubber, she reached the summit. There being nothing she could do about the scrape on the palm of her hand, she wiped the blood off on her trouser leg.

She could see that she was standing on a flat-topped ridge, a pitiless place that in the light of day probably resembled nothing so much as an asteroid. Only the faint whiff of rosemary indicated that it could actually sustain some sort of vegetation.

In the distance she made out a tall tower. That being the only building in sight, she headed in that direction.

As she got closer to the tower, she saw a large canvas-covered truck parked outside, the kind of vehicle one might see on a military base. Hoping it wasn't loaded with armed soldiers, she headed towards it. Trying to keep as low as possible, she hunched over, running in a crouch. The way people scurried about in the movies.

She hadn't gone far when she saw a bear of a man emerge from the tower and head towards the truck.

Boyd Braxton.

Terrified, Edie came to an abrupt halt. Needing a weapon and needing one quick, she snatched a jagged rock from the ground.

Give me strength, God.

The same kind of strength that had enabled Samson to slay a thousand foes with the jawbone of an ass.

Edie glanced at the pathetic stone clutched in her hand.

If only she had the jawbone of an ass.

85

Pondering his next move, Cædmon stared at the watchtower that loomed a hundred yards away. Absently, he stroked the smooth metal of the MP5, wondering if a little shock and awe wasn't in order. That would certainly get MacFarlane's attention.

And, no doubt, get him killed into the bargain. Without ever having set eyes upon the Ark.

No, he needed a far more subtle tactic. Something that would lure MacFarlane's men away from the tower, where he presumed the Ark was stored, enabling him to sneak inside and decapitate the snake. And maybe, if he was lucky, he could then escape with none of the snake's bully boys the wiser. The wily fox outwitting the ferocious pack of hounds.

But how best to create a diversion?

Anywhere else in the world he would have started a fire. However, other than a few wind-blown brambles, there was nothing combustible to be had. He did have the laser light, a last-minute purchase. Perhaps he could do something with that.

Like a man mesmerized by a swaying crystal, he continued to stare at the tower. The Ark of the Covenant was near at hand. Yet completely unattainable.

Had Stanford MacFarlane deciphered its secrets? Had he donned the Stones of Fire, stood before the Ark and communed directly with God?

'We've got a breach on the north-west quadrant. Somebody just tripped the security laser.'

Hearing the disembodied voice in his earpiece, Cædmon's breath caught in his throat.

Edie.

He scanned the promontory, searching for that familiar, curly-haired silhouette, knowing he had to find her before MacFarlane did.

86

Standing as still as a Grecian statue, Edie watched as Boyd Braxton threw back the canvas tarpaulin on the military-style truck and opened the tailgate. She assumed that he was about to unload something. Or else he was getting the truck ready *to be* loaded. Whichever it was, it had to have something to do with the Ark. Of that she was certain.

Taking deep measured breaths, she continued to watch Braxton, curious as to why he suddenly pressed a finger to his ear. Just before he pulled his gun out of its shoulder holster, turned on his heel and ran off.

Something had spooked the man. But what could possibly have –

Oh God! Cædmon.

Swivelling her head back and forth, squinting to better see in the darkness, she searched the rocky promontory. It was like searching the dark side of the moon. Realizing that it actually was a whole lot like being on the moon in that there was no place to hide, she began to shiver.

A few moments later four men emerged from the tower, carrying what looked like a large crate.

Two other men, stubby machine guns at the ready, followed in their wake.

Without being told, Edie knew that the Ark of the Covenant was inside the crate.

Her heart painfully thudding against her breastbone, she watched as it was loaded into the back of the truck. That done, the two armed guards took up positions on either side of the vehicle, the four porters returning to the tower.

Slowly she backed away from her observation post.

She'd taken no more than three tentative steps when a large hand was slapped over her mouth, an unseen assailant lifting her bodily off the ground.

87

'Button your lip!' a distinctly English voice hissed in her ear. 'We don't want them to hear us.'

Releasing his hand from her mouth, Cædmon stepped in front of her, Edie surprised to see a machine gun strapped to his chest. He snatched the rock that she still had clutched in her hand.

'First they would have to know that we're here –'

'They do know!'

Grabbing her upper arm, he unceremoniously pulled her to the ground, the two of them squaring off at a squat.

'Have you lost your bloody mind?' His warm breath hit her full in the face.

'I'm here. Deal with it.'

'I can render you unconscious at any moment, so kindly do not tell me what to do.'

'That reminds me … Did you have to hit me so hard?'

'Be thankful it was me doing the hitting and not one of MacFarlane's thugs. And before you rant at me, I had no choice.' For several seconds he stared into her eyes. Then, raising his left hand, he gently caressed the side of her face. 'I am truly sorry, Edie, that I hurt you.' Both his features and his voice had noticeably softened.

'My feelings are hurt more than anything else. Mainly because you didn't trust me enough to –'

'I trust you with my life. And I will do all in my power to safeguard yours.' He removed his hand from her cheek. Taking her by the elbow, he urged her upright. 'Follow my lead. No hare-brained heroics or I'll stuff my handkerchief in your lovely mouth and bind you hand and foot.'

'If you do that, I won't be able to tell you that they loaded the Ark into the back of that big truck. Oh, and how about giving me a weapon?'

Reaching into his pocket, he removed something that resembled a fountain pen. 'Here.'

'What am I suppose to do with this?'

'Shine it directly into an assailant's eyes. I don't have time to explain the laws of photonics, except to say that it will instantaneously induce a state of temporary blindness. So please be sure the business end is pointing away from you when the light is activated.'

Edie took the laser. 'I was hoping you might give me your diving knife, seeing as how you managed to find yourself a machine –'

Just then she heard the sound – rubber on stone – of a booted foot.

Frantically, she glanced at Cædmon.

Amazingly calm, he put his left index finger to his lips, cautioning her to silence while at the same time placing his right index finger on the trigger of the sub-machine gun.

Suddenly, Edie surprised by his quickness, Cædmon made a lightning-fast about turn.

'Drop your weapon and remove the headset! Now!'

Realizing his pistol was no match for Cædmon's mightier weapon, Boyd Braxton obediently put his pistol on the ground, kicking it in Cædmon's direction. That done, he yanked off the headset and, smiling snidely, tossed it several feet away. 'You didn't want that, did you?'

Afraid the headset might have an open mike, Edie strode over and smashed the heel of her shoe down on the device.

The smile instantly vanished from the behemoth's face. Stepping past him, Edie noticed that the crisscrossed bandages on the side of Braxton's head gleamed surreally in the darkness. Stitches courtesy of Cædmon and a well-aimed bottle. She returned the snide smile.

Braxton took a threatening step in her direction, his right hand balled in a fist.

'Touch her and I'll gladly add a pound of lead to your current body weight.'

At a glance, Edie could see that it was no idle threat. In fact, she was beginning to realize that Cædmon Aisquith never made idle threats.

'She's got you wrapped around her little pinkie, doesn't she?' Braxton snickered. 'Guess you know by now that she's a real prick tease, huh? Hell, my pecker has been standing on end since I first set eyes on the curly-haired bitch.'

His shoulders visibly relaxing, Cædmon slyly smiled at Braxton ... just before he reared back and kicked him in the crotch.

Sounding a lot like a braying donkey, the behemoth dropped to his knees, clutching his testicles with both hands.

'I trust that has given you some relief.' Cædmon turned to Edie. 'My apologies.'

About to say 'For what?' Edie instead went slack-jawed, horrified at seeing a quartet of men, who had suddenly and very silently materialized as though from thin air. Shoulder to shoulder, they stood some ten feet behind Cædmon.

The Four Horsemen of the Apocalypse come to life.

Before she could shout a warning, a floodlight was switched on, illuminating the entire area.

'You would be well advised, Mr Aisquith, to drop your weapon. Very, very slowly.'

Calmly, not so much as peering over his shoulder, Cædmon unclipped the leather strap that held the sub-machine gun to his chest. Holding the weapon in his left hand, his right hand held aloft so it could easily be seen, he bent slowly at the waist, placing the weapon on the ground.

Stanford MacFarlane stepped forward. Retrieving the gun, he handed it to Boyd Braxton.

'Here, boy. You look like you could use this.'

Still doubled over and gasping for breath, Braxton straightened just enough to aim the weapon directly at Cædmon's chest.

Unthinkingly, Edie grabbed MacFarlane by the forearm, knowing he was the only man present who could stop Braxton from pulling the trigger.

'One Christian to another ... don't let him do it,' she begged, ready to throw herself at his booted feet if that's what it took to save Cædmon's life.

'You are not a Christian woman!' MacFarlane bellowed, his face twisted in an ugly sneer. 'You are a harlot!'

88

'And you are a disgusting stain on a snowy white sheet,' Cædmon snarled at MacFarlane, words the only weapon left to him.

Unaccustomed to insubordinate words or deeds, the colonel appeared apoplectic. Like an Old Testament prophet on the verge of an aneurism.

'I want him searched before he's killed,' MacFarlane barked at one of his men.

The situation completely out of his control, Cædmon stood motionless while a muscular man with a shaved pate roughly patted him down for weapons. The torch he tossed aside, the GPS receiver and diving knife he handed to his chief. MacFarlane quickly perused the confiscated items before giving them to yet another of his men for safekeeping.

Still gasping for breath, Braxton rose to his full height, transformed from a wounded bear into a menacing mountain of a man. 'Let's just say I ain't gonna miss you when you're gone.'

Having known all along that this was how it might end, Cædmon defiantly stared his executioner in the face. As he did, Goya's famous painting *The Third of May* flashed across his mind's eye, bloodshed and violence the chain that inevitably linked one epoch to the next.

'Turn your head, woman,' MacFarlane commanded. 'Unless you have a predilection for bloodshed.'

'You kill him, you kill the messenger!'

Hearing that, Cædmon's head swung in Edie's direction.

The messenger?

What in God's name was she up to? A subterfuge clearly, but he had no idea of the nature or direction of the lie. Relegating him to the role of hapless passenger.

Edie startled every man present, including Cædmon, when she next said, 'And something tells me that you'll want to hear what MI5 has to say. They know all about your planned terrorist attack on the Dome of the Rock. Lucky for you they want the Ark of the Covenant, which is why they're willing to do a deal. But all bets are off the table if you gun down Cædmon Aisquith. The Queen's men don't like it when you kill one of their own. In fact, they would take it very personally if any harm came to him.'

Although MacFarlane's face was in shadow, Cædmon could see that the older man didn't appear the least bit surprised to learn of his connection to MI5.

Bloody hell. Edie's stratagem might actually work. No doubt Stanford MacFarlane, like most Americans, stood in awe of the mighty Five.

With a brusque wave of the hand, MacFarlane motioned Boyd Braxton to back off. His eyes narrowing, the behemoth lowered the sub-machine gun. Then, snarling like a rabid animal, he brazenly toggled his index finger over the trigger, wordlessly relaying a very stark message – with the mere press of a finger, he could instantly end his life.

Having no control over Braxton, Cædmon turned his attention instead to the giant's commanding officer. Well aware that the best falsehoods were those crafted from the truth, Cædmon did just that. He told the truth. 'Since we last met, I've used my time wisely. With Miss Miller's assistance, I have put together an in-depth dossier.'

'Complete with photographs, maps, you name it,' Edie embellished, the woman spinning yet another outlandish lie on her improvised loom.

'You're going to have to be more specific than that.' As he spoke, the muscles in MacFarlane's jaw twitched spasmodically.

'As Edie mentioned, Thames House has been apprised of your plan to destroy the Dome of the Rock two days hence on Eid al-Adha,' Cædmon replied, having quickly cobbled together what he hoped was a plausible scenario. 'And, to answer your next question, Five has already contacted its Israeli counterpart. The moment you enter Israel, Mossad will drop a noose around your neck. The Israelis do not take kindly to terrorists.'

'And the deal?' Other than a tightness in his jaw,

MacFarlane gave no visual clue as to whether or not he believed the tale.

'The deal is simple: surrender yourself to the British authorities and you will receive humane and civilized treatment; reject the offer and you will be at the mercy of Mossad. I understand their interrogation tactics are particularly brutal.'

'In case you've forgotten, I'm an American citizen,' MacFarlane declared, as though that gave him some sort of carte blanche.

'Do you think that will matter to the Israelis? To them you are merely a terrorist intent on destroying the most holy site in all of Jerusalem.'

The tick in MacFarlane's jaw became more noticeable. 'And what of the Ark?'

Beginning to think he might actually pull off a bloodless coup, Cædmon said, 'It must be surrendered to Her Majesty's Government. Were it not for the fact that you have the Ark of the Covenant in your possession, you would have been handed over to the Israelis already.' Cædmon glanced at his wristwatch. *10:20 p.m.* 'If you have not surrendered yourself to the British consulate by twenty-three hundred hours, the deal is null and void.' Of course, he had no way of knowing if there was anyone on duty at the consulate. He would cross that rickety bridge when he came to it.

A tense silence ensued, the only sound being a soft *rat-a-tat-tat* as Braxton drummed his fingers against the stock of his MP5. Cædmon purposely refrained from looking at Edie, knowing that any communication, even a silent exchange of glances, would be noticed, MacFarlane in the process of separating the wheat from the chaff.

'Since the beginning I wondered if you would contact British intelligence,' MacFarlane finally said after what seemed an interminable pause. 'But knowing the power that the Ark holds, something told me you'd want to keep MI5 out of the loop. Why? Because I assumed that like most men you would want the Ark of the Covenant for yourself. It's the reason Galen of Godmersham made no mention of his extraordinary find to his brethren, the Knights of St John, even though he was duty-bound to do just that. Instead, he lugged the Ark back to England, where he promptly hid it.' MacFarlane took several steps in Cædmon's direction, the tick in his jaw no longer in evidence. 'So I have to ask myself . . . What makes you a better man than that brave knight?'

Cædmon shrugged. 'I was faced with a crisis that Galen of Godmersham never had to confront.'

'And what crisis might that be?'

'How best to prevent the destruction of the Dome of the Rock. Brave though I am, I am but an army of one,' he added drolly, hoping to recapture the momentum. 'And so I had no choice but to contact Thames House. Better the British Museum has the Ark of the Covenant than a man bent on destroying the world.' Even before the words passed his lips,

Cædmon knew them to be the truth, silently damning himself for not contacting Five. For thinking that he, like Galen of Godmersham, could keep the Ark for himself.

'And when the wretched knight saw this, his death was well deserved.' The cryptic line from the quatrains finally made perfect sense to him.

'Mark my words, doomsday will soon be upon us. And when it comes, we will slay the beast of perfidy with divine revelation.' As he spoke, Stanford MacFarlane compulsively twisted the silver Jerusalem cross that he wore on his right ring finger. Cædmon suspected the ring was his anchor. Seeing that repetitive motion, he feared the scales had tipped. And in the wrong direction.

Edie, who had remained silent, pointed to a string of lights out in the bay. 'Doomsday is coming all right. Dressed in commando black and wielding some awesome firepower. You guys have only got a few minutes left to surrender.' Wearing her bravado like a new suit of clothes, she donned a cocky grin.

Good God. The woman was reading aloud from a Hollywood script.

Without warning, MacFarlane stepped over and grabbed Edie by the hair, yanking her to his chest. Although she desperately tried to twist free, he wrapped her curly locks around his fist and pulled her head back, exposing her neck. He then held out his free hand, palm up. 'Give me that diving knife.'

Cædmon lurched forward, only to be pistol-whipped on the side of the head by one of MacFarlane's men.

Knowing he could do nothing to save Edie if he was dead, he stood immobile. Edie, evidently sensing that she couldn't escape, had suddenly stopped resisting.

'You know, boy, I've got a funny feeling that you and this curly-haired harlot are lying to me.' MacFarlane, his face twisted in a sneer, locked gazes with him. 'Now, I know that you're a trained intelligence officer. So I'm going to assume that you have the mental fortitude to stand by while I hold a gun to your pretty woman's head.' As he spoke, he lightly ran the knife blade along Edie's cheek. 'But do you have the stomach to watch the flesh flayed from her bones in long bloody strips?'

Although her neck was stretched taut as a bowstring, Edie tried to shake her head. Tried to caution him not to reveal that there would be no commandos dressed in black coming to the rescue.

A brave woman. But, more importantly, a beloved woman.

'As I stated earlier, I did in fact compile a dossier outlining everything that has occurred since Jonathan Padgham's murder six days ago,' he confessed, the match lost, his queen taken. 'Included in the report is a detailed threat assessment of your planned attack on the Dome of the Rock.'

'Where's the dossier?'

'In the vault of the Dragonara Hotel.' Having carefully planned for just such a moment, Cædmon now played what he hoped would be their get-out-of-jail card. 'If Edie and I have not returned to the Dragonara Hotel by eight o'clock tomorrow morning, the dossier will be promptly delivered to the British consulate. From there, it will be forwarded to MI5. You are a clever enough man to realize that it would be advantageous to keep us alive. Now, would you please relax your grip on Miss Miller's hair?'

MacFarlane unwound a palm's length of hair. Just enough so Edie could move her neck, but not enough for her to escape.

'How do I know that you're telling the truth?'

'As with your belief in Old Testament prophecy, you must take it on good faith that I am.'

MacFarlane unwound Edie's hair from his fist. Muttering something about 'lying harlots', he shoved her away. Opening his arms, Cædmon caught Edie, clutching her to his chest.

'You and the harlot have a reprieve.'

Without asking, Cædmon knew that he and Edie would be accompanied to the Dragonara by at least one of MacFarlane's men. Once there, they would be forced to retrieve the dossier from the hotel vault and hand it over. Then they would most likely be executed. All told, the reprieve would amount to no more than a few hours. Not unlike watching a killer shark from a glass-bottomed boat, knowing all the while that the vessel will soon capsize.

Hearing the mobile phone clipped to MacFarlane's belt, Cædmon watched as the colonel took the call, turning his back on the assembled group. A few moments later, he ended the call and turned to Boyd Braxton.

'Call in the troops. We're ready to set sail.'

Edie frantically tugged on Cædmon's sleeve. 'The boat that just sailed into the bay, I bet that's how they're getting the Ark out of Malta,' she hissed in his ear.

'I suspect you're right.'

'The harlot is right,' MacFarlane said, overhearing the exchange. 'Not only is my mission ordained by the Almighty, but God is acting through me. How else do you explain that after three thousand years the Ark of the Covenant has been reclaimed?' His eyes sparkling with an inner fire, he smiled, confirming Cædmon's suspicions that Stanford MacFarlane was quite mad, the man suffering from a full-blown messiah complex.

'Yeah, well, I wouldn't be measuring for the drapes just yet,' Edie taunted. 'If you think for one second that the good, sane, decent people of the world will stand by and let you and your misguided followers start the next world war, think again.'

'God spoke through the prophet Ezekiel, his will made known to mankind. I will see to it that his orders are carried out.'

'There is no greater sacrilege than to take upon one's shoulders the mantle of God,' Cædmon said quietly. 'Men like you not only diminish the human spirit, you diminish the very nature of God.'

'Soon enough you and your whore will learn what comes of sleeping with the devil,' MacFarlane retorted. Then, pointing an accusing finger, '"But evil men and imposters will grow worse and worse, deceiving and being deceived." Gallagher, take them away!'

A bald-headed underling, automatic pistol held capably in his right hand, stepped towards them.

'At least we bought ourselves a little bit of time,' Edie whispered.

Cædmon glanced at the lights in the bay. 'Yes, but what of the rest of the world? For them the doomsday clock still ticks.'

'"... if you warn the wicked, and he does not turn from his wickedness, or from his wicked way, he shall die for his iniquity."' As he spoke, Gallagher motioned Edie and Cædmon to take a seat on a nearby slab of limestone.

Cædmon plonked down on the raised stone. 'I've had enough apocalyptic rambling to last a lifetime.'

Wordlessly, Edie sat next to him, while approximately a hundred yards away she could see MacFarlane and his crew piling into the military-style truck. The same truck into which they'd earlier loaded the Ark of the Covenant. She assumed the plan was to drive the truck to the shore and then transport the Ark out to the yacht via a small boat.

From there it would be plain sailing. All the way to Israel.

That thought enraged and terrified her all at once. But it was an impotent rage. And an equally impotent fear. There was nothing she or Cædmon could do to stop the ancient prophecies from being fulfilled. With the End Times hanging over them, the voice of reason had become eerily silent. Instead, she'd reverted to being the terrified child who had feared the death and destruction that was part and parcel of God's wrath.

'Cædmon, I'm afraid. I don't want it to end. Not the world. Not any of it,' she murmured lamely, unable to put her feelings into words. At least not words that made any sense.

He placed an arm around her shoulders, pulling her close to him. 'As the Irish are fond of saying, "At least we had the day."' Edie guessed that he was speaking of their lovemaking onboard the ferry.

Knowing they didn't have much time, she took her fill of him. The thick red hair. The lean rangy physique. The beautiful blue eyes. The relationship over before it ever began.

'I've given it a lot of thought and I've decided that it's more than mere physical lust,' she informed him, speaking in a low whisper.

'Do I detect a deathbed confession?'

'You know, gallows humour has always eluded me.'

'Then perhaps we need to get off the scaffold and shine some light.'

'Yeah, but —' She stopped, suddenly realizing what Cædmon was alluding to.

The laser light.

Cædmon had said that it could temporarily blind a man.

Edie surreptitiously placed her hand over her jacket pocket. The pen-like device was still there. In all of the pandemonium no one had thought to search her for weapons.

'Be ready,' she whispered in a hushed voice, certain that when the time came Cædmon would know what to do.

A few seconds later Gallagher reached into his breast pocket and removed a crumpled pack of Marlboros. Next he patted the front of his cargo pants, searching for a match. Or a lighter. It didn't much matter but it gave Edie the opportunity to slide her hand into her jacket pocket, all the while praying their captor's gaze didn't land on her slow-moving hand.

Her fingers wrapped around the laser. Quickly, she found the small power switch – in the same place where you'd expect to find the clip on a fountain pen. She removed the pen from her pocket.

Gallagher's head suddenly swivelled in her direction.

'Hey, bitch! What the hell are you doing?'

'Bringing you to Jesus!' she retorted, aiming what she hoped was the 'business end' of the laser at Gallagher's face.

A thin ray of green light immediately stabbed out, hitting Gallagher first in one eye then the other. Instinctively he raised his arm to shield his eyes.

'Quick! Turn it off!' Cædmon hissed, snatching her by the forearm to get her attention. The abrupt motion caused the laser beam to shoot heavenwards, making it seem as though the thin green light actually touched the marmalade moon hovering thousands of miles above the earth.

Edie switched it off.

Like a striking viper, Cædmon lunged forward, his right hand whipping out, his fingers wrapping round the barrel of Gallagher's gun. One quick strong twist and the gun was out of the other man's grip. The pistol now in his possession, Cædmon used it to bludgeon Gallagher's bald skull. An instant later, he went limp. Grabbing him by the scruff of the neck, Cædmon unclipped Gallagher's mobile from his belt and lugged him behind the slab of limestone. Out of sight. Edie scanned the area, terrified that the scuffle, which had lasted only a few seconds, had been observed.

Mercifully, there was no alarm. In the distance MacFarlane's men continued clambering into the back of the truck.

'Is he . . .?' She jutted her chin at the man sprawled on the other side of the limestone slab.

Cædmon tersely shook his head. 'But pray the bastard doesn't wake up any time soon.'

Taking her by the elbow, Cædmon headed towards the truck. Not only did they keep to the shadows, but they kept down, crouching as they moved.

About fifty yards from the truck, Cædmon yanked her behind a scraggy clump of dead vegetation.

'Our objective, our *only* objective, is to prevent the Ark being loaded onto that yacht in the bay. If that happens, it will be lost forever. I mean this, love – no heroics.' As he spoke, he lightly held her chin.

'Do you think we've actually got a chance?'

'So long as our escape goes undetected, their success is not a *fait accompli*.'

'If they find Gallagher, they're gonna turn on us like a pack of wolves.'

Still holding her by the chin, Cædmon stared at her. Taking a deep breath, he said, 'The bloodletting, if it comes, will be extensive. And pitiless.'

90

'I don't know about you, sir, but I can't wait to blow the Dome of the Rock to kingdom come.' Fully recovered from his earlier injury, Boyd Braxton positioned himself behind the steering wheel of the six-by-six convoy truck.

'"Vengeance *is* mine, sayeth the Lord,"' Stan replied, knowing that in the eleventh century the Muslim infidels had attempted to destroy the tomb of Jesus, so the reprisal was long overdue. 'Gunny, do you know what the word "Islam" means?'

'No, sir. Can't say that I do.'

'It means "submit".'

Submit or die.

As always happened when he pondered the Muslim faith, Stan felt a hot rage surge up from the base of his spine, his temples pounding with the force of his hatred.

'As God is my witness, I will never be conquered by those people. Never.'

'I hear ya, sir!' Braxton banged his fist against the steering wheel. 'We'll teach those ragheads a lesson! Every last one of 'em!'

Pleased with his subordinate's enthusiasm, the Lord always looking with favour upon those who executed their duty with a glad heart, Stan slammed shut the passenger door. In the back of the truck nine of his men were present and accounted for. The Ark would be well guarded. To a man, they would unflinchingly lay down their lives to protect the holy relic. Although it was doubtful that they would encounter any resistance. The Englishman had admitted that British intelligence was ignorant of their plans. And according to the yacht's captain, the voyage from Haifa had been uneventful.

Soon, in God's name, he would prevail. Then, on the battlefields of that most holy of lands, he would triumph. The Ark of the Covenant was the key to victory. As it had been in the days of old when it was used to bring down the walls of mighty Jericho. 'And so it shall come to pass,' the prophecies of Ezekiel the road map to success.

Nothing could stop him. Not the peaceniks. Not the left-wing secularists who railed against religion. Not the passive wusses at the UN. Not even the stalwart Englishman who had proved such a formidable foe.

Respect for one's enemy, however, only went so far. Stan knew that there was a special hell for men like Cædmon Aisquith and his degenerate harlot. Soon they would discover that God's fire was inextinguishable. The flames of hell burning eternally bright.

'And the serpent will be cast into the bottomless pit ... so that he should deceive the nations no more till the thousand years were finished.'

Out of the corner of his eye, Stan saw a shadow approach. The shadow belonged to Rostov, his communications expert. He rolled down the window.

'What is it?'

An anxious glint in his eyes, the other man said, 'We've got a problem, sir. Gallagher isn't answering his cell.'

The muscles in Stan's belly tightened. He took a deep breath, striving for a calm he didn't feel.

As he silently begged for divine guidance, he saw in his mind's eye the Tree of Life, not seen since the expulsion from Eden, blossoming atop the Temple Mount.

Blessed with that calming vision, he turned to his communications expert. 'Get in the back.' Then to his trusted subordinate. 'We're gonna find 'em and run 'em down.'

'Yes, sir!'

91

Ignoring the vibrating mobile phone clipped to his waistband, Cædmon urged Edie to keep moving, the convoy truck no more than thirty yards ahead of them.

'Maybe you should answer it,' Edie whispered, clearly unnerved by the call. 'Otherwise they'll know something's up.'

Aware that the end result would be the same regardless of whether he answered the mobile or not, Cædmon made no reply as they continued to creep along at a rapid but cautious pace. A few moments later they were outside the watchtower, the wooden door wide open. Time in short supply, Cædmon yanked Edie into the building's protective shadow, the two of them huddling together. He peered out, verifying that the truck was still parked on the other side of the tower.

'I want you to go inside and, if at all possible, lock yourself into a room. I then want you to use Gallagher's mobile to ring the authorities. Understood?' When she nodded, he handed her the now-silent phone. 'Tell them you're an American tourist and that you were abducted from your hotel room. Make no mention of the Ark of the Covenant.'

'What about you?'

'I am off to slay the dragon.' As he spoke, he checked the clip on the Glock automatic. Sixteen rounds. He only needed three. One to blow out a tyre on the truck. One to take out Stanford MacFarlane. And a third bullet to fell the behemoth.

Hit those three, chaos would ensue and all MacFarlane's well-laid plans would come to a halt.

He motioned to the door of the tower. 'In you go.'

'But –'

'No buts,' he interjected, placing a hand over her mouth. With the other hand, he gently pushed her through the open doorway. Then, hoping she would heed his orders, he pulled the door shut.

Stay safe.

His right arm cocked at the elbow, the Glock clutched in his hand, Cædmon made his way around the perimeter of the tower, his plan to approach the truck from the front, enabling him to take out the cab passenger, the driver and one of the front tyres. In that order. And in quick succession. He assumed that, as before, Braxton would be driving with the colonel next to him.

The plan was brazen. Reckless even. But it was the only option left to him. Under no circumstances could he permit MacFarlane to leave Malta alive. Too much was at stake. Too many lives were in the balance.

Suppressing his fear, he crept forward. The truck

was no more than twenty yards away, just beyond the curve of the building.

Suddenly, he heard the roar of an engine. The truck was on the move. He fought the instinctive urge to fire his weapon.

He needed a clean shot. If he botched it, all would be lost.

Knowing he had only seconds, he charged out of the shadows, coming at the truck from an angle to avoid the headlights. Arms locked in a firing position, he found his first target – Stanford MacFarlane – took aim and pulled the trigger.

'Bollocks!' The Glock had jammed. He pulled back the slide on the top of the pistol.

The clatter of machine-gun fire erupted all around him.

Caught in a corona of bullets, he quickly chambered a round, shock and anger hitting him in equal measure.

A heartbeat later shock mutated into fear as he saw a shaky shaft of green light hit the truck's windscreen.

92

'Jesusfuckingchrist! I can't see!' Boyd Braxton yelled, raising his arms to stave off the blinding green beam. 'I can't see a damn –'

The truck swerved. Jerking to the right. Then the left. It began to lose speed.

'Put your foot on the gas!' Stan yelled over the gunny's foul-mouthed screams. 'We *must* fulfil the prophecy! Do not give in to your fears!'

Averting his head from the burning light, Stan leaned over Braxton and grabbed the steering wheel, knowing that fear was the tool of the devil. Fear was what he had felt that long-ago night in Beirut. When his best friend, his comrades, his CO were ripped to shreds by an Islamist bomb. When he had stood shaking in the bomb's aftermath, snot dribbling from his nose, piss puddling at his feet. Afraid to grab his weapon and take action. Afraid to do anything other than drop to his knees and beg God's mercy.

That's when the angels came to him. Gabriel and Michael. The same two angels that adorned the lid of the Ark. They took his fear from him, asking only that he take up the Lord's fight.

And every day since, he had done just that.

This day would be no different.

For he knew no fear.

He had complete and certain faith in the sanctity of his mission.

The same faith that had guided Abraham and Moses in their darkest hour. The same faith that had enabled David to face the mighty Goliath.

'You come at me with a sword and spear. I come to you in the name of the Lord!'

Those were words to live by. Words to die by.

'The battle for the Temple will soon be upon us! Praise be to the Lord!' he joyfully shouted, retaking control of the truck, steering it straight towards the green beam of light.

93

Cædmon ran towards the pencil-thin erratic green glow.

'Turn it off!' he shouted, able to see that MacFarlane had taken control of the careering vehicle. Able to see that he was steering the truck directly towards the source of the beam.

Edie turned her head in his direction. With her curly hair wildly blowing all about her, she looked like one of the Furies in pursuit of the wicked among them.

Her expression resolute, she shook her head, refusing to move out of the path of the oncoming truck.

Cædmon pumped his legs and arms faster, afraid he wouldn't reach her in time. Afraid she would meet her end in a hideous fashion. *Afraid*.

He only had a few seconds, the whole of the world reduced to his pounding heart, the *rat-a-tat-tat* of automatic weapon fire, the roar of the powerful engine.

She was just a few feet away.

He could do this.

He could save –

He was airborne, diving towards her, his arms and legs stretched.

His heart in his throat, Cædmon ploughed into Edie, knocking her off her feet and out of the truck's path. The laser flew from her hands, its beam frenetically arcing through the night sky before disappearing as it plummeted to earth. Limbs tangled together, the two of them rolled across the rocky terrain, the inhospitable surface providing no leaf or blade of grass to soften the impact.

With no time to inquire about injuries, he rolled to his knees. His finger on the trigger of the Glock, his arms locked in a firing position, he prayed that he had successfully cleared the jam. The truck now moving away from him, he took aim at its rear tyres, permitting himself one deep, calming breath before he fired six shots in quick succession.

His aim true, he hit the new targets, blowing out both rear driver's-side tyres, the truck abruptly fishtailing, wildly swaying from side to side as Stanford MacFarlane lost control of the mammoth two-and-a-half-ton vehicle, the truck veering towards the cliff overlooking the sea.

The gun hanging limply from his hand, Cædmon stood motionless, watching in disbelief as the truck reached the cliff edge. For the briefest of seconds its red tail lights twinkled eerily in the darkness before disappearing from sight. A sonorous *boom!* was accompanied by a bright flash illuminating the heavens. A surreal swansong for a madman and the legendary Ark of the Covenant.

'*All was vanity and grasping for the wind.*'

Edie ran to him, throwing herself into his arms. 'Oh God! I can't believe what I just saw!'
'Nor I,' he whispered, holding her tight.

94

As though trapped in a dream from which he could not awake, Cædmon surveyed the wreckage. The explosion having been seen for miles, rescue workers, naval personnel, police and local fishermen had descended in an excited swarm on the rock-strewn beach.

Like many explosion sites he'd seen over the years, this one had the familiar trappings – yellow tape, black smoke, smouldering hunks of twisted metal. At a glance he saw that no man could have survived the blast. Although that didn't deter the local police divers, who were plopping salmon-like from the starboard side of a nearby vessel, aided in their search by powerful underwater torches that cast an otherworldly glow through the dark sea.

'He thought he could walk on water,' Edie, standing beside him, murmured. 'Boy, was he ever wrong.'

'It's over. At least for the moment. Perhaps now the voices of tolerance and compassion can be heard.'

'Or, put another way, God works in mysterious ways.'

'Mmmm,' he grunted, unable to see God's hand in the violent events that had transpired.

He and Edie had kept very much to the sidelines,

two curious but innocent bystanders. To cover themselves they had told the police they were a honeymooning couple who had 'got the wild notion into our heads to spend a romantic night at the ancient tower'. And while they had heard a thunderous explosion, they 'had no idea what caused it'. Coitus interruptus and all that. The lie took, the police not favouring them with so much as a second glance.

'*Deheb! Deheb!*' a grizzled fisherman exclaimed as he charged through the surf, excitedly pointing to a rivulet of molten gold visible in the soot-coloured sand.

Staring at the stream, Cædmon felt like a battle-wearied and defeated knight home from the wars.

The Ark of the Covenant had not withstood the blast. He had failed in his quest. What was left of the sacred Ark of the ancient Israelites was slowly being washed out to sea. He contritely glanced heavenwards. *I gave it my all.* But his all had not been good enough.

Feeling the sting of tears, the crash site turning into a nightmarish blur, he abruptly turned his back on Edie. She'd seen enough. She didn't need to see him break down and cry. 'I need to relieve myself,' he muttered, adding yet another lie to an ever-mounting heap. With a wave of his hand, he headed for the far end of the rocky beach, removing himself from the mêlée and the contorted scraps of smouldering steel.

His vision still slightly blurred around the edges,

he switched on his torch. *So I don't break my bloody neck*, he thought irritably as he navigated over and around the tumbled rocks that had over the years flaked away from the imposing cliff. Like so many orphaned children.

Emotionally and physically drained, he seated himself on a flat-topped boulder. Elbows braced on his thighs, head supported between his hands, he stared morosely at the gently rolling waves.

'How could I have been so arrogant as to think that –' He stopped in mid-castigation.

He bounded off his perch and scrambled over several large boulders, manoeuvring onto his stomach so he could better see the golden object wedged between two mammoth pieces of limestone.

He shone his torch into the crevice.

His breath caught in his throat.

'Bloody hell.'

There, upended, was an elaborate golden lid measuring approximately two-and-a-half by four feet.

The lid to the Ark of the Covenant. What the ancient Hebrews had called the mercy seat.

Affixed to the lid were two winged stern-faced figures. The cherubim, Gabriel and Michael. *'I will meet with thee and will commune with thee from above the mercy seat, from between the two cherubim which are upon the Ark.'*

Without a doubt, it was the most spectacularly beautiful thing he'd ever seen.

'God does truly work in mysterious ways,' he

murmured, thinking that the cherubim were traditionally associated with the primal element of fire.

How ironic.

Utterly bedazzled, he stretched out a hand. Just as quickly, he withdrew his arm, suddenly recalling the fate of the hapless men of Bethshemesh. Worried that a residual spark of the Ark's awesome power might still inhabit the golden lid, he rolled onto his back and gazed up, silently asking, *begging*, permission.

Instead of a heavenly dispensation, he saw the sins of his life flash in quick succession across his mind's eye like so many cue cards.

'Sod it.' He rolled back onto his belly and shone his torch into the crevice. Teeth clenched, he shoved his hand into the rocky fissure and committed the unthinkable – he placed his hand upon the lid of the Ark of the Covenant.

When nothing untoward occurred, he slowly inched his fingers along the rim, detecting some sort of ornamentation. He adjusted the angle of the torch, enabling him to inspect a small incised figure that had the body of a man and the head of a falcon.

'I don't believe it.'

'What are you doing?'

He sat upright. 'Have a look.' He extended a hand to help Edie onto the boulder. Then he directed the torch beam at the golden lid.

'It's the lid!' she exclaimed, nearly toppling back off the boulder.

'Yes, that's what I thought,' he replied, knowing he was about to burst a very large bubble. 'Do you see that row of markings on the rim?'

She inched closer to the crevice. 'Uh huh.'

'Those are Egyptian hieroglyphics.' Reaching into the crevice, he pointed to a line of incised characters. 'This is a rough translation, mind you, but I believe the etched inscription reads, "Ra-Harakhti, supreme lord of the heavens".'

Edie immediately snatched the torch out of his hand and directed the beam into the fissure, evidently needing to see for herself. 'But I don't understand ... Why are there Egyptian hieroglyphics on the Ark of the Covenant?'

'Because it's not the Ark of the Covenant. It's an Egyptian bark.'

'An Egyptian bark,' she parroted, clearly stupefied. 'But ... are you *absolutely* certain?' she demanded, the woman a hard nut to crack. 'And what about the two angels on top?'

'Isis and her sister Nephthys, I suspect. As you may recall, the ancient Egyptians were the originators of a sacred chest known as a bark. Furthermore, I believe an Egyptian bark was the model used by Moses in creating the fabled Ark.' He took the torch from her shaking hand. 'It would seem that Galen of Godmersham uncovered an Egyptian bark, not the Hebrew Ark of the Covenant.'

Tears cascaded down Edie's cheeks. Soon followed by a burst of raucous laughter.

'Bloody hell!' she bellowed.

At hearing the spot-on impersonation, Cædmon grinned.

'Come here, love.'

95

As she stepped onto their hotel room balcony, Edie pulled the two halves of her bathrobe closer together and tightened the belt, there being a damp but invigorating chill in the air. Overhead, a few stars were still visible, shimmering specks of light flung haphazardly across the pre-dawn sky. Glancing up, she sighed, always amazed by the breathless expectancy that heralded the arrival of each new day.

'Enchanting, isn't it?' Cædmon said as he joined her on the balcony. Having just emerged from the shower, he was attired in an identical fluffy white robe. He handed her a cup and saucer.

Catching a heady whiff of bergamot, Edie smiled. 'Earl Grey. Lovely. Yes, it is enchanting,' she agreed as she seated herself at the small table in the corner of the balcony.

So enchanting, she wasn't altogether certain she wanted to leave. At least not yet. After the violence of the night just passed, she needed some down time. Some stress-free, kick off your shoes, sleep till noon, I'm not answering the telephone down time. She didn't know, however, whether Cædmon would be joining her. Other than a brief discussion of what time the hotel breakfast buffet opened, no mention of the future had been made.

Cædmon seated himself next to her. Suddenly nervous, Edie stared at the horizon, the sky now tinted a soft pink. Like the inside of a seashell. On the wharf a few industrious fishermen were already out and about, tossing huge nets onto whimsically painted boats.

'When I was little, I used to think that the stars went into hiding once the sun came up. Of course, being older and wiser ... Well, actually, I'm not exactly certain what happens to the stars come day-break, so just forget I even brought it up,' she said, waving away the silly thought, realizing she was rambling.

'When I was a young lad, I used to wonder what created the rainbow,' Cædmon remarked, his English accent sounding more clipped than usual. Making Edie wonder if he wasn't a little bit nervous himself.

'The mysteries of the universe. Seems we were both intrigued at an early age.'

'By the by, I sent an email to my old group leader at MI5,' Cædmon said, changing the subject. 'Told him that I had caught wind of a plot to destroy the Dome of the Rock on the upcoming Muslim holy day. Trent is a good man. He'll see to it that Mossad and the Israeli public security minister are contacted.'

'You don't think that –'

'No, no,' he quickly assured her. 'I'm just dotting my Is, as they say. The possibility that MacFarlane had a contingency plan is remote. He seemed very much the micromanager.'

Edie fiddled with the delicate handle on her tea-cup, hesitant to broach the next topic. 'You haven't said anything, but I know you're disappointed – that it wasn't the Ark of the Covenant.'

For several long moments Cædmon stared at the early-morning activity on the bay, Edie unable to gauge his thoughts. Or his mood, the small pucker on his brow making her wonder if he was thinking his way out of a quandary.

Finally, taking a deep I've-come-to-a-decision kind of breath, he redirected his gaze in her direction. 'You assume I no longer wish to find the Ark.'

'But I thought that ...' At a loss for words, she stared at him.

'It's still out there. I'm certain of it. Still waiting to be discovered. Still waiting to bear holy witness to an eternal truth that is beyond mortal man's com-prehension.'

'"Thou, silent form, dost tease us out of thought as doth eternity."'

Smiling, Cædmon took a sip of tea. 'How did you know that Keats is my favourite poet?'

She shrugged. 'I didn't. It just seemed –' again she shrugged '– right. So, gosh, this is ... Wow. Guess you can tell I'm kind of speechless, huh?' Crestfallen, she had the sudden urge to glug down one of those tiny bottles of Scotch from the room's minibar.

'The Knights Templar believed that Ethiopia was

the secret resting place of the Ark of the Covenant, the holy relic having been spirited out of Jerusalem by Menelik.'

'Menelik?'

'Yes, Solomon's illegitimate son by the Queen of Sheba. There are several passages in Wolfram's *Parsifal* that intimate as much. The stuff of legends, eh?'

'As I understand it, the Ethiopian highlands are quite lovely.' She wondered if she should wish him luck with his life now or wait until the taxi pulled up to take him to the airport. 'And of course it would make an interesting topic. You know, for your next book.'

'My thoughts exactly. Although ...' One side of his mouth twitched; he was clearly amused by something. 'I will need a photographer. You wouldn't happen to know anyone who would be interested in the assignment?'

'Well, now that you mention it, I do know a photographer who's currently available. Would this be, you know, a strictly professional relationship or ... ?' She crossed her legs at the knee, her robe gaping open to reveal a bare leg well-toned from regular Pilates.

Cædmon stared openly, proving what she already knew, that under the English veneer lurked a man of deep passions.

'You do know that I've always been fascinated by valiant women.'

'A valiant woman and an adventuresome man. We make quite a pair, don't we?'

'Quite.' Then, his jaw tightening, Cædmon figuratively locked horns with her. 'Given your behaviour with that laser, you should be bent over and given a thorough spanking. You came damn close to getting yourself killed.'

'Funny, but you don't strike me as an SM type of guy.'

'Just find me a man who doesn't enjoy being spanked by a beautiful woman.'

Edie slapped a hand over her lips to keep from laughing and losing a mouthful of tea.

Balancing his elbows on his thighs, Cædmon leaned towards her. 'What is it that you want from your life, Edie?'

The question, unexpected and to the point, surprised her. 'Well, like most people, I want security, happiness, a sense of belonging.'

'I can give those to you.'

'Are you sure? I mean, we sorta got flung together.'

Blue eyes twinkling, Cædmon grinned. 'I am quite certain.'

Edie decided to dive in as well. 'Since we're on the subject, I suppose the time has come for me to confess that I'm absolutely crazy about you. You're intelligent, witty, well mannered and considerate. Everything a woman could possibly want in a man.'

'Might I point out that you didn't include "handsome" in your list of attributes.'

'I was saving the best for last.' Edie raised her cup. Holding it aloft, she clinked rims with him. 'Here's to finding the Ark.'

'And if not the Ark then the secret of the Knights Templar.'

'And if not the secret of the Templars then ...' She glanced pointedly at the oversized bed in the middle of the room.

Cædmon also glanced at the bed, its coverlet invitingly turned down. Getting up, he took her elbow, urging her to her feet.

'Let the adventure begin.'

CHARLES BROKAW

THE ATLANTIS CODE

An ancient artefact is discovered in a dusty antiquities shop in Alexandria, Egypt – the long-forgotten trinket soon becomes the centre of the most deadly race against time in history.

The 20,000-year-old relic is inscribed with what appears to be the long-lost language of Atlantis. Only one man would seem to be able to decode its meaning – the world's foremost linguist, Dr Thomas Lourdes – but only if he can stay alive long enough . . .

Meanwhile, an earthquake in Cadiz, Spain, uncovers a most unexpected site – one which the Vatican rush to be the first to explore . . . Perhaps the lost city of Atlantis is finally ready to be found?

But is the world ready for her secrets?

'*The Atlantis Code* will take you to a new level of mystery, wonder, adventure and excitement' Deepak Chopra

CHRIS MOONEY

THE DEAD ROOM

A mother and her son have been executed in their home and fingerprint matches show their attacker died twenty years ago.

But how can dead serial killers return to haunt the present?

The answers lie in the darkest shadows of The Dead Room.

When CSI Darby McCormick is called to the crime scene, it's one of the most gruesome she's ever seen. But the forensic evidence is even more disturbing: someone watched the murder unfold from woodland behind the house – and the killer died in a shoot-out two decades earlier.

The deeper Darby digs, the more horrors come to light. Her prime suspect is revealed as a serial killer on an enormous scale, with a past that's even more shocking than his crimes, thanks to a long-held secret that could rock Boston's law enforcement to its core.

Is it possible to steal an identity? Or are dead men walking in Darby's footsteps? The line between the living and the dead has never been finer.

'A scary breakneck ride' Tess Gerritsen

www.penguin.com

CHRIS KUZNESKI

THE LOST THRONE

Hewn into the towering cliffs of central Greece, the Metéora monasteries are all but inaccessible. The Holy Trinity is the most isolated, its sacred brotherhood the guardians of a long-forgotten secret.

In the dead of night, the sanctity of the holy retreat is shattered by an elite group of warriors, carrying ancient weapons. One by one, they hurl the silent monks from the cliff-top – the holy men taking their secret to their rocky graves.

Halfway across Europe, a terrified academic fears for his life. Richard Byrd has nearly uncovered the location of one of the Seven Ancient Wonders – the statue of Zeus and his mighty throne. But Byrd's search has also uncovered a forbidden conspiracy, and there are those who would do anything to conceal its dark agenda . . .

'Kuzneski's writing has raw power' James Patterson

'Excellent! High stakes, fast action, vibrant characters . . . Not to be missed!' Lee Child

CARO RAMSAY

SINGING TO THE DEAD

Two seven-year-old boys have been abducted from the streets of Glasgow. Both had already endured years of neglect and betrayal - but for Detective Inspector Colin Anderson the case is especially disturbing, because the boys look so much like his own son Peter . . .

Then, with police resources stretched to breaking point, a simple house fire turns into a full-scale murder hunt. An invisible killer is picking off victims at random and, if DS Costello's hunch is correct, committing an ingenious deception.

As his squad struggles to work both cases, DI Anderson learns that deception and betrayal come in many guises. For while the boys' abductor is still out there no child is safe - as young Peter Anderson is about to find out . . .

'A cracker . . . many shivers in store' *The Times* (for *Absolution*)

NICCI FRENCH

UNTIL IT'S OVER

DEAD. UNLUCKY.

London cycle courier Astrid Bell is bad luck – for other people. First, Astrid's neighbour Peggy Farrell accidentally knocks her off her bike – and not long after is found bludgeoned to death in an alley. Then, a few days later, Astrid is asked to pick up a package – only to find the client slashed to pieces in the hallway.

For the police, it's more than coincidence. For Astrid and her six housemates, it's the beginning of a nightmare: suspicious glances, bitter accusations, fallings out and a growing fear that the worst is yet to come.

Because if it's true that bad luck comes in threes, who will be next to die?

'Reads like lightning' *Observer*

'Another nail-biting thriller' *Daily Express*

LUIS MIGUEL ROCHA

THE LAST POPE

Vatican City, 29 September 1978: the world wakes to the shocking news that Pope John Paul I is dead, just a month after his accession . . .

Thirty years later in London, young journalist Sarah Monteiro receives a mysterious package. Enclosed, a list of names and a coded message.

Moments later a masked assassin attempts to silence her forever. It seems Sarah holds the key to unveiling a deadly secret - a plot that implicates unscrupulous mercenaries and crooked politicians, and which goes to the very heart of the Vatican. Sarah has no choice but to run, forced into a ruthless game of cat-and-mouse. She can trust none, especially when her father's name appears on the incriminating list . . .

Sarah finds herself at the centre of a world-wide conspiracy its keepers will stop at nothing to protect.

'An immensely entertaining book' *USA Today*

'Sure to please conspiracy buffs' *Publishers Weekly*

MARTIN LANGFIELD

THE SECRET FIRE

Sotheby's, London, 1936. A paper by Sir Isaac Newton is sold at auction to a bookseller's agent, and within minutes of leaving the auction house he is killed and the paper stolen. For the Nazis are desperate to get their hands on a Newton formula that will unleash the Secret Fire – a weapon beyond all imagining that can wipe their enemies off the face of the earth. And this document is the key . . . unless the French Resistance and SOE operatives also on its trail can stop them.

New York, 2007. Katherine Reckliss learns her grandmother's SOE radio has started picking up disturbing messages from occupied France, warning that a V1 containing the Secret Fire is being launched by the Nazis. Its target? Present day London.

So begins the desperate race to halt the Secret Fire – both in 1940s Nazi-occupied France and modern day London. The clock is ticking as history starts to re-write the future in a new and terrifying script . . .

'A race against time and an ancient secret' *Observer* (for *The Malice Box*)

He just wanted a decent book to read ...

Not too much to ask, is it? It was in 1935 when Allen Lane, Managing Director of Bodley Head Publishers, stood on a platform at Exeter railway station looking for something good to read on his journey back to London. His choice was limited to popular magazines and poor-quality paperbacks – the same choice faced every day by the vast majority of readers, few of whom could afford hardbacks. Lane's disappointment and subsequent anger at the range of books generally available led him to found a company – and change the world.

'We believed in the existence in this country of a vast reading public for intelligent books at a low price, and staked everything on it'
Sir Allen Lane, 1902–1970, founder of Penguin Books

The quality paperback had arrived – and not just in bookshops. Lane was adamant that his Penguins should appear in chain stores and tobacconists, and should cost no more than a packet of cigarettes.

Reading habits (and cigarette prices) have changed since 1935, but Penguin still believes in publishing the best books for everybody to enjoy. We still believe that good design costs no more than bad design, and we still believe that quality books published passionately and responsibly make the world a better place.

So wherever you see the little bird – whether it's on a piece of prize-winning literary fiction or a celebrity autobiography, political tour de force or historical masterpiece, a serial-killer thriller, reference book, world classic or a piece of pure escapism – you can bet that it represents the very best that the genre has to offer.

Whatever you like to read – trust Penguin.